Praise

'This is an outstanding novel, made even more remarkable by its debut status. I loved it, from the first page to the end. Finely textured, deftly woven, it evokes – with confidence and a rare beauty – late eighteenth century England and France. The scene-setting is perfect, and laced with rich, juicy details. The dialogue is period-convincing, and spoken by meaty, believable characters. Hazzard is a tortured hero par excellence, a mixture of conscience, courage and martial skill, a man who can fall victim to arrogance and even cruelty.

'Better than Sharpe, gripping and intense, *Napoleon's Run* deserves to be a runaway success'

Ben Kane, *Sunday Times* bestselling author of *Lionheart*

'*Hornblower* meets *Mission: Impossible*. A thrilling, page-turning debut packed with rousing, rip-roaring action'

J. D. Davies, author of the Matthew Quinton Journals

'This book has it all. Combines great action with really good history, and an engaging and original character in Marine officer William Hazzard, who adds a satisfying dash of the swashbuckling Bombay Buccaneers to some solid scholarship. In many ways this captures the true – and surprisingly subversive – nature of early British imperialism'

Seth Hunter, author of the Nathan Peake novels

'A strong, fast-moving story by an author with a deep knowledge of the period and the narrative skill of a fine story-teller'

Andrew Swanston, author of *Waterloo*

'Hugely atmospheric, *Napoleon's Run* by Jonathan Spencer offers a fascinating evocation of the sights, sounds and smells of the Napoleonic Wars. Thanks to an extraordinary attention to detail and accuracy, it paints a vivid and realistic picture of life on board ship, striking the perfect balance between a thoroughly absorbing history lesson and a thumping good read.

'Packed to the gunwales with action, this fast-paced story is also a very thoughtful thriller filled with intrigue and suspense. Leading a crew of wonderfully drawn characters, Hazzard is not only a convincing action hero, but also one who offers a timeless insight into loyalty, trust and honesty'

Chris Lloyd, author of *The Unwanted Dead*

'This book has a rich cast of characters who will delight, enthral and keep you turning the pages to the very end. A brilliant, thrilling read, with a new – and very believable – hero. This is my favourite historical novel of the year so far'

Michael Jecks, author of the Last Templar Mysteries

'Fantastic … I found myself utterly engrossed in this book, its wonderfully vivid characters and explosive action. There was never a moment's peace to relax and pause for breath, the reader is dragged along on a white-knuckle adventure by Hazzard's Bombay coat tails'

Parmenion Books

'A great read! Well-tempered and well-researched, with well-drawn, well-conceived characters who will, I am sure, be with us for a while'

Rob Low, author of *The Lion Wakes*

Napoleon's Run

Jonathan Spencer is from south-east London, the great-grandson of a clipper-ship captain who brought tea from China. He served in the Canadian army, studied ancient and modern history, and has lectured at universities and private associations on the subject of Napoleonic Egypt. He writes historical non-fiction under the name Jonathan Downs, his major work a revised account of the British acquisition of the Rosetta Stone, *Discovery at Rosetta*, (London 2008; Cairo 2020). He speaks several languages, has trained with the former Russian National fencing coach, and has lived and worked abroad all his life. He currently lives in the Western Cape in South Africa.

Also by Jonathan Spencer

The William John Hazzard series

Napoleon's Run
Lords of the Nile
Emperor of Dust

JONATHAN SPENCER

NAPOLEON'S RUN

San Diego, California

Canelo US
An imprint of Printers Row Publishing Group
9717 Pacific Heights Blvd, San Diego, CA 92121
www.canelobooksus.com

Printers Row Publishing Group is a division of Readerlink Distribution Services, LLC.
Canelo US is a registered trademark of Readerlink Distribution Services, LLC.

This edition originally published in the United Kingdom in 2021 by Canelo.

Published in partnership with Canelo.

Correspondence regarding the content of this book should be sent to Canelo US,
Editorial Department, at the above address. Author inquiries should be sent to Canelo,
Unit 9, 5th Floor, Cargo Works, 1–2 Hatfields, London SE1 9PG, United Kingdom,
www.canelo.co.

Publisher: Peter Norton • Associate Publisher: Ana Parker
Art Director: Charles McStravick
Senior Developmental Editor: April Graham
Production Team: Beno Chan, Julie Greene, Rusty von Dyl

Library of Congress Control Number: 2022933081

ISBN: 978-1-6672-0228-0

Printed in India

26 25 24 23 22 1 2 3 4 5

For Hayley

Despatch to Admiral Jervis, Lord St Vincent, Cadiz blockade fleet:

When you are apprized that the appearance of a British squadron in the Mediterranean is a condition on which the fate of Europe may at this moment be stated to depend, you will not be surprised that we are disposed to strain every nerve, and incur considerable hazard in effecting it.

The Earl Spencer,
First Lord of the Admiralty,
2 May 1798

Africa

August 1795

The wind shifted a quarter-point and roared inland, a cold, hard southeaster – bane of the Cape of Storms. It battered the desolate peaks and crags behind Table Mountain, the scrub springing and bowing to the gale, resigned to its endless power. Winter in the Cape had been a damp, unwelcoming affair; the sun searing hot on the bleak landscape, the Antarctic blast bringing a bone-deep chill.

A shore party of sailors and red-coated British marines trudged along a goat track high on the slopes above the Muizenberg coast, sweating cold in the icy gusts. Fatigue had forced a weary silence. They had crept across the chasms and scree behind Cape Town for too many days and longed to return to the fleet riding at anchor in the bay below. The new war with France had spread to the bottom of the world, and King George had come for the Cape.

At the head of the column, Marine Captain Harry Race stopped, raised a hand and crouched low, cocking his Sea-Service pistol. At once the marines sank into the olive and dun-brown brush, muskets made ready. The wind carried the crash of the surf up the mountainside from the coast road below – with it came the low drone of Nguni cattle, the dull clank of a harness bell, and the sound of human voices. Race extended a small telescope and pushed through the thicket before him, peering down the slope beyond.

At the base of the mountain stood a covered ox-wagon, laden with the lives of a *Boer* farmer and a family of Xhosa herders. Standing shorter than his wife, in buckskins and a broad-brimmed hat, the farmer faced two British soldiers in scarlet: one, the hulking figure of Marine Sergeant Jory Cook, the other some years his junior, William John Hazzard, Lieutenant of Marines.

The farmer looked down in misery, a great sadness written on his sun-beaten features. '*Ons kraal is afgebrand...*'

After six years on the India run with Cook, Hazzard spoke some Afrikaner Dutch, though never enough, he felt. He wished he could say more on this occasion. The farmer's wife began to weep as the boer told his story, Hazzard translating for the sergeant.

'Their homestead was burnt down... workers murdered...'

'*En meisies... verkrag!*'

Hazzard let out a slow breath and muttered, 'Girls raped...'

Cook said nothing but looked away. He was an old hand of the East India Company, where he had met the young Hazzard and taken him under his wing. He had seen and heard far worse in his long years, but few crimes touched him more deeply, soiling the world still further than it already had been. '*Bastards...*'

'*Wie was dit?*' asked Hazzard, *who was it*, hopeful of some confirmation other than his worst expectations, praying some Bushmen had come out on a raid. But somehow he knew they were not to blame. '*Boesmans?*'

The boer shook his head. '*Nee. Nie boesmans nie.*' No. Not Bushmen.

There was something in his tone suggesting he knew but would not say. Hazzard spoke sharply, '*Dan wie? Nederlanders?*' he asked. *Then who? Dutch?* Losing his patience only slightly before recovering, he pressed on, '*Het jy gesien?*' Did you see?

As if sensing Hazzard's upset, a fragile, bare-footed Xhosa elder in a shawl appeared from the rear of the cart, moving slowly, one thin arm taking support from a staff. A boy followed close behind him, protectively.

Hazzard bowed his head with reverence. '*Maqoma-tata.
Kunjani.*' Greetings, Uncle Maqoma. 'It has been many years.'

The old man raised a hand in salute, nodding his head.
'*N'diphilile, Hazar-tata*… yes, many years.'

'*Nie boesmans nie,*' the boer continued. '*Stewel-spore van
soldate.*'

'Soldiers, he said,' murmured Cook.

'Tracks. He saw soldiers' tracks,' said Hazzard. 'From their
boots.' He tried another tack. '*VOC?*' The VOC was the Dutch
East India Company, which controlled the Cape.

But the boer shook his head, reached out and tapped the
wool of Hazzard's sleeve. '*Rooi mantels.*' Red coats.

Hazzard looked at his sergeant. No translation was necessary.
The boer's wife, stifling tears, gestured to them – *kom, kom* – and
they followed her round to the rear of the ox-cart. Old Maqoma
protested, but she raised the loose canvas flap regardless. Two
Xhosa boys and a girl looked out, startled. Between them, half-
shrouded on a litter, lay a girl of no more than ten, blood on
her scorched face, one leg twisted, eyes staring, dead.

Cook looked away. '*Jaysus shite an' all…*'

The boer looked down, fighting some inner turmoil, and
pulled from his belt a torn patch of red serge wool. He held it
out and whispered, '*Rooi manne.*'

Red men.

The stricken farmer's wife, the adoptive mother to them
all, sobbed at them, '*Waarom, Engelsman? Waarom!*' *Why,
Englishman?*

Hazzard accepted the blame in their eyes. He took the patch
of cloth, rubbing it, testing it for weaknesses, for falsehood, but
he knew it was real, and handed it to Cook. 'Sar'nt. There are
no British troops ashore but us. It…'

Cook looked down, saying nothing.

Hazzard took a small notepad from a pocket and scrib-
bled with a small pencil. 'You must go to Cape Town, to
the castle, *na kasteel*? You will be…' His face flushed and he

3

nodded, as if to convince himself – *England could promise them this much* – his anger rising. 'Yes, you will be compensated by the Crown—' Cook gave a doubtful snort, but Hazzard was adamant. 'Damned well better be, Sar'nt…' He pointed back at the gleaming water behind. 'Our English ships in the bay – our guns will soon fire, even while the generals talk peace.'

'*Ja.*' The boer took the scrap of paper, nodding, crushed. '*Mense is mal…*' *Men are mad.*

They gave the farmer their ration of tobacco, out of charity, out of guilt; asked about their food and water. In return, the Xhosa boys urged the girl forward and she offered them dried springbok *biltong* meat from a leather pouch.

The aged Maqoma, his face lined by lifetimes of sadness, touched his fingers to the marines' foreheads. '*Hamba ghashle, Hazzar-tata… Hamba ghashle.*' *Go softly.* His kindness made it all the more painful for Hazzard.

They began up the slope to the heights. Cook remained silent. When they reached a safe distance from the boer and the track, Hazzard stopped, one hand on the gnarled bough of a milkwood tree. He stared at the ground, his face red. '*Swine…*'

Cook handed him his water bottle. It was rum. He drank, and felt it burn down his throat. '*Damn* him… murderous *swine.*' The wind tugged at his dark curling hair. His shoulders sagged, then straightened, his voice holding back the outrage. 'We are the only witnesses,' he said, handing back the bottle. 'I… I still can't believe it.'

As he said it he wondered why – he should not have been surprised to have had his suspicions confirmed. He steadied the heavy double-barrelled Manton pistol slung under his arm, left hand to his Indian sword, as if to be ready, against his thoughts, his fears. 'A smuggler,' he said, 'yes, even petty bloody thievery I could take. But this? It – it is *unthinkable…*'

Harry Race.

'Bombay Rules, sir,' said Cook bluntly in his Bristol rumble and drank from the bottle. 'Natives count for nuppence an' nobody. And Mr Race… he'll be out for trouble.'

4

Hazzard was lost in memory, of Suffolk, of Race the squire's son, always fighting, always envious. When Hazzard went to India, Race joined the Marines, with the help of Hazzard's uncle, just to outdo him. They had later served together briefly in the North Sea and tolerated a perfunctory reunion with renewed rivalry. But this, down here in the Cape fleet, this had been different, and everyone knew it.

As old India hands, Hazzard and Cook had become well known to all – transferred after three years in the East India Company's naval arm, the Bombay Marine – and this had driven Race to further hatred. Hazzard of the dread Bombay Buccaneers, with his Talwar sword, presented by an Agra prince, yet another source of Race's reborn envy. Race had become something dangerous, and rumour had tarred him far blacker still, and left him untrusted even by his own ship's captain.

'I knew him, once. Long ago… as boys.' Hazzard watched the ground as he walked, his hand on the spiked pommel of the Talwar. 'He is my concern, Sar'nt.'

Cook glanced at him. It was as formal a fending-off as he would get. 'Aye-aye, sir.'

What Hazzard and Cook lacked in rank they had earned in service, and their testimony at any court martial would carry some weight. If it came to that. *Otherwise, what*, Hazzard wondered, *must I do?* His grip tightened on his sword.

Harry. What have you done?

They hurried up through the trees to the rock-strewn hillside, keeping to cover along a wooded gully, and skittered down to their rendezvous with Race. They dislodged loose stones and scree as they descended, until Hazzard pushed through a clump of thornbrush and pulled up sharp, coming face to face with the muzzle of a Navy heavy-bore pistol, the finger of Harry Race on the trigger. As Cook emerged from the thicket behind him, Race smiled and put up his gun.

'Given you up for dead, Will,' said Race. 'Or thought you'd gone native.' He peered through red-rimmed eyes, the sun blinding on the sea beyond. 'Well? Who are they?'

Hazzard dropped down next to him. He wondered how to say it, where to begin. He stared, distracted, aware he was busying himself with his kit, his uniform, unable yet even to look at Race. 'Farmers with an ox wagon, Harry, making for Cape Town—'

'Armed?' Race tried to see down the slope, the view now obscured by the *fynbos* brush and treetops below.

'No,' replied Hazzard. 'Only a boer farmer with his wife and a Xhosa family.' Hazzard looked up suddenly, and watched him as he spoke. 'Their *kraal* was attacked. Burnt to the ground.'

Race continued to look down the slope.

'Men killed, servant girls violated...' He waited until Race turned to look at him. 'Then murdered.'

The southeaster had blown the skies bright, clear and cold. Race squinted back at him, into the sun and wind. 'Well,' he said, 'you know these savages. Hotnots or whatever they are. Take anything.'

'No, Harry, they don't,' said Hazzard. 'Not from an elder.'

'Not that old "Macaronio" again.'

Hazzard did not move. 'Did I say it was Maqoma, Harry?' He waited, watching him. 'Because it was.'

'Well, who gives a damn who it is,' muttered Race, with a wave back at the marines waiting behind. 'Tin-pot baboons won't put up much of a fight. Come on.' Race made to get up and move the platoon off.

'I promised them our protection,' said Hazzard. 'And a ticket for Crown compensation.'

Race stopped. 'Protection?'

'Yes, Harry.'

'*Captain* Race in front of the men, thank you, Lieutenant.'

The marines behind shifted uneasily, exchanging looks, Race's men with knowing smiles, Hazzard's not. The platoon had been cobbled together from two groups, Hazzard's division of six from HMS *America* along with three sailing hands, and Race's six from HMS *Stately*. Far beyond the typical inter-crew rivalry, the two groups of men despised each other.

Race smiled suddenly, confident once again. 'Still rankles does it, Will? After so long? Me getting a captaincy ahead of you, eh? Ha.'

'If my uncle saw fit to purchase you a commission in the Marines, Harry,' said Hazzard with quiet condemnation, 'then so be it.'

Race's sun-blistered skin burned redder still. 'Very well, *Lieutenant*, what was in their cart?'

Hazzard did not look away. 'Other than a murdered girl,' he said quietly, 'nothing.'

Someone in Race's file coughed and mumbled something. Race ignored it. 'Nothing be damned! We've been on this recce jaunt of yours for over a week with nothing to show for it. Tasty pickings – want some damn *booty*, man! We've been rotting in that bloody bay for months while these fat Dutchmen wine and dine and bugger the house-boy...' One of his men sniggered. It was all the encouragement Race needed. 'Spoils or a woman – though a *kaffir* slut hardly counts...'

'For God's sake, Harry,' said Hazzard with disgust.

'Your advice is noted, Lieutenant. I shall inspect this prize cargo and claim it for the Marine company of HMS *Stately*, taking prisoners and returning fire if I deem it necessary.' He checked the priming-pan of his pistol and slammed it shut with a clack. 'And I may just damn well deem it so.' He looked over his shoulder at the men. 'Platoon, on your feet!'

All made to rise, but Hazzard barked, '*America*, stand fast!'

Both divisions of marines froze, including Race.

'Sar'nt Cook,' called Hazzard, his eyes on Race, 'no man is to *move*.'

'Aye, sir!' replied Cook.

Race brandished his pistol. 'Belay that!'

'*As you were!*' shouted Hazzard immediately.

Race swung round and snatched at Hazzard's collar, a smile creeping over his sneering lips as he hissed through bared teeth, 'What do they call you, Will, these jolly, rollicking sea-dogs o'yours, eh? "Billy-Jack" isn't it? Worship you, don't they, eh? Hip-hip-huzzah for Billy-Jack, aye-aye and three-bloody-bags-full for the gentleman *bloody* scholar and his pen – just *too damn pale* to draw his *damn* sword...'

There was a rattle of musket locks from behind. Joining Cook, every marine and seaman in Hazzard's division brought his weapon to bear on Race and his men, the sailors with two pistols each and Pettifer leveling a wide-mouthed musketoon blunderbuss.

Hazzard wrenched Race's hand from his collar and held him fast. 'I should have seen it sooner but I would not believe it until we separated but *by Christ*, plundering farms and *murdering children*? Good *God*, Harry! *You* are the looter, the raider we've been hunting!'

Race tried to smile his way out of it. 'What bloody nons—'

'*Yes – that's* what we're doing, Harry! What Blake *ordered* me to do: *find the man responsible*— and it's *you, damn you!*'

Race jerked away from him. '*I* am in command here, not *you.*'

'You are *relieved*, "Captain"!'

'I am *not*—'

'Sar'nt Cook!' Hazzard drew his Manton and held the twin muzzles inches from Race's chest. 'Make ready!'

'*Clear aye, sir!*' Cook aimed his musket directly at Race.

Race watched Hazzard and the Manton, his gaze flicking to Cook with contempt. 'You and your personal bloody rock-ape. You haven't the *stuffing*—'

With his free hand Hazzard cocked the left lock of the pistol's twin barrels. The marines waited.

'What shall I do, Harry?' said Hazzard, his heart pounding, the heavy pistol trembling in his grip. 'For the sake of – for the sake of my uncle? And your father?' He shook his head, angry with him, angry he had forced his hand. '*Damn* you, Harry! The Provosts will *find* you, and I'll *damn well* let them take you!'

'You wouldn't dare...' Race smiled again, and looked back at his men, a joke to be shared. Carefully he reached past the threat of the Manton with his open right hand, and slapped Hazzard's cheek lightly. Hazzard flinched, pulling away.

'See? It's an old game, isn't it, boy?' Race did it again. 'Come on then, eh? Come on, Will, what do you *think* you are *capable* of d—'

The Manton boomed, a cloud of grey powder-smoke blinding them both. A half-inch lead ball howled off into the wind and Race flew to one side with a cry. Pettifer dropped the nose of the musketoon, whispering, '*Christ, he done it.*'

Race's men took their chance and snatched up their muskets, aiming at Hazzard's men opposite. Pettifer swung the musketoon up but too late.

'*Easy, Petty*,' said the man across from him.

Cook raised the muzzle of his musket into one of their faces and growled, '*You dare try it, boy...*'

Race lay still, breathing hard, then gingerly touched his face in disbelief. His fingers came away red with blood, his cheekbone blackened and burned, a strip of blistered skin hanging. '*You utter...*' He half lunged, but Hazzard thrust the twin muzzles hard against Race's chest, the right barrel already cocked. Race stopped and stared down at it, 'Now you've done it, you *bastard*... You haven't the faintest idea what you're meddling with... *not the faintest idea!*'

Hazzard looked at the men, squared off to each other, waiting for the order. Neither squad of marines moved. Pettifer met his eye, the musketoon held rock-steady now: it would kill three at a stroke, but even with that terrible weapon on their side, Hazzard knew he would lose at least four of his own if he gave the order. And he knew he could not, would not.

'*Bargain*,' hissed Race. 'We go, me, my men. No one fires.' Slight panic had entered Race's voice.

9

'You were schooled by my *uncle*, Harry, you *know* us...' Hazzard thrust the pistol against his throat. '*How could you? How?*' Race began to choke, the barrels tight against him, Hazzard watching him until he could bear it no longer and clenched his eyes shut, wishing he could just shoot. '*Damn you...*' He moved back, the Manton still pointing at Race. '*Get out of my sight.*'

But Race did not move, his eyes glancing back at Hazzard's men, at his own. 'By God, Will, if you so much as—'

'I said *go.*'

Race pushed himself stiffly to his feet and adjusted his scarlet coat.

'If the Provosts come, Harry,' said Hazzard, 'I'll see you hang.'

Race's blue eyes stared back, giving no sign to Hazzard of time shared, of any acquaintance or companionship before this, only a bright, shining hatred. 'And I shall see you spitted like a pig,' he said, 'on the *Stately*'s bowsprit.'

He pushed his way through the bushes to the slope beyond, his men backing away, following him, clattering down the hillside. Within a few moments, the scene was quiet.

Cook, Pettifer and De Lisle moved for the bushes at once. A loose volley of shot crackled in reply, echoing across the mountain, musket-balls fizzing overhead: a warning. Hazzard put up a hand to stop them. 'Leave them to the Provosts... when they come.' He sank back, the Manton nearly tumbling from his numbed hands, gulping air as if he had been drowning. 'I can't believe it,' he whispered. 'I can't... It was him.'

'They had us, sir,' said Pettifer.

'*Christ A'mighty...*' muttered one of the marines, then with a mumble, 'Beggin' your pardon, sir.'

Cook took up the Manton, cleared and reloaded the empty barrel out of old habit, and glanced round at the marines, some still staring, wide-eyed. Pettifer and Lacey, Williams, Tyler and De Lisle, the sailing hands Handley, Peckham and Church. 'Well?' said Cook. 'What says the boat?'

'Boat says bloody aye,' said Pettifer without qualm in his rolling Cornish, his hands tightening on the giant blunderbuss. 'We's for you, sir, no fear, and we'll tell Cap'n so.'

This seemed to wake Hazzard from a dull dream. 'I let... I let him go...' He groped for his sword and started towards the slope. 'We must get after him...'

'Gone, sir.' Cook put out a restraining hand. 'We move onto that slope, they snipe us off one by one.'

'Cookie,' called Handley, a tattooed red-haired foremast hand from the *America*, who was gazing out towards Simon's Town through an eyeglass. 'Got company. Dutchies, 'orse an' foot. Bout two 'undred. And signals on the *America*, Mr 'Azzard, sir, seems the admiral's swapped his flag.'

Hazzard took the telescope. In the distance, approaching along the coast road, he could see a cloud of dust rising. Galloping horse and running troops, regulars, militia, black men, white men, all charged headlong down the coastal road away from the oncoming barrage, the remnants of Simon's Town's Dutch VOC defenders. Trees and the jutting headland of the heights obscured Hazzard's view of the Dutch batteries, but there could be little doubt there would be few men left to stand against the invader. A dull, percussive bark sounded in the distance: a signal gun.

He swung the eyeglass out to the bay and sighted HMS *Monarch*. Signals fluttered up her mainmast, and the new flagship HMS *America* responded. Snatches of drumming reached him on the wind. They were all beating to quarters, clearing for action, the red coats of the landing battalion visible as they formed up in Simon's Town. He pulled a watch from his tunic pocket. It was past two. The deadline for the Cape had come and gone. *Monarch* and the other two 74s, *Arrogant* and *Victorious*, ran out their guns.

'Wind change, sir,' said Handley. 'They're in for it now.'

Cook spat. 'Admiral'll blow this bloody hill to Kingdom Come in five minutes.'

Hazzard felt the southeaster die away to an irregular buffeting, mixing with wetter winds from the northwest. Clouds piled high on the horizon. The surf crashed on the rocks of False Bay just below. The coastline stretched out to his left in a graceful arc of marsh and shingle, curving far into the southerly distance. To the right, the peaks surrounding Simon's Town and its small port glowed in the sun. *Monarch* moved into position, her heavy guns rolled out, 32-pounders and 24s, pointing at the shore batteries on the hillside above the town. It would take but a single concerted broadside to reduce the place to rubble. The lighter Royal Navy warships made sail, the northwest wind moving them down the shoreline towards Hazzard, HMS *America, Stately*, the fast sloops *Echo* and *Rattlesnake*, and the low-slung mortar-bombardment vessels, all seeking out the elevated Dutch gun positions of Muizenberg and Kalk Bay just below.

'Sail approachin', sir,' said Handley. '*America, Stately* and the Bombs.'

Within a few minutes, *America* lowered her anchors both fore and aft into boats. The crews rowed the anchors further inshore and put them overboard, the splashes visible even from Hazzard's vantage point on the heights of Steenberg. *America's* capstans began to turn. Hazzard could hear the scream of the cables shuddering under the strain as the ship winched itself slowly into firing position while *Stately, Echo* and *Rattlesnake* glided into range, smaller gunboats in their wake.

'Mr 'Azzard,' reported Handley, squinting into the dazzle of the bay. 'Beggin' your pardon, sir, but ports openin', and they're runnin' 'em out.' He looked back at Cook. 'Time to scarper, Cookie...'

Hazzard swung the scope back to *America*. One after the other, the gun ports were raised. Loosed from captive chains, twenty-six heavy cannon emerged from the darkness, the cries of the gun-crews hollow from inside.

'Very well,' said Hazzard, then zeroed the scope on the road below. The fleeing VOC men had all but gone, a company of

Burgher sharpshooters on horseback bringing up the rear. 'Let's get down to the shore—'

'*Jaysus an' all*,' said Cook, pointing down the slope behind them. 'Mr Race – he's found that *ruddy* boer wagon.'

Hazzard turned, his breath catching. 'Where away?'

'Hard a-larboard, that trail to the coast road.'

Hazzard swung sharp left and focussed. The boer and his family had not headed back to Cape Town as he had advised. Instead they had followed a track to the coast road with the heavy ox-cart and stopped by a clearing in the shade of the trees. Race and his men had intercepted them.

Their white cross-belts bright in the sun, three red-coated marines with muskets circled the wagon slowly, while Race faced the farmer and the old Xhosa headman. The Xhosa boys stood with the girl huddled against the farmer's wife, arms waving as they shouted at them to go away, *hamba, hamba!* In the surrounding brush Hazzard saw Race's remaining three men taking aim. It was an ambush.

'*Good God…*'

Ignoring the flight of the enemy on the coast road at the base of the slope, Hazzard stood in full view in front of the thicket, halfway up the mountain, waving, calling anything to warn the boer.

'*Meneer, hardloop! Gaan weg!*' Run! Get out of there!

Through the eye of the scope, Hazzard saw Race and the boer look up at him. Maqoma appeared, speaking, calming. Race smiled. He drew his pistol, looked up at Hazzard, and shot the frail Maqoma square in the chest. Hazzard nearly dropped the scope.

No.

One of the Xhosa boys ran for the cart and pulled out a heavy-headed *knobkerrie*, the other rushed for a rack of upright herding staves standing at the rear and took down an old *mkhonto* spear. With a rattle of blasts the marines in the bushes fired a volley of musket-shot into the group of figures, clouds of grey smoke bursting from the undergrowth. Their arms flung wide, the boys fell, the *knobkerrie* and *mkhonto* rolling into the dust.

With his hands reaching out, the boer farmer lunged for Race, and Race sank his sword deep into the man's broad belly. The farmer's wife screamed but the surviving girl pulled her away to run into the thicket, followed by one of the marines, diving into the trees after them. The Nguni ox called out in fright, trying to turn, the cart lurching from side to side.

One of Race's men, musket in hand, strolled up to the last wounded boy, now crawling along the road. He stood over him and called something to the others, who laughed. With the brass butt of his musket he then battered the boy's skull until the body stopped moving. Race caught up to the ox and tugged it onwards, and it stumbled up the track, bellowing while the marines squatted to pick over the spoils.

Hazzard's marines stared down at the scene, Pettifer breaking their silence, '*Bloody hellfire…*'

Hazzard felt a wash of ice flooding his limbs and began to shake. The fleet forgotten, the fleeing Dutch forgotten, he drew the double-barrelled Manton once more from its holster. '*America*, to me!'

Every man went over the ridge and hurtled down through the bush of the mountainside, following Hazzard as he dodged through the thorn and shrub. The marines pounded behind him, keeping pace with the three seamen from the *America* shrieking on ahead, arms windmilling wildly, short cutlass blades in each hand.

Hazzard felt nothing, not the ground, not the air, not the brush, running as if caught in a raging torrent. He saw Race at the foot of the slope, no further than a hundred yards at the most and raised the Manton to aim but fell, tumbling end over end. Handley pulled him to his feet and they plunged into the trees and undergrowth at the bottom of the mountain. After fighting his way through the spear-bladed palms and ferns, Hazzard burst out and tumbled into the ditch leading to Race's position and began to run.

14

'*Harry!*'

Hazzard found the track. There lay Maqoma, gazing blank-eyed at the sky, a broad dark stain on his thin linen shawl. Beside him lay the boer farmer, stripped of his buckskin jacket, a livid tear in his abdomen, blood pooling beneath him, and further off, the dead boys, one face-down in the road, his skull shattered.

Hazzard's chest heaved for air, blood pounding in his ears and he was unable to feel his limbs. '*Alive!*' he roared, '*I want him alive! The rest dead on sight, by God!*'

In a gap in the milkwoods and pepper trees he found the Nguni ox, dead, its great horns at a stricken angle, the upturned cart on its side by a grassy clearing. There was no sign of Race or his men, only chests and sacks torn open, spilled grains, blankets and linen blowing in the wind. They fanned out and entered the clearing.

A musket banged to Hazzard's right and the howling bullet skimmed the leaves above his head. He whirled and dropped low, firing a snap-shot, a single barrel of packed pistol-ball shredding the bush, and one of Race's marines cried out and collapsed into the tall grass.

'Spread out!' ordered Hazzard, 'I want them all!'

He heard a scream from somewhere beyond the trees. Cook and Pettifer charged on ahead, Handley and the two sailors coming up fast. Within moments, Cook called out from behind a stand of trees, '*Sir!*'

He hauled one of Race's marines to his feet, the tunic open, white breeches down over his grey gaiters, the unmoving naked form of the black girl at his feet. The farmer's wife lay to one side, stripped to the waist, a jagged wound in her back.

'Rapine and murder, sir!' shouted Cook, shaking the man by his collar, 'The *shite!*'

The marine struggled, '*No, sir – I never—*'

Hazzard strode forward, put the Manton pistol to the man's cheekbone and blew off most of his head.

'*Aye bloody aye, sir!*' replied Cook, and threw down the shattered corpse.

'*Race!*' called Hazzard again, running back to the ox-cart. He tugged out two new pistol cartridges, but a cloud of white blossomed in the trees to his left and Hazzard's left shoulder burst with a musket-shot. He fell, a marine coming for him at the run, in panic wielding his musket like a club.

Struggling to rise, Hazzard rolled against one of the Xhosa staves, his fingers finding the broken shaft of the bladed *mkhonto*. He swung upright and flung the broken spear in a flat, whirling spin. It caught the marine's face as it flew past, knocking him backwards, his hands clutching at his neck. Hazzard dived on him, snatched up the spearhead from the grass and thrust it into his throat again and again as the marine's hands clawed at his face. Hazzard then yanked the blade free and drove the broken haft down into the marine's eye socket where it jammed tight, and the man fell still.

Another marine appeared from the trees ahead, musket rising to the aim. Hazzard flung himself flat and the shot went wide. The marine scrabbled at the cartridge box on his belt to reload as Hazzard got to his feet and drew the Talwar from its scabbard.

'*Petty!*' came a cry from behind, and De Lisle and Pettifer rushed past, shielding Hazzard as they fired from the hip, the packed shot from Pettifer's giant musketoon blasting into the man's abdomen, tearing him nearly in half. What was left of the marine flew backwards into the tall grass. Pettifer turned and helped Hazzard to his feet. '*He's a dead 'un, sir!*'

'Well done, Pet. Sar'nt Cook!' called Hazzard, 'Williams! Tyler, Lacey! Report!'

Cook emerged from the trees with the others at a run. 'Mr Race and two men, headed for the shore and a boat, I reckon.'

'He's making for the landing point,' said Hazzard.

'Spin a yarn for the admiral most like, and blame us for this lot.'

16

'Mr 'Azzard, sir!' Handley joined him with the two seamen. He slapped the reloaded Manton into his right hand. 'Rammed, primed, cocked and locked, aye!'

'Very good, Handley, much obliged – *America* to the beach!'

They dashed through the dark of the low trees towards the light of the sea, the sun blazing across the coast road. Whatever the fate of the retreating Cape forces, the road was clear. They rushed across it and into the bush on the seaward slope to the marshes below, and Hazzard heard one of them shout, '*Ho there! Marines dead ahead – you got 'em, sir!*'

With their red and white standing out bright from the wet sand and marsh grass, Hazzard saw Race and his two remaining men grappling with a small craft. They dragged it through the marsh across the pebbles to the surf where it collapsed and broke apart. Race slammed it down in anger and the others ran off to find another.

Hazzard launched himself down the slope. 'Get them down there, Sar'nt Cook!'

'*Aye, sir! Get yer flippin' arses down that slope! Juldee or dead, as if Davy hisself were after ye!*'

They jumped, grabbing and hanging from splintered tree limbs, dropping from boulder to boulder, stump to stump, the sailors more nimble than the marines, some falling in pain then rising again. Hazzard leapt, dropped, fell, then almost collapsed as he hit the marsh sand and pebble, falling then rising, Cook and Pettifer either side, grabbing him up, his legs pumping, feet pounding, sinking, stumbling, his eye ever on Race, a smear of scarlet against the blue. '*Harry…*'

To their left lay the upturned keels of shattered and abandoned boats. The sailors fell upon them, calling out, '*O'er 'ere!*' but Hazzard did not reply and kept running for the distant figure, not fifty yards away, gazing out to sea at the fleet. Hazzard drew the Talwar, cocked the Manton, and charged.

Race turned. He saw Hazzard tearing across the sand towards him. He tugged his sword from its sheath, raised a pistol and fired.

17

Hazzard threw himself to the left – even with the wind he heard the shot howl past – and fired the Manton in reply. Race drew a second pistol and charged, the two of them rushing each other, pistols raised.

But their action was overwhelmed by a thunderclap of sound, a massed broadside soon overtaken by a barrelling roar: the Royal Navy opened fire.

The slopes of Muizenberg and Kalkberg shook, chalk crags and bluffs bursting, the surrounding waters shivering to the unfamiliar tempest. HMS *Echo* and *Rattlesnake*'s 24-pounders, 18s, and the giant yawning mortars of the gunboats belched thunderheads of writhing smoke and flaming iron high into the deep blue of the Cape skies, to come crashing down upon the coast road and the Dutch batteries. Among the towering bursts of rock and earth, a lone cannon returned fire, its defiance engulfed by the barrage.

Neither Race nor Hazzard broke their stride. Race fired just as Hazzard did, the bullets going wild, their meagre flash and report lost in the cacophony of cannon raging behind them. They threw down their guns on the run and swung their blades in simultaneous overhead attack.

They collided with such force that they spun each other about, the heavy Talwar taking a chunk of steel from Race's blade. Hazzard went down into the surf, whirling round, the weight of the Talwar swinging him up and tight, faster than the taller Race – and he made the first cut. Race cursed with pain but countered quickly with a downward cut to Hazzard's head, Hazzard parrying and hooking it away, dropping his blade in a diagonal strike across Race's trunk. The keen edge of the Talwar slashed the scarlet coat, and Race clutched at his ribs, staggering backwards. He looked at his hands, bright with blood. Hazzard sprang upright but nearly fell again with the force of Race's next blow, hard and to his left, and felt the steel batter away his parry to bite into his arm, a blast of ice lancing up to his shoulder, and he shouted with pain.

Behind them, the 64-gun *America* and *Stately* rocked from beam to beam, nodding with the recoil of their unceasing barrage while the duellists roared in each other's faces. Though no swordsman, Race had the strength to bludgeon and batter. Hazzard overextended and felt a blow slide across his back and strike low to his thigh, connecting as he ducked, parried and twisted, trying to break through Race's guard. Race shouted as he attacked again and again, '*Never as good, was I, eh? Eh? Three cheers, then! Let's hear them, come on! Come on!*'

Hazzard's rage was rising, he could feel it in the clench of his jaw; he pictured the marine clubbing the boy to death, the dead girl, the boer and his wife, Maqoma butchered without a care. He smacked Race's blade flat and to the right, throwing him off-balance, exposing his right side, and swung the Talwar. He cut deep, Race crying out, and Hazzard spun, the curve of the blade slicing *down*, across, *up* to the right, *down* again, slashing Race from hip to chest, his cries taken by the wind, '*Will, wait*—' The Indian sword whirling constantly in a murderous arc, Race's coat flapping, his breeches sprayed red, the Talwar carving a large, bloody X.

Race called again, '*Will…*', eyes wide, sword dropping, until he fell to his knees with a howling cry, a child losing a game, wanting it to stop.

'*Will…!*'

Hazzard paused, the bloodied Talwar poised high. He stared without recognition, his breath hissing from between tightened lips, his chest heaving, ready to deliver the final descending cut. He did not know the Harry Race before him. All memories lost, all forgotten. The Harry of his boyhood had become but a creature, a creature to be stopped. Yet he hesitated, the Talwar still, waiting.

Race searched for his sword in the sand, reaching, missing, then gripping it, his breath rattling to nothing in the barrage of guns. He gasped, his whisper a taunt, as ever, '*Never could… finish, could you…*'

After a moment, realisation returned to Hazzard, the anger rising once again. 'I will *not...*' grated Hazzard, *'give you that final satisfaction.'* He drove the steel guard and hilt of the Talwar into Race's cheek, knocking him backwards into the foam of the surf.

The endless blast of the guns impossible to tolerate any longer, Hazzard dropped to the sand. *'Harry...'* The sky blinding, the seawater lapping, stinging, the ebb and flow tugging at the torn flesh of his wounds.

Race lay not three yards off, breath rattling in his throat. Musket-fire popped, bullets kicking up the earth around him, a boat scraping as it was driven aground, sailors rushing ashore. A far-off call like a seabird, *Mr 'Azzard, Mr 'Azzard.* Hazzard registered the images, the sounds, as if in a fever, a Navy bluejacket and a raised pistol, Cook shouting, somewhere, *Mr Blake—!*

Race was on one knee, the sea beneath him marbled with eddies of crimson. Hazzard watched him from the surf, but did not move, could not, his left knee numb, dead. For a moment, the percussive bark of the guns paused. Race gazed at him from darkening eyes, his voice no more than a grinding rasp.

'Regards... to Sarah.'

A single pistol-shot cracked and Hazzard saw the impact upon Race's back, a burst of powder, blood and grit, an arm twisting, the sword falling. Race fell into the water and lay still. Hazzard watched, expecting him to rise again, as he would when they were boys, playing dead. But Race lay still, the surf pushing then pulling at him, his life draining into the ebb, nothing returning with the flow. An iron door closed inside Hazzard, and he felt immediate relief – soon surpassed by shame.

'Harry...'

The barrage continued, and Hazzard raised his hands to his ears, unaware he was screaming aloud, into the blue above, against the guns, against the Cape. He became aware of Cook and Pettifer leaning over him, their mouths wide, shouting, Cook's face hard, pushing away a hand, pointing at another, calling an order, but Hazzard heard nothing, the bombardment, water in his ears, salt in his eyes, stinging, cooling, biting, a constant shrill filling the void as the guns roared.

Hands moved beneath his head, lifting him up, and he rose, weightless, carried from the water's edge – *Pettifer, De Lisle* – then the hard timbers of a boat, the sharp odour of pitch, salt and lime, the hollow knock of oars on wood, Cook nearby, *Careful, ye blagg'ard, he's my lad, d'ye hear?* Then someone behind, *Get those bodies aboard there!*

'Mr Hazzard…' said a soft voice from above. 'Can you understand me? It's Lieutenant Blake, from the *Monarch*.'

Hazzard blinked, the sun suddenly brighter, the noise crashing in, painful.

'Blake…?'

Blake tucked a folded blanket gently under Hazzard's head, holding him steady, almost cradling him. He smelt of soap and civilisation, wore a crisp white collar with black cravat, and the sun glinted off the gold brocade and buttons of his blue coat. Blake inclined his head in salute. 'The admiral's compliments,' he said with a kindly smile, 'and mine. The finest swordsmanship we have yet seen, and we would have you to dine once again – in one piece, if at all possible.'

Cook swam into his vision. 'You got him a'right, Mr Blake?'

'Yes, Sergeant, we've got him. Be right as your Bristol rain, just you wait and see.'

Cook's hand clutched at Hazzard's and held it tight, his voice shaking through a half-smile. 'Y'hear now? Mr Blake says he'll see ye right, sir, right as Bristol rain…' Then, in a harsher, lower voice, 'You done for him, lad, caught him with the Mughal Cross. Knew y'could…'

'My fault…' His coat burned, on his arm, his leg, burned everywhere, the scarlet like fire. *Rooi mantels*, he heard the boer say again, *Red coats*. 'The boer… Maqoma…'

'He had the devil in him, Mr Race did – you or me or God Himself, he would've done for us all. Admiral'll hear it clear, aye.' Cook leaned over him, his unshaven face tired, even the great oak showing signs of wear.

'I can't ever stop, can I?' murmured Hazzard. *If I'd never found the truth, if I hadn't pushed.* 'Can't stop...' He clenched Cook's hand. *'Get us out of here, Jory.'*

Cook nodded, the use of his first name telling him how bad it was, more than others could possibly know. 'Aye, sir... just you leave that to me.' He rose up, roaring, *'I said get shoved off this bloody rock, ye bone-idle bloody matelots!'*

Hazzard felt his scarlet coat being cut away, a relief, a lightening of spirit. *'It's Dr Simmons, sir, hold tight there...'* Bandages pressed to his raw flesh. *'Sword cuts deep in the fascia, but not deadly... quite a few thorns as well, cutting here...'* Cuffs opening, brass buttons falling, rattling into the scuppers, bouncing away.

Hazzard looked up at Blake. 'Race...'

'Yes, we know.' He sounded heavy with the knowledge of it. The grind of the shore left them and soon they were floating free, dipping and swaying, Hazzard light, euphoric. He sank away, then jerked awake again, Blake still talking.

'...been running quite mad ashore for some two months. He overstepped the mark. Colonel Gordon and the Dutch demanded his head, unofficially. For the negotiations.' He sounded apologetic. 'You were the only officer capable of – how shall I say – dealing with him.'

'He was...' Hazzard's voice croaked, dry. The blast of the guns stopped abruptly. Almost immediately *Stately* and *Echo* took up the onslaught, pounding the rocks now behind them. 'He was...' *What? What was he? Friend? Boyhood rival? Adopted brother?* 'And I... I...'

They dipped in the swell, the Cape mountains bobbing slowly, the rhythm hypnotic. Blake nodded and smiled with some sadness. 'He was to marry a lady of your acquaintance, was he not? Or was that yourself, I cannot recall...'

Hazzard closed his eyes, tears stinging. *Regards to Sarah.* Words came with difficulty, but with sudden realisation: *He overstepped the mark.*

'*You knew...*'

Blake's expression gave little away, confession in itself. 'In our defence, it was a last throw. To create unrest, and then to offer a solution, rectify the situation.' He nodded, solemn. 'Alas, William, a plan gone awry.'

Hazzard watched him, the sun dazzling. *Blake had known. Known.* 'You *ordered* him? You ordered Race *to do murder...*?'

'We had no idea that he would—'

'Innocents *dead*, Charles... *innocents.* H-how could you... for *this*?'

Blake took it upon his shoulders, his head low, yet another burden of his office. 'The admiral had every faith in you, and now we are guests, not invaders. France will never get past the Cape to India again.' He looked away, then back again. 'It is a matter of *empire*, William.'

Hazzard blinked, seeing only the dead. '*Damn* your empire...'

Hazzard could not look upon him any longer. His mind clouded with visions of India, Africa – of home, wherever that was, of Sarah, of the squire's son Harry Race.

Blake was speaking again, 'The Prince of Orange will be—'

But Hazzard interrupted, taking hold of his bluejacket, 'I *'sign...*' his throat ran dry, '...*resign* my commission, Charles... and may God *damn* you all for what you have done...'

The guns fell silent at last. Wreaths of black smoke curled across the sky, deep shadow passing over Blake's concerned features. 'Come now.' Blake kept the tone light. 'Resign? Hazzard of the Bombay Buccaneers? Most unlike.' He smiled down at Hazzard and said softly, 'Fine weather in England, I hear. Time for rest, a spot of leave.'

'No...' The light began to flicker before Hazzard's eyes, sleep descending. 'I will *not*...'

'My dear fellow,' replied Blake, taking Hazzard's bandaged arm and resting it carefully on his chest as he drifted off, 'we could scarce have done it without you.'

Seabirds shrieked and the oars creaked, swung and dipped. Thoughts of Sarah, thoughts of Harry and, before darkness claimed him, a whispered prayer to Cook, *'Get us safe to sea, Jory.'*

1798

Three years later

République

Despite the passing of five years since the Terror, the corridors of the Tuileries Palace were still rank with the sour taint of blood and betrayal. At midnight the vast interior echoed empty and hollow, a polished, torchlit tomb, the ghosts of slain conspirators flitting through arcades of soaring columns and ornamental arches. But the deadliest of its more recent tenants moved through its halls without fear, his heels tapping an eerie, measured tattoo, very much that of the night watchman, and keeper of souls.

Jules-Yves Derrien was a hard, wiry figure in his mid-thirties, bearing scars earned in the victory at Valmy in 1792 – and in darker, unseen battles, in the covert realms of the *Bureau d'information*. In its secret operations he had subverted friend and foe alike in the cause of the Republic, shifting from one faction to the other – eventually to take Robespierre's head, personally. Under the more stable Directory government he had been raised to the rank of 'Collector', and anointed chief spycatcher of France. He had swept the assembly halls clear of any threat, without fear or favour, his eyes and ears everywhere.

The night watch of the palace guard cracked to attention as he passed. His dead, blank expression rarely varied – in his habitual austere black frock coat and cocked hat he was regarded not merely with fear, but dread. To the rank and file he was Citizen *Croquemort* – the Mortician.

Part of Derrien relished the name: the inspiration of fear was the basis of power. He had learnt this lesson well. The Revolution's new Garden of Eden had spawned not one but three serpents, the three chief Directors of France, Lépeaux, Rewbell and Barras – and through Barras, *Primus inter pares*, first among equals, they inspired fear through Bonaparte.

Barras had passed the baton to Bonaparte in the battle for Paris, and let him blast the marching royalists from the streets with grape-shot and become the saviour of the Revolution. It was Bonaparte who had installed the Directors, and Barras who had then given Bonaparte the Army of Italy – which made him conqueror. It was even common knowledge that Joséphine had been Barras's very expensive mistress before he had introduced her to Bonaparte. This was a union too powerful to break, the king and the general, who could summon 20,000 troops with a snap of his fingers – and Barras was wise enough to know who was more beloved of the people. And so too was Derrien.

The palace had been in a state of readiness for weeks since that first night: Derrien had been sent to a lower level of the Tuileries with two Bureau men to wait at a particular spot in a dank hallway where the tall painted panelling concealed a flush door. All he had been told was to meet an 'important visitor' and escort him to Barras's rooms immediately, unseen. Derrien had suggested the rendezvous at the secret door. He had waited, at the appointed time, hands tucked behind his back, the torchlight flickering across his features. One of his men coughed quietly. Derrien turned slowly to look at him in silent rebuke.

With a rattle of keys from the other side came a signal knock, and Derrien had stepped forward, flipped a catch, and swung the door inwards. Out of the darkness beyond stepped two officers in blue cloaks, one, the sunken-eyed and cadaverous *Chef de brigade* Jean-Androche Junot, senior aide of the other, the slight, 28-year-old Napoléon Bonaparte, hero of the siege of Toulon, the 13th *Vendémiaire*, victor of Italy, *Commandant* of the Paris Guard, and *Général en chef* of the *Armée d'Angleterre*.

Junot gave the area a quick check, striding to the corner, peering down the passages. The young general had barely glanced at Derrien at first, his eye sweeping up and down the corridor, before his gaze settled and he gave a sardonic shrug. 'So?' he said, 'I do not know you.'

Derrien noted that he had the impeccable elocution of the foreigner, notes of the Mediterranean carefully smoothed away to almost nothing. 'Today, I am Barras,' said Derrien. 'Yesterday, I was Robespierre.' It was the old custom of the battlefield messenger, declaring for whom one carried a despatch to speed communication. Bonaparte nodded, accepting the tacit compliment that he of all people would recognise a fellow soldier. He looked at Derrien properly for the first time. Derrien bowed his head. 'Battle of Valmy, Citizen General,' he said, 'Captain of Artillery.'

This final comment caught Bonaparte's attention: artillery was the mathematician general's particular speciality. 'Mm. Valmy. Barely a thousand rounds fired. Well done.' Bonaparte took a breath. 'And so. Who would you be tomorrow?'

'Tomorrow, Citizen General,' risked Derrien, 'I would be Bonaparte.'

Bonaparte nodded, satisfied. '*Bon.*'

They set off, their heels echoing dissonantly. Bonaparte said, 'You know Director Barras's intentions.'

'Yes, Citizen General. His intentions are always the same…' Derrien led them up a quiet back-stair.

'And they are?'

They reached the top and Derrien indicated a darkened corridor leading to distant offices. A door opened and lamplight gleamed. Barras stepped out, several figures behind. 'To support the winner, Citizen General.'

Bonaparte turned to go, then stopped. 'You are Derrien.'

He had known all along. Derrien bowed his head. 'Collector. *Bureau d'information.* At the service of the Republic, Citizen General.' He hesitated a moment, then said quickly and quietly, 'Director Rewbell suspects your motives, but Director Lépeaux is ready to retire, and needs only the promise of a bribe to side with Director Barras.'

Bonaparte weighed his advice, then nodded. 'We shall meet again.'

To that same meeting, Derrien had escorted Foreign Minister Talleyrand. Rewbell's derisive clamour had reached out to the corridors, *So! At last you would be king of France, eh, eh!* until Bonaparte's words cut them short, *How many golden baubles more for your mistresses must I buy with the blood of my army! I would push a battle-fleet through a desert with my bare hands,* he had sworn, *if you bookmen would but let me!*

From that moment, the palace had been alive with whispers of an armada – whispers of troops, baggage trains, ships, provisions and guns, yet no one knew how, or where – nor why.

But Derrien did. And he was determined that the whisperers should be silenced. He had doubled the security of the Tuileries and the *Palais Bourbon*, and posted *gendarmes*, militia from the Paris Guard and Bureau agents at every street-corner, watching every secretary, every official at every exit, in the cafés, in the taverns, watching, *listening*. Listening for his special words: *Kléber, Desaix, Monge, Berthollet, Toulon, Marseille, l'Italie, l'Orient,* the ships, the generals, and the greatest secret of all: the target. Any who uttered them were bundled out quickly and jailed for interrogation. *Nothing*, he had promised the Bureau Secretariat, would escape his scrutiny. Thus, by night, his heels clicking steadily on the marble floors with the regularity of a metronome, he patrolled the halls of Government.

On this particular night, he patrolled in the company of a deputy: Citizen Masson, a stone-faced escort with bulging eyes and a broad, mirthless iron trap of a mouth – a dull-witted if obedient bullmastiff.

Dragoon troopers and Foot Guards stood at every archway, atop every stair and at every corner, the Guards with muskets and fixed bayonets, the Dragoons with swords and two heavy 14-bore holster pistols each. Derrien noted their flashings: the 14th *demi-brigade* and the 8th. This was correct for Day Six of his ten-day *décade* roster. He had arranged it so. He would tolerate no deviation, and there never was.

30

'We must confirm every detail,' said Derrien to Masson, like a tutor. 'Constantly.'

'Yes, Citizen.'

'None who is trusted today should necessarily be trusted tomorrow.'

'No, Citizen.'

They walked on, heels clicking. Suddenly explosive in the silence, a concealed door to the service stairs burst open some distance up ahead to their left, the gallery immediately flooded with lamplight. The men and women of the evening-shift cleaning staff clattered out from the hidden passage, mops and buckets in hand, hushing each other as they realised they were not alone. An exit door to the lower levels opened up, and the hall torches flickered in the draught. A Foot Guard ticked them off one by one as they began to file out.

Nôtre Dame sounded eleven and local parish bells clanged in competitive disharmony. Derrien checked his watch. The cleaners were on time. He and Masson moved through them, these malodorous toiling sons and daughters of the Revolution. Derrien was aware of everything, their coarse clothing, their malnourished faces, their fearful silence as he drew near. He was Authority, whether king's officer or people's tribune, he was *power*, and they bowed to him.

Derrien was at the point of telling Masson that the evening shift should not end so early when his thoughts were transported to an arbitrary childhood memory – of summer grasses and golden sunlit meadows, an aunt, a slowing carriage, and a grand lady in a tall white wig handing something down to him as a gift. He stopped.

Perfume.

It was just like her perfume.

The scent lingered as if it were clinging to him, to something familiar. He swung round, his bright, mechanical gaze traversing the group as they began to descend the stairs, their shapes flaring and vanishing in the flicker of torches. One of the

31

women began to push her way through her colleagues, bustling for the door. In her haste she dropped her mop with a crash and all fell suddenly still. Derrien caught her eye.

'*You!*'

The cleaner cried out and ran for the stairs. The guards reacted quickly but had to force their way through the group of startled onlookers. Derrien was soon at the door, his deputy close behind, the cleaners jumping aside. Three Foot Guards crashed down the stairs before him calling, '*Arrêtez, arrêtez!*'

The fugitive woman made the first landing but one of the soldiers reached out for the grubby white neckerchief hanging over her shoulders. She screamed as he tugged her back and she fell, sprawling on the landing.

More guards clumped down the steps as the other cleaners craned over the banister above to watch. Muskets and fixed bayonets levelled, four soldiers surrounded the cornered woman with her back to the wall.

Derrien and a guard sergeant cleared a path. '*Out of the way, damn you, the Collector comes!*' Seeing Derrien, the woman began to shake in stark terror.

'*Ci-citizen…*' she stammered, her hands up, her head turned away from them all, eyes clenched tight shut, now afraid to look. 'Wh–what have I done?'

Derrien examined her. She looked the part, with pitted skin, and lank, dirty hair. She wore a grey-brown bodice over a soiled short-sleeved cotton blouse, lace frills frayed at the elbow, a thin shawl overtop, secured by a filthy knot, an old mob cap with a crumpled tricolour cockade of the *sans culottes* pinned to the front. Her homespun skirt was patched and raggedly stitched at the hem – all correct for one of the emancipated *Parisienne* poor of the new Republic. Derrien leaned over her, and sniffed.

'Perfume.'

His unblinking eyes locked on hers.

'She is nothing, Citizen,' interrupted the sergeant. 'Just a cleaner—'

Derrien corrected him. 'All citizens are of value to the Republic, Sergeant.' He looked at her again. 'Who?' he asked.

'*M-m-m'sieur…?*' she gasped, then blinking, eyes clenched shut, afraid of her error. 'C-citizen…?'

Derrien waited until her breathing calmed. 'The scent. Who gave it to you?'

The woman suddenly cried out, the howl rising to a scream, and tried to claw at the wall for support. Citizen Derrien was unmoved.

'Her skirts.'

The sergeant did not understand. 'I beg your pardon, Citizen?'

'Show me her skirts.'

The sergeant too hesitant, Citizen Masson shouldered him aside and advanced on her. She began to scream more loudly. He tore a corner of the coarse fabric away from its fastening at her waist, then twisted her roughly, revealing an old petticoat beneath. Derrien nodded. 'Again.' And Masson yanked this away as well, revealing plain pantaloons. They were an unusual luxury for one such as she.

'Continue,' said Derrien.

She buried her face in her hands. '*Non…! J-je vous en prie!*' but Masson ripped the pantaloons away with a violent tug and the loose stitching burst, exposing a white belly, unshaven pubis and quaking thighs – and, fluttering around like small birds, fine scraps of paper, large and small, torn notes, receipts – some drifting to the stairs, one settling on Derrien's plain buckled shoe.

Derrien looked down at it. From the varied scrawls before him one word leapt out, one of the most secret in all France, and about whom naught may be said: the commander of the great armada.

Bonaparte.

As he stooped to pick it up the woman screeched, '*Non!*' and shoved him back, then clawed at her breast, tearing at something at her bustier.

33

'*Watch out!*' called the sergeant, pulling Derrien back as the soldiers thrust their spike bayonets simultaneously into the woman's body.

'*Non, non, vous idiots!*' shouted Derrien, but too late.

The woman gave a strangled retch, and collapsed forward, the shocked onlookers on the stairs crying out, the sergeant shouting, '*Get them out of here!*'

The men's bayonets had run her through, one with such force it had become embedded in the plaster of the wall behind. In realisation of their error or in some belated compassion, they tried to pull the spikes free, causing her body to twitch hideously, blood bubbling at her lips.

'No. Hold your positions,' Derrien ordered. The soldiers looked to their sergeant.

'Citizen, surely she is—'

'*Do as I say,*' Derrien whipped back, and Masson drew his pistol. Unhappily the Foot Guards obeyed, and pushed their bayonets slowly back into their victim's twitching trunk. One foot barely touching the floor, she hung partly suspended, her breath rattling, her arms limp, her head lolling.

Derrien bent forward to her bustier and saw that she had tried to reach for a long scrap of paper, possibly to swallow it. He slowly pulled it from between her blood-spattered breasts.

'You live for but a little time longer…' Derrien confided to her, examining the fragment, nearly six inches in length, torn at an angle across the top. He straightened, his left hand taking her hair violently and pulling her upright. The soldiers looked away, one muttering, '*Mon dieu…*' but Derrien continued.

'Unshriven, you will dwell soon in the inferno, beset by demons, to atone for your sins… so they say.'

Her glazed eyes rolled towards him and she began to convulse horribly, sobbing, but Derrien did not relent. 'Who?' he whispered. 'Who has made you do this thing for which you shall burn for eternity?'

The woman tried to breathe. 'Kl–Kla…'

'Yes? Claire? Clément?'

He looked into her eyes and shook her by the hair – as he had done before to severed heads after the guillotine blade had fallen. 'I am here,' he confided. Then roughly, '*Who?*'

Her pupils expanded, and she shuddered violently in a final spasm, the eyes dark, fixed and wide. He knew at once he had lost. He let go of her and the head fell forward, limp.

The guardsmen slowly withdrew their bayonets with a misplaced reverence, and the body crumpled and slid to the floor. The bowels moved, the sight and smell making the guardsmen turn away quickly, *Putain alors*, a hand to their mouths and noses in revulsion.

They protested to the sergeant that the citizen seemed in danger, that they feared she had a dagger, and he turned to Derrien. 'The cleaners,' the sergeant assured him, 'will be disciplined, Citizen. It is a good business, selling scrap paper to the merchants for pulp. Too good.'

Derrien let him think so, but as he read the torn note he knew different. Despite the loss of a witness he was almost exultant. There it was, the scent, possibly a spill from the bottle: the fragment bore an oil-stain from a stray droplet of liquid. He touched it to his nose. It was strong. It was the same perfume she had used on herself, undiluted, the perfume he had detected in the main hall: a forgotten hint of the meadowlands of youth, so very out of place among the soldiery and servant officials, so very wrong on the body of a drudge.

The perfume was important, because it provided a link to the contents: the torn fragment bore a stream of grouped numerals. The first group was broken with apostrophes, much like those of navigation coordinates of latitude and longitude, degrees and minutes, then followed by sets of triple integers. It was a cipher, and he knew it well: it was the mark of their greatest adversary, the British Admiralty.

'A code, Citizen?' asked Masson.

Derrien nodded. 'An impenetrable cipher.'

The cleaner had been no agent – which could mean only one thing: she had not been alone.

The owner of the scent.

'Your orders, Citizen?'

Derrien glanced at the body, the sergeant, the waiting soldiers. 'Arrest the Ordinator General, the cleaning staff and every official who flouted the new incineration directive.'

'And the Bureau duty officer, Citizen?' asked Masson.

'Yes,' said Derrien, mounting the stairs, his attention now fully occupied by the bloodstained message fragment. 'Take them all. And dispose of the body.'

–

In the thrall of his Admiralty cipher, Derrien had not noticed a tradesman's service door on the lower landing of the staircase, opened barely the width of the eye that peered through it. Carefully, the door closed.

Once out in the streets, Tuileries Palace cleaner Isabelle Moreau-Lazare ran through the late-night diners of Paris in her clumsy leather clogs, slipping and stumbling along the gutters and alleyways, trying to avoid militia and *gendarme* patrols, sobbing with fear, her breath coming in short panicked gasps until she reached an alley not far from the *Rue de Richelieu*, echoing to the calls and shrieks of the desolate and drunken.

As if pursued, she raced up the steps of a stinking tenement, running upstairs past other apartment doors – a scream cut short, a laugh, a raging argument – until she came to a tiny back-room by the rear staircase, and fell inside, slamming the door shut and bolting it.

There was barely space for an iron bedframe, washstand and *armoir*, the only light oozing through a grimy broken window, rolled rags stuffed into the holes in the glass to block out the draught.

She tore at her bodice, skirts, cap, *all of it, all, all all!* until she stood naked and shivering, slick in the cold sweat trickling down her bony ribs. She clapped a hand over her mouth but could not stop and rushed to the window, opened it, and vomited into the street below. For a moment she hung there – a raucous cackling and singing and the sound of a breaking bottle nearby.

She leaned on the sill, and the wracking sobs came, in horror, for poor Clarice, until she stood quiet, head down, drained. The cold night air revived her. She rinsed her mouth with water from the jug on the washstand and patted her face dry on a thin towel and wrapped herself in its meagre warmth.

Hands shaking, she unpinned her matted wig of unkempt greying hair, throwing it down, her chestnut curls falling in damp tresses about her pale face, her own concealed spoils of notes and pages falling to her feet, including the handful she had already been given by Clarice. She knelt to gather them, her eye passing over them with practised speed even as she wept.

Administrative slurry much of it, *2 bidons per tenant no more*, and orders for wood and coal, *horses to be stabled not in the mews but at the...* Then more useful, mention of the *demi-brigades* near the Channel ports, headings of *Armée d'Angleterre* and a new group called the *Armée d'Orient*, 'Army of the East'; she wondered, *which east, where?* Others were draft letters, minutes, members attending meetings. *Citoyen La Révéllière-Lépeaux, Citoyen Camot.* Her hands quaking, she stopped at one and reread it. It was a draft of an official letter from the desk of Foreign Minister Talleyrand.

T-Prte Sub

To their Excellencies the Ambassadors of His Sacred and Imperial Majesty of the Sublime Porte of Constantinople – the Republic of France offers assistance in the improved governance of its most favoured khedive

It stopped short but was followed by other drafts:

Ministry of the Interior, the 22ⁿᵈ Germinal,

The Executive Directory, Citizen Minister, instructs you to put the engineers, draughtsmen, and other personnel under the authority of your ministry at the disposal of General Bonaparte, as well as any articles he might require to serve the expedition with which he has been entrusted.

FROM Ordinator-Maritime Citizen Najac –

Should remittances for dock labour not be forthcoming by the 16ᵗʰ Floréal the strike will continue and it will not be possible to ensure appropriate lading of vessels to make the crossing beyond Corsica...

On the reverse was a list. She recognised the names before her at once. Her weeping stopped.

Toulon. Marseille. Gènes. Civita-vecchia. Ajaccio.

Vessels of the First Rank	*Vessels of 74*
Orient – 120 Brueys d.Aig.	*P. Souverain*
	Guerrier
Vessels of 80	*Aquilon*
Gui.ᵐᵉ Tell – Villeneuve	*Conquérant*
Tonnant – Dupetit-Thouars	*Généreux*
Franklin – Blanquet d.Chayla	*Timoléon*
	Mercure
Frigates x 12	*Spartiate*
Polacres x 82	*Heureux*
Tartanes x 75	
Brigantines x 79	

They were warships, classified by the number of guns. She recognised the names of senior naval officers. She knew them all, as she did the names of the government Directors and members of the Assembly. She began to rock on the edge of the bed to calm herself. The evidence before her was clear. This was a battle-fleet, led by three senior admirals, to convey an army.

She whipped on a clean shift and petticoat and pulled on one of her evening dresses, found a pair of damask pumps and a purse, her ensemble more suitable now for an actress and dancer of the *Comédie Française* with well-heeled benefactors – which, among other things, she was.

She could not be late – her cleaning shift had been changed, the timing too tight, and she had little time left. After what she had just discovered she must not miss them, and she hurried down to the rear exit and out, unseen, to the street.

She rushed through the rear yard to a rickety door at the side of a heap of rubbish, then slowed – *breathe, breathe* – and moved briskly around the corner.

Only a few couples were out, militiamen repeating, *Curfew will begin shortly, Citizen, yes, merci*, getting tips for their discretion from the great and good.

She saw a crowd emerging from the theatre up ahead on the corner, and *there*, there was François, looking, waiting, the great Talma, bathed in light from the foyer doors. Polite applause broke out for the grand actor as he doffed his hat and bowed, then he handed a lady up a step and into a waiting carriage, '...*and of course I knew he would get everything fixed, my dear. Your husband is a miracle-worker, besides...*'

But a militia patrol stepped into Isabelle's path, '*Mademoiselle, curfew has begun.*'

The stench of stables and cheap brandy on them, she covered her mouth, then looked past them and waved, 'Joséphine!' It was an old trick, but not tonight, for Joséphine Bonaparte waved back.

'*Belle!* Over here!'

The soldiers turned, saw the Paris Guard escutcheon on the carriage door, saw Talma, saw Joséphine, and bowed, backing away fast. Isabelle hurried past the stinking militiamen, puffing to explain her reddened cheeks and shortness of breath, *Oh what a rush I have had, Joséphine! My aunt, how she can talk!* Trying to smile though she wanted to curl up and weep for Clarice, and because this was her life, taking the hand of the First Lady of Paris, the lady of Napoléon Bonaparte, and lying to her, lying to them all, *Oh, Isabelle, my dear, you look all in! Come join us for a cognac quick, before the army throws us all in jail...*

Talma shut the door and quipped, 'Ah, but only the very *best* go to prison nowadays,' and Isabelle laughed, asking after the children, Eugène and Hortense, and Talma's Lou-Lou, taking her seat as they bumped their way along, out to the wealthy 9th *Arrondissement* and the *Chausée d'Antin*, chattering animatedly as she thought about the bayonets and the scream and Derrien's soulless eyes. And as she listened to their laughter and the surprises of the show they had just seen, she hoped she could signal London, and get out through Toulon or Naples before it was too late.

–

The bells of St Martin-in-the-Fields had long since tolled midnight. Young Marmaduke Wayland, 2nd Lieutenant of Marines, had heard them from his desk in the Admiralty on Whitehall, the clatter of hooves and carriage wheels in the broad road below dying away with the hour, the distant calls of cab drivers among London's late-night supper crowds fading.

On his first administrative posting, Wayland was keen to show he could do at least *something* well, and had stayed long into the dark watches of the night to prove it, if not to his noble father or superiors, who had secured his commission, then at least to himself. In shirtsleeves and waistcoat, he worked through files and correspondence, taking cold coffee to fend off sleep. He turned up the oil-lamp, his eyes sore from strain.

It was unusual for a junior subaltern of Marines to be admitted to the Admiralty for such work, to positions reserved for naval officers of merit, but Wayland had demonstrated unusual abilities. Something of a linguist, within his first week Wayland had been asked quietly one evening in the mess to skim through several French newspapers for any 'items of potential interest' to the Admiralty. His analysis had been so astute that he was swiftly moved from the clerks' pool to the hush of the first floor, and a desk in the anonymous suite of interconnecting offices known only as Room 63. This was the department of Commodore Sir Rafe Lewis – *de facto* head of the most effective intelligence service in the world.

Wayland gathered up various pages he had earmarked for the attention of Sir Rafe and set them aside in the usual tray on his desk. He then used his personal key to open the final despatch box of the night. It had come in just after eight and the change of watch – a nod in the direction of the four-hour watch system practised at sea, though in reality only a few duty clerks were ever left behind in the middle of the night. The building was quiet.

With a flagging heart he flipped open the peeling blue leather lid, but stopped short when he spied the name on the top sheet. It was from a Captain Day, the British Consul in Turin. As a source, Day had rated the 9-suffix in Sir Rafe's special book, meaning '*most reliable*'. After barely a fortnight, Wayland had already discovered that much. Immediately alert, he passed an eye quickly over Day's letter and the attached notes. When he finished he stared at them, horrified.

He rifled through the loose pages on his desk, and then those he had destined for Sir Rafe, convinced he had spotted earlier something now of terrible importance, but could not quite remember where. He used a small magnifying glass and ran down the columns of a cutting he had made from the French paper *Le Moniteur*. Then he found it. He read it again, as if to squeeze some new perception from its contents. Thanks to Day's communiqué, he did. He twisted round to consult the aged wallchart of Europe and the Mediterranean behind him.

Wide awake now, he snatched at a scrap of paper and dipped his pen. Quickly he scrawled the numbers of the demi-brigades in Day's despatch, taking special note of certain units – *NB: 85th, 14th, 69th, 75th* – the numbers of men – *1,800 p/d-b? 3 d-b p/div, div x5? x8?* – and made loose logistical estimates. When he read the results he realised he had been annotating the creation of a hitherto unknown army group. He picked up Day's letter once again, perhaps to convince himself he had been wrong or had missed an obvious explanation clearly visible to better men. There was none.

Only now, in reconsidering his hypothesis with Day's letter rattling in his shaking hands, did his fingers detect something foreign stuck to the back of the despatch: a slip of flimsy browned paper, once rolled tight but now flattened and wrinkled, accidentally gummed by a dark stain. Carefully he peeled it away. It tore at the stain, revealing the impression of a fingermark. It was a coded message. The duty cipher clerk had missed it.

It consisted of six lines of numeric cipher, following three groups of integers: *28'66'96'*. Feeling a lump in his throat, he remembered overhearing Pryce and Lewis say that agents in the field used triple sets of binumeric integers for codenames; he had seen them in the files. If it had come via Captain Day in Turin, it most likely would have originated from within northern Italy or southern France. It was a secret coded message from an agent in enemy territory – and possibly ten days old.

'Good Lord, oh, good Lord...'

Wayland scrambled out of his chair and gathered his notes and cuttings, Day's letter and the encrypted message. He dragged on his scarlet uniform tailcoat, nearly knocking over his oil lamp. He hurried to the communicating door to the adjoining office, took a breath and rapped at it. After a moment, he opened it and looked in.

'Sir Rafe?' He corrected himself, 'I – I mean, I beg your pardon, Commodore?'

Commodore Sir Rafe Lewis was still working at his desk by the light of a green silk-shaded candelabra. He did not look up. 'Mr Wayland. Still here I see.'

Wayland's cheeks flushed. 'Y-yes, sir. I – I think there may be—' he swallowed '—something of an emergency, sir.'

Lewis stopped writing. He was a gruff, businesslike man in a curled, iron-grey wig, with the oaken complexion of the long-serving sailor. 'Well?'

Wayland held out the despatch. 'From Captain Day, sir.'

'Day? Via Hamburg?' Lewis gave it a cursory read, flipping through the attached pages. 'How recent is this?'

'Stamped end of Second Dog Watch, sir, but sent at least ten days ago… if not a fortnight…'

He began to read it again. 'And?'

'Some of the demi-brigades he mentions, the 69th and 75th in particular, are from the *Armée d'Italie*, sir, which is still in the south.'

Lewis glanced at the relevant paragraph. 'Yes. Units marched up north to Picardy for the England invasion force under Desaix.'

'Originally, sir, yes…'

'And now?'

'Captain Day has recorded troop movements, many of these half-brigades have come south once again, down the River Var, along with other elements of the *Armée d'Angleterre*. He believes they are to combine with the *Armée d'Italie*. I, well, sir, I did a rough estimation… it could be as many as twenty or twenty-five thousand men. Possibly a new army group.'

Lewis frowned. 'In the south? Led by Desaix?'

'No, sir.' Wayland hesitated. 'General Bonaparte.'

Lewis looked at him, more alert now. 'By God.' He took it in, but was still unconvinced. 'But he is in the north. There was talk of him taking Desaix's command to invade us instead. Damn sight more pressing for them, surely.'

Wayland looked at his newspaper cuttings. 'Well, sir, I have to wonder, that if…' He cleared his throat nervously. 'If the movements of General Bonaparte are normally secret, then I must wonder why his troop inspections are being reported in

43

the news-sheets so prominently.' He handed him the pieces from *l'Écho* and *Le Moniteur*. 'Tradesmen's complaints about soldiers "for the north", unpaid bills, breakages, and always General Bonaparte, moving from one Channel port to the next.'

Lewis read the cuttings himself, his French sufficient. 'Poor security?'

Wayland hesitated. 'Possibly, sir. But could this not be a diversion? That instead he is heading south? With his best troops, including the 75th Invincibles, and many others still in Italy with Berthier. And his favourite, the 9th Light Infantry, is still guarding Paris for him.'

Lewis considered this. 'Suggesting either he will soon return to them, or just the opposite, that he is leaving Paris in good hands. I do concur.' Lewis set the despatches down with a nod of approbation. 'Well done, Mr Wayland.'

'Yes, sir, well...' Wayland coughed and looked down, embarrassed by his boldness. 'That is, these are Captain Day's suspicions, sir. But also...' Wayland held back from his final unhappy duty, but regretfully handed it over. 'There came this – from the field, I believe, sir. It is still enciphered.'

Lewis took it, immediately angry. 'Why did Mr Blake's clerk not log, decipher and clear it upon receipt?' He began to jot the solution on a blank page.

'It–it was adhered to the back of the despatch, sir. By a–a mark of... of blood, I think, sir...'

Wayland watched as Lewis deciphered the message without recourse to key or code book. When he finished, he set down his pen and read through it.

He reached for a thin, leather-bound folder on the shelf beside him, *Mnemonics – VI*, and flipped through the pages, his finger following down a column to the correct entry. It seemed to confirm an ill-favoured suspicion. '*Damnation...*'

He scrutinised the message again, and made a decision. He strode to the door and yanked it open, bellowing down the lamplit corridors, '*Signals! Look lively there, Mr Pryce, let's be having you!*'

Lewis turned on Wayland harshly. 'You assessed Day's despatch most keenly, Mr Wayland. But that cipher has lain for hours. A week or a fortnight old or not, I cannot say whether you have saved us or damned us, sir.'

Wayland reeled, as if from a physical blow. 'I–I beg your pardon, sir, I do not underst—'

'Invasion, sir, *invasion.*' Lewis thrust his jotted solution to the cipher into Wayland's shaking hands. 'You wished to see real intelligence work, sir, then here it is, in blood, by God, a cry for help.'

> $28'66'96$ – $expos^d$ $p^{ris}1$. *(stop blank revers.^{l})* $rqur^e$ urg^{nt} $xodus$ $cottg^e$ six. *(Stop rev.)* flt $mass^ng$ $Toulon$. *(Stp dbl rev.)* $B^on^ap^art^e$ i/c. adm^s $bruy^s$ $blnq^{dch^a}y$ $vll^{en}v^e$ *(Stp rev.)* $Mars^{lle}$ $Genv^a$ $Cvecch$ $Ajac^{io}$. *(Stp rev.)* 250 $trnspt$ 50 men^owar. $Target$ $unknw^n$.
> $Ends$.

Wayland stared at the message. It was confirmation of his analysis of Day's own conclusions: it was an invasion fleet of some 300 ships. They could embark far more than the 20,000 troops Wayland had calculated. He felt ill at the thought.

'And it explains *this*, sir.' Lewis snatched up a flimsy from his desk and thrust it at him. 'Blockade Despatches, yesterday First Watch, from Admiral the Lord St Vincent at Cadiz, by God – he received the same exodus request from Day direct by courier from Turin.'

> *A fine day's report – (stop rev^{sl}) – party sent to collect orphan.*

Lewis took it back and looked at him hard. 'Pray God they reach our agent before the French. Pray *God*, Mr Wayland.'

The Admiralty burst into life. There came the sound of running feet on the stairs, marching boots, a voice shouting, '*Signals to shutter*,' the blaze from lanterns flashing bright against the dark gleam of panelled corridors.

Duty Officer of the First Watch Lt Pryce bustled in, bleary-eyed, doing up his bluejacket, straightening his white wig, his shoes clacking and skidding along the wooden boards, pencil and notebook in hand. 'Signals, aye, sir, Chart Room being readied, sir.'

'Very good, Mr Pryce, compliments to the First Sea-Lord.' Pryce began to scribble on his pad. 'Note: it is the recommendation of these offices that Rear Admiral Nelson be recalled *forthwith* from sick-leave for immediate duties in the Mediterranean, to reconnoitre Toulon and forestall French invasion fleet – End. Seal and into his hand only.'

'First Sea-Lord'll most like be asleep, sir—'

'*Then wake him up*, sir. Where is Rear Admiral Nelson? Is he still in Norfolk?'

'Rest and recuperation, sir, on account of his arm the sawbones said—'

'Damn the sawbones and ready a rider. I want Nelson back in Portsmouth post-haste.'

Pryce chuckled. 'He'll thank you gladly for that, sir—'

'He can thank the French, Mr Pryce. Next, clear the shutter-line to Portsmouth and send a signal to stand by: I want the Channel Fleet sacked for frigates and sloops and a reconnaissance squadron victualled and armed ready and waiting for Nelson at St Helens, *most immediate* – everything they can muster, no excuses, even Harvey's damned fencibles if need be. Then signal for a despatch run to Admiral St Vincent off Cadiz at the next tide—'

'*Osprey*'s in for repairs, sir, but Tommy and the *Valiant* moored yesterday.'

'Very good, compliments to Tomlinson, make it *Valiant*, turn her about and mark your signal "stellar", St Vincent's eyes only.'

Wayland looked on with the sense of a dark, nebulous terror bearing down upon them, an unstoppable force that he somehow had set in motion, owing to his apparent dereliction. Lewis's comment had stung him deeply, and he stood rooted to the spot in confusion.

'Sir... what if,' he offered hopefully, 'if my report were, well, sir, I – I mean, why launch an attack from Toulon in the south? What if the French are not for us this time, but, but for somewhere in the Mediterranean, or, as I suggested, for India—'

Lewis stopped in mid-flow to Pryce, his voice low, but edged with ice. 'Mr Wayland,' he said, taking Wayland's arm, pulling him away, 'You did well, and it is Mr Blake's cipher clerk who will be scrubbing the decks and not you, sir, but you will address your interpretations to me in private or not at all, clear?'

Lewis paused when he saw the expression on the boy's face. 'Go down to the Registry,' he said, 'and get me a file from the Inactive List, a marine officer, name of *Hazzard*. Then set a galloper to Norfolk and *bring me Nelson*.'

Atonement

1796 – *Two years earlier*

A winter wind had stirred the leafless hedgerows, eddies of snow dancing and tumbling, the poplars whispering high overhead. A lone carriage ground its way along a frosted country lane, the monotony of the horses' hooves thudding through the creaking leather and polished wood of the interior. William John Hazzard gazed through the steamed glass across the white Suffolk countryside, heading home. He shrugged deeper into the collar of his grey cloak, the soft wool of his scarf warming him, but scarcely enough.

It had taken Hazzard four months to reach England, on an old East Indiaman passing the Cape. The ship's Indian surgeon had been appalled at the state of his injuries and treated them again, the contusions so terrible some wounds had to be reopened to drain them of their ill humours, and subsequently restitched. Hazzard spent the first month in a mild haze of Tamil incense and Kashmiri opiates.

When they had reached Deptford customs in January, he contracted a fever, the cold they said, a shock to all old India hands. He was taken to the infirmary at nearby Greenwich Naval Hospital by order of a physician arranged by Admiral Elphinstone – since ennobled to 'Lord Keith' after his conquest of the Cape. Deducing that Keith had known all about Harry Race through Blake and the Admiralty, this generosity made Hazzard's treatment burn all the more bitter.

Upon release from quarantine Hazzard first moved to his rooms in Greenwich, and there completed his scathing report to the Lords Commissioners: about Blake, about Race, and the truth behind their covert shore operation. But instead of a formal response or call to stand witness at a consequent court-martial, a fortnight later he was summarily discharged by the Navy Board and Marine Division HQ in Chatham in Kent. His Lieutenant's shares in prize-money were calculated and he was awarded an invalid's pension, '*For Services Rendered the Crown, in Recognition of Valorous Actions and Wounds Received at the Cape of Good Hope, Anno 1795*'. He wrote in protest, and to his Division CO at Chatham, but had no reply. Hazzard's career was over. His hatred of their Lordships had never burned brighter.

The carriage passed over Jecks Bridge, the old boundary to the parish farmstead, the iron-rimmed wheels vibrating on the frosted stones. He pulled down the window and let in the winter air, closing his eyes to the chill, perhaps trying to refresh, or steel himself. Up ahead he saw the mellow red-brick elevations of the rectory house of St Jude's, its ivy now bare and brown, a light covering of snow in the white windowpanes and doorways, smoke rising from its chimneys. It presided over a modest lawn and snow-dusted beds of rambling shrubs. A path lined with cherry and ancient yew led through a lychgate to the 12th-century church of St Jude's just behind, the whole surrounded by the working farm.

He had often pictured his homecoming: a joyous occasion, a gentle breeze, warm summer sun casting gentle shadow on rolling hills, that quietude of the familiar, amid the embracing green of England. He entertained a rush of memories, his return from school, his return from university.

But this return was different – tainted by Harry Race, Blake and the Admiralty – and he gazed out on a world he no longer recognised, something dead inside him, as cold and rent as the frozen farmland furrows around.

He watched as the front doors of the portico opened and figures emerged in welcome, and doubtless in trepidation. His uncle, the Reverend Thomas Hazzard, stumped ahead of the group on his wooden leg, in his black clerical coat and grey wig, short, broad, the only father Hazzard had ever known. The dutiful estate manager and his wife waited with a very earnest Sam Giffey, head groundsman, the farm's firm foundation. The reverend's glowering old soldier-servant, Moran, stood stiffly behind them all in his old red topcoat, a relic from his days in the 43rd Foot, and beside him was Ellie, the maid grown to become housekeeper, forever young, Moran restraining her enthusiasm with a discreet hand.

But there was another figure, obscure at the back in the shadow of the doorway, out of place, a pale bloom of light under a dark cloak, her blonde hair pulled back, one hand tightening the fur collar at her throat, perhaps in apprehension. Hazzard saw her, and immediately felt all the worse.

Sarah.

The last time he had spoken her name was on the operating table, but now in his memory all he could hear were the last words hissing from the lips of a man murdered, murdered by circumstance, or by Blake – but certainly by Hazzard. He closed his eyes, gripping the bench seat for control.

The carriage came to a stop. The driver opened the door and folded down the steps, his hand out instantly, waiting for Hazzard to take it. The little group waited, hesitant, as Hazzard climbed out slowly, his right hand grasping one walking stick and, in his left, another. They were unprepared for the sight that greeted them.

He stumbled slightly down the steps, the driver murmuring *aye, sir, aye, one more*, and he half fell to the gravel, barely able to keep himself upright, head down in self-disgust and anger, the driver holding him up as Moran and the reverend came forward.

'My boy,' said the reverend, taking him about the shoulder, '*look at you…*' He looked about, back at the others. 'Look at him! Black as mahogany! Black as Jack Tar!' Some tried to laugh, and he clutched him tight again, whispering, '*My boy…*'

'*Uncle...*' said Hazzard, and clung to him, and for a moment no time had passed and he had never left; he was still the boy at home in the stables, in the chapel, on the farm. Then he said, 'Please, Uncle, I am *able*,' his voice scything through their goodwill. 'A little saddle-sore,' he said at last, and tried to smile. ''Tis good to see you, Uncle.'

The Rev. Hazzard stepped back, wiping at one eye, nodding brusquely. 'Indeed, indeed, of course you are, of course.' But he held Hazzard's arm tightly, '*I will not let you go, my boy*, you know such. I lost this leg for Wolfe and as the general said to me, "one leg is—"'

'Is enough, yes, Uncle, I remember.'

'So I be damned, God forgive, to lose yours to another.'

Hazzard gave his thanks to the driver and pushed himself forward, a four-legged beast, a twisted Caliban, bent out of shape, stitched and sewn, a sack of pain, trying to brave an unbidden return.

'As will I,' said Moran, taking a step to his front. 'Your honour is welcome home, Master Will'am.'

'Thank you, Moran,' said Hazzard. 'As you were, Sergeant.' Their old joke, and Moran chipped back a salute in acknowledgement, then Hazzard saw the housekeeper. 'Dear Ellie.'

She was now closer to fifty, he guessed, 'a score afore ye', as she used to say when he was young and she wanted to keep him quiet. He wondered why she had no husband. All housemaids left to marry, he had heard, but she looked as much part of the household as a devoted daughter. She had been his nursemaid, matron, mother, all, and she gazed at him, teary-eyed, then rushed to embrace him. After a moment she dipped in curtsey and said in her warm Suffolk twang, 'Master Will'am, welcome *home...*'

'Have you been taking good care of these two bad-tempered old men?' he asked.

She bobbed, smiling, 'Oh, sir, they not been *so* bad!' Perhaps a little simple, but kindly and generous. 'I've made a tea...!' she declared happily, and hurried into the house, holding up her skirts as she went.

The estate manager removed his hat and greeted him with a bow, his wife dipping, agog at the bronzed traveller returned, and Sam Giffey took his offered hand. 'Sir, I never knew the like when they told me ye'd be back, and I thank the Lord for it, I do, most hearty I do.'

'As do I, Sam, 'tis good to see an old friend...'

They manoeuvred him to the low stone steps and he stopped, not wanting to look up, as if unable to go further. Sarah came forward. She put her hands on his on the walking sticks, just to touch him. 'Are you truly here... I cannot...' His hands were cold and shaking and she gripped them tight. Tears streamed down her face and she put a soft hand to his cheek. 'Oh, William... what have they done to you...'

Hazzard felt the cool of her hand, as if in forgiveness of his sins. His being sighed with relief, and he leaned into her arms. *'Everything they could...'*

She gave a brave laugh, and held him, but in that time of silence, for however short it was, it all returned, the intervening years, the sights and sounds, the fear, and she felt him tense and pull away. She tried to take him by the elbow, 'Come...'

But his arm remained stiff as stone. 'No. Please.'

'Will, let m—'

'Leave me *be.*'

She recoiled sharply, and he glanced at her, softening. More for their reassurance he added, 'I must *try*,' he said, with effort. 'It will pass, they said.'

Laboriously he trod into the house, one stick after the other, one foot, then the other, bent forward, his legs working but weak, quaking with every step, but inside at last. Still unused to the cold, he began to shiver, although he could feel the warmth of the fire from the hall, from the dining room, from the drawing room. Moran and the driver saw to the bags. The reverend paid him, and Hazzard heard him say, *'Tell them, on the road, and at the post, that my nephew is returned, God be,'* his voice broke somewhat and he added gruffly, *'victor, wounded, but whole, God be.'*

The driver gee'd the horses with a click of the tongue and Hazzard heard the wheels grinding on the stones, the carriage taking with it the clinging vapours of London, of ships and powder and war, of India and Africa, leaving only the wind, and St Jude's, and the poplars above. The silence, for a moment, enveloped him.

On the steps, Sarah sobbed, in anguish, in relief, her hand cupping her mouth, trying to keep her pain silent. The reverend took her gently and led her inside. It was a taste of trials to come.

–

It had not been two days before the first upset in the house came, when Moran had drawn a bath for Hazzard in his room, cold water, or nearly cold, as Hazzard's skin could not yet take worse than tepid water without pain.

Moran stepped out to fetch a fresh towel as Hazzard tried to dry himself with his left hand, his right clutching another towel about his waist, when Ellie gave a brief knock and came in.

Ordinarily Hazzard would pay no attention to such an interruption, Ellie having mothered him since childhood. But on this occasion, Ellie stopped in the doorway, a shaking hand rising to her mouth when she saw Hazzard's body. *'Oh no...'*

His back was a latticework of lacerations, from side to side, from corner to corner, as if with great regard to thoroughness, old white scars and new, and further long, red and tightly stitched jagged lines, as if drawn at blind random by a macabre sketch artist: over one shoulder, across the back, at the hip, and across his bare chest. The one leg showing from behind the towel had been cut brutally at the knee and stitched up the thigh, the whole a horror of black, yellow and red bruising, as if not one patch of flesh had been left unravaged.

'Now, me darlin',' said Moran, returning behind her, 'not a sight for such as thee,' and turned her about, and she buried her head in his chest where she shook for some time.

Hazzard suffered another fever in that first week, similar to those he had endured at Greenwich, a mad wandering through fantastical fears, faces looming over him, silent or deafening, as he shuddered with cold under blankets before a roaring fire – and amidst it all, Ellie always there with renewed devotion. Sarah could not bear to stand by while he suffered, and the pair clashed by his sickbed.

'Thank you, Ellie, I will tend to him now—'

'Beggin' your pardon, mum,' said the matron, 'Master Will'am says only to be I and Moran who tend him owing to his wounds—'

'But, Ellie – that is nonsense surely, come, let me—'

'I do regret, mum, Miss Sarah, that—'

Hazzard stirred in the bedclothes.

Sarah moved to his bedside. 'Will… you're awake…'

Hazzard looked round, hollow eyes wide, and saw her, 'No, *not here, please…*'

Ellie held her back. 'Please, mum, we upset the master—'

'William, let me tend you, in the name of God, *please*—'

'*Harry, Harry…! Marshes…*'

'What does he say, Ellie? What does that mean?'

'It's the *fever*, miss! And you mustn't catch it if'n it be you'rn and you be for taking it home!'

'For heaven's sake, Ellie, quickly, his sheets are soaking and need changing, he…' As she raised the blankets she saw his body. 'What are these… *these marks…*'

'*Get out, get out! Must not…*'

Shouting, somewhere in his mind, and Sarah clutched at herself as if struck, '*Oh God…*' and ran from the room.

Over the following weeks they communicated briefly by letter, Sarah ever enquiring about his recuperation, her concern never waning, but deepening when she received no word. After three months they had seen each other only on four occasions, his recuperation more maddening than he had expected, though he had moved from using the two walking sticks to only one. With summer, the strength began to return to his legs, and they managed a ride on the adjoining parish estates. On the third ride she watched as Hazzard's mount, Agamemnon, a dappled grey, slowed up ahead to a walk, then came to a stop by the trees, Hazzard slumped forward onto the horse's neck. 'William…? Are you all right?'

She rode up beside him, her gloved hand reaching out to take the rein. 'Will…?'

'That… *smell*…' he gasped, his eyes tight shut. '*The damp… in the wood…*'

She took his arm, as bunched and hard as iron, the muscles quaking with tension until the fit subsided. He straightened abruptly and pulled the rein away, and she followed, never understanding what had happened, the episode serving only to take him further from her.

By day he sat at his desk in his study, gazing at his books, anything to take him away from where he was, to somewhere safe, somewhere known, seeking solace in the past. Continuing his work from his days at university, he began to read again – Herodotus, Tacitus, Polybius, all of them. Without him knowing, his uncle contacted his old friends from Jesus College, Dr Edward Clarke and his assistant John Cripps, and they tried to convince him to return to Cambridge, at least to work among conducive surroundings.

Cripps was excited at the prospect: 'Consider the things you have *seen*, sir…' He indicated Hazzard's study and his souvenirs of travels to alien worlds: carvings of Hindu deities, a curved Omani *khanjar* dagger, a hide-covered Ndebele shield and Xhosa warrior's *mkhonto*, its leaf-blade spearhead gleaming black with the housemaid's polish. 'This is a treasure trove. You must be proposed to the master, surely.'

'Quite right, John,' said Clarke hopefully. 'I have said so many times, Will. The college would welcome you with open arms. Your work on Egypt alone warrants it – no one else has been there, for God's sake…'

'I am only an amateur, Ned,' said Hazzard, 'Jack of all trades, master of none.'

'Stuff and nonsense,' retorted the ebullient Clarke. 'I'll have you at a lectern within the month.'

Relenting, Hazzard did give a lecture on his findings of ancient scripts, Syriac, Coptic and hieroglyphics, but the distraction left him unsatisfied. Despite their protests, he returned home, to work, he claimed, but really he knew it was only to escape.

One morning in June, while putting his books into some order, a yellowed note slipped out and dropped to the desk. He looked at it, heart thudding, for he knew what it was.

The New Republic Constitution:

Item: to sail away and discover a new world for no one else but us;

Item: to find a new way to the Indies without getting one's feet wet;

Item: to find rivers and lakes with no fish and fish in them; Item: to host balls with only the very best people, (just us ourselves alone!), and Item: always to be silly happy there!

Half of it was scratched out, rewritten, and he could hear her laughter while they composed it, Sarah, as they grew up together, at sixteen, at seventeen, in France. She was with him on that slope with the oak overlooking the valley from Grenôble, her French impeccable, better than his, laughing at his inability to say 'Bordeaux' without sounding like a Gascon or an *anglais*. He read it, remembering, remembering all of their promises to each other. Promises shattered when he went to India a year later. Shattered by William John Hazzard.

He reached for pen and paper, dipped the nib, but hesitated over the page. He rose stiffly, taking up his stick and swung quickly to the door. He headed for the stables and asked Sam to saddle Agamemnon.

Within twenty minutes he had done two miles, his rising trot weak, thanks to the left knee, and a canter near impossible, but the rhythm was helpful, and soon he reached the gates of Minster House, Sarah's home.

As he rode up the drive he saw her father's footman emerge with trunks and cases from the distant dower-house. The man raised a hand in greeting and Hazzard returned it – but was seized with a sudden fear. Eventually he met Sarah in the rose garden.

She came, head down, eyes restless, unwilling to meet his. Before she could say anything, he held out the note he had found. 'Do you remember this?'

She opened it and, after a moment, laughed, then shook her head, '*Oh, Will...*' she said, and flung her arms about his neck and he held her, at last a proper reunion, he feeling more himself.

'There now, come,' he said, 'I had not intended to do this to you...'

She pulled away, wiping her eyes, taking a handkerchief from him. 'It is not that... it's...' She drew a breath, closed her eyes and stood straight. 'I am going, Will. On a tour.'

He watched her face, his mind not grasping her words. 'A tour? A tour of what...? I don't under—'

'We go to Naples first, then Athens.'

Hazzard blinked, trying to adjust. '*Naples?*'

'A group of us, artists, and scholars, enthusiasts.' She looked away. 'It was organised through the Antiquarian Society, and it is safest to travel in a group—'

'*Safe?*' He leaned on his stick, suddenly not strong enough to stand. Again, he tried to understand. 'Sarah, Italy is at *war*—'

She sounded dismissive but would not look at him directly. 'Only in the north, William...'

'*What?*'

'The Society has made all enquiries—'

'All they need do is read a newspaper!' He sank onto a stone bench seat. 'The War Ministry would never permit it – they would stop you at Customs and Excise at Deptford or, or—'

'*Will*,' she said with finality, 'I am *going*.'

'For God's sake, Sarah – Bonaparte has been fighting the Austrians in Italy for months.' He closed his eyes, wishing she could *understand*. 'Sarah, it is sheer *lunacy*. It is *not* – not...' The idea of her being anywhere near a battlefield made him feel light-headed with helpless fear. 'If Bonaparte turns on Rome he could be at Naples in a *week*, good God, you know that! Despite London gossip about Lady Hamilton and her gowns it is *no* place for fine society and *concerts*—'

'Oh, yes, of course, for that is surely the only reason I would go. Oh how I would *miss* my grand piano.'

Then he remembered: almost eight years previous, at this same spot, tormented with guilt, he had told her of his departure for India and his commission in the Bombay Marine of the East India Company. They had both felt just as pained then, but some slow poison had since wrought its destruction between them.

Then, his final attempt, and he regretted the words the moment they passed his lips: 'We were to wed.'

She stared back at him, astonished. 'Yes, we were, Will, to wed, for years we were to wed but when, how, with you away at sea? Coming home on leave only twice? And look what you've become. Bitter, ill-tempered, bewitched by, by some unspeakable anger, locked in your study or that fusty old college day after day. You would not let me tend or even *visit* you for these past months – hiding I know not what from me when I wanted to comfort you...'

He said nothing and she looked far away. 'Why may I not do as you did?' she said quietly. 'Travel, and see this world... as we had promised.' She mumbled something else but he could not hear. Her face crumpled in misery. 'Though you have returned it is as if you have left me once again,' she added, 'as did poor Harry.'

She knew nothing of their duel. It had been tearing at him since his return. He had kept Harry's secret. Let him rest in what little peace his twisted soul could find, he thought, at least in her imagination, and in his uncle's. They had been spared the ordeal of meeting the family, for Race's father and mother were long dead, and no others remained, Harry the final echo of a fading line, now silenced.

'Harry promised he would marry me if you did not. Then he ran off as well…'

He would not tell her. He refused, for whose sake he was unsure, his own perhaps more than hers. Let Harry stay that other boy, reckless, envious – but not the rapacious savage he had become. 'Harry was not… worthy of you.'

'Is that why you left him?' she cried in accusation, the dam finally bursting. '*Left him to die in that awful place!*'

'I did my *duty*,' he lashed back, a coward's answer, he thought.

'And see what your duty has done to you!'

Tears streaming down her cheeks she ran from him, a hand to her mouth, running from her sadness, from him, from every-thing, it seemed to Hazzard. And he let her go, unwilling to face her any more: her beauty, kindness and care a constant reminder of his failure to save Harry, his failure to become the husband she needed – and he took up his stick, a sense of horror washing over his crippled heart.

He wrote to the Secretary of War, to the Admiralty, to the harbourmaster at Tilbury, anyone and everyone, demanding they forbid her passage, blockade the hapless tour groups who knew nothing of what could await them. He gathered the latest despatch reports from periodicals, which all painted a dire picture for the survival of Venice and the city states, and rode the next morning to *show* her, *convince* her.

But one of the groundsmen met him at the gate. He confided that the house was in turmoil: Sarah had gone. She had left the previous afternoon, just after they had parted, a brief note left for her stricken mother and father.

Hazzard had ridden from the scene, heart in his throat, unable to think, and rode, rode through the wood, past the river, and died another death, for Sarah, for Harry, all over again.

–

Within six months, the pain had dulled, though it beckoned him daily, a constant ache. The truth, which he could never bring himself to admit, was that Sarah had become a reminder of his last violent moments with Harry Race. In his absence abroad, Sarah had rejected suitor after suitor, awaiting his return, a patient Penelope to his Odysseus – but when at last he did return, he could not bear to see her, and Sarah could watch only from afar. Harry Race had won after all, he thought, his venom striking him through the heart. And now she was gone – driven from him by the same dark spectre that haunted him daily.

They did receive a reassuring word from her father that following winter that she had been in contact and was safe, and the family had passed Hazzard her accompanying personal letter. It never left his side:

> …Greece! How wonderful a prospect! Just as we had spoken of for so many years, my dear clever sea-soldier-scholar. I do miss you so.
>
> Sir William has said he can help with the Ottoman formalities, as Athens lies under their unloving care. But Heavens, his lady wife, Emma, is a dear – with a different gown for every moment of the day, each as éxotique as the next. I should never introduce you for

she is such a beauty she would surely steal you away from me…

Each word he knew by heart, all at odds with their parting, an absolution of his final sins against her. To see her hand was something of a connection, as if the note bore some physical remnant of her through the very script penned on the page, and he could still feel her presence. From time to time he would look at it, his eye casting over the letters, not reading, merely seeing, sensing her. Then he would thrust even these thoughts aside, and regain himself and begin his self-recrimination once more.

He collected news of every clash in Bonaparte's Italian campaign, Piedmont, Lombardy, Liguria, and the threat to the Mediterranean, searching for any hint of potential danger to Sarah in Naples. He and the family had all signed and sent petitions to Sir William Hamilton, the ambassador to the court of Naples, enquiring further of her whereabouts, but had received no reply, the waiting endless, the hope exhausting.

–

After another year, it had sunk deep within him, casting a pall over the household, his reverend uncle growing more distracted, lost in a world of his own. On one occasion, they were discussing the latest reply from the Foreign Office when Hazzard was struck for the first time by the change in him.

The old man stood at the windows, looking out over the side garden, his long white hair peeping from under the grey wig. 'Sir William Hamilton knows nothing, he says. Nothing. Ambassador, or pleni-potentate, or whatever he is…' He looked round, a thought occurring to him, as if he had only just seen Hazzard sitting at his desk. 'Did you know we have not a single ship in the Mediterranean, sir? Not a one. Jervis should know better, and does.'

'I'm sure he does, Uncle,' said Hazzard gently.

The old man sighed, reaching out to touch the cold glass. 'Sarah was as a daughter to me…' he murmured, far away, shaking his head in wonder. 'Not a single ship…'

Hazzard's only consolation was parish work, seeing to the tenants, seeing to the harvests and tithes, the poorhouses, helping his uncle, both grateful for it, the farmers and labourers blessing him for his care. But still he kept to himself. His peers in neighbouring estates were uncomfortable in his company. At his last society dinner, having endured a stream of glib complaint about war and privation, he had snapped the stem of the wineglass in his hand, shoved back his chair and stalked out. Now they passed him quickly by in their gleaming two-seater phaetons – a social pariah. So it suited him all the better, and he rode the parish estates alone, an isolated figure. Although time had healed many of his wounds, it left a livid scar on the last.

He continued to grow stronger, returning to fitness slowly over the following months, a faint inner voice urging him to health in case Sarah needed him, as if he could somehow intervene and still protect her – which he had so clearly failed to do. He accepted the post of Fencing Master at the Academy in Portsmouth and kept his hand in, drilling cadets and training with masters – but he resigned a short time after: he had beaten a visiting Austrian instructor to the piste, not hearing the cries to stop, not realising where he was until he was pulled away.

Otherwise, among the gentle hills of Suffolk, the war with France seemed at times a remote drama, enacted by unseen players on a distant stage. With Bonaparte's endless victories in Italy, it now came to call, sudden and loud, the king's troops and swaggering coffeehouse officers seeking recruits, adulation and free drink in the taverns. When French troops entered Rome, some two years to the day of his return to England, the talk in the press was of nothing but the Navy and Bonaparte, always Bonaparte – and invasion.

More than ever, he wanted to reach Sarah, find her, get her *back*. When Sam Giffey told him there was an impressment in the village, marines rounding up men for the Navy, Hazzard had gone immediately to the village green and tried to re-enlist. He was diffidently refused – on medical grounds, they claimed, but he had heard their whispers, the sergeant recognising him, and he detected the unseen hand of the Admiralty. He would give his life for England, at sea or on land, in the ranks if need be – but he would never trust the Sea-Lords of the Admiralty ever again.

Though surrounded by his artefacts and texts at his desk, his eye staring out upon the lawns and winter woods of walnut and elm, he heard them constantly, the guns, always the guns, booming from the dark recesses of memory. Cursed to sit idle as Bonaparte now stood poised to attack, he watched the fallen leaves blowing in an endless ebb and flow, his bitter heart sinking into a black frost.

With spring, a new determination overtook him, and he began to walk regularly, for hours at a time. It was on one of these excursions, one cold April morning, that his world changed for ever. He walked the four miles from St Jude's to the village: the left knee feeling stronger, tighter, his footsteps smoother, his balance better, his walking stick now a mere gentleman's accoutrement.

He strode along the High Road and eventually into Sheep Street, heading to the green. He passed the old market pavilion with its mouldering thatch, returning the greetings of familiar faces seated outside the Black Swan tavern, '*Mornin' ay, Mr 'Azzard!*' – '*Morning, Isaiah, save some for the rest of us,*' their laughter following him, awaiting his regular arrival for a noon refresher before his homeward journey.

But, on this day, something was different. One of the field labourers' boys saw him and ran down the road, past the forge and around the corner. Hazzard followed. He saw a waiting carriage, four horses in harness, stamping, their breath steaming in the fresh spring air. Hazzard stopped.

It was not the Bury coach, nor the London mail bound for Colchester or Ipswich. It was an official carriage, the horses bobbed and trimmed in military style. Talking to a figure through the open window, the boy pointed back at Hazzard in the road. Taking a coin, the boy then ran off. The carriage door opened and out stepped a Royal Navy officer in full uniform, cocked hat, white gauntlets, and swirling cloak. Inside was a Marine officer in scarlet.

'Mr Hazzard...?'

Hazzard tensed. 'Yes.'

The Navy officer put his heels together and bowed his head, as one might to a respected gentleman squire. 'Commander Montgomery, sir, and Lt Soames. Attached to Chatham Division.'

Hazzard took a tight breath. Chatham had been his old Marine division.

'Yes.'

Montgomery tucked his hat under one arm. 'Concerning your recent letters to the Admiralty and the Secretary of War – there has been... a development.' Politely, he indicated the interior of the carriage with a gloved hand. 'Could you spare us a few moments, sir...?'

Toulon

The port of Toulon was bursting with troops. Every bed had been billeted, every hostelry filled; tent-lines crowded every yard and quad in town, and encampments stretched across the surrounding clifftops and hillsides. The sloping, cobbled streets were clogged with infantry, sappers, cavalry and fusiliers – and the eager *Toulonnais* merchants who sought to serve them.

The sea was covered from Le Mourillon to the outer harbour by a vast forest of masts, 74-gun ships of the line, 80s, frigates, corvettes and armed merchantmen: the battle-fleet of the Republic, stark, bright-painted, the Revolution on the wave. Rowing-boats, tenders and barges plied between them, booms swinging bulging cargo nets high over decks, scrabbling hands and boathooks reaching up to take livestock, stores, kegs of biscuit, kegs of powder, charges, rounds, carriages and guns for the ordeal ahead. And across the decks and throughout the town there was but one name on every lip: *Bonaparte.*

Derrien surveyed the scene from artillery ramparts on the heights. He hated Toulon. To him it was a stinking warren of smugglers and black-marketeers, a haven for *ancien chouan* royalist sympathisers, dreaming of the return of a king. He determined to visit the Revolution upon them in a way they would never forget. As Bonaparte had saved the Republic, so too would Jules-Yves Derrien, and kill a spy.

He had wasted little time in Paris. The enciphered message fragment had been sent with its oil-spot for immediate inspection to a trusted apothecary near Grasse, the centre of perfume manufacturing. In the same laboratory that had provided

65

Derrien with poisons, gaseous ethers and powders, the chemist had identified one of the scent's chief components, a blend of lavender and China tea-rose, mixed with the sandalwood casks in which it was transported. The consignment was sold to just seven *parfumiers*, five of whom were not far from Grasse, in small country towns. But only one lay in the very heart of the French Navy: the old and respected *parfumier* Ablondi of Toulon. There was no better site for an Admiralty spy network, and it was too much of a coincidence for Derrien to ignore.

It had taken Derrien three days to reach Toulon down-river by barge, but within only an hour of his arrival he had commandeered an escort of twenty-five Flemish and Dutch '*Patriotten*' grenadiers, happy to take blood money from the powerful Republic. They now stood rigidly to attention behind his waiting carriage, in gold livery, tall mitre caps and white wigs, gleaming arms shouldered, their sergeant a motionless block of granite.

But peering at them with suspicion from atop his high horse was a *Chef de bataillon* colonel of the local *gendarme* cavalry, resplendent in full dress, gloved fingers brushing first a flowing moustache and then a magnificent gold-inlaid *Savoyard* sword at his hip. He was flanked by two other *gendarme* officers, each reminiscent to Derrien of pantomime dragoons from the stage.

'You have seen enough, *m'sieur*?' demanded the colonel, pinching his nose, as if itching from snuff.

Derrien wondered if the Revolution had touched this pompous Franco-Italian fool. He very nearly ordered him to address him as 'Citizen'.

'Yes.'

'I have sent to Paris, *m'sieur*,' he continued proudly, 'To confirm your credentials. *Ha.*' He waited for a response to this impressive display of authority. When he got none, he fingered his moustache angrily. 'You will not have any of my *gendarmes* without proper authority from the *département*.'

'They would be useless to me.' Derrien headed to the carriage, uninterested. 'Your ranks are infested with royalist insurgents.'

'How dare you,' said one of the officers. 'You will withdraw that remark, *m'sieur*, at once.'

Derrien stopped. The door of the carriage clicked open and Citizen Masson emerged, with two heavy men in dark coats, stout pewter-topped sticks held ready like clubs. They moved either side of Derrien and showed the pistols in their waistbands to the *gendarmes*.

'*Ma foi*,' scoffed the colonel. 'You threaten me with common bailiffs? Hired bully-boys from Marseille?' His face reddened, his eyes bright. 'It is *my* task to keep the peace in Toulon!'

'And it is my task to keep the Republic from destruction.' Derrien looked away, waving a hand. 'You and your operetta officers are dismissed.'

'*You* dismiss *me!*' The colonel put a hand to his splendid sabre.

Derrien nodded back at him. 'I do. And in future, *Chef de bataillon*, you will address me by my associated rank of *Général de brigade* – unless you wish to be posted to the Frisian Isles with your fine peacocks here.'

The *Patriotten* grenadiers still looked to their front, but some allowed smiles to creep across their faces. They knew the Frisian Isles.

'*Pah!* Enjoy your moment in the sun, *m'sieur*. It shall not last.' He snapped his fingers. '*Troupe. Marchons.*' The colonel had put on a brave show, but Derrien caught the shadow of fear cross his face. His officers followed, their mounts' prancing hooves clopping on the cobbles sloping down to the town below.

Derrien climbed into the carriage, joining the nervous Citizen Montfort, his local Bureau liaison man, who sat in a ridiculous powdered wig and ill-fitting coat. He was clearly terrified of his visitor from Paris.

'Y-you have seen the, the heights, and streets, *m'sieur*? I mean, Citizen?' Montfort stammered. Citizen Masson and the bailiffs sat on the banquette opposite, staring at him woodenly.

Derrien ignored his question, folding his hands in his lap, aligning them carefully with the seams of his coat-pockets. 'How many sales of the scent were made by the *parfumier* Ablondi?'

Outside, the grenadier sergeant barked an order and the carriage moved off, the grenadiers following as they descended the hill. Montfort nodded to Derrien, as if recalling facts learned for an exam. 'Sales, yes, of course, yes, three, C-Citizen? Two were to naval officers, n–now at sea, I fear... But – but yes, we learned that the scent was also created for one elderly customer alone—'

'One?'

'Who has since died, Citizen,' Montfort apologised. 'An old woman, I believe in her eightieth year...' He glanced at the bailiffs and swallowed. 'But y–yes, though, we have questioned the other regular patrons...'

Derrien looked at him. 'You have done what?'

Montfort backed away into the corner. 'We, that is, w–was I not to? I sought only to assist—'

'Citizen Montfort, you have no idea of why I am here, or what information I seek. How can you have questioned prisoners?' Montfort could not bring himself to respond and Derrien looked away in disgust. 'Perhaps you shall learn.'

They followed the winding road down to Toulon's Le Mourillon district, entering a connected series of small fountain-squares. The narrow streets were thick with troops, in uniforms of all descriptions, and the grenadiers forced a path through the crowds, the occasional fist beating on the back and sides of the carriage as it passed, a drunken soldier or staggering whore, Derrien thought, and he seethed with revulsion. When at last they pushed their way into the final market-square, and he saw the corner shop marked '*Parfums, Ablondi et fils*', Citizen

Derrien was more than ready to mete Revolutionary justice upon Toulon.

Inside, the shop was cramped, only a few simple displays of testers and exotic crystal scent-bottles on a high gleaming counter, with stairs to rooms above and below. The old Ablondi, a small, white-haired man in his sixties, stood behind his counter in a stained black leather apron, his spectacles raised like goggles, interrupted in the process of his craft. Captive between Masson and the bailiffs were his two youngest sons, both of barely twenty, both with sullen, downcast expressions. Derrien took them to be nothing more than a pair of Provençal bumpkins.

'You sold a bottle of scent,' stated Derrien, leafing through Ablondi's large leather-bound customer register, 'identified by the distillers of Grasse as your particular admixture.'

'A decoction?' asked the old man uncertainly.

'You sold it to a woman now deceased. Or so you claim. This is insufficient information.'

The old man lowered his glasses and peered at the book. 'Ah, yes, I recall the questions by the *gendarmes*. Madame Plancher – what of her, *monsieur*?'

Derrien did not like his French. It sounded nasal and foreign, almost Spanish or Italian, adulterated with the local Occitan language – he said '*hoc*' instead of '*oui*', not the least of his linguistic sins. 'I am not "*m'sieur*", but "Citizen Derrien". Do you understand?'

The old man nodded, frightened, and replied formally in the tongue of the north, '*Oui*, Citizen Derrien.'

Derrien continued. 'You sold it to someone else. To whom?'

Ablondi shrugged slowly, his hands rising plaintively. 'But, the ledger, Citizen Derrien… it says I did not. Perhaps the scent, it was passed to a little one, a daughter or grand-daughter, from poor Madame Plancher?'

'Citizen Plancher had no family.' Derrien turned another page in the book. 'You sold it to another.'

The old man shrugged again and laughed gently. 'But, ah, how, Citizen Derrien? If my ledger, it says no, then—'

Derrien spoke without looking up from the page before him. 'Search the premises.'

Within minutes the soldiers swarmed over the building. Masson and the bailiffs pushed Ablondi and his sons to the back door and threw them bodily down the cellar stairs. They were dragged through the basement workshop, out to the square and forced to their knees. The grenadiers tossed items from upstairs windows into the square below, books, clothes, bed linen and belongings, even a table smashing to the cobbles. The gathering crowd moved forward, shouting insults at the grenadiers. Derrien nodded to the grenadier sergeant. 'Palisade, Sergeant.'

'Yes, Citizen.'

Montfort watched open-mouthed from inside the carriage, moving from one window to the next, as ten grenadiers formed line, the crowd shrinking back. With one command they charged their bayonets and slammed to attention, unmoving, a wall of polished spikes holding back the crowd. The people began to scream.

Derrien ignored them, watching the Ablondi sons, pistols to their necks. Derrien knew they were guilty of something. All he needed was a modicum of leverage. When it came, it came from an unexpected quarter. The grenadier corporal appeared at the shop door to the yard.

'Citizen.' He held up a sack, then set it down on the ground before Derrien as if it were dangerous. Masson bent down and pulled the neck of the sack clear of the object inside. It was a large earthenware jug.

The boys began to whisper, one cursing the other. 'But this, this is not ours?' said the old Ablondi in confusion.

Derrien crouched and pulled out the jug's broad cork stopper. It was coated with a white, gluey substance. Carefully, he sniffed. It was not perfume.

'And this, Citizen.' The corporal held out an old pistol, missing its trigger, flint and strike-plate, the butt cracked wide, quite useless.

Derrien studied it momentarily then got to his feet. 'Citizen Ablondi!' he declaimed, as if in court, so that the small crowd could hear him. 'In contravention of Article 19 of statutory ordinances set by the Committee of General Security and Ministry of the Interior, you have been found *guilty* of possession of a firearm and a quantity of unlicensed opium milk, for the manufacture of black-market apothecary's laudanum.'

'But no – it cannot be so—'

Derrien waved a hand. The sergeant dragged the old man to his feet and stood him against the wall of his shop. Four grenadiers formed line in front of him and stood to attention. The crowd pushed against the spiked ramparts of grenadier bayonets, calling more loudly.

One of Ablondi's sons broke free and tried to run from the square but Citizen Masson doubled him over with a fist to the stomach. The boy hurled a curse in Occitan, which Derrien could not understand, then spoke in a garbled rush. The sergeant translated into French.

'He says he did it, Citizen. He says he took a bottle of the scent from his father's bench. Gave it to a servant girl.'

'We have no servants in the Republic, Sergeant,' corrected Derrien. 'We have officials.'

'Yes, Citizen. He gave it to an official, a girl at a local residence.'

'Which local residence, Sergeant?'

The boy said no more.

Derrien snapped his fingers. 'Sergeant. Firing party make ready.'

The sergeant gave the order and the corporal roared out, '*Apprêtez!*'

The crowd grew louder still, several NCOs and officers pushing their way to the front, shouting past the grenadiers, asserting their superior rank, to no avail. The grenadiers did not move. Their cries rose to a crescendo when a mounted *gendarme* officer appeared at the end of the lane leading to Ablondi's shop, a platoon of militia infantry behind. It was the captain from the heights, without his colonel.

'*What is this?*'

The crowd cheered, sensing an ally. Derrien turned, hands behind his back. The militiamen formed up across the cobbled street, their muskets shouldered.

'*You!*' called the captain, 'You will depart this place at once!'

Derrien called over his shoulder, 'Sergeant.'

By the sergeant's command the remaining grenadiers formed up and marched, manoeuvring to make two ranks in front of Derrien, blocking the *gendarmes*' path to the shop and square. The iron studs on the soles of their boots rang out as they crashed to a halt. Behind, the corporal continued with the firing-squad. *Kogel in loop! Balle en canon!*

'*Citizen!*' the captain tried again. 'You will answer for this! This is not the procedure!' The militiamen shuffled uncertainly in their files. 'Who are these grenadiers, these *Dutchmen*? I do not recognise their authority to bear arms in this *département*! As such I hereby place them *under arrest!*'

Derrien did not take his eyes from the captain. 'Sergeant. The militia shall not pass.'

'Yes, Citizen.'

With another barked order from the sergeant the grenadiers ported arms, their muskets held before them, bayonets bright. The *gendarme* militia shrank back, looking to their officer. They were not the equal of grenadiers.

'Corporal,' said Derrien over his shoulder, 'on my order.'

'*Ja, meneer!*' He turned back to his men. '*En… joue!*'

The firing squad raised their muskets and presented. Derrien kept his eye ever on the *gendarme* captain. 'Citizen Masson. Ask him again.'

Masson cocked a pocket-pistol and put the muzzle against the boy's head. The old man began to call out, now in French so Derrien could understand.

'*Ne lui dis rien, mon fils!*' *Tell him nothing, my son!*

The captain's mount stamped nervously at the disquiet of the crowd. 'This is *monstrous, m'sieur!* Sentence without trial is the mark of tyranny!'

The son fell to the ground, his brother wailing at him, both babbling a stream of Occitan to the sergeant. Derrien looked on, waiting, his hand raised, ready.

'Citizen,' said the sergeant, 'he will take us. They do not know the name of the house, but they know where it is. He is an idiot, straight off the water.'

Ablondi continued to shout to his son, '*Non! Non!*' Then, red-faced with defiance, he spat upon the ground and uttered the final blasphemy at Derrien's back, in the clearest, purest French he could muster, the old battle-cry of Toulon:

'*Vive le roi!*'

Long live the king.

The crowd fell into a deathly hush. Derrien raised an eyebrow at the *gendarme* captain. Here was all he needed. He dropped his hand. The corporal complied.

'*Feu!*'

The muskets cracked with a double report and four .65 calibre bullets smashed into the old man's chest, his shattered remains thrown to the cobbles. Ablondi's sons raged against the hands restraining them. '*Non non non! Papa! Papa!*'

A voice in the crowd screamed, some turned and ran, a stall toppling, goods trampled. The grenadiers remained impassive in the face of the square on the verge of riot.

Derrien nodded at the *gendarme* militia and the captain. 'You may now disperse the mob, Captain.'

The captain looked down with contempt. 'Get your *Flamande* dogs to do it. I have no fear of you, *m'sieur.* I marched from here with Schérer and Kellerman through the *Porte d'Italie* and returned in glory. Where is *yours*? *Butcher*.' He called to his men, '*Sergent de la troupe! À vous! Alignez!*'

The militiamen shouldered arms, formed files and turned about. Derrien glanced at the grenadier sergeant and pointed idly at the prisoners. 'Bring them. And let them carry the body.'

Citizen Montfort looked on in horror as home after home was sacked. Derrien went wherever the girl official had worked, inflicting his own personal reign of the Robespierre Terror, the militia unable to stand against him. The grenadiers dragged old men, wives and daughters from their homes, beating them with their muskets in the street. Derrien stood over them with a small screw-barrelled pistol, dispatching those whom he saw fit or taking prisoners for interrogation later. Eventually a name was given: a governess of the family Bartelmi.

'And you have seen this visiting governess?' asked Derrien of an old washerwoman in a yard.

'Yes, Citizen, a *Parisienne*,' she replied, eyes wide, her jowls shaking. She clutched her shawl protectively about her.

'You speak a very fine French, Citizen, a pleasure to hear in these southern parts. Are you from Paris yourself?'

'St Denys, Citizen,' she admitted, more anxious now than before.

'Excellent.' He turned to the bailiffs and the sergeant. 'Take her. If she has lied, kill her.'

–

As evening fell, Derrien's carriage climbed out of town into the surrounding country, deep into a gathering gloom. The grenadiers marched the prisoners behind in silence, grim pall-bearers to Derrien's funereal procession.

A few miles southeast of the port, on the road to Le Pradet and Hyères, they reached a hillside affording a view of the entrance to the outer harbour of Toulon, packed with ships. Silhouetted on a rise against the slate-grey skies was a grand old house.

'The home of Hugues Bartelmi,' mumbled Montfort, his voice low, cowed by the events of the day.

Derrien looked out at high iron gates and a fine neoclassical *maison de maître* of stone pediments and pillars. 'Who is he?'

'Philanthropist,' said Montfort. 'A wife, two daughters. A shipping magnate, servant of the *département*. He assists with the *Ordinnateur Maritime*, Citizen Najac, pays for the school, the curate, takes in students, homeless sailors, the poor, they—'

'Students?' Derrien's face transformed with the light of realisation. 'Of course...' He looked out of the opposite window at the sea-traffic of Toulon, at the lights burning on the cliff-sides, on the rocky islands encircled by boiling white amid the darkness, the sound mingling with the wind. It was the perfect vantage point.

The grenadiers clanged on the gates with the butts of their muskets, the tolling of so many alarm bells, until two Arab servants hurried out to open for them, scuttling aside, heads bowed. The carriage entered and slowed at the front steps. The gentleman of the house appeared in the elegant portico, a dinner napkin in hand, lamps casting a welcoming glow behind him. He was dressed in pale grey, a fashionably knotted white cravat at his throat, the image of genteel prosperity. Derrien loathed him on sight.

'Good evening, Citizens. How can I be of service? A warm drink on a cold evening?' He laughed. 'I think the spring rain is coming...'

Derrien climbed out of the carriage. The wind began to rise, and it tugged at his cocked hat. 'Citizen Bartelmi,' he said, 'I am Citizen Derrien of the Ministry of the Interior. May I see your writing desk?'

Bartelmi smiled, bemused, 'My writing desk? Well, I...' and then opened his arms. 'But of course, Citizen, but, may I ask why?'

'You will see.' Derrien nodded to the grenadiers. 'Sergeant,' he said, staring at Bartelmi, 'sack the house.'

As the rain started to spot the cobbles, the grenadiers stormed into the candlelit interior. Within moments, the screams began.

—

At her dressing table upstairs, Isabelle Moreau-Lazare heard the cries below, and froze, pen in hand. The grenadiers' boots banged on the stairs. Her breath catching, she rushed to her door and closed it. There was the sound of breaking glass, a shriek. *Claire*, she thought.

Bartelmi's instructions had been clear – she knew what she must do. Moving quickly she wiped her pen, put the top on the ink, and crumpled the coded cross-written note she had been writing:

> *6 Rue Victoire, Paris, Dearest, do thank Joseph for that wonderful* BLANK *carte M8191 delta and Sinai canal silting 15 degrees* BLANK *occasion on that last*

Folding it, she stuffed everything into the front pockets of her smock. Heart pounding, she pulled her small packed valise from under the bed, snatched the cloak hanging on the back of the door and threw it on, pulled open the casement windows, pushing the outer shutters wide.

The cold wind hit her and she gasped. She tossed out her valise and watched it fall and bounce, first onto the lavender borders then the gravel and into the grass. She climbed out onto the sill and took hold of the cast-iron downpipe, trying to pull the window shut behind her, but nearly losing her footing, her cloak flapping wildly, toes probing through her silk shoes, slipping across the rough texture of the wall before finding purchase. The wind battered at her, the rain striking faster, harder, stinging her eyes. She began to climb down.

She stopped just above the tall window directly below her own, its shutters closed, and heard further cries as doors were

76

kicked open. A foreign language – *German?* – then in French, '*Below! Get below at once.*'

A pistol cracked and three muskets boomed, followed by a cry and a crash of furniture. In her fright she slid downwards, her hands catching the bruising edge of an iron bracket, then fell.

Her stomach floating, her breath not coming, she crashed into the lavender. The woody stalks drove up her wet skirts like so many sharpened stakes, scraping her legs as she struck, cried out, hit the earth hard, and rolled onto the gravel.

Scarcely able to breathe, she clawed her way to her feet, grabbed for her valise, *missed* the handle, grabbed *again*, pulled the cloak's hood over her head, her mind urging, *go quickly*, and raced for the bare heath and the stables, *faster*, her legs pumping, feet flying, terror driving her onwards as she ran into the rain, hearing her own mocking voice, *Run, spy, run.*

–

Inside, Derrien, Masson, Montfort and the bailiffs trooped upstairs with the bloodied Bartelmi, the sergeant holding him by a thick twist of rope round his neck and a dagger to his spine.

On the half-landing they passed an open chamber filled with screams, three grenadiers tearing the gown from the lady of the house and throwing her to the floor by the bed, one groping at her swaying breasts as he tried to mount her, then looking up, seeing Derrien. Coming to attention, his comrades quickly tried to block the scene from view.

'*Louise!*' cried Bartelmi, but he was pulled up sharply by the noose at his throat.

Derrien glanced in and said to the sergeant, 'Not here. And gag him.' The sergeant put the rope between Bartelmi's teeth and dragged him up the stairs. The screams resumed.

On the candlelit gallery above, Derrien found a fine mahogany *escritoire*, complete with blotter, pen, inkstand and letter-rack. He saw with some satisfaction that it was filled with blank stationery.

He took the wallet from his inside pocket and withdrew the torn coded message fragment. 'This,' he said to Bartelmi, 'is Amalfi paper. Very fine, as you know.' He took a fresh sheet from the stationery on the desk and laid it beside the fragment. 'The King of Naples banned its use in official documents. It was too soft, and prone to dissolution in water...'

Bartelmi looking on, Derrien bent over the two sheets, comparing them through a small magnifying glass. 'This old paper was most popular among counter-revolutionaries and spies for clandestine communications. The evidence, you see,' he said, glancing at Bartelmi, 'can be destroyed, turned to so much pulp, without recourse to fire.'

He bent to the paper again, noting the texture and weave, examining the watermarks.

'However, this torn remnant here – can you see? – is stronger *post*-edict Amalfi paper.' He almost smiled. 'Used in error. It failed to destruct.'

Bartelmi began to breathe harder against his gag, his eyes widening, flicking to the paper and back to Derrien. It was clear he knew precisely what Derrien was talking about.

'And this remnant,' he said, just for a moment relishing his success, 'bears the same watermark as the paper on your desk. Do you see the cipher written upon it? By an agent of the British Admiralty?'

Bartelmi struggled to get free, frantic, but Derrien continued. 'This spot of perfume, here,' he said, showing him the mark on the enciphered fragment, 'tells me that a woman either wrote this note, or was present during its execution. Which?' he asked. 'A wife? A lover?' Derrien waited. 'Or perhaps a *governess*.'

At this last mention Bartelmi gave a guttural scream behind his gag, '*Non, non!*' struggling to pull away, shaking his head fitfully, his eyes clenched shut.

Derrien turned back to the paper, content. He had enough. 'Take them.' He took a steadying breath. *Yes.* 'Take them *all*.'

Confused, Montfort hesitated. 'All? But—'

Derrien rounded on him, his violence exploding. '*ALL of them!*'

They shoved the gasping Bartelmi back to the stairs, and Derrien stood still at the desk, staring at the fragment. He folded it away neatly into his wallet and, just as he replaced it in his inside pocket, felt a cold draught at his feet, from an unlit passage to his left. He had no idea why, but he recalled the soaring arches of the Tuileries Palace.

She is here.

He lunged down the passage to the distant door as if in a dream, his legs impossibly heavy, his movements impossibly slow – too late, he knew somehow, too blinded by his success – his hand reaching for the intricate scrollwork of the brass latch, grasping it, wrenching at it, bursting the door in until it bounced on its hinges.

It was a makeshift bedchamber and boudoir, the shutters swinging in the wind, the rain blowing in on a small dressing table, sheets of paper strewn on the floor. He moved to the open window and looked down, the rain lashing at his face, chastising him, and saw the crushed lavender below, the deep scuff marks in the gravel, and the curving arc of wet tracks across the trampled grass.

'No…'

He gripped the window frame almost to breaking point, imagining his quarry reaching the harbour, getting a boat, to Genoa, to Naples, to freedom. The only proof of her existence floated on the damp breeze around him: the merest gossamer trace of that delicate scent, created by the late *parfumier* Ablondi.

–

Under cover of a foggy and moonless night, a small black jolly-boat darted across the swell of the outer harbour of Toulon, leaving a smear of misty silver in its wake.

The six occupants appeared to be a party of sailors and their officer from one of the numerous men-of-war at anchor. But the swift, practised movements of their short paddles suggested something altogether different.

A patrol ship emerged from the drifting fog, its lanterns swinging, a bell clanging. Then it disappeared, engulfed once again in the dragon's breath of Toulon. The boat slid past unnoticed.

Two of the oarsmen scanned the harbour roads through blackened telescopes. One of them spotted a fire-beacon high on a distant shore, no more than a dull glow.

'*Contact*,' he muttered.

The officer leaned close and whispered, 'Where away?'

'Starboard bow, east-nor'east, sir.'

'Very well.' He looked to the man on the tiller. 'Come to starboard and follow the shoreline east-nor'east. Into the fog.'

'Starboard, aye.'

The boat disappeared into the cold mist, their only guide the sound of breakers on the rocks. The coxswain pulled the tiller gently and guided their strokes, '*Hard down on your portside, easy a-starboard, lads*.' The boat spun slowly into line with the cliffs as the fog parted, revealing a towering ridge rising dark before them. Above lay the shore batteries, thick barrels of 24-pounders black against the night sky. They passed underneath, looking up, silent. Off-duty sentries leaned in doorways, clustered by braziers, faces lit by the flicker of flames and the glow of pipes, their quiet laughter drifting on the breeze. The six rowed past, undetected.

They drew in to a sheltered cove, jumped out and pushed the craft into the lee of rocks and the lazy bobbing of a tidal pool. They waited motionless in the deep shadows, the only sound the surf and the drag of pebble and shell. '*Clear?*' said the officer.

'*Clear aye,*' murmured Marine Sergeant Jory Cook, late of HMS *America* and the Battle of the Cape. '*On me in twos.*'

He hurried across the shingle beach to a ridge of sand and rock, the others close behind with the officer, Marine Lt Gideon Bagnall. They were rigged like French sailors in long-tailed caps, neckerchiefs, baggy *culotte* trousers and short woollen coats – all concealing a plethora of weapons.

'Make ready,' said Bagnall. 'We find our man, and depart.' He was young, his voice breathless, excited. 'We shall save the day afore it's lost. All clear in the boat?'

'Clear aye, sir,' they murmured.

Bagnall raised his pistol. 'Right. Godspeed.'

Marine Privates Pettifer and De Lisle caught Cook's eye. Pettifer was built like a Cornish drayhorse, De Lisle the opposite: lean and wiry, with the shifty eye of a fox. '*God save Bristol,*' muttered Cook to them both with a nod.

Bagnall leapt over the ridge and ran. The marines followed, dashing across the deserted coastal heath.

Half a mile inland up a steep slope stood a stone and timber barn, a signal fire in a tall beacon marking its position. Cook saw it first but was wary. The fire burned bright, throwing eerie shadows, the only sound the snap of flames. Cook wanted it dark, always dark.

Taking the lead, Bagnall ran to the rear corner of the barn by a dilapidated low door with a broken cask lying to one side. He hit the stone wall and dropped low, his features garish in the flashing orange of the fire. The marines split into their teams, two disappearing into the long grass, Pettifer and De Lisle covering the tall double doors at the front entrance. Bagnall cocked his pistol and drew a blackened, razor-edged smallsword.

Cook headed for a distant rise overlooking the eastern approaches to the inner roads of Toulon harbour. He was not prepared for what he saw.

'*By Jaysus, shite an' all…*'

The channel was packed with dozens of merchantmen, barges, tenders and tugs – all scuttling between the disciplined lines of a battle-fleet: the black, spiked masts of broad 80-gunners, 74s, frigates, 44s, 24s and 16s – and towering above them all, a three-decked giant, mounting 60 gun-ports on one broadside. Foundry furnaces sprayed clouds of sparkling flame into the night as the smelters poured, cannons swinging on booms, billowing clouds belching into the hellish sky. Vulcan was at his anvil.

Cook drew a large-bore Sea-Service pistol and crawled back to the barn. '*Sir*,' he hissed, but Bagnall was still crouched at the front, ready to go in. '*Sir, we've got to recce the port*—'

Bagnall made a cutting gesture with his hand, then hissed at the doors, '*Liberté!*' There was no reply.

Cook watched. Bagnall reached for the rusted clasp of the tall barn doors. Pettifer and De Lisle crawled closer in the darkness, Pettifer readying his bell-mouthed musketoon.

'*Liberté*,' Bagnall repeated.

Still no reply.

Not liking it, Cook tried to call him away. '*Sir*—'

Bagnall banged on the door. '*Come on, blast you…*'

He tugged open the clasp. The doors swung wide, creaking on old hinges. The cavernous interior was dark but for the penetrating flicker of firelight through gaps in the walls and roof. They could see an earth floor, jute sacks, hanging tools and humped shadows – but it stank of all things dead.

Bagnall recoiled, covering his mouth and nose. '*Good God.*' He looked out at Cook. 'Make ready, Sar'nt.'

'*Sir, wait*—'

Impatient, Bagnall rushed inside, pistol and sword ready. A lamp shutter clanged open and Bagnall was caught in a sudden blaze of light, a musket blasting from a corner, the flash bright, spinning Bagnall in a circle, but not before he loosed a round from his pistol towards the lantern.

A figure fell, tipping over a table with a crash, the lantern falling, throwing crazed shadows. A second shot exploded from the opposite corner. De Lisle ran inside and a Dutch *Patriotten* grenadier charged out of the dark, fixed bayonet reaching for him.

De Lisle dropped, a four-barrelled pistol ready in both hands, and fired his first round into the man's chest. The grenadier fell from full height, breathing a last fetid breath in De Lisle's face. The shots had echoed all over the hillside.

Cook came at a run as Pettifer rolled Bagnall onto his back. '*Agent…*' whispered Bagnall. '*Agent… find the…*' But when Cook bent lower to listen, Bagnall's eyes rolled and stared into nothing.

Pettifer glanced at Cook, 'Is he?'

'Aye.'

De Lisle suddenly jerked away and pointed over their heads. '*Jaysus shite, Cookie…*'

Hanging from the main beam, now brighter in the glow of the fallen lantern, what had at first looked nothing more than sacks, were five bodies. Ragged strips of burnt clothing hung from scorched limbs and charred bare feet, one face no more than a skeletal grimace, the flesh torn away by rats and corruption, long, matted hair trailing.

Pettifer stared. 'Christ God, Sarge… three of 'em's littl'uns…'

They found the suspending ropes and lowered one of the corpses. On the chest was a stained fly-bill fastened by a long carpenter's nail hammered into the breastbone. Across the top were daubed the words *Mort à Bartelmi* and the call-sign Bagnall had used, *Liberté!*

Cook took the flyer and read it. 'Death to Bartelmi all right… This must be him, our poor bloody passenger. We're rumbled, lads.'

Pettifer let down one of the girls. 'Just a littl'un…' he kept mumbling, 'Not ruddy right, Sarge… not even the *Frogs*'d do this… not to their own kind…'

There was a whistle from out front. They could hear the rush of boots and the clank of equipment coming up the track fast. Cook looked down at the dead girl, her face a mask of horrors, one ear missing, a pure white eye turned inwards to save its soul from further torment. He looked out down the track, then pulled Bagnall's body out of sight. 'Get ready to clear out.'

Pettifer brandished his blunderbuss. 'Come on, Sarge, these bastards're *ours*.'

'Too right,' muttered De Lisle.

Cook swore and pulled Bagnall further into the darkness. It was already too late. 'Into the ruddy barn then.'

Two silhouetted ranks of the *Patriotten* grenadiers doubled across the gravel and formed line in the wide doorway of the barn, the NCOs bawling, '*Qui vive! Zone interdit!*'

After a moment, Derrien and Montfort appeared, each holding a lantern, Citizen Masson a bulking shadow behind. The grenadier sergeant gave the command, '*En joue!*' The grenadiers presented their muskets, ready to fire.

From the depths of the barn Cook roared out, '*M'rines by twos!*'

The cry in English surprised the grenadiers and Derrien. Four quick shots rang out from the two marines concealed in the grass behind them and four of the rearmost grenadiers staggered and fell, the ranks loosing a ragged volley into the barn in reflex, one man in the front losing his head to a shot from behind, a cloud of powder, blood and bone blowing black in the lamplight. Cook and De Lisle fired their pistols as Pettifer stepped out, '*Have that!*' and fired his musketoon.

The torrent of shot from the packed blunderbuss muzzle ripped away the midriff of the grenadier sergeant beside Derrien and the right hand and hip of Montfort, who dissolved in a wailing scream. Derrien spun and toppled against the doorjamb, raging, '*Anglais! Anglais! You are Englishmen!*'

'*Scram fer it!*' shouted Cook, and hefted Bagnall's body onto his shoulder. The two lone marines tore through the grenadiers from behind, short-bladed sword bayonets slashing at exposed throats as they went, before plunging after Cook into the flickering darkness of the barn's interior, the fallen lanterns throwing crazed shadows.

The grenadiers recovered and formed line, their second volley thundering, the stinking barn alive with shot, and Cook went down, Bagnall's body falling. The enraged grenadiers charged into the dark after them but Pettifer had reloaded, and stepped out once again to give another salvo. The walls burst with stone shrapnel and splinters, the blast drowning the grenadiers' cries. He hauled Cook to his feet, '*C'mon, y'old lump!*'

But Cook struggled to take Bagnall. '*Dead man, Petty!*'

'He's garn! We got to leave 'im, Sarge!' and they dived through the shattered planks of the rear door. Lt Bagnall's body stayed propped up in the doorway, a final lookout for his first and last command, his marines dashing to safety across the heathland scrub to the steep hill road.

The surviving grenadiers stumbled round the barn and formed line once more, Derrien shouting, '*After them!*'

The Dutch commands of the corporal were whisked away by the wind, '*Twee rangen! Snel verdomme!*' *Two ranks! Quickly, dammit!*

De Lisle broke off from the others and delved into his pack, pulling out a rolled woollen bundle with a length of fuse. He yanked the cap of a snaplock and the quickmatch flared. '*Bag o'tricks! Hit the deck!*' He hurled it hard, low and fast at the Dutch troops.

The grenadiers presented arms just as the bundle bounced several yards from the front rank and exploded. Compacted iron fragments flew in all directions, the lime-powder core flaring white-hot, blinding any not killed by flying scrap-metal, the oil-soaked wool belching a furious cloud of choking smoke.

Pettifer and De Lisle pulled Cook along and they half tumbled down the slope, scrambling to the boat, distant shouts drawing closer. They fell into the craft and shoved off, their paddles plunging into the black water, *One two, one two*, quick, hard and shallow, powering them out into the deep, the wind hitting them, stinging their faces with spray.

Cook turned and watched the distant ridge. Derrien screamed at the few surviving grenadiers who staggered blind, retching, hands to their faces. A troop of *gendarmes* appeared, a mounted officer shouting down at Derrien, pointing a pistol at him, the grenadier corporal taking aim at the figure, a *gendarme* shooting the Dutchman dead. Derrien waved madly at the sea and they rushed to the ridge, some of the militiamen kneeling and firing at the fast-disappearing marines, their bullets spattering harmlessly into the waves far behind. Within moments the tar-blackened boat was swallowed up by the darkness of the waves.

'*God save bloody Bristol…*' breathed Cook.

De Lisle fell back, a dark patch on the shoulder of his coat. 'Bloody mantrap, Sarge,' he whispered. 'Bloody *shite* of a mantrap.'

'Aye,' muttered Cook. 'For that poor bloody soul, whoever he was.'

'S'a *family*, Sarge…' said Pettifer, badly shaken, 'Hangin' there… *whole family.*'

'But we di'n't give up the boat,' said Cook. 'Prayers for the dead… By land, by sea, Jack or Jolly.'

'*Jack or Jolly,*' they intoned solemnly as they rowed.

Cook looked back over his shoulder at the smoke-laced coast around Toulon and pulled out the stained flybill taken from Bartelmi's desecrated corpse. The others watched him, each silent with their thoughts.

Cook cast back, over the past two years, the battles, the losses. Nelson and Lord Jack had tried to stuff the devil himself back into his bottle at Cape St Vincent – and now Toulon had become Lucifer's forge yet again. *It was all for nothing*, he thought. *Bloody nothing.*

But this, he reckoned, looking at the flybill, *this would be enough to get him back*. Get back the only officer they had ever trusted – now alone with his wounds, alone with his bleak memories, adrift, somewhere in England.

Mission

The Royal Navy carriage hurtled along the High Road at full gallop, heeling around corners, Soames rolling against Montgomery on the bench seat as he continued explaining: '*...and that shore-party raid by the marines took place two weeks ago, sir,*' he called over the noise of the road. '*What they discovered, they impressed upon me, was far beyond what any of us had feared. It would be no breach to tell you we have recalled Nelson as well.*'

'*But what can that have to do with this!*'

Hazzard looked at the crumpled note in his hands and reread it:

> *William. The situation is grave. Come in uniform and ready to sail if at all possible. We have news of Sarah. Room 63.*

Montgomery looked grim, 'Perhaps all will be made clear, sir.'

The driver lashed the team of four to arrive at St Jude's in less than fifteen minutes. The wheels slewed across the gravel and Hazzard jumped out, his heart pounding. *Good God, good God.* '*Moran!*'

He tore open the front door and called through the house. 'Moran! Get my sea-bag and uniform from the trunk in the attics!' Montgomery and Soames followed, waiting on the threshold. Hazzard passed quickly through the hall to the gun cupboard in the study. 'Where is the double Manton?'

The Reverend Hazzard appeared from the French doors to the side garden. 'William...?' He had not seen his nephew so animated. 'What–what is it? What's afoot...?'

Hazzard indicated Montgomery, who held out a message bearing a Ministry crest. 'Uncle, read this. It is over two weeks old…'

The elderly reverend examined the note, a printed summons from the War Office, blanks written in a flowing, round hand:

From the Offices of the Secretary of State for War
NOTICE OF ATTENDANCE 10th April 1798
Name: Hazzard, Wm. J., H.M. Marine Forces
(Chathm – Reinstated Active –)

Is hereby commanded to present himself at:
the Admiralty Buildings London with Immediate
Effect from 10th inst. Failure to report for roll
within 7 days will result in Disciplinary Proceed-
ings under the terms of…

It was signed and sealed by both the under-secretary and Lord Melville, the Secretary of State himself. The Reverend Hazzard looked at Montgomery and Soames. 'What is the meaning of this? I – I thought him not on strength…?'

'No, the other note.' Hazzard thrust the slip of paper into his hand and went to the foot of the stairs. 'Moran! Have you found it? I leave at once!' He felt a swelling fear, the same that had hammered at his chest when he rode from Sarah's house that black morning eighteen months ago. The paper shook in the old man's pale hands.

'News of Sarah…? But how came you by news of this poor girl, sir? I–I do not understand…! Where is she…?'

Montgomery bowed to the old man and said smoothly, 'I fear I am not permitted to discuss such matters, sir, merely that we are to convey Mr Hazzard as swiftly as possible to the Admiralty.' He looked at Hazzard. 'If it is convenient, sir, you may ride ahead with Mr Soames, your bags and equipment to follow in the coach.'

Hazzard stopped and stood still a moment. *Admiralty*. Having read the summons from the War Office it had not crossed his mind that he was in fact not to report to Lord Melville or Chatham Marine barracks – but to the Admiralty. Seeing Sarah's name on the note had blotted out all other considerations – including the use of his first name. He felt his heart pound. 'Who gave you this?' he asked, his words barely above a whisper, that old dread slowly creeping inwards. 'Which officer?'

Soames looked uncertain how to reply. 'It was handed on by a junior, sir—'

'Was it Blake?' demanded Hazzard. '*Was it a Lieutenant Blake?*'

Montgomery cut in, 'I know of no such officer, sir, only that the matter is of the utmost urgency to the Crown and that your attendance was requested *in camera* at the very highest level. As we had no address other than your rooms in Greenwich, riders were sent to Portsmouth, Dartmouth, Tilbury and Chatham. Through your publications we reached your old college tutors at Cambridge, which led us here.'

The Reverend Hazzard gripped his nephew with shaking hands, his eyes wide with fear. 'Now, now, my boy, please, listen to me, *listen*, Jervis has plenty sons for this work, *plenty*, and you have – have done more than enough… *please – more than enough…*' The old man clung to him, his head down, quaking.

'Uncle, I must. It is Sarah,' he whispered, his breath tight in his chest, *Sarah*, and he nearly choked the words, '*God above, it's Sarah…*'

There was movement in the hall. It was Moran on the stairs, bringing down Hazzard's packed canvas seaman's bag, and an old, long-faded red uniform coat over one arm. Ellie the housekeeper came after, with reddened eyes and cheeks running with tears. Clumsy, brutal and crude in her slender arms was his heavy Indian Talwar sword with belt and hanger.

Moran fumbled under the scarlet coat and pulled out the old leather sling and holster, gleaming with polish. It was

Hazzard's double-barrelled Manton pistol. 'Cleaned and cleared for action, Master Will'am.' He held it out with a firm hand. 'If this be for Miss Sarah,' he said, 'then just you go and get 'er back.'

Hazzard took it. 'I will.' He turned to Montgomery. 'How fast are your horses?'

Montgomery nodded. 'As the wind, sir.'

–

Hazzard and Soames rode on ahead through the day and by four they saw the distant chimney smoke of London. They stopped at a post-house near Lincoln's Inn and Soames sent warning of their imminent arrival. By five they trotted their mounts through the mews off The Strand and down Whitehall. It seemed that every other man was in uniform, the city an armed camp. Just before Horse Guards' Parade they stopped, and Soames passed them through a cordon of marine guards at the protective Screen wall. They entered the vast courtyard of the Admiralty.

Hazzard looked up at the old building. He had felt hope and pride when he had first reported for duty all those years earlier – and now only a deep distrust. Two towering wings jutted forward either side of a high-pillared portico set like a grimace, its columns so many bared teeth ready to devour the world. Knowing what he did of its tortuous depths, Hazzard felt sick at heart that Sarah's name could ever have been spoken in its halls.

Two grooms ran to meet them and Hazzard slid out of the saddle while Soames busied himself with the formalities. In his battered leather riding coat he passed the curious gaze of still more marine guards as he mounted the broad stone steps and entered the great hall. There was a smell of polish, sweet tobacco and soiled wool – and the hint of panic. It was crowded with bluejackets and civil servants hurrying in all directions, red-coated marines guarding every door. A group of naval officers spotted him, fell silent and stared. 'Where is the duty officer?' he asked them.

One took an amused step towards him, light glinting off an immaculate buckled shoe, and looked Hazzard up and down with fascination. 'And what, pray, might you be?'

Hazzard removed his coat. His officer's uniform cut away by the surgeon at the Cape, Hazzard had come in his old cotton and linen Bombay Marine jacket – its salt-stained scarlet and braided bastion loops long faded, each bullet-mark and sword-cut roughly stitched. On the breast were several jewelled orders, a silver Mughal star, a brooch of crossed swords, and a cluster of diamonds orbiting a ruby and gold tiger. He wore tasselled black Indian boots, his black bicorne hat not in the regulation side to side manner but fore and aft, the crushed crow's beak hanging low over his face, casting his features in darkness, suiting his mood. 'None of your damned business. Where is the duty officer?'

'My dear chap,' the naval officer continued. 'You do *not* come to the Admiralty dressed like a, well, a Zanzibar pirate – and what on *earth* is that?'

He pointed at the sword hanging at Hazzard's hip. Hazzard put a hand on the spiked pommel, its curved scabbard bright with silver-threaded Hindustani Devanagari characters.

'It is a Mughal Talwar, as you might well know had you ever sailed beyond Portsmouth in your vaunted career.'

There were chuckles from behind and the man coloured more deeply than the dots of rouge on his cheeks. 'I *beg* your pardon—'

'I am Hazzard, William John. Former Lieutenant His Majesty's Marine Forces and Captain-Lieutenant the Bombay Marine. Where is Room 63?'

To hear 'Room 63' was enough to still the officer's tongue, but to hear 'Bombay Marine' was almost a threat. More heads turned. The officer backed away, wrong-footed. 'One moment,' he mumbled and moved off just as an older, bare-headed marine officer in scarlet and white cross-belt approached, Hazzard noting the empty sleeve pinned up at the shoulder.

'Mr Hazzard? Major Carteret, 35 Company.'

Hazzard came to attention. 'Sir.'

'As you were,' he said. 'I think you're frightening the natives.'

They headed down the vaulted south corridor, their boots echoing. Hazzard looked about, at the chandeliers, the oak panelling. The place had become a cross between a First-Rate ship of the line and a Parisian hotel.

'Didn't think we did Captain-Lieutenants any more,' said Carteret.

'We don't, sir. But it's enough to shut up the Navy.'

Carteret laughed as they headed upstairs, a great skylight dome above displaying a cold, grey evening. Eventually Carteret stopped at a door marked by a small tarnished oval plate, and a barely legible '63'. His hand on the latch, he hesitated then said, 'Look here. Some of us knew Harry Race for what he was, and raised a glass to you at the Cape. You did the job and got your chaps out. And that's what counts. My advice: clear for action, and stand-to.'

It was an unexpected welcome and made Hazzard feel less alone than he had in years. He nodded his thanks. 'Aye, sir.' Carteret knocked once and Hazzard went in.

To one side was a cold fire grate under a smoke-blackened mantel. Sitting at a long, polished table before a tall window overlooking Whitehall, cup of coffee in hand, was the elegant figure of Lieutenant Blake, in braided blue tailcoat and spotless white collar and breeches; the Admiralty officer from the Cape who had rung the death-knell for Harry Race, and nearly destroyed Hazzard in the process.

Blake paused, the cup halfway to his lips. He smiled warmly, perhaps even gratefully. 'William.'

Hazzard very nearly turned on his heel to go, but Blake rose from his seat, prepared. 'Do hear us out, William, please, I beg of you.'

Hazzard was unequivocal. 'I made it very plain I would never countenance your orders again.'

A communicating door in the far corner opened and Sir Rafe Lewis strode in. He closed the door and banged a stack of files on the table. 'What about mine then, sir?' He pulled out a chair and sat. Hazzard looked back at him. Lewis waited for an answer. 'Well?'

'And you are, sir?' asked Hazzard.

'Commodore Sir Rafe Lewis, Mr Hazzard. And this is Room 63.'

Beneath the dark curls of his grey wig a leathern, sun-browned face looked out, and Hazzard recognised a serving seaman of considerable experience. He nodded. 'Sir Rafe.'

'My compliments on the India pattern.' Lewis pointed at the uniform.

'It's seen some days.'

'Haven't we all. Is that a Talwar?'

'Yes, sir.'

'Hm. A gift I understand.'

Hazzard wondered what else he knew. 'Presented by the Wazir, in Agra.'

There was a brief silence, Lewis not taking his eyes off him. Hazzard threw his riding-coat and hat on the table and sat, stiff, reluctant. Blake sat down, his chair scraping.

Lewis consulted his notes. 'You are the same Hazzard who wrote a monograph on Egypt, hieroglyphical scripts and so forth, and – what was it?'

'Coptic, sir,' said Blake.

'Yes,' said Hazzard.

Lewis nodded, reading through his notes. 'You have lectured at Cambridge and Somerset House, and write for... the *Gentleman's Magazine*.' He made it sound seditious. 'As does Dr Johnson, so I believe.'

'On occasion.' Hazzard saw one of the pages before Lewis. At the top it said, *Hazzard Wm J. (Chatham)*. The first entry he could read upside-down was underlined: *Orphaned. French mother. Father Maj. R.F. Hazzard HEIC killed active service Maleh. French educᵗᵈ. Master of Sword, the Academy Portsmouth. Qualified Mariner. Knowledge of Languages. Knowledge of Literature. Knowledge of Histories. Knowledge of Geography. Knowledge of Navigation. Knowledge of—*

'Why did you transfer from the East India Company to the Marines in '93?' Lewis asked this without looking up.

'The declaration of war on France.'

'Nothing to do with a poor assessment in the Bombay Marine?'

Hazzard stiffened further. 'That assessment came before the letter of the Wazir.'

Lewis nodded, seeing a note: *Regarded highly by Presidency, Wazir and Nizam of Hyderabad.* 'Very well. You wanted to fight despite having a French mother.'

'My mother was of Huguenot descent and forced to flee, pressure from the local bishopric. She married my father in India. Her loyalty to England was never in doubt. She acted as agent against Hyder Ali and the French. She died when I was a child, shortly after my father. But then you know all of this because it lies before you plain as day.'

Lewis looked up at this. 'Impertinence will get you nowhere, sir.'

'I do not recall asking your advice.'

Lewis considered this a moment, watching him, then seemed suddenly satisfied and slapped the file shut. 'Very well. I have been instructed by the First Sea-Lord and the Secretary of War to put a certain proposition to you.'

'I was told there was news of my fiancée, Miss Sarah-Louise Chapel. I am here solely because of—'

'We shall get to that shortly.' Lewis leafed through more of his papers. 'Your original oath and employment as a seconded officer to these offices binds you to that agreement even now, and what follows here shall then not be repeated outside these walls, is that understood?'

Hazzard nodded. 'Very well.'

'Good. One of our clandestine agents recently felt in danger of exposure and arrest in Paris and fled the city, sending word of a large French fleet massing at Toulon in the south. We have since heard similar tales from local sea trade of Marseille, Genoa, Ajaccio and Civita Vecchia, amounting in total to possibly 300 transports and 50 men o'war.'

Lewis waited, his opening broadside having its desired effect. Hazzard stared back at him. This was not in the press. 'In Toulon. I thought they were massing a flotilla at Boulogne.'

'That flotilla is but a pipedream. Toulon, however, is an invasion fleet, Mr Hazzard,' said Lewis. 'I tell you these things for I believe you can understand them better than most. It is a fleet large enough to land over 30,000 men, wouldn't you say?'

'Yes.'

'Quite. Further, it is to be commanded by the hero of Italy and the Revolution himself, General in Chief Napoleon bloody Bonaparte.'

Hazzard felt a chill.

'Bonaparte.'

'Mm. I thought that would pique your interest.' Lewis continued, 'It could be bound for Naples, Sicily, or even Turkey – or worse, to overwhelm Lord St Vincent at Gibraltar, join with the Spaniards blockaded in Cadiz and land on our own south coast, just as they tried last year.' He looked away, some dark bitterness burning inside him. 'We are weak, Mr Hazzard. We have no ships in the Med; only the Cadiz blockade fleet, spread thin all the way up from Gib to the Tagus at Lisbon. Since the Spaniards joined the French two years back, all Spanish-controlled ports are effectively closed to us, including Naples,' he said, 'leaving the French free to gallivant about the Med as they please. And there is little we can do to stop them.'

A distant alarm sounded in Hazzard's mind, more and more insistent, but he could not identify its cause. His mouth went dry with some nameless fear. 'I still fail to see what this has to do with—'

But Lewis went on. 'Our agent gathered vital information regarding the target of this fleet, this... this damned *armada*, and demanded evacuation while lying in wait at a safety-house outside Toulon. But neither our man Captain Day in Turin nor the other consuls have been able to make further contact.'

Blake put a handkerchief to his mouth to cough, but said nothing.

Hazzard knew Toulon. In his youth, years before the Revolution, he had once stayed nearby. And he knew that Lewis and Blake knew this. *French mother. French educ^{td}*. 'Where, in Toulon? Towards Marseille, or Hyères...'

'Overlooking the gulf,' Lewis said with some apology, admitting a dark truth, '...and the Isles of Hyères.'

Hazzard's nerves tingled with a creeping cold, and perspiration sprang to his forehead. Lewis continued, somewhat more quietly, more urgently, as if to convince Hazzard they had acted properly. 'A fortnight before the War House issued you that notice of service and we set out to find you, Lord St Vincent sent a party of marines to rescue the agent. We learned only yesterday the operation was a failure. It was a trap,' said Lewis. 'The shore party lost their officer and came back empty-handed. It appears the French were lying in wait, having learned of the safety-house.' His voice dropped. 'This is partly why Commander Blake here suggested we contact you.'

Hazzard felt himself tighten from head to foot.

Blake rose from his seat and opened the door to murmur a few words to Major Carteret, who was waiting outside. Hazzard heard footsteps. For a moment he had the irrational hope that Sarah would appear – but she did not. Instead he heard a heavy footfall behind, a pair of boots, well drilled, stamping to attention.

'At your ease, Sergeant,' said Lewis.

Hazzard turned and found himself looking up at the tall figure of Marine Sergeant Jory Cook, in red coat and black neck-stock, white cross-belts and breeches, gaiters and gleaming parade boots. He needed a moment to place this most familiar face from his past, so wrong in the present.

'Jory?'

The big man smiled down, his familiar Bristol rumble a welcome sound. 'Aye, sir. On deck.'

For all his pain in those past two and a half years, Hazzard had not counted the loss of Cook. Despite his wounds he had felt nothing so sharp. Immediately he was standing, clutching his hand tight.

'My fault, sir,' said Cook. 'All this. I told the lieutenant – beg pardon, sir – Commander Blake. Looks like I rattled the 'locks.'

His close-cropped hair had greyed more at the sides, and receded from his broad brick-red forehead, emphasising his thick neck, and the bags under his eyes told a harsher tale than his years would ever admit. Hazzard clasped his hand for a moment longer, not wanting to let go. 'You great oak. Still in one piece.'

Cook nodded. 'Aye, sir. God save Bristol.'

Hazzard smiled at his ancient oath. But there was something else, something wrong. The big man cleared his throat, his eye sliding from Hazzard's, downcast.

'Sar'nt, if you please,' said Lewis, indicating a chair, 'Toulon.'

Cook bowed his head and they sat. 'Own eyes, sir,' he said confidentially, speaking only to Hazzard. 'Outer roads of the harbour stuffed with men o'war and armed merchants. 74s, 80s, and a big bastard 120 – the old *Dolphin Royal*, as was, looked like. Big as the *Santísima Trinidad*, if y'ask me, three decks o'murderous guns.'

'Army?'

'Aye, all over the shop. Tents across the hills, forts fit to bust. It's like they just can't keep up with all the bloody men they gone and got for theirselves. But...' Cook reached into his coat pocket. 'From the RDV. I remembered you'd spoke the name, from years back, when we were out in the Bombay Bucks.' He looked down. 'We found them, in a barn, sir, all. Nothing we could do...' He laid out the bloodstained flybill from Bartelmi's body on the table between them. Hazzard put a hand on the browned crackling page.

> Traitors to the Republic
> For the heinous **Crimes** of Consorting with
> Enemies of the State,
> Harbouring Fugitives from Justice, for Sedition,
> and Counter-Revolutionary Activity,
> The Lives, Persons and Worldly Goods of
> THE FAMILY **BARTELMI**
> Are hereby declared <u>Forfeit</u>
>
> Liberty, Fraternity and Equality!
> Long live the Republic
> By Order
> Citizen Derrien, Judge of Instruction,
> Ministry of the Interior

It was a printed form, the name of the victim scrawled on a line across the centre. He read it again, his eye dwelling on the dried smears.

Hugues Bartelmi.

Lewis watched Hazzard from the other end of the table. 'I believe you knew him.'

Blake added, 'Your mother's family... guardians, if I recall.'

'Yes,' Hazzard was disoriented, not seeing the connection, expecting that the grave news concerned Sarah, not Bartelmi. 'He was a friend of my mother's. A great man – he sent me to Grenôble for study, sent Sarah to...' Hazzard looked at Cook. 'What happened?'

Cook's voice tightened with every word as he related the shore-party landing. 'Children and all, sir. Worse'n ever we saw in India.'

Madame Louise... Pépin, Cécile and little Claire...?

'Citizen Derrien,' said Blake, 'is not a magistrate, or *Juge d'Instruction* as he claims, but what they call a "Collector" in the *Bureau d'information*, a covert executive of the Ministry of the Interior. We believe he is solely responsible.'

'But what has...' Hazzard tried to speak but his words stuck, cloying in a tight, dry throat. The answer to his question had already risen in his mind, cruel and unbidden. 'What has this to do with Sarah?'

Blake looked to Lewis. Hazzard waited.

Lewis explained, 'Our Paris agent escaped the Bartelmi household and reached Naples. And there passed a message to someone else, someone above suspicion... such as a young lady, on a grand tour, believed to be returning from Naples via a safe route to England.'

Hazzard stared at him, finally seeing.

No.

Blake's voice was carefully modulated, as if accustomed to giving solace to the bereaved. 'Miss Chapel was last sighted with our agent in Naples, boarding a carriage with two French émigrés after a dinner at the home of our ambassador, Sir William Hamilton.' He put his handkerchief once again to his mouth, as if to hide his words. 'The carriage was discovered on a southerly road, overturned, its escort killed. The occupants... missing.' He dabbed again at his lips with sorrow. 'I am truly sorry, William.'

Hazzard remained very still, a look of perplexed horror on his face as he listened to Blake. Cook watched him. Streaks of the dying sun glowed through the windows as evening fell, sounds from the street whistling faintly down the cold chimney, echoing then fading.

'Mr Hazzard,' said Lewis in the vacuum, 'the French are closing in on any sources that might disclose the course of that fleet and its target. And we *must* know where it is headed so that we may plot a course, intercept and destroy it. We know not even whether it still lies in port or has sailed. You are one of only three natural French speakers on the roll and have conducted secret shore operations before. Find Derrien and this fleet, Mr Hazzard, and you find our agent – find our agent and there you will find your lady.'

Hazzard heard him as if under water, the voice muffled, booming slow and dull in his ears, until he burst through the surface and exploded from his seat, hands reaching out for Blake. But Cook knew his man and caught him fast, both arms tight in his grip.

'*Damn you, Blake!* God *damn* you!'

Blake leapt back in his chair and Lewis got to his feet. 'You will control yourself, sir!'

'*What lie is this?*' shouted Hazzard, struggling in Cook's grip, addressing Blake alone. 'Did you make her a courier now? Play on her *patriotism*? Lure her into service to some unknowable greater good? Then abandon her as you did my men and me? How *dare* you! *How dare you!*'

Blake sat, head bowed, taking the beating, but Lewis struck back.

'How dare *we*? How dare *you*, sir! A serving officer of His Majesty's Marine Forces *resigning* in the midst of war? Shame on you, sir! Shame!'

Hazzard tugged himself free of Cook. 'Shame? *You* speak to *me* of shame? Bloody treachery and dishonour, by this man and Admiral the most wretched *Lord* Keith, damn his name! Landing troops all the while talking peace at the Cape, at the cost of innocents and my own...' With mention of the Cape and the memory of Harry Race Hazzard faltered. 'Dropping me like a dog into a pit to tear him apart... and absolve you of all sin.' He looked back at Lewis. '*That* is shameful, sir. And *wicked.*'

Blake closed his eyes, pained, 'For God's sake, William...'

The door opened and Major Carteret looked in, two marines ready behind him, but Lewis shook his head quickly. The door closed.

'And I did not resign, did I, Commodore?' continued Hazzard. 'I hardly had the chance. Division and the Board saw to that, did they not? Took my confidential report of Admiralty activities, tossed it aside and me with it – pensioned off, invalided from wounds received, *outcast*.'

Lewis kept his voice low. 'It may not be shouted in the *Times* or the *Gazette*, or cast abroad in the penny papers but, *damnation*, we are at the point of *breaking*, sir! Europe has left us to fight France alone, Spanish, Dutch, Austrians, all fallen, gone – speechified, treatified, and we shall be next. Damned ambassadors making excuses, for kings and cowards...'

Shaking, Hazzard watched him, his face hot, his immediate anger dying away. Lewis seemed as angry as he was.

'You tried twice to re-enlist,' said Lewis. 'After the battles of Cape St Vincent and Camperdown. Sawbones wouldn't pass you.'

'It was damned nonsense—'

'You had a stick and *could scarcely walk*, man! Then when you could, you damn near carved a visiting sword instructor to pieces at the Academy and had to be hauled off him, raving!'

Hazzard looked away, rebuked, infuriated. They regarded each other in silence for a moment.

'You fit now?' demanded Lewis.

'Of course.'

'Good,' continued Lewis. 'Want to get back to it?'

Hazzard leaned on the edge of the table for support, with an overpowering urge to draw the Talwar.

Lewis went on. 'Go to the Cadiz blockade fleet. Form a company of marines on the flagship, the *Ville de Paris*.' He nodded to Blake who unfolded a stiff sheet of paper from his files and slid it towards Hazzard. It bore a crown seal and ribbon, and was signed *Melville*. 'From the Secretary of War. Leave to form your own independent company with warrant to move across the war zone as you so choose. Your sole discretion.'

Hazzard looked at him hatefully. 'You must be joking...'

Cook pulled out a folded piece of paper, urging him to believe. 'Look, sir, fifteen names, solid okes they are. Three attack parties of five.' He put the sheet under Hazzard's gaze. 'Good lads. Steady hands. Me and Admiral Jack thought it up.'

Lewis continued, tempting him. 'Call them 9 Company, invisible, off the roll. Don't exist. Recruit or demobilise as you see fit.'

Hazzard stared down at the table, his faded Bombay cuffs, his shaking hands, the names on Cook's list blurring. 'I *vowed* I would *never...*' He closed his eyes, Cook's voice close, low, calming.

'We'll get her, sir,' he said. 'We'll get 'em all. After that bloody barn, I want 'em, as does Lil and Petty.'

At the sound of the old names Hazzard looked at the page. At the top of the list were Pettifer and De Lisle. At least they were still alive. He took a breath.

Cook nodded. 'Best we got. Dark as night, quiet as the grave. Some French and Italian in there too. No Chatham square-bashers, just the best. Dark, fast, in, out.'

'Nine Company. Invisible,' Hazzard muttered to Lewis, 'thus you may cut us adrift when it suits you as though we never existed.' Hazzard thought of the Cape skies, the bombardment, the mountains shaking, blood in the surf.

Lewis sent a packet skidding across the table to him. 'French identity, passport, sovereigns, *francs, assignats, escudos, lire*. Admiralty orders, full reinstatement and made up to Captain of Marines. Pay backdated to your return from the Cape in '96. Least I could do.'

Blake gathered the material into a pile and pushed another slip of paper towards Hazzard.

'Your cipher, William. The standard six digits, with the alarm reverse for the final integer if compromised. Communications to precede with this codename cipher, if you please.'

Hazzard looked at the slip: *34'18'89*. But for the 89 it was the latitude and longitude of the Cape of Good Hope.

'Just, for memory's sake,' explained Blake apologetically.

'I will not,' said Hazzard, 'serve the Admiralty again. *Never.*'

Lewis watched him, Blake sitting silent. 'This occasion you will abide by *my* terms alone.'

Lewis swallowed his outrage. 'Refuse your *king?* Sedition now! By *God* you test me, sir—'

'Do I.'

'Oh *damnation*, very well! Retain your retired status, but on full pay. Take the damned rank as a cloak legend, call yourself a duke if you like – but you will sign an undertaking to His Majesty as a commissioned Exploring Officer.'

'And Sergeant Cook to be paid up to the equivalent rank of Company Sergeant Major in the 1st Foot Guards.'

'The Marines have no such rank—'

Hazzard lashed back at him, 'Well they damn well *should.*'

Lewis took a moment then waved this concession aside. 'Very well. Report to the lugger *Valiant* at Portsmouth to catch Nelson. He took *Vanguard* to Cadiz ten days ago. It took us long enough to find you from your rooms in Greenwich.'

'And if we cannot catch him up?'

Lewis paused a moment, savouring his final executive order. 'You will discover the target of the French fleet, Captain Hazzard, and report to Rear Admiral Nelson. But if you fail to, or become separated from his command, then you and 9 Company are to intercept and engage the enemy *independently.* In all measures possible.'

Hazzard felt Cook shift behind him with a surreptitious, *Christ Almighty*, but Hazzard seemed unmoved.

'And if I find Derrien?' asked Hazzard.

'Do with him whatever you damn well please.' Lewis turned and opened the communicating door behind him. 'Come, sir,' he called. 'My final condition,' declared Lewis. 'Your second in command.'

Lt Marmaduke Wayland stepped in, red-cheeked, shame-faced, as if guilty of some misconduct but unsure which, his left hand groping to still the sword which clattered in its scabbard at his side with every move.

'He has seen action at the mutiny on the Nore,' continued Lewis, 'and has language and gunnery skills.'

Wayland glanced at Lewis then Hazzard, head down. 'Sir... I – great, *great* honour, sir, yes, sir...' Wayland stuck out his hand to Hazzard from too far away, leaning forward, nearly losing his balance, then slowly withdrew it.

Hazzard did not seem to notice him. In the ensuing silence Blake offered him the folder with the Admiralty orders and identity papers. 'These are the reports, William,' he said, 'with charts, times and dates. In Naples, trust the *Lazzaroni* rebels, but remember, the city and court is a nest of vipers. King Ferdinand is our friend though bound by circumstance to refuse us, therefore do watch Sir John Acton. He is English, but serves as the Neapolitan Prime Minister in a very difficult situation...' He fell silent and, after some consideration, kindly extended his hand. 'I wish you the very best fortune, William...'

Hazzard looked at the hand, then with sudden violence seized the lapels of Blake's coat and drove him backwards against the wall, shaking him. '*Damn* you, Charles!' he raged in vicious despair. 'It's *Sarah*. How *could* you? *How could you? You bloody murdering fool!*'

Cook tried to haul him back, '*Easy, sir, easy, save it for the Frogs, sir,*' Wayland watching open-mouthed as the door banged open and Carteret and the marines rushed in, boots crashing.

Hazzard felt himself taken round the shoulders and pulled from Blake, Lewis cursing in his ear, '*Damn* it, Hazzard! *Damn it, man.*'

Blake nearly collapsed, one hand to his throat, his expression sorrowful, accepting his terrible burden, a pall of grief passing over him. '*William...*'

Hazzard stopped struggling, and after a moment they let him go, his chest pounding, his face a bone-white mask. But Lewis was remorseless. 'For *God's* sake. *Find* them, *stop* them, *sink* them. Get Derrien – then you'll find your lady. It is the *only* way.'

Hazzard looked from Lewis to Blake. 'If she has come to any harm, Charles,' he said in a quiet, even tone. '*Any* harm… I will come for you.' Hazzard took up the files, his coat and hat, gave a last distracted look at the cold room, at the marines, at Blake and Lewis, his eye settling on neither, as if they were not really there. 'Both of you,' he said, 'I swear it.'

He pushed past Carteret into the corridor. Cook followed, Wayland hurrying to catch up. In Hazzard's mind the French fleet was already burning to the sea-bottom – with Derrien and Blake lashed screaming to the helm.

Launch

The *Valiant* was a twin-masted lugger of sixty feet, stripped for speed, her sharp-nosed prow cutting the waves like a blade, as if driven by Hazzard's own furious demons. They left the Isle of Wight in a streaming wake of foam, the masts of warships at anchor off St Helens soon no more than a memory on a bright, stony blue horizon.

A darkness had settled upon Hazzard, which neither Cook nor Wayland could penetrate. He dined with Cook or on deck with the men of the watch, looking out to sea, saying virtually nothing, the petty officers aware they were not on just another despatch run. For hours of the first day he stood alone at the bows, gripping the creaking stays behind the flair of two billowing spritsails, the hands on one occasion hearing him, '*Come on… come on…*'

Lieutenant Tomlinson, commander of the *Valiant*, had been alarmed by Hazzard's orders, thrust at him on the quayside by an Admiralty escort – Hazzard essentially had permission to commandeer the ship if need be. Neither had he liked Hazzard's menacing silence, nor the looming presence of Cook. He could not wait to be rid of them. The crew did not share his forebodings; to keep occupied Hazzard lent a hand, hauling sheets, in the rigging, clearing tackle, at the foremast lookout, wherever, anticipating need before it arose. He had a weather-eye, they said, and respected him for it.

At dawn on the second day, Wayland found Hazzard already on deck, a boat-cloak over his shoulders, hunched on a stool at the portside rail with Perry, the Bo'sun, and two hands perched on upturned kegs beside him, each oiling and clearing block-pulleys of fouled skeins of rope. None spoke, each content in his business. Cook was behind him, cleaning a brace of pistols. When Wayland went forward and looked back, he saw Hazzard, hollow-eyed and staring, his skin raw with windburn in the rising sun, his lengthening sideboards merging into the stubble of an unshaven jaw.

Lewis's demand for secrecy had prevented Wayland from discussing any mention of his work at the Admiralty – and his orders to make diary notes struck him as odd. To Wayland it felt disloyal to Hazzard, a secret betrayal. When he had found his file in the Inactive List he could not believe that here was the man of whom he had heard so much at the Academy, the famed Master of Sword, from India, Basra, Madagascar and of course the Cape – who had even taught him briefly as a cadet a year earlier.

And now here was Hazzard himself, his dear lady caught up in ghastly circumstance, purely by dreadful accident, it seemed to Wayland; truly an appalling prospect. He wanted to offer hope or support, to pledge his all to his cause. He wanted to do something for him, anything, if only to see him breakfasted, or at the least wish him well for the day. But after another look at him, thought better even of this.

Lt Tomlinson met Wayland amidships. He had only five years on Wayland but an ocean of experience separated them. Tomlinson offered the younger man the best of the morning.

'Good morning to you too, sir, Lieutenant—' Wayland shook his head in self-condemnation, 'I mean, forgive me, *Captain*, I am sorry.'

'Quite right, Mr Wayland, Lieutenant I am, quite right, a lieutenant who is the Captain, and your Marine Captain who is called Major when aboard. Very confusing, yes, yes, welcome to the Navy.' He looked forward and saw Hazzard. 'He is troubled.'

'Yes, sir.'

'I should think we all heard him last night.'

'Nightmares, sir,' said Wayland in apology. 'I do not believe he slept above an hour. He has seen many actions, in Africa, and... other savage places...'

'Mm. The hands don't much care for that, spirits taking a man in his sleep, lost souls come up from the deep and so on. But few serving marines of my acquaintance know their way about a ship of sail as does he. And fewer still could entice Mr Perry there to stay on after a cold Mid Watch and share the dawn.'

They looked at the group sitting silent but for a few murmurs as they exchanged tools and materials. He could smell their pipe-smoke, sweet on the wind. 'You are new to the Marines, Mr Wayland.'

'Yes, sir. A year.'

'With Major Hazzard?'

'No, sir. Though I once saw him at the Academy...' He watched Hazzard's back. He had only just noticed that Cook had positioned himself to guard him. 'Captain Hazzard is—' He broke off. 'Sorry, sir, the major—'

'Quite right, quite right.'

'He has been with Sergeant Cook for ever, it seems. They hardly speak, knowing each other's minds.' Wayland looked at Hazzard again. 'I would gather that the major is like me, sir... or rather, I like he...'

'Book-learned, you mean.'

'No, sir, no, I meant merely...' He gazed at the deck a moment. 'Alone. Or, just, by himself.'

Tomlinson watched him, then looked up at the brightening sky as streaks of pink gave way to pale violet and blue. 'Perhaps we'll get you up to the tops today, hm? Get your blood moving, hm? What do you say?'

'Yes, sir, thank you.'

The exchange seemed to have ended and Wayland moved off before Tomlinson, then caught himself. 'Dash it.' He stopped, his eyes down. 'I beg your pardon, sir.'

'As you were, Mr Wayland, at your ease. And worry not,' he added with a harsh smile, 'I know a marine stands fast, when the time comes.'

–

It was later that same day, as they heeled past the Breton peninsula, that a cry went up from the forward lookout. Tomlinson stepped out from the helm and readied his glass. 'Where away!'

The bo'sun ducked beneath the forward lugsail and moved to the rail, his arm signalling the direction out to sea. '*Starboard bow, heading west-nor'west, Cap'n…!*'

Tomlinson raised his telescope and Hazzard moved to the starboard rail beside him. He saw the ship, a two-masted sloop tacking to starboard, trying to beat up to the northwest, her sails luffing in the wind, the Republican tricolour flapping astern.

'*She's French! Clear for action!*' called Tomlinson, and the crew hurried to their two swivel-guns and four 9-pounders. Tomlinson raised the scope again, aware of Hazzard at his elbow. 'An *aviso* from Brest, Mr Hazzard, probably headed for Ireland with despatches for rebels—'

'We have not the time,' said Hazzard flatly. 'We must catch Nelson, sir.'

With the blowing of the wind Tomlinson did not seem to hear. He took his eye from the glass and looked back at him. 'What was that?'

'I said we have *not the time*. We must leave her, Captain.'

Tomlinson stared at him, but Hazzard did not look away. 'You question my orders at sea? In sight of the enemy? Good *God*, sir—'

But Hazzard had already assessed their chances. 'She's heading for open sea under full sail—'

'Aye, quite right, quite right, so it happens, Mr Hazzard!' called Tomlinson over the wind. 'And we shall engage her according to standing orders, what else!'

Tomlinson tried to push past him but Hazzard did not move. Tomlinson stepped back quickly, appalled. 'God above, sir, you will stand aside *this instant*.'

Cook moved in behind Hazzard and Tomlinson stared, incredulous. '*Captain*,' shouted Hazzard, the wind howling through the stays, 'we must get after *Nelson*.'

Tomlinson looked out at the *aviso* and back again, but Hazzard had given him pause. 'She's tacking to starboard! We can overhaul her easy—'

'And if she turns?' argued Hazzard. 'If she turns to larboard, runs before the wind and out to open sea to escape?'

Hazzard could tell Tomlinson knew the answer as well as he. It would involve a chase that would take them miles off course, costing them precious hours, perhaps even days if the wind then changed.

'We could tow her to Lisbon,' insisted Tomlinson. 'She'd be our first prize since... My men would...' He turned away to the rail, unwilling to show Hazzard that he knew he was right. 'Damnation. *Damnation*.'

'With every moment lost I fall behind Nelson. Do not force my hand, Captain, for the sake of your crew and my regard for your command.'

'Your *regard*?' Tomlinson choked it back and stared at him. 'What *are* your *damned* orders about, sir? I have run too many spies and secrets in my time and seen too many men perish for paltry gain—'

'Then you should know better than to *ask*, sir!'

'*Cap'n*,' called Perry from forward, '*she's changing course!*'

'Very good, Mr Perry!' called Tomlinson, not taking his eyes off Hazzard. The wind hammered them and they clung to the braces. 'What's her heading?'

Perry climbed onto the rail at the bow, leaning through the foremast stays, peering through his eyeglass. '*She's gone to lu'ward, sir, sou'-sou'west! She's runnin' with the wind!*'

Tomlinson nodded, still watching Hazzard.

'Very well, Mr Perry!' He glanced over his shoulder at the fast-disappearing ship and swore again. 'Blast you, Mr Hazzard, and blast your secrets…' He raised his glass, pretending to look. After a moment he called out, 'Too quick for us, Mr Perry! And we have orders for Nelson!' He lowered the glass and called out, 'Must've got a whiff of Foyle's cooking, what!'

'*Aye, sir .!*'

There were curses from some and laughter from others and Foyle grinned sheepishly along with them. Tomlinson put a good face on it, but this time he pushed angrily past Hazzard and Cook. 'How will you repay me for *that*, Mr Hazzard, I *wonder*.'

Hazzard had no answer for Tomlinson, only what Lewis had told him, and that seemed scarcely enough for the captain of a fast ship in action. He watched the French sloop disappear into the glowing blue haze. Within moments, it was gone.

He let go of the rigid stays of the straining mainmast, and found Cook hovering like a bad conscience.

'Don't say a bloody word,' said Hazzard, and moved off. After a moment he headed back to his old place at the bows.

Wayland saw Cook ease the lock on a short-barrelled pistol he had held ready under his jerkin – in case Tomlinson had disagreed with Hazzard's reasoning.

—

The winds obliged them in Biscay and they reached the Mediterranean Fleet patrols off Lisbon at the Tagus estuary within four days, and were passed on southwards to Cadiz. They rounded Cape St Vincent, the last promontory of Portugal jutting into the Atlantic, and found the offshore squadron of the British blockade some nights later, fleet lights winking in the darkness, glinting on the shimmering waves, sails ghostly and pearlescent in the gloom. The torches of fortified Cadiz burned bright, the Spanish navy trapped in its harbour, England, their ancient enemy, once again at the gates.

When Wayland and Cook emerged on deck with their bags, the crew of the *Valiant* were gathered at the rails, pointing, some calling and whistling at the great 74s, the *Goliath* and *Culloden, Zealous* and *Audacious*; some waved their hats at the *Bellerophon*, known to all as the pugnacious 'Billy Ruffian', her topsails puffing as she charged past, the rigging hands waving back in response.

When eventually the fleet boat reached them, the weather closed in and the wind picked up. Wayland and Cook made their way down the steps with greater care than usual, the boat pitching to and fro. His faded Bombay scarlet buttoned on for the first time since boarding, Hazzard pulled on his old leather coat against the weather, just as Tomlinson joined him.

Tomlinson caught a brief sight of the Indian orders pinned to his tunic, and the Talwar at his hip before Hazzard did up his coat and covered them. The decorations seemed to make him relent, standing down his guns, prepared for some final barrage of condemnation. He cleared his throat, looking away.

'I have no notion of your task, Major,' he called over the wind, his hard eyes narrowing, 'but Admiral St Vincent takes specially against indiscipline. After the fleet mutinies of last year he now segregates his marines and sailors and would hang a man a week if he thought it necessary.'

It was a warning to a fellow officer, something of a compliment from Tomlinson, given the friction between them. Hazzard wedged his black crow's-beak hat on tightly. 'Thank you, sir. I understand.'

Tomlinson continued, 'And I have heard tales, sir, from the southern oceans, of men who kill their superior officers in duels. And he will not be pleased to encounter one whose infamous conduct has been bandied about as an example by mutinous seamen.'

The wind lashed Hazzard's cheek. Though he took it as a warning, Tomlinson's reminder of Race was harsh and uninvited. 'And you believe what you have heard, Captain?'

Tomlinson considered the question. 'I would say that discipline sits hard upon your spirit, sir. Though my crew might take issue, I would never rely upon you.'

Hazzard took up the guide-line to follow Wayland and Cook down the steps into the boat rocking on the waves. 'Very well, Captain. Thankfully for your crew, I would not say the same of yourself. Godspeed back to England.'

Hazzard went over the side into the plunging stern of the boat below. He knew Tomlinson's attitude was a foretaste of the reception to come, and something he had not anticipated. It darkened his mood.

The midshipman at the tiller gave the order and they shoved off from the *Valiant*, the oars dipping into a rising swell. Hazzard watched the diminishing figure of Tomlinson in the light of a swinging lantern above the *Valiant*'s rail, and saw him turn away. Then, as if having fought off a determined disinclination, Tomlinson returned, raising a hand in silent farewell. Hazzard was grateful, and doffed his hat in response, wondering if indeed he might be fortunate enough, one day, to rely upon Tomlinson of the *Valiant*.

The wind rose and the boat bobbed like a cork on the choppy sea. By the time they reached the fleet lines, the Atlantic rain struck hard and cold, and they rowed to the lee of the warships. Hazzard shouted to the young midshipman wielding the tiller. 'Where is *Vanguard*?'

'Sir?'

'The *Vanguard*, Admiral Nelson's ship – which is she?'

A gust blew spray across the pair and the boy wiped his face clean. 'I–I think she's sailed, sir—'

Hazzard cursed under his breath. 'When?'

'Sir?'

'*When did she set sail?*'

The boy replied uncertainly. 'I think his lordship might better address your queries, sir—'

'It is the protocol, sir,' called Wayland, eager to help, 'and we do carry word from the—'

114

'*As you were, sir*,' snapped Hazzard. 'I shall have no loose talk, is that clear?'

Wayland lowered his eyes and Hazzard felt he had struck a dog with a whip. He hunkered deeper into his collar, his mood darker still.

They passed the 74-gun *Culloden* and soon made the broad stern of the flagship, the giant First-Rate *Ville de Paris*, a 110-gun castle of wood, iron and sail over three decks, reaching 200 feet into the air. Wayland stared upwards into the rain with wonder, the rebuke forgotten.

They passed the stern gallery windows high above, their lamplight warm and inviting, each row adorned with painted balustrades like so many balconies on fine London townhouses. The crew shipped oars and they bumped against the bulging port broadside. The midshipman called up, '*Ahoy the* Ville,' and the reply came down from above, '*Hulloa the fleet boat*,' and two knotted lines were dropped either side of the boarding steps.

The small boat pitched and heaved beneath their feet, two oarsmen using hooks to hold her steady, but the swell was too strong. Hazzard took the steps first and Wayland followed, Cook coming behind with both Wayland's and Hazzard's bags over his shoulders, but the boat slid out from beneath them and the big man slipped. Hanging from one of the lines, Wayland snatched for his arm.

'*Sergeant*—'

Dropping the bags back into the boat, he caught hold, his boots kicking on the slick planking. He hung over the waves from Wayland's straining hand, Hazzard reaching for him, the midshipman calling to the crew, '*Lay your hooks! Lay your hooks and bring her in!*' until Cook's scrambling feet made the first step.

'*Thank ye sir! Gettin' too old for this…*'

'Get up here, y'old salt,' called Hazzard as he and Wayland pulled him up, the rain lashing at them.

Reaching the midships gangway, they nearly fell to the deck. Hazzard struggled to his feet, cursing, the rain sheeting off his coat, and he beat his sodden hat against his thigh. A number of officers and men had joined them from the quarterdeck and gathered round.

'Good evening to you, sir,' called a young officer in cloak and cocked hat, 'I am the Third Lieutenant, Lt Markham. May I say who it is—' The lieutenant flinched as a sudden gust of rain lashed at them. As he straightened he saw the slung Manton pistol and spiked Talwar swinging under Hazzard's coat. '…or, should I say "what"…'

Hazzard found himself facing a pair of lieutenants, a petty officer and two captains. He replaced his hat and threw an open-handed Marine salute to the foremost of the two. 'Permission to come aboard, sir. Major Hazzard, 9 Company Marines, with orders for Rear Admiral Nelson.'

'Nelson?' The captain looked over his shoulder at his colleague behind. 'Have we a Nelson, Sir Thomas?'

'Name certainly rings a bell…' said his companion wryly.

The young third lieutenant broke in, '*Hazzard?* Not Hazzard of the Cape?'

Another gust brought rain and spray crashing over them, and they all held onto their hats, clutching their cloaks tight round their necks and ducked. When they straightened, they saw that Hazzard, Wayland and Cook had remained stock-still.

Lt Markham continued his belated introductions. 'May I name Captain Bathurst of His Majesty's Ship the *Ville de Paris*…'

Bathurst smiled and gave a brief bow. 'You seem to have brought an ill-wind for someone, Mr Hazzard.'

'I hope so, Captain.'

'And Sir Thomas Troubridge,' added Markham, 'Captain of the *Culloden*.'

'Quite all right, Mr Markham,' called Troubridge, coming forward to shake Hazzard by the hand. 'We are old acquaintances. Got you back, did they, William?'

'And into my pirate suit, yes, sir.'

Troubridge swept him with a delighted glance, looking inside the coat. 'My heavens so it is. This, gentlemen, if I may,

116

Major,' he declared, 'is the old uniform of the fearsome Bombay Buccaneers. Complete with sword-cuts and bullet holes I see.'

'No, sir,' said Hazzard. 'Moths, most like.'

Amid the laughter as they were led below, the whispers shot round the crew in an instant: Sgt Cook was back, and with him had come Hazzard, from the Cape.

–

The admiral's dayroom in the stern of the upper gundeck was bright and warm with candlelight and gleaming brass. Reflections twinkled in the dark row of galleried windows, the torchlit forts of Cadiz visible in the distance. Troubridge and Bathurst sat in low button-backed leather chairs, a silver tray of sherry glasses and a crystal decanter hard by on a large carved desk of polished walnut. A discarded napkin from their interrupted dinner lay alongside – the sounds of diners on the other side of the folding bulkhead filtered through to Hazzard's ear, along with the Spanish voices of several ladies.

Behind the desk sat the vigorous former knight Sir John Jervis, known to some hands as Lord Jack, but to all as Admiral of the Blue, the Earl St Vincent, commander of the Mediterranean Fleet. He had a broad, rough, yet amiable look, not unlike a Suffolk farmer, thought Hazzard. His presence did not fail to impress: *here was Hercules himself*, he thought, *guarding the pillared straits to the world*.

Before him on the table lay Hazzard's Admiralty authority and papers. On the other side stood Hazzard, Cook and Wayland, waiting. The admiral read, peering through a pair of tiny, wire-framed spectacles.

'You say you have dined, Mr Hazzard. But are you certain Mrs Humphries and the washer-ladies below cannot offer you a dry change of clothes, at least for the interim?'

One of the sailors' wives had taken Hazzard's leather coat and Cook and Wayland's boat cloaks down to be hung before the galley fire, but the three of them were, as ever, still wet. 'If we have the time, sir, thank you. But I would rather be off as soon as possible, under cover of night.'

Lord St Vincent nodded slowly and continued to read. 'Captain Bathurst tells me you command the 9th Company of Marines,' he said in a distant tone. He looked up at last. 'Which, to my reckoning, has never reported anywhere?'

'Perhaps not, sir.'

St Vincent turned and looked at Troubridge. 'What did you say about this, Tom?'

Troubridge nodded. 'Perhaps Major Hazzard is to *form* 9 Company, sir.'

'Mm. The Phantom Major,' said St Vincent, looking up at last. 'Yet here you stand, Mr Hazzard,' he began, casting his eye over him. 'Every inch a Barbary pirate, dripping onto Captain Bathurst's rather good Turkey carpet. What are you then, sir? A trick of the light?'

'No, sir.'

'No indeed, sir...' He glanced at Cook. 'See what trouble you have caused us, Sar'nt Cook.'

'M'lord.'

'Always knew I shouldn't let you out at weekends.'

'No, m'lord,' said Cook with a soft laugh.

St Vincent shuffled through the papers again. 'Lord Melville has lent his weight here, I see, comes near to threatening us all, Mr, Mr *Hazzard*,' he paused, savouring the name, then read aloud from a note by the Secretary of War. 'This officer... *et cetera, et cetera*... is to be accommodated by *all* members of His Majesty's forces, *regardless of rank*, and be permitted to operate at his *sole* discretion.' He peered over the glasses at his two captains. 'Countersigned by Mr Pitt the Prime Minister, no less. But not the Honourable Mr Fox.'

They chuckled at St Vincent's stab at the Whigs, and the wayward nature of Westminster and the Admiralty. He laid his hands flat on the pages.

'Very well, Major. I am sorry to relay that Rear Admiral Nelson has sailed, to the resentful chagrin of certain of my other senior officers, threatening duels and all sorts.'

Troubridge murmured a comment about that, *disgraceful affair, my lord…* and Bathurst, *hear hear.*

But Nelson's departure was news Hazzard had not wanted to hear confirmed. 'Sir.'

'We had word of a massing at Toulon from passing traders, Danes, Americans and the like, hence Sergeant Cook's swift return to the Admiralty. As soon as the admiral arrived in *Vanguard* we were sore relieved, and duly sent him to reconnoitre with a squadron. Sir James Saumarez and *Orion*, Ball and the *Alexander* among them. They have a five-day start on you. Your new report confirms our somewhat grim situation.'

'A sloop, sir. It's all I need.'

St Vincent turned to Troubridge and Bathurst. 'Have we any such left? Nelson could find barely a few frigates. There's Hardy and the *Mutine* but we need him here…'

Bathurst shook his head. 'Retallick took the *Bonne Citoyenne* sloop with Nelson, my lord.'

'There is the *Esperanza* brig, sir,' said Troubridge. 'That Spanish prize, a blockade-runner captured sneaking into Cadiz a week ago. Her bo'sun swears blind she's fast and she's been well armed.'

'That will do us fine, sir,' said Hazzard.

'Very well…' said St Vincent. 'I dare say your expedition is fully *sub rosa*, Major, so I shall not pry – and though I smile upon the initiative of sending you three and this company of Oddfellows you wish to collect, I fail to see what you can do that a squadron under Nelson cannot.'

'Reconnoitre and destroy are only part of my orders, sir.'

The admiral regarded Hazzard warily. There was something of a threat in Hazzard's presence, and St Vincent did not like it. 'We are not unaware of your name, Major. Nor of the curious devotion which certain of the marines and seamen seem to display for you.'

'I know little of that, sir—'

'It is a compliment, sir. And the highest, in my book. Take it as offered.' He was almost angry. 'Yet I would ask you to consider the effect that tales of the Cape might have played in the fleet mutinies this year past.'

It was just as Tomlinson had warned. It was the swat of a bad-tempered bear, but Hazzard was no longer the timid and dutiful lieutenant of three years previous.

'If you will pardon me, sir,' he said carefully, 'I will not be held accountable for the ignorance of some, nor the brutality of others.'

Hazzard thought he heard Cook whisper, *Christ Jaysus*, under his breath, but could not be certain.

Troubridge and Bathurst stirred uncomfortably, but St Vincent merely grunted. 'Such injustice of responsibility comes with rank and influence, Major. And it seems you now have both.' He grumbled to himself, 'Still, we have spoken with Lord Keith, and a Mr Blake at the Admiralty... slippery fellow, but he knows eggs is eggs.' He gathered the pages together once more. 'Nevertheless, these are incendiary times. I feel we must get you off this ship and at the enemy's throat as soon as we can.'

'Thank you, sir, my thoughts precisely.' Hazzard gave a curt bow of the head to accept the unspoken apology. 'And if I may request,' he added, 'that we be excluded from the ship's log, m'lord. Best we were never here.'

'I wholeheartedly agree.' The admiral then frowned in sudden recollection. '*Hazzard*... was there not a father? A country parson, called Hazzard?'

'Sir?'

'Used to minister to the wounded in Lowestoft, or Yarmouth? Lost a leg in '59 with Wolfe at Quebec?'

Hazzard caught Wayland's interested expression and Cook glanced at him.

'My reverend uncle, sir,' said Hazzard. 'The Rector of St Jude's, Thomas Hazzard. Was with you on the St Lawrence

River in Canada, landed with Wolfe and the 60th Royal Americans. Disapproves of our pulling out of the Mediterranean, m'lord. Thinks you soft on the French.'

Troubridge swallowed a laugh and St Vincent looked surprised. 'Goodness me. And I thought the *Times* was harsh.'

There was a knock at the door and St Vincent shouted to enter.

Lt Markham appeared with the Marine commander of the *Ville de Paris*. 'My lord. Major Duncan, as requested.'

The major, in full dress of fringed epaulettes, glowing white cross-belt, sword and metal gorget and chain, plumed hat braced in the crook of his left arm, marched forward and banged to attention beside Hazzard, throwing a quivering parade-ground salute. His hair, or wig, thought Hazzard, was set in a fringed Plantagenet bob, and shimmered as he moved.

'*Sah!*'

St Vincent was irritated by this display – as was Cook, Hazzard could tell, who inched away with stiff dislike.

'Major Duncan, this is Major Hazzard. You will release to him those marines of the new draft—' he glanced at Hazzard '—for a raid of sorts.'

Duncan bristled. 'I see, sir. Of how many are we to be deprived, m'lud?'

'Fifteen,' said Hazzard.

Duncan looked at him, astonished. '*Fifteen?* M'lud, that is the entire draft – they've been incorporated into platoons, their wages and stoppages calculated…'

Hazzard heard Cook mutter '*Stoppages?*' under his breath and look away with disgust.

'The new draft, Major, was intended specifically for Mr Hazzard, not us,' corrected St Vincent, nodding at Cook, who produced his list. 'Sar'nt Cook and we captains three considered the matter hard, did we not, Tom? Read on, Sar'nt.'

'M'lord. Privates De Lisle, Pettifer, Underhill, Cochrane, Duggan, Porter, Farmer, Fielding, Kite—'

121

'*Kite?*' said Duncan. 'That blackguard? Irish Cockney from the docks of London? He's not even a true marine – from the 69th Foot – a cut-purse and a fiddler—'

Troubridge murmured quietly but clearly, 'He was one of the first onto the *San Nicolas* after Nelson at Cape St Vincent actually...'

Duncan spluttered hopelessly, 'But—'

Cook continued, 'Rivelli, Craddock, Napier, Simcox...'

Duncan sagged. 'M'lud I must protest, Napier is a brute and nearly broke a man's neck in a boxing match last week...'

'...Anderssen, and Hesse,' finished Cook.

'Hesse? The *Austrian*?' asked Duncan with incredulity. 'He barely speaks English and fails to understand every command I give him.'

'Perhaps,' said Hazzard, 'but he does speak German, French and Italian. As do Mr Wayland and I.'

Wayland made to correct Hazzard out of modesty but Cook jabbed him with a thumb and he kept quiet.

Lt Markham turned to Captain Bathurst and the admiral. 'My lord, forgive me, but in support of Major Duncan, surely this man Hazzard is a renegade, best remembered for the Cape where he attacked his commanding officer, a most respected—'

St Vincent banged the flat of his hand on the table and the decanter and glasses jumped. The voices of the diners next door stopped. 'You will be silent in my presence, sir!' He rose and moved towards him. 'It is not *you* who dictates to *us*, sir, but *we* who dictate to *you*! Is that understood?'

Bathurst concurred with the admiral. 'Lieutenant, you will withdraw your remark, doubtless spoken in haste and, certainly, ignorance and ill-founded rumour.'

Markham reddened and stammered an apology. 'Y-yes, of course, sir. Forgive me, my lord...'

'Perhaps he might gain valuable experience commanding the brig of which we spoke earlier, my lord,' added Bathurst.

'Can he handle such a one?' asked Troubridge. 'He is but third lieutenant, despite his age...'

Blushing scarlet, Markham stared at the floor, a humiliated schoolboy.

'I wonder,' replied St Vincent. 'With luck Mr Hazzard will teach him some manners.'

'M'lord,' said Hazzard, 'I would rather only a few hands and the marines – the prize crew will do, as I am more than capable of command at sea.'

'I am growing surer of it by the moment, Major Hazzard, by comparison to what we see before us.' St Vincent took his seat once more, his anger subsiding, and he nodded to himself in confirmation of his own thoughts. 'But no, no, this will leave you free for tactical matters. *Esperanza* is after all a prize, and has been accounted for in shares. She should not be lost to us in your operation if at all possible.'

Markham glared at Hazzard with nothing short of tight-lipped hatred. Duncan then took up the cudgels himself. 'M'lud, what sort of raid requires linguists and,' he laughed obsequiously, 'truly, some of the least disciplined men of the fleet battalion?'

'I need marines, Major, not toy soldiers,' said Hazzard.

'*My* men,' Duncan replied, 'are the finest drilled troops in the world. Not a rabble of highwaymen,' he muttered, 'or mutineers...'

Wayland took a step forward, but Hazzard put out a hand and stopped him. He could feel the sinews tensing in the younger man's wrist.

St Vincent brought a halt to the duel arising before him. 'Gentlemen, this will cease at once. Major Duncan, you will gather the men required by Major Hazzard.'

Duncan had begun to tremble, with anger or nerves, Hazzard cared little. 'Yes, m'lud.'

'And *you*, sir,' continued St Vincent to Markham, 'will send for, supply and victual the *Esperanza* brig, and convey Major Hazzard and his men wheresoe'er he requires, do you understand me, sir?'

'Yes, my lord, very good, my lord.'

St Vincent seemed satisfied with his show of submission. 'Very well. Be about it then.'

Markham bowed his head and Duncan stepped back, saluted, turned about, and marched to the door beside the lieutenant. The door banged shut behind them.

'So, Mr Hazzard,' said St Vincent, coming round the desk. The captains got to their feet, the interview concluded. 'You shall have your Oddfellows. Brutes or cut-purses as they may be, I hope they serve the turn.'

'I'm sure they shall, m'lord.'

Troubridge offered his hand. 'I wish you the Luck of the Bucks out there, William. Do send for *Culloden* should you need us, and we'll be there in a trice.'

'If we can spare you,' warned St Vincent, then to Hazzard, 'Seems we both bear a weighty responsibility, do we not?'

'Sir?'

The admiral's features creased into a grim smile and he took Hazzard's hand. 'Not to disappoint the good Rector of St Jude's.'

–

Just outside the door Wayland stopped behind Cook and Hazzard, one hand out for support on the newel post of the staircase to the lower decks. 'Odd's *teeth*, sir. Forgive me, but, Major Duncan – I could take no more of it...'

'He's a bastard of a pen-pricker, sir,' rumbled Cook. 'Stop-pages indeed, for men who've just transferred duty? Stopping their wages for boot-black and petty goods they already got? Ruddy thief more like.'

Hazzard agreed. 'Both of you go below and see that Duncan roots out those men as promised... we want to shove off soon as we can, and I don't trust him an inch.'

'Yes, sir,' said Wayland and headed after Cook.

Hazzard watched him descend then on impulse called after him, 'Mr Wayland.'

Wayland turned. 'Sir?'

The niceties of command had always been difficult for Hazzard, and over the past two years he had grown still further from them. But he knew something was required of him, if only to repay the boy's loyalty. 'Quick thinking,' said Hazzard, 'on the steps. Coming aboard, with Sar'nt Cook. Well done.'

Wayland nodded, pleased but doing his best to conceal it. 'Sir.'

Hazzard moved through to an officers' wardroom of sorts, its furniture stowed to one side as if the floor were cleared for action, a tip-up table, several chairs, two seamen passing through and heading quickly below, giving their compliments, '*Sir, aye.*' Their warmed and dried coats and cloaks had been hung and left with their bags.

He leaned against the polished oak bulkhead wall, alone. Before him was a door leading out to the upper gundeck. He could hear the calls of the men, a woman laughing. *Dog Watch*, he thought, *dinner time*. He tugged at the black cravat at his throat to loosen it; it was wet. He lifted the heavy Manton and its sling over his head and set it down on the table with relief. He felt like a newly press-ganged landsman, utterly out of place.

Being back among the Navy had affected him more than he had imagined possible. He had forgotten the foul smells, the conditions, the perpetual damp. He had certainly forgotten depot martinets like Duncan and popinjays like Markham and their reign of terror over lower ranks. It was only now he realised how he had hated it all. The *Ville de Paris* was far bigger than the Third-Rate 64-gun *America* at the Cape, but he had never felt more trapped, and wanted to get aboard the sloop and get off on his own to find Sarah – and Derrien.

He opened the door to the upper gundeck beyond, and came face to face with Duncan, the rain lashing at him from the open grilles above. After a moment's pause for recognition,

Duncan burst through the doorway and grabbed Hazzard by the jacket-front, shoving him backwards against the doorframe, his fist almost in his throat – all in full view of the working seamen not ten paces behind among the 24-pounders of the gundeck. The rain and spray gusted in, striking Duncan's twisted features, bouncing off his oiled wig.

'How *dare* you subject me to that, that *humiliation!* I know your type, *Hazzard*,' he said, spittle flying from his lips, 'I've seen it time and again, *ill*-disciplined, *moneyed layabout* "gentleman" *swine*, gets a wound or two and thinks he's God Almighty! I've heard all about the Cape and I think it's *disgusting!* These damn dogs here sing *songs* about it because of y—'

Hazzard seized Duncan's wrists and drove his knee hard into his groin, and Duncan collapsed forward, the air blowing out of his lungs. One of the gathering sailors behind raised a clenched fist in triumph, *G'arn sir, give it 'im!* A midshipman dashed off for help.

Hazzard took hold of the metal gorget at Duncan's throat and wrenched its gleaming chain hard until he began to choke. The soft white folds of Duncan's face darkened, the eyes bulging. '*How bloody dare you*,' rasped Hazzard, 'What do you do to *them*, Duncan, if you think you can lay your *filthy* hands on *me*?'

Duncan croaked, 'No, *no*…! I… I—'

The sailors were cheering and shouting by now, but Hazzard heard the thud of bare feet running on the gundeck behind. In the next moment the chipped blade of an old whittling knife was put to Duncan's throat by a calloused hand. Over his shoulder in the blowing clouds of rain behind him, Hazzard recognised the bright blue eyes and ginger stubble of a sailor peering out from beneath a tatty woollen Monmouth cap.

'Everythin' all right, Mr 'Azzard, sir?' he asked. 'I 'eard you was aboard.'

It was Handley, formerly of the *America* and the last battle with Harry Race. 'Good to see you, Handley,' replied Hazzard, staring into Duncan's sweating face. 'Care to come on a trip?'

Handley leaned round, putting his red bristle intimately close to Duncan's shrinking cheek. 'Would be a bloody honour, sir.'

Cook appeared over the other shoulder. 'Should I be callin' the surgeon, sir? Seems Major Duncan's had some sort of fit.'

Duncan choked. '*Cook*, my God I'll see you *hang* for this! There's... a *dagger*...' Duncan gasped '...*in my—my stomach! A spike*, it's – *cutting me—* I'm, I'm *bleeding*...'

Suspecting it might well be true, Hazzard pushed Duncan away into Cook's arms. It had been the spiked pommel of the Talwar. They all looked to investigate, but there was no blood. Handley made the joyous discovery.

'Why, Major Duncan, sir,' he reported merrily, 'I do believe you 'ave pissed yourself.'

The crowd of seamen behind hooted with laughter and Duncan staggered away a few steps, plucking at his clinging breeches. 'I – oh *God*...'

Whimpering in private torment, he tottered onto the gundeck and scuttled down the stairs to his cabin, keeping his legs apart as he ran, the sailors whooping and whistling behind him.

'Much obliged, Handley,' said Hazzard. 'Or what is it these days? You must be a senior petty by now.'

'Only a Mate, if you please, sir,' he replied. 'They don't knows a good thing when they sees it.'

'Now there's a truth,' muttered Cook, shaking his hand. 'Wotcher, Andy.'

'Well I do,' said Hazzard, gathering his coat and the slung Manton, 'so consider yourself a warrant, and Ship's Master of this new brig of ours, ready to sail our backsides out of trouble when we get into it, which we will.'

'A pleasure, sir,' said Handley.

'Get the best scroungers in the marines to find powder-kegs and shot, pistol and musket, buck and ball, quickmatch, wadding, flash-lime, langrage and nails, anything you can find...'

Cook recognised the materials. 'Bag o'tricks?'

'Yes. We need every scrap we can get and the armourer won't give it up easily.'

Handley smiled. 'Any idea where we headed this time, sir?'

From down below they could hear Wayland and Sergeant MacDonald calling the last names of the marines. There was a short silence, followed by a cheer.

'Yes, Handley,' said Hazzard, 'we're off to fight thirty thousand Frenchmen.'

The rain trickling from his grizzled chin, Handley grinned from ear to ear. 'Blimey, sir,' he said, 'my 'eart goes out to 'em.'

Brig

The *Esperanza* cut a swift course east-northeast between Algiers and the Balearics, heading for Sardinia and the long road north to Toulon. By the first morning at full sail she was making 15 knots, loaded as she was.

There had been reports of a privateer off Menorca and Hazzard took full advantage of the news: *Esperanza* was a twin-masted brig, and in true Royal Navy fashion the foremast and the mainmast tops had been square-rigged – but rather than square-rig the mainsail, the prize crew had retained the huge gaff rig on its boom, swinging like a giant fish-tail over the helm on the raised afterdeck. To Lt Markham's anguish and the crew's jubilation, Hazzard demanded the gaff sail remain for improved manoeuvrability, and struck the colours.

'With that ghastly rudder of a gaff waving over my head and *no ensign*, sir, we shall look a dashed pirate ourselves!' complained Markham. 'They are called *brigantines* for very good reason, for they are sailed by *brigands!*'

'That's the idea, Mr Markham,' Hazzard had said. 'And I want every stitch of canvas up, even if we set kerchiefs and bed-linen to the tops, for I *will* catch Nelson.'

Wayland watched with fascination as Handley worked the ship with McGovern, the experienced bo'sun of the small prize crew. The crew numbered only forty hands, though it should have been eighty at least – and they were not best pleased with the replacement of their own captain just to make way for Hazzard and his marines. But their complaints were forgotten once the marines proved their worth on the heave and haul of the sheets and braces, their quick reactions to orders and their evident pleasure at being released from the tedium of the blockade fleet.

Markham ignored Handley but followed Bo'sun McGovern everywhere only to concur with his wise suggestions as if he had thought of them first. He issued petty orders to tidy stores or coil lines, strutting about behind the wheelhouse like a diminutive Drake on the Spanish Main.

Wayland meanwhile kept the company of the quiet yet attentive Midshipman Greaves, who was barely fourteen. Markham had brought him from the *Ville de Paris* for reasons best known to himself – and dark speculation grew daily. While he was inspecting the decks with Wayland all had heard Markham howl from the stern, '*Mr Greaves!*'

Greaves had flinched as if struck, then recovered himself. 'Mr Wayland, would you be so kind as to watch the shrouds to the foremast tops?'

'Of course, Mr Greaves.' He peered up at the lattice of rigging uncertainly, trying to remember. 'Those ropes up there?'

'Yes,' he said, then explained, 'With the staysails hoist, the lines can foul on the extra tackle. We are short of hands to keep them clear, you see… do call on the bo'sun if they give trouble. I am much obliged.'

Wayland and several marines watched him go fearfully and heard the inevitable stream of invective: '…*just not good enough Mr Greaves, not, sir. If you will gallivant about the ship with marines how must I find you when I need you, sir!*'

There was little escape for the boy: what with the marines, the three upturned attack-boats stacked and lashed amidships, and the brig's eight snub-nosed 32-pounder carronades, conditions were cramped. She was not much bigger than *Valiant* had been, at 100ft from prow to stern and 27ft in the beam. She was low and fast, and built like a spearhead – and there was little room to hide.

Hazzard had not noticed the confines of the *Esperanza*. He felt confined in other ways. His first night had been plagued by dreams of Blake, Derrien, Bartelmi and Sarah, a sightless spirit, trapped behind a wall of weeping glass: the closer he drew the more remote and irretrievable she became. When he emerged from the aft hatchway to the main deck that first morning to address his new company, he was in no mood for the task.

The marines had been formed up into their three sections of five between the stout carronades along each side, and across the beam before the mainmast and wheelhouse. Their heads snapped up as Cook called them to order.

'*Eyes in th'boat! Look t'yer fronts... P'rade!*' he barked, '*P'rade... 'shun!*'

Drilling like Foot Guards, they stamped the deck with a single dull boom, their ordered muskets rattling as they racked them back and upright, the buttplates cracking on the boards at their sides in unison. For this first parade they wore full uniform of red coat with buttoned-back tails, white breeches and tall spatterdash gaiters and boots, white cross-belts, cartridge pouches and bayonet, with plumed black round-hat 'toppers' and stiff black leather neck-stocks.

Unlike Guardsmen, however, they remained dead still on the deck of the flying brig, despite the roll of the sea and the bursting spray. Cook and Wayland stood off to the portside shrouds, watching.

The white haze of the mountainous Mediterranean skies was almost blinding. Hazzard breathed in the warmth of the May air, the wind soft and enveloping, then settled the beak of his cocked hat lower over his dark-ringed eyes.

'At ease, Sar'nt.'

'*P'rade!* Stand-at... *ease!*'

They brought their heels down with a single report, the ordered muskets thrust forward at an angle, their free hand smacking their belts in the small of their backs. The sailing hands gathered to watch, a gala display for all.

Hazzard looked at each of them. They were men he did not know – but who apparently knew him. It made him feel exposed, resentful of Lewis, of Blake, and partly of the men themselves, that they had intruded on his reclusive world and his personal mission. It could all have been simpler, just Cook and himself, as he had briefly hoped. Yet here they stood.

'We are now 9 Company,' he began, but too quietly, the wind and spray too strong. He tried again. 'We are now 9 Company. Should you be required to identify yourselves by any senior officer or NCO, naval or marine, you will tell them that alone, and no more.'

They waited, staring dead ahead. Some smiled: his words had smacked of rebellion.

'Let me be very clear,' he called. 'I did not want you.'

The Talwar hung heavily at his left hip. The double-barrelled Manton pistol bumped and swung across his chest. He removed his hat and ran a hand through his blowing hair.

He moved across the ranks, watching their expressions but not seeing their faces, not wanting to, letting them blur. 'You were chosen because you are not cattle who need the lash, and can survive on your own. If you're not everything Sar'nt Cook and Lord Jack himself has said you were, I'll cut you adrift at the first chance.'

More of the *Esperanza* hands clustered in the rigging above to listen. Markham and Greaves appeared from the afterdeck, Markham shocked at Hazzard's lack of formality.

'I am not a regular officer. And we are not regular marines, are we? We do not stand to attention and wait like ducks in a fairground while the enemy brings his guns to bear – and hope Jack Tar knows what he's about to save our hides.' Someone in the rigging laughed but was hushed. 'I'm not here for glory or prize money.' The words brought his anger to the surface. 'I'm here to find an enemy fleet… and *burn it to the bottom*.'

Some in the ranks whispered, *Aye…*

'Boats dark, clothes dark, weapons black. That is now our way. Sar'nt Cook's way. And he taught me everything I know. Pistol, blade, bag o'tricks – hit them hard, then out, fast.'

Some began to nod, slow smiles spreading. Hazzard saw a flash of bare skin at one marine's throat. Square-jawed, long, dark sideboards, his round-hat tipped forward like a gaming-house rake, he had the ironic twist to his lips of the dockside Cockney. Hazzard stopped in front of him.

'It must be Private Kite.'

Kite banged to attention with a bright smile. 'Aye, sir, so it is, sir.'

'*Mind yer lip, that man…*' grumbled Cook from the sidelines.

Hazzard looked him over. 'You found us our powder.'

'Buck and ball, sir, the lot,' he said, grinning proudly. 'Middies on the *Ville* won't have no shot for their little pistols.'

The company nearly broke into laughter again, cut short by Hazzard. 'So you've done this before?'

Kite thought a moment. 'Well, sir, there *might* be a unfortunate Chinee, short o'Pennyfields down Lime'ouse, what lost a bag o'pearls… but, *strickly* speakin', they wasn't really *'is*, legal-like, was they, 'im bein' only a Chinee…?'

More laughter but Cook shot them a quick *Silence on p'rade…*

Hazzard reached forward and pulled open Kite's red coat. Instead of the regulation shirt, under the bastion lace and brass buttons there was only a white collar and false shirt-front, a square of stiff sailcloth. 'What's this?'

'Improperly dressed,' growled Cook.

Kite's manner abruptly changed, a steel shutter going down. 'Purser, sir. And stoppages. Short supply, he said.'

'No undress shirt?'

Kite hesitated then clearly threw caution aside. 'Kit inspected afore roll, sir, then parade for inspection. Can't wear it as it's counted in kit. If missing, it makes kit improper kept, sir, get a fine.' Then added, 'Major Duncan, sir.'

Hazzard recalled Troubridge's words about Kite: *First aboard the* San Nicolas *at Cape St Vincent after Nelson.*

'Do you know Rear Admiral Nelson, Kite?'

Kite looked dead ahead and raised his chin. 'No, sir, and he don't know me neither.'

While Jervis and Nelson had been lionised for their victory at Cape St Vincent, Kite and the nameless other ranks, who had boarded the Spanish ships, had remained unknown, unremarked, unrewarded.

'No one thanks the watchdog, Kite.'

'No, sir.'

'Undress shirt next time. No kit inspections. I am not Duncan.'

Kite glanced at him. 'Aye, sir.'

The man next to Kite was in the same bad state. Hazzard jerked open his tunic front as well. It was worse – he had no cotton lining to his coat at all. 'Name?'

Dark Mediterranean eyes widened with surprise and he cracked to attention. 'Rivelli, sir!'

'The Italian.'

'Sir! Salerno, sir. Well, Isle o'Dogs like Mickey 'ere.'

Hazzard tugged the jacket open further. Rivelli's neck and shoulders were raw with livid sores. He was bare-chested with one of Kite's false shirt-fronts, but the thick wool serge had chafed and burned, the lining cut out, a commodity doubtless sold off, for what, wondered Hazzard, gaming debt, drink, or 'necessaries' charged double by Duncan or the purser on the *Ville de Paris*, so proud of their stoppages.

'Painful?'

Rivelli stood still, his open coat a strange source of pride. 'No, sir. Fit for duty, sir, aye.'

'No undress shirt either?'

Rivelli hesitated. 'Purser on the *Ville*, sir…' Then, in a rush, with mustered courage, 'But wanted to fight with Mad Billy-Jack, sir, and no mistake, sir, aye.' He looked down, reddening. 'Sorry, sir.'

Others murmured, *Hear hear*, and *Aye*.

Hazzard looked at them. *Mad Billy-Jack? Was that what he was?*

'All right. Draw a spare shirt from Sar'nt Cook. All of you—' he stepped back to address them all '—from now on, no leather neck-stocks, just kerchiefs for the sweat, undress shirts instead of redcoats and soft caps instead of toppers. Spatterdashes off as well, if you go overboard you need to kick your trews off or you've had it.' He turned to Cook. 'And get them to cut off these damn silly tails from their coats, Sar'nt. They're too heavy when wet and I want them ready to move fast. Get Pettifer or De Lisle to show them theirs. Short jackets from here on.'

'Sir, Major Duncan took 'em, sir,' said Pettifer, stepping to attention. 'Said they wasn't regulation, sir.'

'Then cut the arse off these new ones and damn his eyes. We're not Piccadilly swanks looking for bum-boys.'

There were whistles and laughter and a few cheers, Markham looking horrified. Pettifer called back happily, 'Aye-aye, sir!'

Hazzard glanced up at the sky, soaking up the heat, *how he had missed the sun*, and waited for them to settle.

'Right, enough, quiet in the boat. You've been divided into sections under Corporals Pettifer, De Lisle and Second Sergeant Underhill. I want firing drills perfected, reloads brought down to fifteen seconds or less, even with buck and ball. Every man will practise the sword and how to cut a fuse and set quickmatch to powder.' He looked at them all again. 'Some of you think you know me…' he began, 'but you do not.' He raised his voice, his eye catching Markham. 'Any questions.'

It was more of a challenge than an invitation and they knew it – but for one. A figure at the far end of Three Section came to attention and took one pace forward.

'Warnock, sir. 69th Lincs. With Kite, sir,' he added. 'Simcox on sick-parade. Replaced him.'

Warnock was a 'burnt' man, his short-cropped hair revealing skin charred by the sun and the blast of powder-burns. His left ear was missing, gnarled scar tissue in its stead. At his hip hung a native tomahawk from the Americas. There was something in the thrust of his chin and his dry, Thames-side voice – a testing of Hazzard against some secret yardstick of his own.

'Well?' said Hazzard.

'Is it true, sir?' he asked. 'About the Cape.'

Hazzard looked him over. Cook was ready to kick him to the deck, but Hazzard was not surprised by the question. They all wanted to hear the answer. But Hazzard did not oblige.

'You'll find out.'

Warnock looked directly at him. 'Sir.'

Hazzard nodded at Cook. 'Sar'nt.'

'*P'rade!*' roared Cook, '*P'rade, 'shun!*' They came to attention. He then bawled, '*Never give up the boat!*'

The marines shouted back in unison, '*Never give up the boat!*'

Cook repeated it. '*Never give up the boat!*'

'*Never give up the boat!*'

'Clear!'

'*Clear aye!*'

'Clear!'

'*Clear aye! Aye, Sergeant!*'

But for the roar of the wind in the sails overhead and the crash of the spray, there was silence.

Hazzard looked them over again, his eye lingering on Warnock. 'Work them hard, Sar'nt Cook,' he said, 'Bombay Rules.'

'Aye, sir… Bombay Rules it is.' He stiffened. '*P'rade! Eyes in the boat… To your sections! P'rade! Dis… perse!*'

They broke up, going to their tasks, their voices low with whispers. As Hazzard went past him to head below, Cook murmured, 'We don't have spares for Rivelli to draw a shirt, sir…'

'I know,' he said. 'Give him one of mine.'

The first few days at sea saw Hazzard wandering about the ship, moving from rail to rail, to the helm, up to the tops, where he would join the lookouts without a word, watching, or in brief conference with Handley and the bo'sun. Much as he had on the *Valiant*, he hung onto the stays by the bows, staring out to sea, lost in silent storms among the brilliant blue all around.

He utterly ignored Markham. At the first night's dinner at the captain's table, a cramped anteroom between the galley and the stern cabin, which doubled as a wardroom, Hazzard said not a word to anyone. Though he apparently despised him, Markham sought to curry his favour – yet received none from the preoccupied Hazzard.

On the second night, Markham waited in silence ten minutes for Hazzard to appear before throwing down his napkin and rising in frustration. Taking this rejection keenly, Markham thenceforward ate alone in his cabin. Consequently, Greaves and Wayland enjoyed their meals with Handley and McGovern.

The marines busied themselves mastering the jolly-boats, towed in line behind the racing brig, their exercise chiefly to paddle hard enough to make the towline drop slack into the water at least once – an impossible task, it was agreed, as was any hope of marksmanship from the flying boats afterwards.

Wayland did better than expected. He ordered the gunlocks for the eight carronades be kept dry below, wrapped in oilcloth, each ready for immediate use. He conceived of staggered and angled firing ranks, reloads all timed to the second by his grand-father's watch. He also solved the problem of the standard-issue Sea-Service musket. A workmanlike version of the Short India Pattern, it was still too long: without its bayonet it was nearly five feet in length and, Wayland realised, too clumsy for drill on board or covert operations ashore – it was almost as tall as Private Hesse, the Austrian. He informed Hazzard, who simply replied, 'Sort it out then, Mr Wayland.'

137

Duly Wayland enlisted the carpenter and a gunner's mate from the prize crew. To the horror of Markham and the glee of the marines gathered round, they managed to saw through the barrel and forestock, shortening the musket to just over a yard. They refitted the sling-swivel band and cut down the brass ramrod, creating an entirely new weapon. With this lighter, handier musket, some managed to fire four rounds per minute from the hip; when they dragged in their shredded floating target to cheers all round, Kite declared they had 'Done for it, good and proper'. Wayland dubbed it the 'Shorter India', was himself pronounced 'the Professor', and became something of a hero.

Though the men had a paternal fondness for the young officers Wayland and Greaves, they continued to regard Hazzard with caution as he picked his way slowly through their tasks, intervening in a knife drill here and a sword practice there in curt monosyllables – then back again.

On the first few nights at sea, Cook trained Hazzard in sword drills, the men of the watch looking on. Using a pole to nudge a net bag slung by Handley from a yard, Cook called out the cuts, *ready – moulinet one to quarte, up to two, to tierce – faster, lad*, to describe his infamous X, what they had come to call the Mughal Cross. Below decks, conversation would stop, and the marines would look up at the deck above their heads, listening to the dissonant *thwack* of the blade as it grew faster and faster, until they heard the inevitable thud of the severed bag hitting the deck.

On one evening, Wayland joined him with Midshipman Greaves. Greaves watching by the glow of swinging lamps, Hazzard put Wayland *en garde*, Wayland smiling his embarrassed smile. Within one beat, a parry and riposte, Hazzard disarmed the boy, the sword clattering to the deck. Wayland backed away, his hands out in amiable surrender with his apologetic half-laugh – but this was abruptly cut short.

'Now what do you do, sir?' demanded Hazzard. 'Bow to your opponent? Take a glass of champagne?'

'Well, sir.' Wayland stood still, mortified, rebuked once again. 'I–I pick it up—'

'Yes, sir, you *pick it up*. But should I retreat, lower my blade and allow you to do so?'

Wayland had gained some confidence in his days with the marines, and he stiffened. 'Yes, sir. That would be the gentleman's course.'

'Would it?'

'Yes, sir...' Wayland looked down after a moment, regretting his words immediately.

'*There are no damned gentlemen here*, Mr Wayland, *none*. No lords or ladies despite dreams of glory with Nelson. This is a place of *murder and fear*, and you will feel it soon enough. If your enemy loses his sword, then *that* is your moment.'

Wayland cleared his throat and raised his chin. 'To what, sir?'

Hazzard thrust his own sword into the bag. '*To kill him, damn you*, what else!'

Hazzard stalked off, the sailing hands returning to their tasks, the First Watch moving away, a consoling hand patting Wayland on the shoulder, his hero now somewhat tarnished. They agreed with Hazzard, but felt he had been a mite harsh with the lad. They would never see the pair fence again.

For most it was enough that he was Hazzard of the Cape, and he became the embodiment of all that they had heard. To others, he was a dark, mythic figure, aloof and potentially more dangerous than any officer they had known.

On the fourth night some of the men from One and Three Section sat back among the stacks of crates and kegs in the long forward hold, the low ceiling fogged by rolling clouds of blue smoke from their pipes, their tankards filled with the small beer Hazzard had permitted, or contraband rum smuggled aboard from the *Ville de Paris*.

They were mostly quiet, gathered in twos and threes, the odd lone figure among them. They were old marines of some experience: there were no eager innocents in their number keen to learn from older hands, and none would ask of another's past. Each had troubles of their own.

Voices drifted down from the upper deck: "'But, pray you, be these bullet-holes and sword-cuts,' asks Sir Thomas. 'No sir,' says 'e, cool as Christmas... 'Moths!'"

There was a burst of laughter from above and they listened. Warnock was one of the lone figures, a sense of enforced isolation about him, a mistrust of others. He wandered into the midst of a group and drank a draught from his tin mug, his face already flushed with it. As he had done on deck that first day before the whole company, he dripped his dissent into the stillness. 'He's a bloody tarp.'

Whether it was Warnock's sneer or the term he had used, a chill went through the gathering.

'No, he ain't, Knock-Knock,' replied Kite with a sigh, tired, as if he had argued this before with him. He did not look up from the lock he had disassembled and was busy cleaning. 'Correct me if I speak false, Brother Lambert,' Kite continued, nodding at a sailing hand in their number, 'but a tarpaulin is a old officer, come out o'retirement for one last fling, afore he can't give it what-for to the missis no more.'

There were sniggers and Lambert nodded, his sing-song Welsh coming through strong. "'Tis true, aye. A tarp is a proper Pooper, he is.'

'Bollocks, Mickey,' said Warnock to Kite, drinking again, the rum doing its work. 'Gives Riv the shirt off his back and you lot go soft on 'im, officer's pet.'

'Oh come on, Knocky,' said Kite, 'Riv didn't know, did he, and he needs one.'

Rivelli was squatting on a cask playing dominoes with Napier. 'Give over, Knocky mate, it's from stores, Cookie said so hisself.' He fingered the collar of the shirt, his black eyes wide and earnest.

'Look at it, y'alfwit – it's a *gent's* shirt, double-two cotton or nothing. Me ma used to stitch 'em. Why'nt you nick 'im a new one, Mick?'

Kite took a swallow from his own tankard and looked at it philosophically. 'Cos I was distracted by the mariner's seabird, wot alighted in splendour upon yon portside rail, what d'you bloody think? We didn't have the stores, so stuff off.' There were chuckles all round.

'Twat.'

'Pipe down…' muttered Pettifer. 'Speakin' of yer officer…' The big Cornishman looked round at them from his place on the floor, where he sat with Hesse the Austrian, their backs to a pair of posts, cleaning pistols.

Warnock drank again. 'He's a bloody tarp, no mistake.'

A quiet lament issued from a dark corner, 'Call him Samuel call him Saul, and he shall be shamed as us all…'

Warnock nearly spat. 'Oh belt up, y'old misery.'

Marine Private Cochrane hunched his thin back at them, his face close to the lip of a jug of watered-down ale, his half-closed eyes staring into unseen worlds. He had pulled two men from the water in the attack on Tenerife, but could not remember doing so. Talk said he had been a hangman in Belfast, the illegitimate son of a country parson, and locked in perpetual, mournful penitence.

Warnock was determined. 'After he carved up that sod Rice or Race, he couldn't walk after for two bloody years, they said. Had a bloody stick.'

'Call 'im what y'like, Knocky,' said Kite. 'But a stick don't make 'im no tarp.'

'What of it anyways?' demanded Pettifer, banging down the pistol and threatening to get up. 'You got an ache for him, Private? We was *with* him, me, Lil and Andy, runnin' down that ruddy mountain – then he hits two men in a blink with pistol ball at *twenty yard* he did, took another with his bare 'ands and a ruddy *spear*, then cut that Race up like a Sunday brisket.'

'An' I done my bit too, mate,' Warnock threw back at him, holding up his tomahawk. 'I got scalps for the Mohawk, I did, with *this*.'

'He did,' said Kite, 'stank like a pig's bollocks for a week...'

They all laughed again, but Warnock angrily pressed his point. 'We got to look out for usselves, as no other bloody bugger will, specially no tarp.'

But Pettifer got to his feet. 'That's ruddy *it*. That's incitement, that is!' He turned to a figure in the corner, one boot up on a crate, smoking a long clay pipe, his scarred face wreathed in smoke. 'Bloody *tell* 'im, Jeremiah, and shut 'im up for good or I'll read him the King's Regs I will and march him out.'

Sergeant Jeremiah Underhill shook his head. 'Still now, the lot of you. Clucky little hens...' With forty years under his belt, Underhill was the oldest. Some said he had sailed beyond Sumatra, and could speak Chinese. He wore a trimmed beard but had a shaven upper lip in the Quaker style – permitted owing to cuts and burns to his face. Gunsmoke and wounds had left him with a hoarse London whisper. 'Clucky little hens,' he muttered again.

'Go on, Sarge, tell us,' urged Rivelli.

'Tell us *what*?' sneered Warnock.

The rest of the hold was quiet, the remainder in darkness but for the yellow pools cast by their lanterns. The *Esperanza*'s planks creaked, the sea rushing against the hull, most of the sailing hands swinging in their hammocks, asleep. A few men roused themselves slowly, turning to listen.

Someone raised a lantern. Underhill's expression darkened steadily. 'All right. But not a word goes out.' He took another drag on his pipe. 'Who remembers the *Oude Kasteel*?'

Most shook their heads, but De Lisle said, 'Dutchman... captured from the island. Some problem with her.'

'Aye, a Hollander manned by Frogs, nosing round Ceylon from Port St Louis, got pinched by the Bombay Marine, renamed the *Oldcastle*. Fifty guns, sailed like a brick. Cap'n

Isaiah Merrick took her on. A more hated captain I never heard of. They'd been at sea a week when one day, a Marine corporal paraded his section before the mast for morning roll – with one man among 'em loaded and rammed.'

Rivelli said, 'That's chargeable—'

'No, boy,' Underhill corrected, 'in the Bombay Buccaneers that's mutiny. And Merrick was a wicked man, fearin' evil all about him. As only the truly wicked do.' He put a taper to the lantern at his elbow and relit his pipe. Clouds of fragrant smoke billowed. 'Tiger sharks in the wake, devil-fish at the bows, dark omens the Lazcars said, stayin' below, prayin' in mumbles. And they were right.'

'You been to China too, right, Sarge?' asked Rivelli, excited.

Underhill's features creased in a hideous grin but he did not reply. 'The sergeant wanted to shoot the private and corporal both, right where they stood, to show he was not complicit. But the platoon's young Second Lieutenant of Marines, barely three months in his scarlet, stepped forward and told this shite of a captain a great lie: that 'twas he to blame, and not the corporal. But Merrick knew. To teach the young officer his lesson, for standin' in for another, or for bein' more generous of spirit than he – he had that boy strung from a rig in the full heat of the Indian sun, and beat, within an inch of his life.'

They listened in awe. 'Floggin' an officer…'

'The private he hanged, out o'spite, so's the boy could watch while he were bein' beat.' Underhill cut through their surprise with another. 'And who was it gave the beating? Not the bo'sun, as normal practice, but that Marine corporal, thus sufferin' the crueller punishment. An' when that corporal slack-ened off, could take no more of it, Merrick hisself stepped in and finished the evil task.' He stared off into the distance, remembering. 'Forty lashes, they said, but that lad took *fifty*, and then more with a Syrian scourge, till the white of his ribs showed.'

He fell silent for a moment.

'That boy come down from his scaffold and swooned dead away to the deck, all hands reaching to carry him. It was all the Middies could do to stop the crew killing the Cap'n there and then, while the Lazcar witch-doctors summoned demons to feed upon Merrick's black soul.'

Rivelli stared. 'But why'd he say he was to blame?'

'Because, boy, that lad knew the private and corporal would sures be hanged for the infraction – though he, bein' an officer, would not. He held such an ordeal a fair trade for the life of a common man.' He looked at Warnock. 'That ain't no tarp, boy.'

'That's the major,' said Rivelli excitedly. 'That's him, a-right, isn't it, I bet on it. And Cookie's the corporal?'

'Bollocks,' scoffed Warnock. 'He's havin' you on.'

'Must be true, Knocky,' said Napier, his big battered face swinging up to look at him. 'Oke on the *Victor* said Mad Billy never lets no man see his back, for it's hard as flint and flayed like nothin' by God's hand.'

'Yeh – them Buccaneers seen more 'n anyone,' added Rivelli. 'That sword of his, like nothing I never seen.'

'It is from India,' said a foreign voice from somewhere to their left. Warnock peered round into the darkness. 'It is called the Talvar.'

The source of the voice was sitting on the floor, near Pettifer, still propped against his post, paring an apple. Marine Private Hesse was small and dark, with moustachios waxed into points like a grand hussar. 'It is the sword of Arjuna,' he said. 'It will cut a man in two.' He nodded at Warnock before popping a piece of apple into his mouth. 'Even you, *Nick-Nock*.'

'And you, mate,' muttered Warnock, 'sound like a bloody Frog.'

'Austrian, *Scheisskerl*,' said Hesse, smiling nastily as he chewed. 'I *eat* ze Frogs, *m'sieur, mmm-mwah!*'

Rivelli and the others laughed, mainly at Warnock's expense, but Pettifer wanted Underhill to continue. 'Tell 'em what happened.'

Underhill smoked again. 'Back in port Merrick was examined by a court martial in the Black Castle of the Bombay Marine, acquitted of all censure. But a Mughal prince had heard, and sent his finest *Sushruta* surgeons aboard, and they took the boy off to heal his wounds – no one dared interfere. That night, after four bells of the Mid Watch when all were a-bed, the Indies come back – but they weren't no doctors. These were blood-faced Marattas, sons of Kali with *pishkabs* and *khanjar* blades. No one 'eard a sound. Not a marine, not a pisser in the waists, not a rat. Next day, the captain was gone.' He laughed, a dry cackle. 'Two days after, we found his 'ead, floatin'.'

The crowd sat back, satisfied, nodding, *aye*. But Warnock continued to fight his corner. 'Listen to 'im: how'd we know any o'that's true?'

Underhill laughed, his dead dry whisper the sound of a snake shedding its skin. ''Cause I'm the one who found the 'ead, boy.'

Underhill returned to the shadows, his eyes narrowing, as if to peer at further memories. Kite looked about. 'Well, if y'ask me, Mad Billy's republican views have come to bite him one in the arse. And he's been guv us lot, the Awkward Squad.'

'Who you callin' awkward?' demanded Warnock.

'Oh come on, mate – Riv's a dago ice-cream pedlar, Mr Napier there near knocked a bloke's 'ead orf, I'm a fugitive from the law and you, Knock-Knock, are 'alf earless, what makes yer hat fall off in a strong wind.' The laughter nearly rocked the prow of the boat and Kite raised his tankard in salute. 'And that's what I calls awkward, mate.'

But Warnock saw nothing amusing. 'And bollocks to you too, Mickey, if you reckon on me servin' a flamin' tarp just to please Cookie for the look o'the thing!'

As though his words had conjured him from thin air, the company fell quiet as the hulking shape of Sergeant Jory Cook emerged from the darkened hold, caught in the yellow wash of the lanterns. Men in their hammocks quickly turned away, feigning sleep.

'What's him that says so...' he whispered.

Kite saw the danger first. 'Jaysus, he's had a skinful...'

'*I said, what's him that says so.*'

Pettifer tried to get in his way. 'S'all right, Sarge,' he said. 'Only an oke relievin' himself—'

'*Mr* Marine Private *Knock*-bloody-*Knock*,' said Cook. 'Simcox on sick-parade is he, eh... so he volunteers to take his place... get off reg'lar duties, get off th' *Ville*, get away from *Duncan*... and leg it for a cosy billet ashore.'

Warnock stood ready. 'I done no ill, Sarge. Man's got a right to his thoughts.'

'Not in this navy, boy...'

Cook swung a bunched fist, but Warnock ducked, and smashed Cook hard in the ribs out of reflex. But Cook seemed hardly to notice.

'*That's done it, Knocky!*' Napier called. '*You're for the rope now.*'

'That's defence o'meself, that is—'

Cook's left crashed into the side of Warnock's head and the heel of his right swung upwards and connected with his chin, the blows driving Warnock first downwards, then up and back, enough to break any other man's neck. It lifted his feet from the boards and sent him against the plank wall. He spun and bounced, toppling crates before staggering back, but Cook doubled him over with a blow to his midriff and dropped him on the way down with a back-fist.

'That's Bombay Rules, laddie,' laughed Underhill.

Pettifer seized Cook's arms and Kite held him back as he raged at Warnock, '*Get up again and yer a dead man, y'hear!*'

Underhill stepped forward and put a boot across Warnock's neck, pinning him to the floor. 'Easy, bye, lie ye still now...' Underhill looked at Cook. 'He's down, Jory,' he said, 'I see that fist's still a smithy's hammer, eh, boy.'

Cook sagged in Pettifer's arm-lock, tired, not merely from Warnock. 'God's blood, 'Miah – talkin' of their *officer*.' He nursed his hand.

146

'Clucky little hens is all, Jory,' said Underhill lightly, looping an arm round Cook's shoulder, leading him off. 'Come along now, thou old Methuselah. Let's be finding a bottle and slingin' thy hook somewhere in this fine, fine hostelry...'

When the pair had moved into the darkness and up to the deck, Kite took a lantern and leaned over Warnock. 'You dozy *bloody* bugger, Knock-Knock. He could have you twitchin' from the highest yard if he wants.'

Warnock pushed himself onto all fours and spat blood on the floor. 'Bloody Cookie. I could've had him... An' that old goat and his bloody yarns—'

Shadows jumped. There was the sound of crunching bone and Warnock dropped to the boards once more, this time unmoving. Kite lifted the lantern higher to reveal Hesse standing over him, in his hand a soft leather pouch filled with lead shot.

'*Verfluchte Scheisskerl...*' he spat down at him. 'One word more against him, *Herr* Knock-Knock,' he said, 'and I remove your heart.'

—

By the sixth day, *Esperanza* flew north, coming abreast of the vast isle of Sardinia, devouring the miles, lone merchantmen rising and fading on otherwise uninterrupted horizons.

When Midshipman Greaves called the noon meridian, a sail was sighted off the port bow. It was not a warship, but a fishing boat, her single mast broken, well out of her regular grounds and prey to the currents, her crew waving for help.

As a basic precaution Hazzard gave the order for scarlet uniform to be kept out of sight, and Cook brought him a flamboyant blue-grey Spanish tailcoat they had found in the hold, part of the booty of the *Esperanza* prize crew. Wayland stood in shirtsleeves and waistcoat, the marines in blue and white undress shirts, canvas and denims, leaving only Markham and Greaves in the universal navy bluejacket.

Markham grew excited at seeing the ship and peered through his eyeglass importantly. 'Put a shot across their bows,' he called to no one in particular.

'Belay that, Mr Greaves, Mr McGovern,' said Hazzard and looked at Markham. 'It is a fishing boat. With a jury-rigged mast, hailing us in distress.'

They looked out at the waving figures, hearing their calls. Markham reddened and hissed under his breath, 'Dash it all, sir, you *will* acknowledge me, you *will* call me *Captain*.'

Hazzard kept an eye on the boat and its crew. 'Then I advise, Captain, that you reef sail to slow our progress and bring us alongside. Unless you intend to ram them...'

'Dash it, Hazzard, I had every intention to give that order *presently*,' insisted Markham. The deckhands looked the other way. 'Mr Handley, Mr McGovern! Douse sail, if you please, and bring us alongside. And, well, be quick about it.'

'*Aye-aye, Captain!*' called Handley, not without some irony, '*Douse sail it is! Mr McGovern, douse sail and ease your helm, rudder amidships...*'

McGovern took the relay and the rigging hands shinned upwards, *Let go yer braces, sheets and halyards!* Within minutes the *Esperanza* slowed for the first time in a week.

'God...' said Markham, wrinkling his nose as they approached. The stench of rotting fish was overpowering. 'Look at them...'

The boat was listing badly to starboard and its single sloping lateen boom had been contrived from two spars on a splintered mainmast, loose lines trailing in the water behind, nets hanging from two stern gaff booms. There were seven crew at most, all in tatters, four men, three women – who stood protectively over their rotting catch, long filleting knives ready in their hands.

The boat was made fast and the captain helped aboard. Unkempt and ragged as he was, he had the quiet bearing of responsibility – but Hazzard noticed that he kept his eyes down, glancing at the carronades, muskets, and Hazzard's uniform.

To Hazzard it was fear, the hallmark of the down-trodden – former victims, doubtless, of a seapower, Genoa, Rome, Naples perhaps – or France. The man bowed his head several times in quick succession and took Hazzard by the hand as if to kiss it. '*M'sieur le capitaine. J'vous remercie.*'

Hazzard corrected the man's grip and shook his hand. '*Ne vous inquiètez pas, m'sieur le capitaine.*' *Do not worry, Captain.* He asked if he had come from Corsica, though judging by his accent Hazzard guessed probably not, but he was certainly not French either. He tried Italian, '*O siete dalla Sardegna? Preferisce parlare in Italiano?*' *Or are you from Sardinia? Would you prefer Italian?*

The captain exhaled slowly with relief and nodded with a laugh, and they switched to Italian, '*Sì, che Dio sia lodato! Siamo della Sardegna – sei da Roma, signore?*' *Yes, may God be praised, we are from Sardinia – are you from Rome, sir?*

Pettifer passed them cups of water and Wayland moved in beside Hazzard. 'Sir, my Italian's rather rusty to say the least…'

'Sardinian fishermen,' murmured Hazzard in reply. 'Let's get them some timber for repairs, Sar'nt Cook, and check below how many casks of water and biscuit we can spare for them,' he said, then added to Cook under his breath, 'and best give me a fine salute to make it all look very official…'

'*Oui, Capitaine.*' Cook stepped back smartly and swung him a quivering Portsmouth salute, then called for two marines to follow him below.

'Hold hard there,' whispered Markham. 'You are not the *capitaine* at all, dash it. This is outrageous. It is I who should be saluted, and I… I shan't permit His Majesty's stores to be *pilfered* for a lot of, well, scruffy Dago-Frog fishermen.'

'They may provide us with information,' said Hazzard quietly.

'Oh, what could a revolting fisherman possibly—'

But Hazzard turned his back on him and asked the Sardinian captain straight out, '*Capitano, Lei ha visto qualche navi inglese?*' *Have you seen any English ships?*

149

The captain looked from Hazzard to Markham, detecting something amiss. '*Sì*...' he said carefully, 'a British frigate... it captured the French privateer, *La Pierre*.'

Hazzard translated quietly and Wayland whispered, 'He must mean HMS *Emerald* or *Terpsichore*, sir – they were in Nelson's squadron. A midshipman on the *Ville de Paris* told me so.'

'Where was it?' asked Hazzard of the fisherman in Italian.

'Off Cap Sicié...' The captain watched as provisions were brought up from below, and lengths of timber passed to his overjoyed crew. 'Yesterday,' he said, 'or the day before, Captain. The news, it is everywhere. The *Pierre* was, how you say, the big fish in these waters.'

Midshipman Greaves came forward with a chart and they gathered round, Markham trying to see from the back of the group, standing on tip-toe.

'Here... *Tolone* – Toulon,' said the Sardinian, then indicated the headlands to the west of the port, 'and here is Cap Sicié, *secondo me*, in my opinion, two days' sail.'

'He is not inaccurate, sir,' said Greaves quietly, his finger indicating their progress on the chart. 'This is our course and current position by dead reckoning, twenty-five nautical miles north-west of San Pietro in Sardinia. Two days' sail at most. We are very close.'

'More like a bloody whisker away, sir,' murmured Handley.

Hazzard examined the chart and agreed. 'Well done, Mr Greaves...'

Markham watched, furious, trying to elbow his way forward. 'Dash it all, why do you *whisper* so? What's he *saying*?'

Hazzard looked at the Sardinian captain. The man was clearly sympathetic, as if he knew some secret. 'Has there been news of the great fleet?'

The Sardinian looked at the chart. 'It lies at Toulon and Marseille, Genoa, and Ajaccio. Some here, some there... fifty in each port, maybe a hundred – transports, frigates, merchantmen...' He shrugged. 'They wait only upon the winds. But surely, *Capitano*, everyone knows this?'

150

'*Jaysus shite...*' muttered Cook. 'Five ports? The Toulon fleet's big enough on its own.'

'It is what you seek, hm?' The Sardinian shrugged again, their secret clear to him. 'And your great *Nelsone* as well.'

Hazzard glanced at him. Despite Hazzard's Roman accent, but possibly thanks to their whispers and Markham's outbursts, the Sardinian had guessed they were neither French nor Italian. Hazzard removed his hat and bowed his head in apology and acknowledgement. 'Yes, Captain, it is. Welcome aboard HMS *Esperanza* of the Royal Navy.'

The captain blinked, smiling, shaking his head, and waved a hand at the stores being handed over. 'Who else would sail a gunship like this, with no colours, yet give aid to poor fishermen? The *Napolitani*? Or *Genovesi*? *No*. And the French, hm, they take first, and ask last.'

Hazzard felt a terrible sadness emanate from him. 'Would you have a brandy, sir?'

The captain shook his head quickly. 'No, no, I would like it too much, yes, but no. Not good when short of water, hm? As you are now, thanks be to us. Come.' He flicked a finger at the chart, a debt to be repaid. 'Look, Cap Sicié, the wind, it changes fast and the *tramontane* or *mistral*, it will come. If the fleet sets sail, the great *Nelsone* would be in danger. You see?'

'He's right, sir,' said Greaves. 'If the Marseille and Toulon fleets put to sea simultaneously...'

Hazzard looked at the chart. The cliffs of Cap Sicié lay dead centre between Marseille and Toulon. Nelson would be trapped between the two.

'Which must not happen,' insisted the Sardinian. 'For how could we stand against France alone?'

Haggard, his lank hair blowing, but with signs of renewed hope, the captain took Hazzard's hand, bowing and touching it to his lips. '*Le bacio la mano, commendatore...*' then clasped it, and in broken English said, 'Thanks be to you. The good fortune to you, and *lo grande ammiraglio*.' He turned to his crew and clapped his hands, '*Marco, Gianni, dai, dai, veloce! Andiamo!*'

As the fishing boat pulled away, the captain raised an arm and waved, one of the young men jumping to the rail and shouting '*Viva il re Giorgio! Viva il re!*'

Greaves watched them in wonder. 'Long live King George…?'

Wayland nodded. 'Indeed, sir.'

Markham looked through his glass as the boat pulled into the distance. 'Well, sir,' he said in an affected drawl. 'Caught between two fleets, eh? The great *Nelsonay* indeed has come unstuck again, just as at Tenerife, what?' he said, adjusting the telescope. 'As Orde said: after all his boasting, it is all merely loud noise from an ordinary little man…'

Hazzard turned and smacked the scope from Markham's eye and knocked the hat from his head with the back of his hand. They tumbled to the deck and Markham stumbled backwards from the rail and fell into a stack of kegs and rope, blinking, shocked.

'You *fool*,' said Hazzard, 'it is Nelson who stands between you and an enemy fleet of *four hundred* ships and thirty *thousand* men. Even that wretched fisher-captain understands. If Nelson is sunk, sir, then so by God are *you*.'

Two of the hands looked to McGovern, who stared, just as surprised as Markham, but Kite, Pettifer and Hesse stepped up behind Cook, sawn-off muskets held loose but clearly ready, and the sailors remained still.

'*H-how dare you*…' gasped Markham, flinching behind raised arms. He looked at them all, at Wayland and Greaves, snatched up his hat then got to his feet, shaking. 'You defy me, sir!' he stammered. 'Y-you defy me!' He pushed Greaves out of his way to run aft, tripping over a coiled line, clutching for the hatchway ladder to hurry below.

Every man on deck watched. When Markham had gone, they shuffled about, embarrassed. Handley joined Hazzard.

'Bout time and all,' he muttered.

'Get us out of here, for God's sake, Handley,' said Hazzard. 'Mr Greaves, you are officer of the helm,' he said, turning to the boy, 'Cap Sicié, on this good southerly, fast as we can.'

'Aye-aye, sir.' Greaves hurried aft, his commands echoing across the ship, 'Master Handley! Set headsails, staysails and coursers, and make your helm nor'nor' by west if you please!'

'Aye, Mr Greaves, sir, nor'nor'west it is! Heads'ls, stays an' coursers aye!' Handley relayed the commands and McGovern touched his hat brim and bawled, '*All hands make sail! Jump to yer sheets an'alyards and haul away!*'

With a renewed zeal the hands leapt to the rigging, and the canvas cracked open and billowed overhead. *Esperanza* charged forward, her sharp prow turning towards France, and Nelson.

–

That night Hazzard sat at the folding table in his makeshift cabin, a small storeroom stacked to the ceiling with crates of dry provisions. He had snatched barely three hours' sleep from Mid Watch and tried to work through the final hour before dawn.

He pored over Blake's intelligence reports once more, reports of courtiers and informers, of espionage, of Sarah caught in the machinery. He consulted a chart of the Neapolitan coast: *Sheet M3/337a – Being a Representation of the Bay of Naples With All Islands, Shoals and Shewing All Batteries, Anno.1793.* Beside it lay a miniature of Sarah in silhouette with curling tendrils of hair at the nape of an elegant neck, all in shadow, the face secret, hidden, kept from him.

> *...from Sir Wm Hamilton Kt & Plenipotentiary, French informant the Countess De Biasi in company Englishwoman and agent 28'66'96.*
>
> *Item: Boarded carriage Naples 11Hpm –*

Item: Carriage discovered turned over to south of city on Rapallo-Salerno road,

Item: Horses missing presum.d taken; coachman dead; armed escort dead; Mortal traces int. of carriage a quarter past 1H, date the morning 9th instanter.

Item: Spoor of cavalry troop; French shoe farrier marks,

Item: French coin found — suggest interception by army scouts or agents of French Gendarmerie Extraordinary.

French troops had occupied Rome since February, but Naples was still a free independent kingdom, controlling the whole of southern Italy and Sicily. Hazzard knew he had to go direct to Sir William Hamilton in Naples, the remaining safe haven for fleeing French and Italian nobles. Hamilton was the only hope, the last person who had seen Sarah.

And if nothing there, then what?

The pain had dulled but with every surfacing thought of her he felt more and more the weight of guilt. He looked at her silhouette. How little he had known of her, he decided. The dark outline of her miniature seemed to taunt him.

The sealed orders from Lewis merely confirmed his verbal instructions: *If parted from Med. Sqn, Oi/c Nelson R.Adm., 9 Company Marines Oi/c Hazzard W^m. J. Capt. will engage the enemy independently in whatsoever measure possible to prevent enemy attack or invasion.*

He had known all along that if they missed Nelson, and made Toulon before finding Sarah, they could well find the French fleet riding at anchor. With a bloody-minded recklessness he had never known before, he decided he would then be true to his word to St Vincent and Lewis, and attack. Fifteen marines in French kit would be sufficient to infiltrate, blow powder magazines, set fires and wreak general havoc. Enough to sink their best ships or at least delay their launch until Nelson arrived with reinforcements, and bring in St Vincent with heavy guns.

Failing that, their chief value to Nelson would be to track the French fleet and, if given opportunity, harry their progress with covert night attacks. As they drew closer to Cap Sicié he feared it would be more the latter. But to plan for such an event left a sour taste; it was an acknowledgement of his failure to find Sarah.

He made a note: *Spanish Armada 1588 – 130 ships. Marseille and Toulon combined: 200 ships. Assume Ajaccio, Genoa. Assume Civita Vecchia. Bonaparte controls Venice, ergo, assume Venetian Navy. Assume only 50 ships at each remaining port: total ca. 350 ships.* Another ten at each port would make 400. Given the sea-room between ships in convoy, and given two lines of battle for escorting 74s and 80s on the perimeter to give full vent to their firepower if challenged, troop-transports protected in the centre, Hazzard calculated the fleet would cover roughly four square miles of the Mediterranean. And each warship mounted sufficient armament to reduce a city to rubble.

Good God.

Xerxes, he thought, would have been envious. And only Nelson and 9 Company stood waiting, a new Themistocles at Salamis.

The target of the fleet still eluded him. It was too big a fleet for merely taking Naples – if they had Rome, they could simply march on Naples. If England, why had the French not massed at Lorient, Brest or La Rochelle on the Atlantic coast? From Toulon they would have to break through Gibraltar and get past the Mediterranean Fleet – just as they had attempted the previous year, leading to their defeat off Cape St Vincent. And if Hazzard knew anything of the old Sir John Jervis, he knew he would never allow them to try it again. If Lewis had any theories, he was keeping them to himself. *Malta, Sicily, Ottoman Turkey?*

He looked through the folder before him and came across a small volume, gathered accidentally into his own things somehow, aboard the *Valiant*. It must have been Wayland's, a

155

copy of Defoe's novel *Colonel Jack*. Tucked inside was a scrap of paper.

> HMS Valiant, 10 May. Upon greeting the Blockade Fleet at the Tagus, Portugal.
>
> Looking out upon our brave sailors and knowing their gladsome Hearts, their Fearless Duty, and seeing our great ships, this Wooden Wall standing against tyranny for the sake of All Humanity – seeing our guns, our troops, I reflect upon the Foolhardiness of our Enemies whom we face alone without fear, trusting in God, the King, and His Glory – and I am filled with a pride I can not contain.
>
> Upon seeing such spectacle, who would be anything, I wonder, but an Englishman!

Hazzard set it down, sorry that he had read it. It was fanciful, young and, worse, familiar – he wondered if he had ever enthused in such a way when he had been scarcely nineteen himself. Doubtless he had. He considered Wayland, whether he could trust the boy, whether he were Lewis's creature, an Admiralty spy, watching, noting everything for some future reckoning.

But Wayland was utterly without guile, his inability to conceal his thoughts and feelings all too obvious. The diary entry made that plain enough. He thought of their last clash and his angry words in swordplay, and pledged to do better.

At the bottom of his bag he found a small silver pendant on a long leather lace. Ellie must have put it there. He smiled. It was appropriate: a figurine of St Jude, the Patron Saint of Causes Lost. He thought of her and her care, her tears for his pain. He looped it round his neck.

His French identity documents and Toulon passport bulged from under the lining of his tunic, *Capitaine Louis-Martin St Juste of the 30th Infanterie de Marine, on confidential assay from the Ministry of the Interior. Born Grenôble, 27ᵗʰ November 1767*. He could feel their flat lump against his ribs, the false legend impeccable, drawn from known facts of his own life, an uncomfortable reminder – a burden of memories, rather than a potential means of escape. But escape had not yet entered his thinking. *Escape to what?*

There was a knock at the door. He looked for his watch, hidden beneath the loose pages. It was nearly four. Wayland would be coming off duty and he would take over himself. He opened the door.

But in the passage stood one of the marines, Porter, a bespectacled Yorkshireman. Hazzard knew him only as the oddest of St Vincent's Oddfellows, but he had yet to speak with him properly. 'Porter, isn't it?'

'I were just passing, sir,' he said in a quiet lilting voice, 'and glimpsed your light...' He adjusted his round-framed spectacles, they seemed tight to his face, and enlarged his eyes. He held up a small bottle. 'I cannot but help notice, sir, that y'not be sleeping well, and I bring you this, as a relief.'

It was a small glass vial filled with a brown liquid.

Hazzard took it. 'What is it?'

'Tincture of Valerian, sir, in a brandy suspension. Touch of hops and *passiflora*. Ten drops in water is a powerful soporific, suitable for one watch of four hours' sleep. Twenty drops will put you down for a full night, sir, if y'could but bear it.'

'Who tells you I can't sleep?'

Porter blinked behind his lenses. 'Well, sir,' he said apologetically, 'the dark circles round the eyes, the pallor of the skin, and of course the nightmares when you kick the house down should you actually fall into sleep, sir.'

Hazzard wondered if he were trying to be funny or whether it was just his way. 'Do I cause a disturbance?'

'Oh no, sir, we little angels sleep the sleep of the dead.'

Hazzard looked at the bottle. 'How do you come to be dispensing medicines? Are you a physician?'

Porter was one of those men who looked permanently weighted down by a secret, painful wisdom. 'I were an apothecary's assistant, sir, in a York emporium,' he said. 'But wife and young ones died of fever, despite that. When a squadron put in at Whitby I took the bounty, sir, to get away. Sold me soul for sixteen pound and stoppages. I can read, write, do sums. And, alas, can hit a man in the fighting-tops from a rough deck.' He said this last as if he wished it were otherwise.

'Did you assist the surgeon on the *Ville de Paris*?'

'No, sir, Mr Tainsh on the *Theseus*. If he had a mind t'ask, that is. But Captain Miller took heed, as we had ulcers among the crew, and recommended onions and lemons. I had anti-spasmodics, carminatives, treatments for blisters, boils, shock, but most never understood...' He searched through his shoulder bag and Hazzard could hear the clink of small bottles. 'Got much of it from a man in Tangier, used to come to Gib and leave it for us...'

They both stopped and listened. They heard singing. A fiddle started up, a jaunty John Gay tune, and boots began to thump in time. It was Kite, leading one of his customary songs.

Wot the 'ell is that in fair Polly's slot,
Called the bo'sun from his gin...
Why bo'sun, sir, says Jolly Jack,
Tis a ship's be-lay-in' pin!

I'm... Jolly Jack, I'm Jolly Jack, I'm Master of the Fleet – and if
yer lurkin' round the 'eads, I'll have yer arse, me sweet!!

I seen 'em big... and I seen 'em small,
An' I seen 'em foursquare loooong...
But I never seen a belayin' pin
Wiv bloody bollocks on... Hoi!
Ohhhhhhh, I'm... Jolly Jack, I'm Jolly Jack, I'm Master of the
Fleet...

158

Porter looked away and cleared his throat, then glanced back with a wry smile. 'Not exactly High Church, is it, sir?'

'No,' agreed Hazzard. 'But more honest.'

They both stopped once again. Kite's songs apart, they heard something else, something entirely foreign to the sounds of the brig.

Porter strained to hear. 'Sir – is that...'

Hazzard moved a pace into the dark passage, towards the ladder. It was the unmistakable sound of a schoolmaster's birch, delivering a slow, rhythmic whipping.

There was a shout, a scuffle and a heavy fall. They looked into the darkness of the passage towards the two stern cabins – one had been taken by Markham, the other shared by Wayland and Greaves. A thin film of light escaped from beneath the door on the right, Markham's cabin.

There was a muffled cry, followed by another crash. Markham's door was yanked open, yellow candlelight flooding the low-beamed corridor.

Barefoot and wearing only his over-sized man's shirt, the young Midshipman Greaves burst into the passage and hit the opposite wall, whimpering, his breath coming in panicked gouts, his naked thighs and the back of the shirt dark with stains seeping through the cotton. Sobbing, the boy tore at the latch of his cabin door and threw himself inside, slamming it shut behind him.

Markham appeared in his open doorway, a frayed switch in his hand. He too wore only a shirt, his waxen face and hairless legs slick with sweat in the dull gleam of a stinking tallow candle. He was not wearing his powdered wig. Hazzard saw the man was almost bald, with only sparse tufts of thin, patchy hair. Markham turned and saw them, in his expression that open-mouthed surprise of a soul caught, at last, in the full realisation of its own evil.

'*Hass... Hazzard...*' he gasped. He staggered backwards and fell inside, crying out, gibbering, shoving the door closed and bolting it.

159

It took Hazzard a moment to understand what they had just witnessed.

'Good *bloody* God...' He lunged past Porter back into his cabin and snatched up his sword belt and the Talwar. '*I'll kill him.*'

But Porter blocked his path, his hands out, 'Sir, now, *sir.*' He shook his head. 'There's nowt to be done, sir, nowt of any good, not at sea. I'd say he's gone, sir, lost his wits.'

'Of course he has! That boy's soiled himself! *Whipping* him? Good *God*, what *else!* I'll see him *dead* for it—'

'Aye, sir, aye, I'm sure y'would, true.' Porter nodded, blinking, his voice quick but gently calming, the task clearly nothing new to him, stepping between men and their darkest intent. 'And what of all that follows, sir? Not thoughts to be entertained by God-fearing men, sir.'

Hazzard looked at him, baffled. '*What?*'

'Shall you turn a yardarm into a gibbet? The men fearful, conflicted?' He looked down, silent, his eyes on him.

Hazzard stared back at him, frozen into inaction. 'It is the *damned law!*'

'Aye, sir.' He nodded.

'God's *blood*, man — we cannot simply...'

He could arrest Markham, confine him to his cabin, and waste a marine to guard him. Beyond that, he knew Porter was right.

Porter took a cloth and bottle from his bag. 'Best I see to the lad, sir. I shall see to the captain too, sir, never fear, and pronounce him unfit. As the only medical staff aboard it should satisfy Mr McGovern and Master Handley. And the court in Gib. Should we ever return.' He smiled with a philosophical tilt of the head. 'Ah well, but that's ne'er been a fear we had, is it, sir? Returning, I mean.'

The death-knell pronunciation of his last remark hung heavy between them. 'All right,' said Hazzard. 'But if that creature sets foot on deck I shall send him straight to Hell.'

'Never fear, sir. A few hours' treatment,' he said sadly, 'and I'll send him there meself, without disturbing poor old Lucifer one little bit...'

Porter moved down the passage, humming, rummaging in his bag. Hazzard turned and dropped his sword on the papers on his desk – *God's teeth*. He looked down at the sword, two inches of the engraved blade already loosed from the neck of the scabbard, ready for a lightning draw and cut. He slammed it shut.

As he did so, he heard the note of the wind change, and the ship pitched, making him stumble. Boots clattered down the steps outside his door. It was one of the young foremast hands.

'Sir, Master Handley says for you to come quick...' His shaking voice echoed the shine of terror in his eyes. 'Storm, he says, sir. Big as a India sky.'

Armada

Many said it was the *mistral*, but wiser heads said it was the *tramontane*, howling out of the north. Whatever its source, it blew hard enough to bring a renewed frenzy of activity to Toulon harbour: the wind had come at last. The fleet could set sail.

The flagship *Orient* rose high into the bright white-streaked skies, a fortress mounting 120 guns, her highest topgallant yards almost invisible in the morning glare. Peering at her critically from a distant quayside further up the harbour road, *Sergent-chef-major* Achille Caron, Senior Warrant of the 75th *demi-brigade de bataille*, 'The Invincibles', stood surrounded by troops, carts and carriages. He watched the raised quarterdeck of the great ship, braided officers placing a podium at the rail, others gathering with loudhailers. It bore all the hallmarks of an address.

'*Putain,*' he cursed.

The fleet admiral and a number of flag officers encircled a central figure. They parted, some leading the way to the rail, indicating where the figure could stand, where he could take hold. After a moment, Caron recognised the man mounting the podium. He had not seen him since a freezing morning inspection in Picardy three months earlier, when galloping messengers had brought them the trouble now laid out all around them.

'*Sacre...* at last,' he whispered, '*Bonaparte.*'

Caron knew Bonaparte personally, from the Battle of Arcole in Italy. So did the *Alpha-Oméga*, his finest skirmish *chasseur à pieds* platoon of the 75th who had distinguished themselves in too many battles to care much for anyone or anything but themselves. They were now spread in lazy disarray across the pier among the cargo, some sleeping, some passing round a bottle, others staring, bored or drunk, in various stages of half-dress – some with tattered trousers, one a woollen sailor's cap, others with prized Italian and Austrian equipment torn from corpses in the Alpine snows. At their centre were the oldest survivors, the trio of Rossy, St Michel and the giant Pigalle. They sat on ammunition crates playing cards, unconcerned with the grand sights swelling before them.

'*Putain…*' Caron spat. 'Who has wine? Rossy? Did you leave me any Richebourg after the *foie gras?*'

There was laughter but Rossy ignored them, first brushing his moustaches with theatrical skill, then rearranging the grimy and dog-eared playing cards in his equally grimy hand, his little finger cocked delicately, poking from fingerless gloves. 'I have given up drink, *Chef*,' he said, scratching at his unshaven chin, concentrating on his hand. 'But only for summer. Or until next week. Indeed, I am also considering taking holy orders, just to get out of this place. Perhaps an English convent, with a fireplace and naked nuns with fat, white English *derrières*. *Mwah*.'

There was more laughter and Caron grunted, fiddling with his pipe and tobacco pouch. 'English arses. They will never be big enough for Le Pig.'

There were whistles all round. Caron patted Pigalle on the shoulder, the giant of the group. Pigalle frowned with heavy concentration at his cards, tiny children's playthings within his huge ham-like fists. They said his cloak was made from those of two regular men's, stitched together.

'*Tiens enfants*,' continued Caron, 'Le Pig, he is our special *garçon*. Wherever he plants his boot, that is where the line shall stay.'

'If I am somewhere,' murmured Pigalle, 'why should I want to move…'

'*Chef*,' said Rossy. 'I say Malta.'

'I say Sicily,' said St Michel, pushing his spectacles up the bridge of his nose. Long-sighted, he was the best shot in the 75th.

Caron nodded. 'Some say we are for the Turks.'

Rossy shrugged, unconcerned. 'Then I shall have some arses with Turkish Delight.' He slapped down a card. 'Threes. Pig?'

Pigalle grunted. 'What is this one?' he asked, and showed it to them. Everyone laughed.

'That is a king. You see his magnificent crown? You should play it now.'

Pigalle looked more closely. 'Why does it not say R for *Roi* then, in the little box in the corner?'

'Because these are German cards, Pig. They do not speak French.'

'They should.'

Rossy nodded thoughtfully. 'You are quite right, *M'sieur* Le Pig. Everyone should.'

Caron looked around at the massed troops. 'I bet you very soon many will, who never spoke it before.' He puffed at his pipe. 'Trouble, *enfants*, she has found us again...'

Rossy raised a dented tin cup in salute to the harbour and the hills. '*Pauvres salauds*, poor you, whoever you are, we did not mean to do it.' They continued their game, disinterested Roman soldiers at the foot of an unremarked cross.

Captain Moiret joined Caron at the waterside. A rare commodity in any *demi-brigade*, Moiret was a seasoned and popular company commander, a young man, now aged by campaign experience. 'So. Another rousing speech. At least this time we go, *enfin*. Are the men watered and fed?'

Caron nodded. '*Oui, Capitaine*. Before assembly. They might need to piss.'

'Let them,' said Moiret. 'Into the harbour. With malicious zeal.'

There was a cheer from the thousands already aboard the ships in the harbour and the further thousands still ashore, their shouts echoing around the hills. They watched as Bonaparte guided a female figure to his side. Joséphine Bonaparte waved a hand and the men cheered still more loudly. The batteries fired in salute and clouds of white smoke drifted across the rocky basin.

Caron watched as Bonaparte let her step down again and she retired several paces to join the other ladies. Bonaparte readied himself.

'*Soldiers of France…*' began Bonaparte. '*It is my honour to address you today…*'

He had already spoken to them, ten days earlier, when the wind had denied them launch. This would be a reminder of their glory. 'His address fires the nation, eh, *Chef*?' said Moiret, dutifully.

'Mm,' said Caron. 'Though Rossy asks where his six acres of land will be, which the general promised. Paris, he hopes. Near a good brothel. Or at least a good café.'

'Very sensible.'

'*…No greater armada has ever set sail from the shores of Europe. You are one of the wings of the Army of England – you have made war in the mountains, plains, and cities. It remains to make it upon the ocean!*'

Caron listened with half an ear and glanced at the faces of the troops. Bonaparte would never go easily, he decided, and these men would hold onto him with devotion: in their hearts, he knew, they believed that here before them stood a god.

'*…Soldiers, the eyes of Europe are upon you. You have great destinies to accomplish, battles to fight, dangers and fatigues to overcome…*'

Moiret looked out at the ships. 'What is the last count?'

At dawn Caron had tired of going beyond 67, but had heard on the grapevine that there were at least 150 transports in Toulon harbour alone. 'Thirteen ships of battle, *Capitaine*, forty frigates, gunships and *avisos*… and seventeen thousand men. Too many,' he said, 'for this to be over quickly. There must be another fifty or sixty ships at Marseille. And only the good god of whores above knows how many more men await us…'

'That is most apt, *Chef*,' said Moiret.

They looked along the quayside while Bonaparte continued his speech – an incongruous group approached, and heads were turning to look. Cloaks and mantels flapping in the cold wind, half a dozen top-hatted civilians emerged from among the assembled troops and carts stationed along the road. They approached the quayside barrier, uncertain, deferential, lost, behind them a wagon-train of luggage. At their head was an older man, the rest very much his junior. He met Moiret, raised his hat and extended his hand.

'You are *Capitaine* Moiret? My name is Jurat, of the—' Moiret took their passports. Jurat continued, in explanation '—of the Engineers and students of the *Polytechnique* and *École des Ponts et Chausées*.'

Moiret glanced at them, curious. 'Bridges and Highways?' he said. 'I hope we find some for you to study. So… you are the *savants*, hm?'

'*Savants?*'

'The scholars we were told of.'

'Ah! *Savants*, yes, but of course,' laughed Jurat. '"Those who know", eh! Haha, well modesty forbids, of course, but scholars, certainly.' He indicated the two boys beside him. 'Our finest and youngest, Citizen Jollois there, and Citizen De Villiers du Terrage.'

De Villiers du Terrage could not have been more than seventeen. He gazed at everything around him, the cliffs, the batteries, the ships, the banners – and Jollois peered back at Moiret over a pair of large round-eyed smoked glasses, his dark hair blowing from underneath a low-crowned top-hat pushed to the back of his head. He looked like an anarchist, and somewhat unimpressed. 'We need the *Franklin*, I think, Citizen Captain,' Jollois said. 'That is my scholar's opinion…' he added drily.

166

'Is Citizen Le Père arrived?' asked Jurat, looking about. He was excited. 'We were allocated this quay by the *Général de brigade* Caffarelli…'

Moiret read his passport and ticket. 'Citizen Jollois is correct. You are to join the *Franklin*. You need another quay, for we are bound for the *Spartiate*. Perhaps I can get a tender over here for you—'

'When do we sail, Captain?' asked De Villiers, then apologised, 'I beg your pardon, Citizen Captain.'

Moiret looked him over. He had seen younger in uniform, but not a so-called civilian 'expert'. 'Your guess, Citizen.'

'Perhaps you know,' asked Jurat hopefully, 'where it is we are all going?' He smiled expectantly.

Someone hissed at them to be quiet while Bonaparte spoke. Caron asked him, 'You do not know?'

'No,' said Jollois with some irony, 'they tell us *savants* nothing. But Citizen Monge did say I should bring these,' added Jollois, tapping his sunglasses. 'To see if they work.'

Moiret caught Caron's eye. This was more than even they had been told. 'My compliments, Citizens,' said Moiret, 'to sign on for an uncertain fate. None of us know.'

'*Alors*, it was our duty,' said Jurat brightly, shrugging it off. 'An honour. I only hope we get a good view at sea.' He looked out at the ships in the harbour, trying to spot the *Franklin*.

Moiret handed back the passports and added, 'I think we can guarantee you a good seat, Citizen.'

Someone shouted, '*Vive la république immortelle!*' Other voices ranged about the harbour joined in. Moiret called for a runner and tore a sheet off a notepad to order a tender for the engineers. Jurat was already striding off, calling for men to assist with their wagons. Caron watched him go.

'Where do we go, *capi*, that is so rare and untouched, that we need builders of bridges and highways and scholars with pens.'

'Yet without hot-weather kit.'

'Or water bottles.'

Moiret looked at him. 'No bottles?'

Caron shook his head. 'Some fool said they would be issued aboard ship but I think he was sucking it out of his thumb. We scrounged a handful from the *gendarmerie* barracks when they were not looking. But it will not be enough.' He muttered to himself, 'Pigalle is not so stupid as he seems.'

'Meaning?'

'Today Pigalle asks me why we have so many books with us.'

Moiret did not understand. 'Books?'

'When we escorted the heavy old one, that Citizen Monge – the foundry scientist, hm? *Putain*. Here, at the warehouses,' he said, 'I saw them, stacked into the sky, books, more than twenty *thousand*, he said, very proud, all in a special crate which they turn and use as the shelves, in an instant. We are now a *biblio*, hm? The mobile *Académie*. We must be going where there are no books for the scholars to read. Or, *c'est à dire*, rather, no books that the scholars *can* read.'

Moiret looked up at Bonaparte as he considered their least favoured conclusion. '*Bon dieu*... it is not Malta or Sicily then.'

'*Non*. Turkey?'

Moiret looked worried. 'We do have interpreters, Turks and Levantines...' He gave Caron a glance. 'What if it is the other place...?'

'*Putain*. That would be a madness. A madness...' Caron watched Bonaparte. 'God in heaven has long forsaken that land... Let us pray we are not to be forgotten there as well, *Capitaine*.'

Bonaparte finished and the massed troops began to sing the 'Song of Departure'. Rossy and Pigalle sang with the others, waving their beer and wine bottles, the patriotic hymn ringing across the harbour, loud enough to shake even Caesar from his everlasting night. Moiret and Caron joined in and raised their voices to match the marching bands playing on the quayside, if only to lift their spirits, and reinforce the faintest of faltering hopes.

168

A gun boomed and signals fluttered up the masthead of the *Orient*. Across the harbour the leafless forest of masts burst into flower, blossoming with billowing white canvas: the fleet began to set sail. Already towed into position from the quaysides, one by one the ships weighed anchor. More guns saluted, and cheers rose up. Slowly, the great warships manoeuvred into line with the transports, and processed past the flagship, Bonaparte taking the salute at the rail.

Behind him, Jules-Yves Derrien watched the gathered fleet officers and General Staff crowding the elevated poop deck, chattering with ladies in pale gowns and parasols, so many mock Marie-Antoinettes wishing their husbands were king – or better, like Bonaparte, the next master of the world. How he pitied them. He remembered that first meeting with the general, in the basement passage of the Tuileries, and recalled with some pride that Bonaparte had been true to his word: they had indeed met again. Jules-Yves Derrien would now safeguard the expedition itself, ever on the alert.

Bonaparte took the salute from *Spartiate*, then *Guerrier*, and the 80-gun *Franklin, Conquérant*, and the great *Tonnant*, her beloved captain Du Petit-Thouars bowing formally, each quarterdeck ranged with officers raising their hats. The batteries in the hillside forts around continued to fire, grey plumes dissipating in the blustering wind, and the battleships returned the honour in confident *au revoir*.

Bourrienne, Bonaparte's discreet private secretary, leaned in close behind him, 'Should I whisper "remember, thou art mortal"?'

Bonaparte smiled at his old friend, and considered the point as he gazed out at the ships, *his* army, *his* men, *his* handiwork. 'Thank you, Louis-Antoine. Marcus Aurelius was quite right. At times like these it is difficult,' he said, 'to remember.'

The short and plump Bourrienne adjusted his spectacles and looked out as the 74-gun *Heureux* and *Mercure* processed slowly past, the crew waving, troops at attention in ranks, then offering the salute. 'However, they would be envious of this,' murmured Bourrienne to Bonaparte, 'even on Mount Olympus.'

Those going ashore filed down the gangway, the ladies and servants, and Joséphine went with them. Bonaparte remembered their first meeting, at the salon with Barras – Bach or Boccherini drifting across the late summer evening, her gloved hand in his. '*I think, m'sieur, you will truly conquer the world,*' and his reply, '*I must, to prevent it from conquering me.*'

She had remembered it too and, as they embraced at the gangway, breathed in his ear, 'Keep the world from conquering you, *mon cher.*'

'I shall,' he had promised, 'and will lay gods at your feet.'

She had looked back at him as she was escorted along the quay, his Joséphine, and his eye followed her until the last possible moment, not without some pain. It would be his longest day, this time spent so far from her, and he felt the pangs already. Her son Eugène stood at his side, a touchstone of memory for him, the boy waving his goodbyes, too excited with the coming adventure to register the parting or its consequences.

Derrien watched her go; beside him stood Colonel Junot. They exchanged glances, something about her known between the two of them, but neither admitting it, for the sake of discretion. 'We must endeavour to see he is not upset, Citizen, by this parting,' said Junot. 'Perhaps, we could arrange some sort of distraction.'

Derrien nodded slowly in mutual understanding. 'I had thought the women were banned, *Chef de brigade,*' said Derrien correctly. 'Distractions might be troublesome.'

'Indeed, Citizen,' said Junot. 'But so many have been smuggled aboard in uniform or as galley-wives it seems hardly worth the effort of enforcing the ban...'

'Something, then, would be possible.'

'Indeed,' said Junot, and ambled away, leaving it to Derrien.

It took eight hours for the great fleet to pass in salute. Bonaparte did not move from his post. After the rearguard sailed by,
contre-amiral Villeneuve bowing low on the quarterdeck of the
vast *Guillaume Tell*, Bonaparte stepped down gratefully from his
podium to applause from the gathered staff. He bowed, an actor
on his stage. Moments like these, he had long recognised, were
to be writ large, and he was determined that everyone lived up
to the occasion. He had fought off the initial onset of seasickness
for the sake of the procession – but he would resist his bed for
just a little longer.

'My dear admiral,' he announced to the patrician figure now
before him, with more than a nod to theatre. 'The task force,
the fate of my army, and that of France, is now in your hands.'

The elegant Admiral Brueys d'Aigalliers doffed his plumed
hat. 'My general,' he replied, 'it is my honour.'

There was further applause. Brueys turned to the younger
Captain Casabianca at the quarterdeck rail overlooking the great
crowded tweendecks stretching away before them, and relayed
the order: '*Prepare to make sail.*'

There was a cheer from the assembled troops and passengers.
The anchor chains rattled and ground against the capstans and
the headsails and vast mainsails dropped from their yards, the
dazzling canvas bright in the sky. Bonaparte felt the decks creak
and move beneath his feet. The heavily laden keel shuddered
against the shoals, heaving itself forward, driven onwards by the
urges of the north wind. Within moments, Bonaparte and his
invasion fleet were launched.

He stepped to the quarterdeck rail and looked down at his
men. They looked up at him in silent anticipation. Seized by
the moment, he snatched off his hat, thrusting it upwards at
arm's length. In reply came a rolling roar, *Vive la France! Vive
le général!* his legions cheering in response, clenched fists high,
and they began to sing the 'Marseillaise'.

No, Joséphine, he thought, *I will not be conquered this day… not
this day.*

In a far corner of the crowded quarterdeck, Jules-Yves Derrien watched all, a dark furnace raging with a secret pride. There was nothing, he decided, *nothing*, to touch them now. Not the winds, not the seas, not the English, not God Himself. *Nothing*.

Soon the *Orient* edged into the channel and out to sea, and became the largest vessel sailing on the face of the earth.

--

A mountainous swell heaved around *Esperanza* as the *tramontane* howled across the sea. Hazzard burst out of the aft hatchway to find two men grappling with the wheel, the hands hauling the starboard braces tighter on the port tack, their shouts snatched from their lips as the air was sucked away in a tidal vacuum. Hazzard gasped for breath in the plummeting pressure and half fell towards the binnacle, groping for a handhold, the compass spinning wild.

McGovern and Handley appeared next to him, each fighting for a purchase on the tilting deck as *Esperanza* lifted and crashed, spray bursting from windward. '*We've got to strike sail or we'll be took abeam and capsize!*' called McGovern. '*On the tack this wind will have 'er over, sir!*'

'*Can we not brace the gaffsail to hold her?*'

Handley shouted, '*Mr McGovern's right, sir – we haven't the draft or keel to hold her trim!*'

'*Very well!*' called Hazzard above the wind. '*Douse sail but keep her helm true to wind'ard to meet the swell head-on – we'll come about to nor'-nor'west on the starboard tack if we get the chance!*'

'*Aye, sir!*' McGovern went forward and called to the foremast hands, '*Douse yer sail! Let go yer braces, sheets and halyards, Mr Hopkins!*'

Regardless of their efforts the wind struck them with the violence of a broadside. *Esperanza* swung about, the foremast courser collapsing just in time before she was taken aback and shoved sternmost into the sea, the skies a blistering purple, the sea erupting into heaving cliffs of granite. The large gaff broke free and lashed like a monstrous tail, two men lifted from the deck by its braces and McGovern knocked down by a loose line.

'*Douse the mainsail!*' called Hazzard. '*Or she'll have us over! Let go your mainmast halyard!*'

The gaff topyard dropped, two men thrown against the mast as the sail collapsed, other hands diving on it to make it fast. Three others on the wheel, they lashed rope round the horns to hold the brig steady.

Hazzard fell against the midships rail, Wayland suddenly at his side, clinging to the shrouds for a hold. '*Sir! We're taking water below!*'

'*We must keep the sailing hands on deck! Marines to rotate by section working the pumps, Mr Wayland!*'

'*Aye, sir!*'

The bows rose and smashed into the towering waves, the bowsprit and yard snapped away like so much matchwood, the mist and spray blinding, loose lines snapping like whipcord, an unseen coach-driver flogging madly at the waves. In the foremast tops a seaman was calling, his arm waving to the starboard bow.

'*Sail ho!*'

Hazzard clambered to his feet and Handley gave him a telescope as they threw themselves at the rigging and climbed the flexing ratlines, the sea plunging at sickening angles as they ascended.

'*Man o'war, sir!*' cried the lookout and Handley put an arm out eastwards for Hazzard.

He raised the scope. The world had gone mad, waves breaking upon waves, spray spinning into whirlwinds, rampaging peaks of black iron rising and crashing beneath the dull glowing grey heavens. Hazzard tried to control the bouncing image in the lens.

There.

'*Three masts, she's riding low, sir!*'

In the grey pre-dawn light he could make out a 74-gun ship of the line, listing to port, rocking in the wind as badly as *Esperanza*.

'*Colours?*' called Hazzard.

Handley called, '*Could be the recce squadron, sir! But she's miles off course if she is…*'

As Hazzard watched he saw the yards squared away and mainsails reefed, the captain fighting to keep her bows to windward for fear of foundering – a swell so large could smash into the stern galleries and flood all decks, dragging her down. The signal flags flapped against the dark grey sky but he could not read them, until at last the stern taffrail and galleries came round and there was the red ensign. It was the *Alexander*, from Nelson's squadron.

'*She's one of ours!*' cried Handley. '*It's the* Alex*!*'

'*Range?*'

'*I'd give her more'n a mile, sir! P'raps two an'alf thousand yards!*'

'*Any other sail?*'

The *Esperanza* dropped suddenly into nothing and Hazzard felt weightless, his legs lifting, floating, his chest dropping, and he grasped at the rail before him, until the brig crashed onto the surface of the sea as if it were stone. He fell to his knees and cracked his head, sliding round, his feet through the struts, hanging out into space.

'*Sir!*'

Handley and the lookout pulled him back in and he clung to the rail, the scope swinging round his neck on its lanyard. He could see nothing but red – a gash on his brow had formed a curtain of blood over his left eye. '*Get down to the wheel and hold our course for the* Alexander*, Handley!*'

Before he did, the lookout beside them called out – it was another ship. '*Sail ho! Second man o'war!*'

It was another 74, bucking like an unbroken horse, its tops torn away, the rigging flying. Whipped by sudden lashing rain,

Hazzard held the scope to his right eye. He saw the stern as it swung round and read the painted name: *Vanguard*.

Nelson.

'*There she is! Flagship ho!*'

Esperanza sheared back to starboard, an undersea demon taking her keel in hand, throwing her across the waves. '*We're being blown suth'ard, sir,*' shouted Handley from inches away. '*We'll be thrown on the rocks o'bloody Corsica at this rate!*'

Hazzard watched through the glass as lines were cast from the *Alexander* to *Vanguard*, angry signals rippling up *Vanguard*'s mast. Handley struggled to read them, '*Cap'n Ball, sir! He's trying to tow the Vanguard!*'

'*We've got to reach Nelson, Handley! Or we're on our own!*'

'*We have to stay bows to wind'ard or we'll be turned and took a-beam! She's built like a schooner above but she hasn't the keel below! She'll go over if she has to!*'

Wiping the blood from his brow Hazzard swung the glass back and looked. The two ships of the line were now mere dots, the giant swell pulling *Esperanza* further away. With doused sail they had only the rudder to keep the helm true, and if *Esperanza* was turned, she could either capsize or be swamped by a wave and pulled under in minutes.

'*Set the gaff mains'l and foremast courser to maintain our position on the starboard tack, Handley! We've got to try!*'

Handley pulled him in close, his voice low. '*We'll never catch their sail, sir. And if we don't turn fast enough a foremast courser will take us aback and push us under arse-first. They're as good as gone, sir. That's as is.*'

Hazzard lowered his streaming face, the spray whipping at him, the heave and pitch of the ship exhausting, throwing him up, throwing him down. There was not a star in the sky, nothing for Handley to fix upon, nothing but the crashing waves all around them – they were off-course and running wild. Of the *Orion* or the rest of the squadron there was no sign, and four hundred enemy sail out there, somewhere, ready to attack.

Below, on deck, the marines hauled on lines with the crew, Cook bellowing over the wind, a purple-grey whirlpool above become glowing fiery cloud, sky become sea. Hazzard watched as *Vanguard* and *Alexander* disappeared, the miles between them stretching out by the moment.

Nelson, gone.

Handley and Hazzard picked their way down the rigging to the deck, the wind tearing at their limbs, the rise and fall of the waves easing, then smashing them again. Every man was thrown across the decks, only their lifelines saving them from being swept overboard. Cook struggled to the wheelhouse and hung on beside him.

'*Two Section under Mr Wayland working the pumps, sir,*' he gasped, water sheeting off his soaking back. '*Regret Capt. Markham very sick, sir. Must be something he ate, says Porter.*'

Hazzard barely heard him. Nelson was no longer in danger at Cap Sicié. He thought of the *tramontane*, and realised with a lurch that Bonaparte's fleet, now doubtless hurtling southwards, would be running with the wind.

'*Jory – the French. The fleet would have set sail!*'

'*What?*'

'*They could be on us any moment.*'

With his thoughts came the proof of them.

'*Sail off the starboard bow!*'

Hazzard pitched into the wheelhouse wall as the deck suddenly heaved to port, as if to bear away from this new threat. Handley, Cook and Hazzard fought their way forward to McGovern at the starboard rail. Hazzard saw a light frigate ploughing through grey crags of towering waves, coming straight at them, her mainsails billowing, her bows submerging with every toss of the sea as the cyclone shoved her from astern, flying high behind her the French tricolour bright in the unearthly light.

'*Second enemy sail ho!*'

Esperanza lifted and fell and Hazzard nearly flew from the deck, Cook and Handley hanging by the stays, each grabbing and holding him fast. The second frigate was running astern the first.

'*Corvettes, sir,*' called McGovern. '*Or armed pinques! Twelve guns apiece, six 18s or 12s a-side! Clear for action, sir? Got to ditch them jolly-boats o'yourn, sir, no mistake!*'

Hazzard took them for fleet scouts. There was now no doubt: Bonaparte had set sail. He assessed the *Esperanza*. She had lost her bowsprit and yard, but the standing rigging was otherwise intact, the running rigging under control. The brig was still afloat, the decks cluttered with equipment and the three upturned boats still lashed amidships, their deadly explosive cargo watertight within, the covered guns unmanned. They could shove everything overboard to clear for action, but they had only minutes to do so. If they lost the attack boats, they lost everything. He then remembered they were running without colours on a Spanish brig. If they cleared for action the corvettes would take them at once for an enemy.

He turned to Cook, '*Jory! Get the Spanish gear up here, at the double! We'll bluff them out!*'

'*Bloody have to, sir,*' Cook moved across the rolling deck to the midships hatch.

The leading corvette charged, her tops reefed, her mainsail puffing like a bellows in the gale. A flash, bright in the purple sky, burst from her starboard bow-chaser and a plume of spray flew upwards, fifty yards shy of *Esperanza*'s prow, demanding she heave-to.

Hazzard called, '*Mr Handley! Mr McGovern! We must not clear for action! Hoist that Spanish ensign, and look as if we're in distress! He's got to think we're allies and come in close so we can use the smashers! Man the guns but keep them covered! Set some hands to stand by on the gaff mains'l and set the foremast hands to stand by ready to drop the foremast courser on my command – clear?*'

McGovern looked uncertainly to Handley but Handley liked it. '*Aye-aye!*'

Cook, Underhill and a squad of marines emerged from the midships hatchway with Wayland, all clad in their plain or checked shirts, smocks, blue coats or cloaks.

'*One and Three Section, rammed and locked, sir!*' called Cook, and handed Hazzard and Wayland a cloak and hat each.

Hazzard pulled a grey cloak over his Marine scarlet. '*I want us to confuse that damned corvette as much as we can! So we're their Spanish allies from here on, clear?*'

Underhill smiled. '*Bring him in and blast him, sir?*'

'*Aye, smashers at the ready! Mr Wayland! Gunlocks to the mounts and set the marines behind the rails ready to fire buck and ball!*'

Underhill smiled. '*That's good India, sir!*'

'*It's all we've got, Sar'nt!*' Hazzard had taken no chances: the four carronades had already been double-shotted, the first with grape, the second with chain and langrage scrap, the third with canister-shot of packed musket rounds, and the fourth with a 32-pound ball. Powerful as they were, they were short-barrelled and effective only at close range – Hazzard's plan would lure the corvette into a killing ground. The marines loosened the oiled canvas covers on the guns, ready to tear them off at the command, and crouched behind each, hanging on tightly to each other as the brig rose and crashed down.

'*Mr Wayland! I shall command the guns but you shall command the musketry!*'

Wayland nodded. He was shaking.

'*Mr Wayland! Do you understand!*'

'*Yes, sir! I mean, aye, sir!*' he cried, but did not move from the shelter of the hatchway.

'*Mr Wayland! No one could have prepared them better. Keep them under cover until the very last moment – then cry "Havoc!"*'

Wayland's eyes lit up at the expression. '*Yes. Yes, sir, cry havoc it is, sir!*'

Hazzard ran forward up the pitching deck and took hold of the forestays as Wayland made for the stern. High atop the mainmast he saw the pale banner of His Catholic Majesty of

Spain flutter overhead. Cook roared out, one arm up. '*Guns ready, sir!*'

The bow plunged, the spray blasting Hazzard from head to foot but he hung on, visible to them all. He called to the crew, '*Stand fast the marines! Stand fast the* Esperanza! *And wait for the command!*'

The Frenchman's spritsail was flying loose, torn from its mount at the bow, fouling on the stays and driving the prow from side to side like an animal shaking its prey. The ship reared again but held her fire. The Spanish colours had worked.

'*She's run 'em out, sir!*' It was Handley, beside Kite, crouched with Warnock and Cook behind the first carronade, the pair clutching their weapons, waiting.

'*Hail them, lads!*' called Hazzard. '*Wave for help!*'

The deckhands called and whistled, waving their arms, fellow mariners in distress, allies reaching out, and the corvette surged in towards them, lookouts pointing, drawing closer to starboard.

The brig heaved up the crest of a wave and crashed down again. When she righted herself the corvette had closed the distance. Hazzard could see the French crew, their sodden coats, their knitted caps, their bare feet. He put a hand to the Talwar at his hip, ready to give the order.

But climbing unsteadily from the midships hatchway came Lt Markham, in full uniform, with sword–belt and cocked hat – in his hands the red ensign of the Mediterranean Fleet.

'*En'my in sight…*' he cried drunkenly, falling, his hat whisked off by the wind. '*Run up… th' colours… Mis-Mister G'eaves…*'

Hazzard jumped down to the deck. '*Handley! Get that bloody fool below!*'

Markham tried to draw his sword but it fouled on his sash belt and he tugged at it, stumbling. '*F'rward the f-fleet!*' He saw Hazzard and waved the sword at him. '*Y'sh-shall call me Capt'n but once, sir!*' he screeched. '*R'n up the c'lours!*'

Esperanza lurched and threw Markham to her decks, Warnock and Kite diving on him, trying to hold him, but the deck rolled and Warnock fell. '*Mickey! Get him!*' Markham pushed himself up, Kite grappling with him, then collapsed to his knees and vomited, dropping his sword – and the ensign. The wind snatched it from Markham's feeble grip and flung it high into the rigging. The colours cracked open, snapping blood-red in the gale.

Markham scrabbled for his lost sword to meet his foe but the damage had been done. The French captain opened fire with the first three of his starboard guns.

Two 18-pounder balls of round-shot went wide but the third tore away the starboard rail and part of the stays at the bow, throwing Hazzard against the jolly-boats lashed to the deck. He got to his feet, threw off the Spanish cloak to reveal his scarlet and drew the Talwar. The corvette, he decided, was close enough.

'*Starboard guns, stand by!*'

McGovern, Cook and Handley bawling across the decks, the gunners tore the covers off the carronades. Hazzard could hear the cries of the French over the wind, *Anglais, anglais!* but it came too late. The corvette reared alongside, not twenty yards off, shuddering with the impact of the sea, rising still higher upon heaving mountainous waves, presenting her profile to Hazzard, a tableau frozen in the moment: the captain, one boot on the rail, clinging to the stays with sword in hand, a shining order and cockade pinned to his blue tunic, his mouth formed in a shout to his enemy.

'*Qui-êtes-vous-anglais?*'

Who are you, Englishman?

Hazzard swung the Talwar. '*Fire!*'

One after the other, the carronades blazed from the *Esperanza*, shredding the corvette's sails and blasting her crowded gundecks into clouds of splintering wood and iron. The foremast disintegrated and the French captain disappeared. Wayland screamed out, '*Nine Company! Staggered firing pattern first and second ranks! Rapid fire! Fire!*'

The marines blanketed the rigging with rattling shot and crewmen fell to the flying decks and into the sea. Markham ran towards Wayland, waving his sword, calling, but neither Wayland nor Hazzard heard him as the three remaining guns of the corvette fired their passing broadside in response.

The first round-shot smashed through the deck and ploughed up the planks into a knot of sailors at the base of the foremast, one of the carronades rising, tipping and crashing onto its side. The second ball struck the starboard rail amidships and gunners and marines flew backwards with the impact amid flying slivers of wood. The third ball smashed through the covered boat lashed to the starboard stern quarter, and took Markham's right shoulder and arm with it, sweeping what was left of him screaming into the boiling sea.

Hazzard found himself face down on the deck, pushing himself upwards, heat on his forehead, a new gash, jagged splinters in his arms and side. Greaves helped him up, a seaman lying across him in a heap of timber, *The jolly-boats*, he thought, *exploded*. Napier with a man hanging from each arm, then Warnock and Kite, a cascade of seawater knocking him down – and Hazzard called out to Handley, '*Hoist the mains'l gaff and brace to starboard! Drop your foremast courser!*'

The mainmast gaff boom flew up the mast and the sail swung wide to starboard, McGovern himself hauling on the braces. '*Pull, ye buggers, or we're done!*'

Moments later the foretopmen dropped the foremast mainsail from its yard and the world jarred to a sudden halt.

The *Esperanza* tipped upwards, taken aback, then the gaff caught the wind and spun her sharply to starboard. Hazzard and Greaves were thrown sideways to the rail, Greaves half over the edge, Hazzard hanging onto the boy, two men falling on them, pulling them back in. The *Esperanza* now lay broadside-on between the two corvettes, her starboard guns facing the stern of the first, and her portside guns staring down the jaws of the second.

Wayland saw Hazzard at the rail, looked out at the corvettes and understood immediately. He shouted down the line, '*Double broadside rake, port and starboard guns – fire!*'

The carronades boomed out both sides of the brig. The bows of the following corvette burst into a storm of shrapnel and splinters. But the stern of the first vanished in a cloud of shot, iron rounds blasting through it from end to end, men flying overboard, its shattered remains collapsing before their eyes, the waves tossing her broken corpse to pieces. The *Esperanza* hands cheered in savage satisfaction. The waves then hit them and the wind caught the dropped courser, and *Esperanza* rolled to starboard, presenting her exposed port side to the second French corvette. They had come about nearly full circle.

'*Douse the foremast courser!*' It was Greaves, shouting beside Hazzard, blood in his mouth, his hand tightening on Hazzard's, fear in his eyes. '*Let go your foremast halyards!*'

'*Well done, Mr Greaves! Ready the guns!*'

Wayland was calling the reload, the second corvette closing, her six 18-pounders ready to deliver the death-blow. Hazzard watched, powerless, as the end came.

Though mauled by the raking attack, the muzzle-flashes of the French cannons rippled down the broadside of the corvette as she slewed to leeward and battered *Esperanza* in a perfect passing attack.

Regards to Sarah. Regards to Bartelmi.

Esperanza heeled over and the round-shot smashed through her exposed hull, the air filled with flying debris, splinters and screams from below, and Hazzard flung himself over Greaves. '*Get down!*'

Cook was blown back to the foremast and Handley landed across one of his legs. Hazzard tried to call out, but had no voice, no strength. The three assault boats had been destroyed, the stern and starboard rails nearly blown away, and she was listing, skidding on the waves, Hazzard lying among the remains, water sheeting across the decks.

Blake's reports. Admiralty orders. Gone. To the bottom.

Hands began dragging him out, calls from all sides, *'She's going down!'* He got to one knee as the corvette moved off, driven by the gale.

'Mr Greaves! Mr Wayland!'

Hazzard's head was ringing, the howl of the wind and the blasts rendered to the muffled tolling of a bell. He heard the cries of men trapped, some crawling out, Wayland loping forward, looking for him. Wayland fell, then righted himself, his face dark on the one side, his hand outstretched.

'Sir…'

Hazzard collapsed, a sailing hand lifting him by the arm, then pointed to starboard, his mouth forming words to Hazzard but making no sound, *Man o'war.*

A warship charged past but did not open fire. It was not the corvette, but bigger, a frigate, a new arrival. Hazzard waited for the *coup de grâce.*

The orange flicker of her bow guns flashed bright in the storm – the shots burst all around the fleeing Frenchman, peppering the corvette's stern. The frigate rose high on a wave, showing bright copper hull-plates flaring in the gloom and Hazzard knew at once she was not British. The corvette returned fire but was blasted again, her mizzen mainsail shot to ribbons as she ran south with the wind.

From somewhere came Handley's voice, *'Abandon ship!'*

It brought him round, the world suddenly at full volume. *'Mr Wayland! Marines to me!'*

All around him, the dead, pushed and pulled by the roll of the brig as the water slapped at their stiffening limbs, Markham's bid for glory lying tangled in broken timbers, the red ensign now a torn rag amid splintered wood. Cook shook him to his knees, lifting him up. He had fallen again.

'Sar'nt…'

Faces behind him: *Pet, Lil, Hesse, Rivelli… others, good.*

Someone said it, *'Never give up the boat, sir.'*

And he heard himself shout, head down, '*We* are the boat...
We are the—'

The wind dying, the sea cluttered with floating men, burning wood, the flames now a scattering ring of ghostly campfires on the surface of a rolling sea. The storm had died, its work done.

So it ends.

A broad wall of wood and iron glided slowly into his vision, its great mass blotting out all else. Hazzard stared, barely registering it.

Frigate.

Tall, with two gundecks, 18s and 24-pounders, their gaping mouths still smoking, still sending their odour out to him. The storm had been sucked into nowhere, the silence roaring in his head. He could see lanterns glowing, hands waving from above, voices calling down.

Ropes dropped from the rails, their heavy knotted ends splashing into the water, and voices hailed them. Hazzard called out then fell, and Kite helped him up. Hazzard shook his head, *must do better than this.* 'Come along, Kite.'

'Think we're rescued, sir...'

'Jolly good.'

Cook beside him, Handley, Wayland – *where was Greaves? Oh yes.* The boy lay nearby, unmoving, his only command action to douse the courser and save what was left of the ship. Hazzard thought of Markham sinking in terror. 'Bring Mr Greaves... we must... bring Mr Greaves...' and he clutched at one of the stays and looked up as men climbed down, offering their hands.

'*Per aquí! Sí, sí, aquí, aquí! Dóna'm la mà!*'

Spanish. They had been saved by their enemy, and would all soon be captives.

'Are we done, sir?' asked Wayland in a dead voice, suddenly close to his ear. Hazzard could not blame him, torn and bloodied, left hand hanging limp, propped up by Porter instead of an Admiralty desk.

'Porter... get him aboard and carry on...'

'As ye'say, sir.'

They were pulled aboard and a line flashed in front of Hazzard's face, a different voice from above, '*Señor, aquí!*'

But Hazzard turned back to the wreckage, waist-deep, wading, calling, '*Lambert! Anyone! Esperanza hands... to me!*' Sinking, swimming, he went down the hatchway ladder, calling, endlessly calling, '*All hands... come to my voice – this way...*' the black water rising, trapping the dead.

He submerged, swimming beneath the bodies, the clouding grey water stinging his eyes as he bumped into them and tugged at their limbs to see if they would respond until he could take no more of the darkness, the light of lanterns from above turned a dull luminescent green. A staring face, eyes wide, mouth open – *Farmer? Fielding? Anderssen?* – and a hand took his coat from behind, pulling him back.

Hatch ladder. He hit it with his shoulder and grabbed at it, *handrail*, crooked treads in his hands, slipping, fighting a rising panic, *drowning, always been afraid of drowning*, until he was pulled out by Cook, his grey, scarred face grim.

'They're gone, sir.'

'But Greaves was—'

'Gone, sir.'

Cook and Handley dragged him to the Spanish nets but Hazzard shoved them forward, kegs and crates floating with the dead all round. He retched for air, coughing up water. He had one final look, then took the last line, a loop, a large noose, some part of his mind remembering to put it over his shoulders, under his arms, *pain, splinters*, and he was lifted bodily. For a moment he hung there, a hanged man, free, weightless, rising slowly past a gun port, his legs trying to walk the broadside, failing.

Hands pulled him over the rail and laid him on the deck, his constricted throat dragging in the air and choking, then breathing, his chest aching. He rolled over and heaved up the last of the sea in his lungs, the deck cold against his forehead. He kept his eyes shut then breathed again, the panic ebbing.

No, Mr Wayland, I am not done. Not till I am dead.

In the light of a lantern the Spaniards saw Hazzard's scarlet coat, its braided collar facings, the empty Talwar scabbard, and backed away, calling out. A sword scraped from its sheath and muskets were cocked. Hazzard heard only a hushed silence, so welcome after the gale and the guns. He lay gratefully still, breathing.

A pair of boots clumped slowly towards them along the deck, the unhurried pace of authority. Hazzard heard a scuffle and an impact, the butt of a musket, someone falling to the deck, one of the marines – *Cook? Warnock?* – another muttering a curse and the man in the boots snapped in Spanish to his crew, '*Ya basta!*' *Enough*. Hazzard turned his head stiffly to one side, opened his burning eyes, and looked up.

A man some years his senior, with long, straight dark hair pulled back in a tail, wearing a pale cutaway gentleman's coat, dark waistcoat and tall dark maroon boots, a jewelled Toledo blade at his side, looked down upon him. He smoked a slender cigarillo. He squatted beside Hazzard, examining him mournfully from head to toe, shaking his head.

'You seek for the living among the dead,' he murmured in Spanish, 'even as your ship sinks beneath your feet. And you refuse the hand of help, until you are the last. If I knew nothing more of you, this would tell me enough.'

It was high Castilian, spoken in a quiet, reflective tone. To the assembled English it might have sounded like a prayer. He gave a command, '*Elena,*' and a blanket was brought and laid over Hazzard's back. Hazzard felt a woman's presence hovering behind him, a caring softness. A gentle hand was put to his neck, so alien, it enveloped him in warmth.

'You sail the Spanish ship,' the man continued in thickly accented English, 'but you, *señor—*' his fingers touched the soaking fabric of Hazzard's sleeve '—you wear the British coat of blood.'

Very slowly, Hazzard pushed himself up onto one elbow, all he could manage. '*Me llamo...*' he began, then coughed. '*Me llamo el Mayor... Guillermo Juan Hazzard, infantería de Marina de su majestad britanica...*' he said, his breath coming in slow gasps. '*Un gran placer... a conocerle a Ustéd...*' *A great pleasure, to make your honoured acquaintance.*

The musket barrels dropped, the crew looking to their captain in confusion upon hearing the Spanish. In response, the Spaniard rose and looked down at him, then performed a short, formal bow.

'*Para mí también.* And I,' he replied in English, to repay the compliment, 'am Don Cesár Domingo de la Vega, *capitán* of the *Volpone.*' He looked about at the survivors. 'And you, *señores*, are my most honoured prisoners.'

Revenge

Hazzard was carried into De la Vega's cabin between two men and propped in a dining chair at a dark, carved table. Most of the large splinters had been removed from his right arm and upper back but every movement was painful. One of the Spaniards held a flagon of water to his lips and he gulped in deep draughts.

Tapestries hung from folding bulkheads and silver glowed on every surface – from the tops of crystal decanters to small chased gilt boxes marked with noble coats of arms. Jewelled rapiers and smallswords hung on racks beside displays of pistols. A cot was slung between the ceiling beams supporting the poop deck above, swathes of silk hanging either side. It was more an exotic baronial home than a fighting ship.

The deckhands tried to remove his red coat, but there were still several splinters preventing it, and they stopped trying. He collapsed forward, holding onto the table for support, and gasped, '*Cómo están mis hombres…?*' How are my men? But they had no answer for him.

The door opened and a woman entered, dressed all in black, her headdress wrapped from crown to chin like an Arab, revealing only a pale, closed face. She was followed by Elena, the girl from the deck, carrying a bowl of water, cloths draped over one arm. Elena was dark-skinned with jet-black curls, a large burn scarring one side of her face, her eyes cast down, from Hazzard perhaps, or from everyone.

She set her bowl down on the table and uttered a few words to the woman in black. The woman said nothing, her eyes not leaving Hazzard's. They set to work, removing the remaining splinters from his arm and shoulders, and pulling off his red coat, blood springing from fresh tears and punctures. The woman in black drew a small dagger and took rough hold of his hand and began to slice open the bloody shirtsleeve.

Hazzard sagged with the pain as they pricked at the skin with sailcloth needles, plucking out deeper shards of wood, sweat trickling from his scalp. He grimaced, bringing a smile to her pale lips. 'Ha,' she mocked, '*El hombre grande...*'

De la Vega entered. He dismissed the two watching crewmen in a Spanish dialect Hazzard could not follow, then sat heavily at the other end of the table, swinging his feet up and banging his boots on the polished surface. He lit a cigarillo with a taper from a lamp, blowing out a lungful of smoke, and regarded Hazzard quietly.

'Christina,' he said at last in English, 'and Elena, the little one. They have the blessing of *la Santa Maria*, for the *curación*, the healing. You say this? Healing? In Zaragoza they are holy,' he said, 'or put to death, by those who are more holy.'

Hazzard watched them. Elena's eyes flicked up to his.

'My crew...' he said.

De la Vega nodded, a grand wave out to the tweendecks of the ship beyond. 'Eating, taking water. The two witches have seen them already.' He nodded at him in salute. 'My compliments. You have the wounds, but ask after your men.'

Hazzard nodded back formally. It seemed to be the way. He had forgotten the formality of Spain. 'I thank you. Can you send my sergeant? I need a roll-call. Count our dead.'

'You now have twenty *marineros* and eight *soldados*,' said De la Vega, ready with the answer. 'And we find thirty-one dead, left by the sea, *señor*, and more French. We bring them up still. You are,' he said, 'the deadly adversary.'

Half the marines were gone, over half the prize crew also dead. Hazzard felt crushed. He ran the events of the night yet again in his mind, each time wondering what he could have done differently. But for Markham, it might well have worked.

De la Vega sighed and shook his head, leaning forward, suddenly in earnest. '*Madre de Dios*. What do you seek to do, hm? Turn over your ship to sink the two Frenchmen? Attack both *al mismo tiempo*, the same time? *Madre*. Ask Alfonso. I say to him, here, I say, is a true *Capitán: loco, agresivo, furioso*.' He blew out another cloud, and rubbed his eyes, tired, angry. 'It is the bad trick of Fate, *duro* – *no, malo*, that you are an *inglés*. For we could do well, you and I, hm?' His humourless nurse drew back, one hand covering an eye with her fingers, warding off some evil spirit. De la Vega pulled a face at her and she returned to her work with a secret smile.

A stream of inconsistencies pricked at Hazzard. Not a man among De la Vega's crew or his officers wore uniform or insignia of any kind, and the women were armed. The black-clad Christina carried a small pistol on a belt, and God alone knew how many daggers.

'You are a privateer,' said Hazzard in realisation.

'*Cómo?*' De la Vega nodded. 'Ah… *sí*. Pray-va-teer. Hm. With, how you say, the letters of marque, from my King Carlos.'

'A king allied to France.'

De la Vega shook his head. 'The king, he may be the friend of France. But I, Cesár Domingo, cannot say the same. And now, ahh, I am Cortés, I think.'

Christina began to murmur and mumble to herself as she gripped Hazzard's left arm tightly. Elena began to wrap the wounds with strips of clean linen. Immediately he felt better. He looked at her and thought of Sarah, the two so very different. '*Muchisimas gracias, señorita*,' he said, but got nothing in reply.

'I take the grain, the rice, the pepper,' said De la Vega, watching them. 'Or guns, or opium. I take from the Sardinian, Greek, Turk, and French – and *sí, los Españoles*, the Spanish, yes. When I must. But not from my brothers, *mis hermanos de Barcelona, los Catalanes*.'

It was a mark of pride, thought Hazzard. Barcelona would then have been his home: Catalonia, the foreign language he had spoken, Catalan.

'And what of the French?'

De la Vega examined his cigarillo. 'That *bastardo* French frigate, *Pierre*, he takes two of my prizes. The captain says they go for their great fleet, for this general – this *Buonaparte*.' His anger was obvious but contained, as though experience had taught him to expect such iniquity. 'But when I see *L'Esperanza de Cádiz* being bombarded by two *corvettas Francesas*, I bring down fire upon them, with gladness.'

He made a cutting gesture with his hand. It had been a final decision, irrevocable. He smoked again, and relaxed. 'So. Now the *Franceses*, they hunt for Cesár Domingo. *Hijos de puta*,' he cursed. 'And I become Cortés, who has burned his boat.'

De la Vega had saved their lives, and put his own in jeopardy as a consequence. Even though it was through De la Vega's own desire for revenge, Hazzard felt responsible for the mistaken identity – and try as he might, he did not sense De la Vega was his enemy.

'Forgive me,' said Hazzard. 'My apologies. *Lo siento.*'

De la Vega did not understand at first, then waved a hand at him. 'Ah, no no. No no no. Not between *caballeros*. For you, I am certain, would have done the same for me.'

They sat in some silence, considering their positions.

At last, De la Vega asked wearily, '*Madre, hermano.* Will you truly fight this *Señor Buonaparte* alone? Or his great secret fleet, with your little hands-full of soldiers?'

Hazzard looked back at him. He had no idea what to tell him. Or indeed what he could. He felt a fool. And De la Vega had his answer. The Spaniard cursed again, throwing up his hands, exasperated by a younger brother. '*Dios mío.* It is true! You are the *mad* one. *Loco inglés.* They say this fleet it is more than three hundred ships, some say *four hundred*. This is the battle I would never choose, *amigo*, for I love life above death.'

Elena and Christina lifted Hazzard's shirt to wrap a corset of bandages around his ribs, but when they saw the scars they stopped and pulled back quickly. De la Vega saw their reaction. He rose from his chair and looked at Hazzard's back. Hazzard let him.

'*Madre de Dios*... what *are* you, my friend? *Who are you?*'

When Hazzard said nothing, De la Vega busied himself with another cigarillo, then threw it down. He leaned on the table then looked at him. '*Franceses?* The French do this to you?'

Hazzard shook his head. 'No one you would know.'

Swallowing her fear, Elena applied the bandages, Christina holding herself away, more apprehensive, as if Hazzard were afflicted by devils. As they worked, he felt stronger and steadier with each breath.

'I cannot stop trying.'

'*Ya basta, sí?* Enough now. The *armada*, she has gone. So you have no battle. Your duty to your mad King George is full, *completo, terminado.*'

Hazzard looked up quickly and Elena noticed, stopping her work. 'Gone?'

'Sailed these three days past. The *ingleses* sail around, *Nelsón, sí*? Looking, looking... oh *sí*, milord, oh *no*, milord.' He mimed Nelson, searching hopeless far horizons. 'Like you, he finds *nada* but the great storm. I have the ears too, my friend, and they work better than the eyes of *El Nelsón.*'

Elena dabbed at Hazzard's head wound and he held her hand a moment to stop her, for a last question. 'Where was it headed?'

Elena did not pull away, and he could feel her staring into him. The older Christina watched, then made the sign of the cross.

De la Vega lost his patience. 'Genova, Ajaccio, *todas partes*, everywhere, like they lose the north, *lost* – like you, *inglés*, who fights the winds.' Christina and Elena gathered their things together. De la Vega watched them, his storm blown out. Frustrated, he sat back and banged his boots back up onto the table. He smoked and calmed himself.

'Christina is *loca, sí*? But Elena,' he said, 'she likes you.'

Hazzard looked at her. She stared back, not afraid of the evil eye. 'Did the English harm her? The French?'

De la Vega shrugged. 'She understands little of such things. But, to answer, no. It was not the matter for nations, only men, and their wrongs, Spaniards and Catalans. They did this, peasants from Zaragoza.' He frowned. 'You say this? Wrongs?'

'Yes.'

When he was not looking, Elena continued to stare at Hazzard. Then both she and Christina bowed and left, Hazzard watching her go.

'*Hazard*,' pronounced De la Vega, without the Castilian lisp. 'A good Spanish name. From the Arabic, you know? I learn such things, with my sailing, and Cervantes and windmills. But here, at sea, there are no windmills, *amigo, sí*? And you are not Don Quixote.' De la Vega noticed the pendant round his neck. He sat back again and drew on the cigarillo, calming. 'An *inglés* with a saint.' He asked, 'You are *católico*?'

'No. It is St Jude,' said Hazzard, feeling as lost as Don Quixote. 'Cervantes would have liked him.' *Lost causes indeed.*

De la Vega sat up, tired of diplomacy. 'Why truly are you here, *amigo*?' His dark eyes bored into Hazzard's, not letting him escape. 'You fight like a *torero*. Two enemies at once, one not enough. But you did not come for the *armada* with just this little Spanish boat. Truly, you did not, hm?'

Hazzard gazed at nothing, the lamplight warm, comforting. His failure in battle, his wounds, his fatigue, had stripped him of any reticence he might formerly have had. There was in De la Vega a quality that fostered a complete ingenuous trust. Perhaps, thought Hazzard, that was De la Vega's gift.

Before he had gone on deck in the storm, he had thrust the charts and intelligence reports into a weighted despatch bag, and left them to sink in the *Esperanza*. But he had saved one item, along with his identity papers. He reached into the buttoned inside pocket of his red Bombay coat lying on the table beside him. Seawater had seeped into its glass and stained the white background, but it was still beautiful. It was the oval miniature silhouette of Sarah.

He looked at it in silence a moment, then held it out to De la Vega, and heard himself speaking to the Spaniard with more honesty than he would ever normally have allowed to Cook or, indeed, to himself. De la Vega took it with suitable reverence.

'I have come for a lady,' said Hazzard quietly. He felt ashamed. It seemed too selfish a reason to have lost a ship and the men entrusted to his care. This perceived fraud fuelled his bitterness all the more. 'She would be my wife, if she but lives,' he said. 'She was kidnapped by the French, by a murderer. And I am to blame.'

De la Vega watched him. 'So. *La verdad*. The truth.'

Despite his burden of guilt, Hazzard realised he was determined to go on. 'My orders are to find the French fleet, to find a missing spy. But first I will find the man who took her. And destroy the fleet if it stands in my path. But I *will* find her.'

De la Vega seemed less interested in the strategic goals of His Majesty's Navy than he was in the personal, the real. 'So you fight for no king, but for your lady.' De la Vega peered at him through the smoke of his cigarillo, fascinated. 'You would burn these four hundred ships, and *fifty* thousands of men? To save her?'

With the light-headed clarity of confession, Hazzard had no doubt.

'Yes.'

Derrien. Dead.

De la Vega nodded slowly. He handed back the miniature of Sarah with care. 'Then, my friend, I, Cesár Domingo, will be honoured to help you.'

He stood and moved to a cabinet. He opened a decanter.

'No,' said Hazzard, 'I have put you in enough danger. There are also English ships out there now. Lend us a boat and we'll go to the first port we find.'

De la Vega almost laughed. '*Loco inglés.* Let me ask you, *señor*, this *Buonaparte*…' he said, pouring two glasses. 'He makes the treaty, *un acuerdo*, at Venezia, hm? But then he takes Venezia. There is treaty with Roma, and they take Roma, and make the prisoner of *el Papa*? The Holy Father?'

'Yes,' said Hazzard. 'They did.'

'This *Buonaparte*, he has, *cómo se dice, ha roto su palabra*…'

'Broken his word, his parole.'

'*Sí*. Broken his, ehh, *parole*. Good French word.' He joined Hazzard at the table and pulled a chair next to him. 'There is also the treaty with my king. So, one day, will he not break this word with Spain, and come to Burgos? To Barcelona? Or Valencia?'

Hazzard knew what De la Vega was trying to argue. But Hazzard could not deny him. He was right. 'Yes. He could.'

'So,' continued De la Vega, 'it is my *duty* to help you. Where do we two *republicanos* go, *amigo*, in this world of kings? Toulon, with "the guns ablaze" but no *armada*? Or with fire, like *El Draco* at Cádiz? We burn the four hundred ships and I find my prizes, hm?'

The light of morning broke through the stern gallery windows behind them, lighting the cabin in rose and orange.

Last seen boarding coach with comtesse de Biasi after dining with Sir William Hamilton…

'No. We should go to Naples.'

De la Vega sat back, content. 'Ah, *Napoli*. Better than Toulon,' he said. 'No fireships necessary. Come. It is a new day, *amigo*.' He pushed a glass towards Hazzard and raised his own. 'And now we are Cortés together.'

–

Sir Thomas Troubridge, Captain of the 74-gun HMS *Culloden*, was roused by a flickering candle suddenly bright in the darkness of his quarters. He sat up in his cot. It was Tyndall, his wardroom valet.

'Sir, got a signal from the *Mutine*. Cap'n Hardy's headin' back out, sir.'

He handed him the note and Troubridge squinted at the rushed hand. *Advised enemy fleet put to sea. No sign Vanguard after NW gale, am proceeding last target.*

'Is she still with us?'

'Yes, sir – squadron runner's also here, having himself a nice tot – well,' he added dubiously, 'that Porto plonk, the '91, if y'don't mind, sir…'

Troubridge threw off his blanket and climbed out, reaching for his coat. 'The damn year doesn't matter, Tyndall, for heaven's sake…' He dressed and Tyndall lit the way to the wardroom.

The Second Lieutenant and the duty despatch runner of the squadron, a midshipman, rose from their chairs and bowed.

'Good morning, sir.'

'I trust it will be.' Troubridge moved to the sideboard and poured himself a brandy and water and knocked it back for a quick sting. 'Very well. Reply to the *Mutine*: *Reinforcement squadron will await you at rendezvous to combine.* Copy to Signals. Nelson will want the entire squadron, not dribs and drabs haring off in different directions. Off you go. Captain Darby of the *Ruffian* may burst his spleen but we shall be waiting and praying rather than charging and hallooing.'

'Yes, sir,' said the boy. After a brief hesitation he asked, 'If the French fleet heads southwest, for Gibraltar, sir, and we have gone north to the rendezvous, could they not overwhelm his lordship at Gib and make for England?'

It was just the thing Troubridge had feared since they had departed Cadiz. 'Perhaps. But as we know, his lordship will place himself in their path more squarely than the white cliffs of Dover.'

The lieutenant was not so convinced. 'It is said they number in the hundreds, sir…'

Troubridge thought of Nelson, alone, of Hazzard, alone. He felt the kinship of their loneliness, despite the guns at his command. 'Should make them all the easier to find then, sir.'

Troubridge strode out into the cold, the first streaks of dawn visible in the distance. He climbed to the poop deck and looked astern at the bow waves of the ten ships of the line trailing behind, the hunt howling at his heels, and he the Master of Foxhounds, without so much as a whiff of the quarry.

The officer of the watch on the fo'c'sle of *Goliath* saw him. With an exaggerated slowness so that Troubridge might see it clearly, the officer reached up for his cocked hat and raised it in greeting, the gesture striking Troubridge with funereal solemnity.

Troubridge returned the salute. He looked out over the decks, over the officers and men of the watch staring steadily out to sea. He raised his glass and focussed on the unbroken horizon.

'Easier to find…' he muttered to himself, 'then find them, my dear fellow…'

–

Seven hundred miles to the east, *Capitaine de vaisseau* Luc-Julien-Joseph Casabianca and flag officer Lieutenant Gilles-Michel Marais moved to the rail of the broad quarterdeck of the 120-gun *Orient*. They looked out into the cool darkness before dawn, surveying the fleet formation, the sea churned into phosphorescent wakes streaming far behind.

By the shrouds stood a solitary figure, almost invisible in his black coat and hat but for the nearby glow of the compass lanterns. He turned at the sound of Casabianca's approach.

'Citizen,' said Casabianca to Jules-Yves Derrien, 'I take it all is in order.'

Derrien bowed. 'Yes, Citizen Captain.' He did likewise to Marais. 'Citizen Lieutenant…'

'Citizen,' said Marais.

Casabianca exchanged amused glances with Marais at this clumsy Republican protocol. These little slights did not pass Derrien unnoticed, but he treated Casabianca with care. He was the toast of the fleet, a sturdy man with stern and noble Romanesque features, undisturbed by the weight of command, nor the heady purpose that propelled them ever southwards along the Italian coast.

'You left the admirals and generals at dinner, Citizen Derrien,' observed Casabianca.

'And the ladies...' added Marais, suggesting some sort of unnatural inclination. It had been noted that Derrien had not yet engaged in any amorous shipboard dalliance. Most were not surprised. There was talk he was a sexless monster or eunuch.

'Matters of State, Citizen.'

Casabianca nodded out to sea. In the furthest reaches of his telescope were coastal lights, their distant twinkle lost amid the night glow of the horizon. 'Not even a scout to investigate. Naples lies quiet and stinking as we pass.'

'Very wise of them,' murmured Marais.

'It was put to them to remain so,' said Derrien, with quiet satisfaction.

They looked at him. Marais bowed his head briefly in acknowledgement. 'My compliments.'

They believed him. Derrien's position was unique, accountable to none but Bonaparte – and perhaps not even then. His presence on board had been felt with a suffusing pall. That the advisers to the court of Naples might have felt the same threat was no surprise.

'Then we will be on schedule.' Derrien nodded, feeling more than pride: *power*. They were the gods of the sea, unstoppable, irresistible. And he had made it so.

Tinkling laughter and a footfall on the ladders behind heralded the approach of several late-night revellers from below, three army officers and two ladies. At four in the morning Derrien decided they must have been gaming – at one thing or another.

The officers saw Casabianca and Marais and brought themselves unsteadily to attention, and exchanged bows and salutations. 'You look very cross, Captain,' teased one of the women, more than a little drunk. 'You must be speaking of weighty matters.'

'Captain, *Madame* Dutoit, of your acquaintance,' said one of the escorts, slurring only slightly, noted Derrien. He dripped with braid and gold fringe, and had heroically dishevelled hair as though he stood in a divine breeze in a grand portrait – a major, Derrien recalled, a muddied clod of the 9th *demi*, and not the woman's husband. Casabianca bowed.

'The business of war, *madame*, not a topic for gentle company.'

She looked like a child to Derrien, a child rouged with paint on a skin blotched by wine and juvenile intrigue. He turned from the group with contempt. How these men could sniff up the skirts of such a creature was beyond him, playing mistress-and-master in and out of each other's cabins every night, having smuggled them aboard, or 'found' them still aboard 'by accident'. Now they had been underway for over a week, wives of favoured officers were coming out of the very woodwork. He thought of the sailors' women below, toiling as their husbands did. A few had tended his mounting desires – brief, harsh and fumbling though the liaisons had been in the sweating waists of the ship. In those furious moments he saw them differently, draped in the tricolour, becoming the Republic in his very hands as he pounded into them with fervour. His devotion was for them, he knew, not for these bourgeois *faux-aristos*.

Marais moved to Derrien's side. 'He plays all parts, Citizen,' he murmured in defensive explanation. 'A good leader must.'

'Must he?'

'Yes. And he has saved the navy for the Republic as a consequence. He is our De Suffren, our new hero.'

'I understand, Citizen Lieutenant,' said Derrien, 'I do not read the newspapers. I write them.'

A sharp-nosed sloop cut across the fleet lines and a call went up as it drew alongside. A few minutes later a young ensign began to climb the boarding steps.

'Citizen Captain,' said Derrien, 'my time has come. I shall see you at our first port of call.'

The breathless ensign came running. The officer of the watch passed him up to the quarterdeck steps and he saluted.

'Despatches, *Capitaine*, from the scouting squadron.'

Casabianca took the satchel but asked him direct, 'Well?'

'The English are reduced to three ships of the line after the storm and are scattered. But one of our corvettes, the *Héphaestus*, was sunk by a stray brigantine, the *Athène* badly damaged by a frigate, both privateers, position lost in the gale, *Capitaine*.'

'Only three English ships?' snorted the muddied major. 'How very paltry of them,' he sniggered.

Casabianca glanced through the despatches. 'Where there are three,' he said, 'there will soon be more, Major. If but a dozen of them were to encounter our transports, there would be slaughter.' He looked up from the pages in his hands and glanced at Derrien. 'So come the English, Citizen. So comes Nelson. Though you promised he would not.'

Derrien was unperturbed. He indicated the fleet all around them. 'And so comes Bonaparte, Captain. "Like a Jove", as their Shakespeare might say, I believe. Nelson's squadron will be merely a token force, Citizen, for reconnaissance. Their milord Admiral at Gibraltar will not leave his station for fear of leaving the approaches to England undefended. By which time,' he concluded, 'it will be too late.' He bowed to Marais. 'Citizen Lieutenant.'

Madame Dutoit paid Derrien a glance then pointedly looked away as if bored, and his eyes glittered with amused loathing. As he passed, he added, 'In view of the losses, Citizen Captain, the navy may be short of men,' he said. 'I am sure the lady's bed could spare at least a few.'

The army officers spluttered, one reaching for his sword, the clod of the 9th snatching a glove from his belt, ready to demand satisfaction, 'Have a care, *m'sieur*...'

Marais took a swift step between them. *'Messieurs.* The captain is on deck. You will respect the rank.'

Derrien smiled at the heroic major. 'Quite so,' he said, 'honour cares little for its consequences. But you should.'

Derrien bowed to Casabianca and Marais, and disappeared down to the waiting sloop, making a note to send in the major with the first wave of troops.

—

'Who is this, I wonder?' he said.

'She is the niece of the Dean of Norwich.'

They watched the carriage approach, a young Harry Race's arm resting on his shoulder, the practice sabre dangling carelessly.

'Is she a beauty?'

'Oh yes.'

'Then I shall steal her from you.'

'And I shall thrash you back to the fields, villain!'

'So you think, m'sieur! Have at thee!'

Their blunted swords clashed and Harry ran to the chestnut tree, William after, the sun beating down, each seeking to best the other before the carriage rounded the corner, and claim her as the prize of a hazy summer's afternoon. Harry's face twisted in a rage, *'Always better, aren't you! You take everything and everyone…! Regards to…'*

But the red surf washed over him again, filling his wounds with a liquid pain, carronades raking the French corvette.

Harry!

Elena was shaking him awake, her wide, frightened eyes shining, bottomless black wells, her hair tumbling around her bare shoulders. She lay naked beside him in the cot, her hot, scented skin tight against his in the heat, in some hope that she could drive the demons from him, a protective crucifix clutched in her hand.

The door was flung open and De la Vega and Wayland stood with a candle, spitting a low, dull gleam of yellow on their faces, casting crazed shadows on the plank walls. Hazzard lay bare-chested, bright with sweat in the Italian night, his dressings soaked, the freshly stitched cut on his forehead throbbing.

'We heard you shouting, sir...' said Wayland.

They're all dead. Harry, Sarah, Bartelmi, father, mother. This endless war had killed them. *Derrien* had killed them.

Derrien.

'Another nightmare, sir?' said Wayland.

Hazzard sagged back into the cot and closed his eyes.

'Elena...' he said to De la Vega, 'Cesár, I had no idea...'

De la Vega stilled his protests. 'She is the gypsy child, *la pequeña Elena*, my mad little one...' Elena rested her head in the hollow of Hazzard's neck, her bare, soft breast hot against him. Wayland looked away out of propriety but she did not notice. She whispered a prayer in Catalan, but Hazzard could understand none of it.

'You have drunk the black blood, my friend...' De la Vega said, as if Hazzard were cursed. 'Only steel will vent your humours.'

Derrien.

Hazzard could taste it, yearned for it.

'Where are we...?'

'*Napoli, amigo,*' said De la Vega, 'City of vengeance.'

Rapier

The Bay of Naples lay broad and open, the frigates of the royal fleet riding quietly at anchor under flickering torchlight to the north, coastal luggers cutting swift paths to the city-states, while merchant barques plied the sea-routes to Sicily and Sardinia. The city hummed with business as usual, giving only a fearful glance over its shoulder at the war that rocked the whole of Europe. Its ashen beard white in the starlight, Vesuvius looked down from its jagged summit upon it all, a smouldering column rising high into the night sky, Vulcan's threat to snuff out the sweating kingdom.

They had sailed for seven days, avoiding Corsica and the Strait of Bonifacio, instead skirting the southern coast of Sardinia to cross the Tyrrhenian Sea. When Hazzard saw the charts he calculated the *Esperanza* had been blown nearly seventy-five miles to the southwest by the storm, just as Nelson in *Vanguard* had been dismasted and driven from Toulon.

The Catalan crew were mistrustful of anyone – French, English, or indeed Spanish. But what tension there had been with their British guests was soon overcome by their unified determination to strike back at the French navy, and their evident respect when, those days earlier, they had prepared the three dozen bodies of French and British sailors for burial at sea.

The marines had stood in line either side of a bier wide enough to take three men together, and drilled for each burial, Cochrane murmuring his litany in Latin, the *Volpone* crew, heads bowed, understanding every word. Markham had not been found, as it was with many others, and Underhill, who gave the roll, had declared '*Claimed by the sea*' for these unfortunates, and '*Visited by God*' for those who had died of wounds. Hazzard had recognised the body of the French captain, the cockade, the order pinned to his breast, and the marines had fired a salute, as they did for Greaves and McGovern, the Catalans satisfied that at least these few Englishmen had some religion within their souls. At a stroke, it had bonded them against two common enemies: the sea, and the French.

Now, Hazzard watched from the portside rail on the quarter-deck. The *Volpone* glided in on a humid onshore breeze, under the guns of the Castello Aragonese soaring high above, perched on its island clifftop, and headed to the darkened reaches of the quiet Gulf of Pozzuoli and Capo di Posillipo, to the northwest of the royal city. They readied a shore-boat, the heat hanging heavy like a fog, fetid and dense. De la Vega called for his weapons, and held out a sword to Hazzard. '*Para ti, amigo.*'

It was a light Toledo rapier, just under a yard in length, with a jewelled swept hilt and short crossguard. 'It's magnificent,' said Hazzard gratefully, having lost both his prized Talwar and the Manton in the wreckage of the *Esperanza*.

'It is the *espada ropera* of my youth – Toledo steel, *el mejor* – the best. I think you will be good together, for you are the quick hand, I think, *amigo.*' Hazzard took it.

De la Vega next held out a pistol. 'And this,' he said, 'is a Lorenzoni. You know of this?'

'An Italian pistol.'

'No no no, my friend. Not just the pistol. It load for you, itself, *sí*? *Mecánico?* You fill the powder, here.' He opened a small cover on the breech above the trigger to reveal a long chamber in the iron frame; he took a powder flask from the sailor and poured. 'And *las balas*, the pistol-balls, in here, seven, *sí*? No more.' He took seven heavy-calibre rounds from a pouch, putting them one by one into another circular chamber, and Hazzard watched them drop and roll out of sight into the interior. They looked like 40-bore, nearly half an inch in diameter.

204

De la Vega closed the magazine cover and held it out. 'The muzzle held down, you move this, the, the... ehh, arm, *sí*? Try.'

Hazzard took the gun in his right hand and cranked the stiff lever forward with his left, feeling the springs and action click, first opening the powder chamber. As he pulled it further round, it cocked the flint and the priming pan closed with a clap.

'So. Ready,' said De la Vega as Hazzard eased the cock forward. 'No ram, no, ehh, *cómo se dice*, pack or prime? Seven shots, *sí*?'

Hazzard hefted it. It was the most sophisticated weapon he had ever seen. 'It is extraordinary...'

'You want the secret landing, hm? No *Franceses* to see us, no spies? *Bueno*. If the *Camorristi* come, we may need such a *cañón*, my friend. Seven men, *boom boom boom*.'

Hazzard and Cook had chosen Kite, Hesse and Rivelli – both the latter spoke Italian, Rivelli's London family hailing from Salerno, further down the coast, and Hazzard had an idea they might need a good cutpurse: Kite could prove useful. Wayland and Underhill were to remain aboard with the rest of the marines. Alfonso, De la Vega's first officer, would take command of the *Volpone*.

'Clear aye, sir,' said Wayland, before the assembled marines, somewhat uncertain, but gathering his courage for the task.

'Could still be o'service, sir,' said Warnock, but Underhill snapped back at him, quick and low, '*In* line, lad, *as* ye were...'

Warnock racked himself back to attention with a terse '*Sir.*' Hazzard spared no concern for their petty grumbling, too preoccupied with his own intentions. The boat was lowered away, Hazzard thinking only that this was his last chance: Naples, he knew, was the key.

They rowed towards the outer harbour markers, the Spaniards experienced at their craft, swift, silent. Within half an hour they reached a small sea cave, one of De la Vega's regular landing spots. He swung the tiller and they headed towards the dark mouth, the black waters breaking, the boat dipping on the swell. Fending off the rocky walls with their oars, they entered the echoing darkness, hearing the roar of a waterfall.

Ducking beneath the dripping ceiling they passed into a vaulted rock chamber, the rush of water suddenly loud. De la Vega opened a shutter of his dark lantern. What they had thought was a waterfall was a barred tunnel grate, at least the height of a man, the white glow of frothing water belching from its rim, a dim light glowing somewhere in the distant interior. The stench was appalling. It was one of the many outlets of the Neapolitan sewers, carved through the rock forming the northern arm of the bay, carrying with it the stinking detritus of the port. Leaning outboard from the boat in the full force of the rushing water, it took two men to lever the creaking grille open.

'Come. *Vámonos*,' said De la Vega and led the way with his lamp, climbing into the tunnel. Hazzard and the others followed, wading knee-deep against the current – they wore dark shirts, jerkins, boots and breeches and lightweight cloaks, the marines in labourer's caps and homespun – soon soaked by the rushing water. The boat pulled away, the Catalan crew slipping back into the bay and the *Volpone*. ''Ere,' whispered Kite, ''Ow do we get a cab back 'ome then?'

'Do not fear, *amigo*,' said De la Vega. 'They know.'

Hazzard estimated they had moved through the tunnel for nearly a hundred yards before it branched out, a flow of seawater entering a junction complex, washing down six other channels. Rivelli stopped and pointed at the wall. De la Vega raised his lantern higher. It was a glyph, a stylised M in a circle, a diagonal line at its top.

'It's a clan, sir, of the *Camorra*,' Rivelli whispered to Hazzard, glancing at Hesse and Kite. 'You don't poach on their manor. Cut yer throat they will.'

Kite nodded. 'Do yer collar up then.'

De la Vega urged them along. 'Nothing to fear, *muchachos*. The *Camorra*, they are my best customers. Most of the time.'

'You know this mark?' asked Hazzard.

De la Vega pointed at the wall. 'This one?'

'Yes.'

He thought a moment. 'No.' He shrugged. 'It is new. We go faster, hm?'

They passed through the labyrinth, finding vaulted Roman brick chambers, quaysides and canals, groups of the home-less clustered around fires on stone landings beneath gratings, turning away in fear as they passed, a tattered one-legged woman with a crutch sitting a silent watch. Lone figures stood in distant corners, smoking pipes, marking the group's passage, as they marked everything above their heads on the streets. 'The watchers. *Camorristi*,' De la Vega whispered, '*Ndrangheti*. *Lazzaroni* rebels, who knows.'

After another hour of turns along the foul, stone-lined rivers, they came to a halt at a shaft and an iron ladder. De la Vega and the marines kept an eye on the branch passages as Hazzard climbed to a dripping grille at the top, its edges thick with grease. He pushed it open easily.

He looked into a mews behind a cart shed, the sharp tang of horse dung and slick streets in the air, the heat dissipated by the promise of a salt breeze off the bay, flickering torches on walls, lamps burning. He pushed the grille aside and climbed out. The Lorenzoni pistol cocked and ready, he crouched in the road by the opening as the others emerged one by one, dashing for the shadows.

'Guns hidden, *amigos*,' said De la Vega. 'The royal militia hunts down the *Lazzaroni* and the *Camorra*. To be a band of armed men in *Napoli* is, how you say, not wise.'

They followed De la Vega through the darkened streets to the foreshore. They came to a series of quays and jetties, small boats with hanging lamps bobbing gently at wharves. Behind them rose the city, great hills studded with tall, square-topped villas, wealthy onlookers jostling for a sea view over the heads of crowded slums. De la Vega stopped them at a corner.

'*There*,' he whispered. 'But we go *cauteloso*, hm? Careful…'

Between dilapidated warehouses, light spilled from high windows onto the crooked planking of a broad wharf reaching out into the bay from a waterfront tavern. They moved to the back and found a large yard, fed by a descending lane from the higher main road beyond, and an alley leading to a rear storage area of rubbish and piled crates. At the back door was a rotting portico, an old coach lamp glowing dully overhead.

'This is the tavern for the, *cómo se dice, los barqueros*, the, ehh, boatmen,' said De la Vega.

'Hesse, take the side entrance, eyes open, Rivelli, with me,' said Hazzard. 'Sar'nt, you and Kite take up positions and cover this portico.'

Cook looked at the place with its dark alley behind. 'You're not ruddy joking…'

De la Vega led them through the back door. Though the place was open on three sides to the bay, the heat was worse inside, the air thick with tobacco and the smell of boiling olive oil and frying food. It was bare, a planked floor and stone walls missing large slabs of fallen plaster, heavy, tarred wooden beams exposed through neglect.

There were a number of watermen in the far corner, some sitting singly, some eating in silent pairs, bowls and rough wine before them. Ostensibly they were waiting to ferry late-night passengers to ships, or from one side of the large bay to the other. They were instead the backbone of the smuggling operations of the local *Camorra* faction. The graffiti on the beams showed several clan glyphs. Their eyes flicked upwards at the newcomers, then away.

Posts and panelled divisions abounded in the tavern, providing shadows and dark corners. De la Vega led the way to the darkest, close to an exit. Hazzard could hear Rivelli suck in his breath behind him. These were not his people but he knew their ways, as much as he did those of Londoners, from Limehouse to the Isle of Dogs. Hazzard sensed he was expecting trouble.

They sat in high-backed bench seats in a corner. A heavy woman appeared from a doorway to the back.

'*Salve*,' said De la Vega, offering her a gold coin, then continued in Italian, 'Tonino. Send him my greetings, and say Cesár Domingo has come.'

The woman looked at the coin, impressed, and nodded. She kept her eye on him but called loudly, '*Gian-Franco, vieni qua.*' A boy of barely ten appeared and she mumbled something to him. He ran off. She shrugged at them, '*Un ora – o due, possibilimente. Del vino?*'

'*E del pane*,' said De la Vega and she left to bring bread and wine. 'We wait,' he said to Hazzard. 'One hour. Or two, she says. She has not decided. But wine, bread, it is better than, eh, *nada*.'

'Sir,' murmured Rivelli to Hazzard, 'three blokes in the corner. They got gang marks. Watching us.'

Hazzard glanced at them. He saw a tattoo on the back of one man's hand, and bowed to Rivelli's experience. 'Well done, Rivelli. Hesse will keep an eye on them.'

A moment later Hesse entered and sat quietly nearby, not looking round, fishing in a purse for coins, as any man would. The watermen glanced at him, the soiled clothes, the unshaven face, drooping moustache, the slump of his shoulders, then looked away, uninterested. A taverner called to him and he called back in a hoarse voice, '*Grappa*…'

Rivelli grinned. 'Nice one, 'Essy.' He murmured to Hazzard, 'If they come, sir, they come in close, with the knife or wire from behind. Don't let 'em close with you.'

'Understood. But they won't be as quick as Hesse.'

The woman brought glasses and a carafe. The clock ticked to two. More watermen came in, went out, then drunken wharfingers and a red-cheeked woman hanging off them, laughing, other men muttering to each other in desultory greeting passing bags to each other. None spoke to the three men Rivelli had spotted. A few bedraggled prostitutes ventured in and said the name of a ship, and one boatman rose to take them out. Rivelli watched, and they waited.

Eventually a man entered quietly through the back door, a young woman at his side. The taverner nodded at De la Vega and they approached. Rivelli got up, ready, his right hand on the butt of the knife in his belt. The unshaven young man wore a leather coat, and brought the taint of horses and humid streets with him.

'You are *signor el Capitán*?'

De la Vega nodded and replied in Italian, 'But you are not Tonino.'

They sat down, looking over their shoulder. 'You come for Antonino,' said the man. 'I can take you to him.'

'He always meets me here himself.'

'I am Alberto, his nephew – this is my cousin, Marietta, *sì*? We came back from Castellamare to help my uncle.'

The taverner woman returned to their table, bringing more glasses and a bottle of clear liquor. De la Vega nodded at Hazzard, indicating the floor was his. Hazzard spoke, his Italian quick and staccato.

'Do you remember hearing of a carriage, attacked on the 20th of March on the road to Rapallo? A young Englishwoman, taken by French horsemen? Men killed?'

Alberto looked blank for a moment, glancing at Marietta, who shrugged. Ignoring the wine, he poured the *grappa* into their glasses instead, his hand trembling slightly. 'Where you from? Rome?'

'*Ehi, Napoletàno, un po' di rispetto*,' warned Rivelli, not caring much for Alberto's etiquette: *a little respect*. 'You say, *"where you from signore"*,' he corrected.

Alberto noticed him and heard the Salerno accent. He nodded slowly, spreading his hands in apology. '*Va bene. Mi dispiace*. Forgive me, *signor Salerno*. May I enquire,' he asked Hazzard more courteously, 'where you are from, *signore*? *Roma?*'

Hazzard nodded. '*Sì*.'

'*Bene, bene*.' Alberto nodded with approval. Rome was a fabled exotic land, now filled with resistance fighters facing the French. He raised his glass to them. '*Salute – al Papa*.' They all drank, toasting the captured Pope. Alberto wiped his mouth. 'But, a carriage? To Rapallo in March?' He shook his head. '*No. Secondo me*, it could not be.'

'Why not?' asked Hazzard, his accent sharp by contrast to the soft southern sounds of the Neapolitans.

'*Ehi*,' he replied, spreading his hands wide with a shrug, 'The rockslide.'

'Rockslide?'

Marietta explained. 'In the second week of March the road through Rapallo was blocked by rocks and mud. Everyone knows this.'

'We have been away,' explained De la Vega.

Alberto nodded. 'No one could get in or out, only on the long cliff road. They cleared it this month past now.' He shook his head. 'If a carriage with an *inglese* was attacked, the English ambassador, the great Sir William, *il grande signore*, he would tear down the sky. If she was taken, then by who? Which clan? There would be a ransom, demands, the Royal Guard, *tutti*. Uproar. And, *ehi*, we don't like the uproar.'

Rivelli leaned forward and whispered to Hazzard's ear, 'He's meetin' your eye, sir. Tellin' the truth, I reckon.'

Hazzard pressed the Neapolitan. 'Not Rapallo then. On another road perhaps.'

Alberto shook his head again. 'No. *Impossibile*, my Roman friend. We are *Camorra*,' he said proudly but quietly. 'We fight the *Francesi* spies every day here. We fight ourselves. We fight everyone. If an enemy attacks a carriage, we *know*, because we must have our share, a taste, to wet our beak, hm? Nothing, not April, not March, not February, *no*.'

'But it has to be—'

Alberto was adamant. '*Impossibile.*'

De la Vega put a hand on Hazzard's arm. The heat rose up around Hazzard's face, suffocating, and he stared at the table before him, trying to think, his throat constricting with the realisation. He saw the Admiralty building, the forecourt, the portico's pillared teeth.

Blake.

Lewis.

Lies.

For a moment Hazzard lost his breath and tried to swallow, the air catching in his throat.

You utter, utter fool. Fool for believing them again.

'Come, come,' said Alberto, 'it is important, hm? You, ehh, an officer from the Guard? *Il Vaticano?* For a price, maybe we can find the truth, but ah, it costs, the messengers, the informants…' Detecting Hazzard's distress, he suggested in a businesslike tone, 'Come. We go to Antonino, and he will explain. He will help.'

Rivelli looked at De la Vega and gave a tight shake of his head. De la Vega was inclined to agree with him. 'No,' said the Spaniard, 'better to bring him here.'

Alberto chuckled. '*Ehiiii*, we are all friends here, hm? We hate the *Francesi*? *Bene*, you follow us, and *tutto bene.*' He wagged a finger, 'You do not summon Antonino, ha?' he laughed, shaking his head.

'No, please,' said Marietta, easing the tension, 'Antonino says to come, but we must hurry. He watches the French tonight. A ship is going, perhaps to their fleet which sailed by these two days past.'

Hazzard looked at her. He could not think clearly. According to Blake's reports, there was a *Lazzaroni* contact – though not De la Vega's Antonino. But now Hazzard wanted to test everything Blake had provided – *because Blake had lied about the coach.* He decided to test the two *Camorristi* in front of him – with a trap. 'Is Don Canucci with him…?' asked Hazzard hopefully. He looked away, adrift, uncertain, 'I must... I *must* speak to Don Canucci...'

Alberto frowned. 'I think, you know, there was a man of that name some months ago, but—'

'Really?' Hazzard shook his head, as if despairing, 'But he is a great man, I was told, a man of affairs, a man of honour. He told us to come here, for Antonino...'

De la Vega glanced at him and understood at once. He put a hand to his sword, very casually. '*Sí, sí*. We must find, eh, this Don Canucci, but we go carefully, *amigo mío*...'

'Many of the Dons, they moved away.' Marietta smiled, then touched Hazzard's hand lightly, her dark eyes lustrous, inviting. 'But perhaps Antonino will know where he is. Come, I will take you.' She put her hands gently on Hazzard's arm, squeezing. She smelled of rose oil and blossom, her cheeks flushing, a Calabrian beauty, hints of red in her black hair. Few men would say no to her.

'Yes, we must hurry,' said Hazzard distractedly to De la Vega, 'Shall we?' Hazzard met his eye and De la Vega flicked a glance at the butt of the Lorenzoni in Hazzard's belt.

As they got up, a group of travellers blew in the main entrance behind, a gaggle of young men and women following. They made boisterous calls for wine and passage, laughing and banging down their trunks. Rivelli tugged at Hazzard's sleeve, his face white.

'The three blokes, sir. They're gone.'

Hazzard gave a quick look. And Hesse had vanished.

Once outside they followed Alberto – not up to the *piazza* on the main road but instead into the alley and yard to the left, the lane rising to their right. There was no sign of Cook or Kite.

Marietta smiled and took Hazzard's hand in hers. 'Perhaps,' she said, 'we will put your fears to rest. And you can tell me of Rome. I always like the *Romani*, so brave, so... *strong*. In *Napoli* we admire strength.'

'Yes,' said Hazzard, then stepped behind her, twisting her arm up and round her back, putting the muzzle of the Lorenzoni to her neck. '*There is no Don Canucci, signorina.*'

'*I know,*' she gasped. '*Surrender.*'

Three men emerged from the shadows of the old portico, each one drawing two long-hilted daggers apiece – Veronese duellists, or Venetians possibly, guessed Hazzard, preferring the blade to the pistol. From their right, six others came down the lane, silhouetted in the torchlight of the main road and waterfront houses beyond. They strolled towards them confidently, Hazzard hearing them speaking French. He twisted Marietta's arm tighter. '*So – the French pay you? To take Antonino and his territories?*'

She gasped at the pain. 'He is dead, *signore – like you.*'

Four shots rattled off in quick succession and the three Venetian daggermen fell dead to the slick cobbles. Cook and Kite charged out from the rear of the alley, Kite dropping on the third with a lightning swing of the arm and the flash of a short blade, down at the neck and the ribs, a dockyard kiss. The approaching figures stopped, then came running with pistols, muzzles blazing.

Marietta slammed a hand back at Hazzard's chin and broke his grip, then tore away from him, trying to run for the group of Frenchmen. But she was flung backwards by the impact of a bullet and fell, retching and gasping for air. De la Vega spun Alberto about, 'For your treachery, *hijo de puta,*' he hissed, and slashed him with a downward sweep of his sword. Alberto collapsed to one knee clutching at his throat, blood pumping through his fingers, his free hand reaching for a pistol.

From behind, Hesse and the three tattooed watermen came running, '*Rivelli, la pistola!*'

Rivelli shouted, '*Got him!*' and dived on Alberto, shoving his own knife down and into his neck, spitting a final curse in his face, '*Maledetto traditore!*'

Hazzard aimed the Lorenzoni and its 40-bore blast boomed in the close confines of the alley, one man going down, another knocked down by his flailing limbs. Hazzard cranked the lever and felt the action reload. The second shot blew a leg out from under another who fell screaming. But in seconds the remainder were among them. Out of reflex Hazzard holstered the pistol and drew the *espada ropera* and cut in the same action, its light blade opening one man's neck and slicing across the face of another. The three *Lazzaroni* watermen with Hesse leapt on the wounded Frenchmen, stabbing down at them, cursing, finishing them off.

Five more men came running down the slope from the top of the lane, one hanging back, looking up and down the main road to the *piazza* beyond, calling orders in French. Cook charged one in mid-draw and threw him into his companion, ramming the blade of his sword-bayonet through the throat of the first and seizing the head of the second. With a swinging jerk he yanked the man up and to the left by his chin and the snap of bone echoed loud.

Hazzard saw the glint of lamplight on gun-barrels and yelled '*Down!*' as the French pistols cracked and bullets rattled off the walls. Cook shouted out, snatching at his leg in pain, but Rivelli was caught in the open, not fast enough, his eyes staring as a bullet crashed into the centre of his chest. He fell, grasping his midriff and crying out with a wail, '*Mickey…!*'

Kite ran to him, '*Riv!*' and slid across the cobbles, trying to catch him, but Rivelli sank to his knees and toppled backwards, his last breath a whisper, '*Mickey…*'

A bullet hit De la Vega and he spun, '*Madre…!*' overbalanced and stumbled, one man raising a blade at his exposed back. Hazzard lunged with full extension from the shoulder and drove the *ropera* blade between the man's ribs and into his lung, the razor-sharp steel sliding free in an instant.

'*Jory! Out!*' called Hazzard, pulling De la Vega to his feet. He called to the watermen, '*Lazzaroni! Andiamo!*' Let's go! and they ran to Kite and Rivelli. Two of the remaining French lunged at Hazzard in simultaneous attack. Neat parries to *quarte* and *sixte* long gone, Hazzard cut in a tight, whirling figure of eight, opening the first man's wrist, his sword clattering to the ground, blood spraying black in the half-light as Hazzard's spinning cut whipped across his companion's forehead and he fell, blinded, both hands to his face. Hazzard disengaged and plunged the *ropera* into his throat, already looking for the next assault, a blade slashing at his neck, missing, striking his shoulder. He thrust into folds of linen, and another fell.

Watching Hazzard's fast approach, the last man in the lane stopped in a sudden skid, his boots slipping as he went down backwards onto the cobbles, his sword hand flying out behind him on the sloping street – and saw Cook. He gasped in recognition.

'*Englishman!*'

Even in the flicker of torchlight, Cook knew him at once, from the hell of a stone barn in the raid on Toulon. He pointed and roared out, '*Bartelmi!*'

Hazzard turned and saw him. He understood immediately who it was.

Derrien.

Jules-Yves Derrien tried to scramble to his feet but could not find sufficient purchase. Hazzard charged him and lunged, the blade tip reaching, quivering so close to Derrien's chest it drove him backwards again but Derrien beat it away, staggering, slipping – Hazzard flicked the sword-tip up and over the beat, then down in a diagonal cut to Derrien's throat, catching only his chin. Derrien cried out as he spun away, his smallsword clattering to the road as he stumbled to his feet, scrabbling for the sword.

Two of the wounded French raced past Hazzard and gathered up Derrien, pulling him away as he called, '*Anglais!*' he cried, '*I see you now! I see you!*'

'*You will know me, Derrien!*' shouted Hazzard, chasing, stumbling, falling to one knee, '*You will know me!*'

Get up. After him—

He tried to run, but Cook was on him just as the two Frenchmen turned, guns raised. '*Sir! Down!*'

They dropped as the muzzles flashed and bullets chipped the stones beside them. When Hazzard looked up, Derrien was gone.

He turned for De la Vega, his left hand slick and sticky with heat and he looked down at his blood. *Must be cut*, he thought, *idiot, course you are.* The watermen came to his aid, Blake's words reminding him, *Trust the Lazzaroni*, and he wondered — *is that a lie too?* — as the elder of them took him by the arm and lifted him carefully, his lined and weathered face looming close, splitting into a terse grin.

'*Ehi, bravo, ragazzo, bravo — un attimo, un attimo.*' *Well done, boy, just a moment.*

Hazzard tried to catch his breath. '*Siamo inglesi — amici dei Lazzaroni,*' Hazzard told him, *We are English — friends.* Looking for the others: Rivelli lying dead and staring over Kite's arm, Cook and Hesse supporting De la Vega, men crowding round to get them up and away, '*Su, su, veloci!*' *Quick — hurry up.*

Hazzard heard a horse's hooves clopping, and the *Lazzaroni* half-carried them, limping, to the back of a cart, to take them to the only place the English go, they said, the place of their great prince, *il grande signore*, Sir William Hamilton.

–

They pushed past the frightened kitchen maids roused from their beds, two of the watermen carrying De la Vega between them. The cook, an older woman with a cool head, lit the lamp on the table, wiped her hands on her nightgown as if it were an apron and snapped at her staff to clear some space, be quiet and wait.

They guided De la Vega to a hard-backed chair and he sat heavily, clutching his bloody arm. Kite and Hesse put Cook beside him, and Hazzard sank onto a stool in the corner, the shock of the entire affair slowly sinking in. The cook rapped an order at one of the maids; staring wide-eyed at De la Vega and the blood, she ran to get help from upstairs.

Hazzard's right hand was shaking. Elena's dressings across his ribs had come loose, soaked with sweat or blood he could not tell, his wounds hot, pricking like needles. He heard the ring of a bottle on a glass and the cook brought them brandy, then shoved a cloth under Hazzard's jerkin at the shoulder where blood had seeped through the shirt. He handed his brandy on to Hesse first who pushed it back at him, *mein Herr*. Hazzard drank, the rim rattling against his teeth, the fire in his throat forcing his eyes shut and he saw Derrien again, falling, the sword flashing, missing.

Missing.

'That *hijo de puta*,' spat De la Vega, 'That Alberto, he killed Antonino... and went to the French. But *how? How* did they know?'

'The taverner,' murmured Hazzard, 'she sent the message.' He thought of the little boy running off into the streets with whatever note she had given him, *Foreigners at the wharf, Alberto, come quickly, they ask for Antonino.* And Alberto duly brought his special henchmen, fresh from his new partners in Rome, the French. And Derrien.

'That man, the *Francés* in black,' asked De la Vega quietly, 'is he the one you seek?'

Hazzard stared. 'Yes...'

And I missed.

The leader of the *Lazzaroni* watermen came in. He was clearly an old hand, with a face of beaten bronze, heavy-set, scarred and saddened. 'Your man, *signore*,' he said, 'we take him to Padre Damiano for the rites, with all honours, for a soldier who fought the *Francesi*.'

'His name,' said Hazzard in Italian, 'is Marine Private Carlo Rivelli, of Salerno, and London.' He thought then of an immigrant family in the slums of dockland London, so proud of their son in the scarlet uniform of their new home, and how they would never see him again. 'A loyal soldier of his king.'

The waterman watched him with sad eyes. 'Who could die better, *signore*?' He touched two fingers to his mouth, an oath taken. '*Commendatore, non ce lo scorderemo mai.*' *My lord, we will never forget.*

Their lanterns flashed, swinging in the darkness as they ran out to the street and the horse and cart, the sound of hooves fading into the night.

The stairs soon echoed with voices and quick footsteps, candlelight playing on the walls and faces. Several footmen appeared, helping Hazzard with De la Vega as Hesse and Kite gave an arm to Cook and they limped up to the wide stone steps of an arched hall.

They found a tall figure waiting in elegant evening frockcoat and white wig, whispering to another gentleman, a pair of attendants either side, each holding a silver candelabra. Hazzard was in no doubt: this was Sir William.

Hazzard had heard much of Hamilton, a vigorous, older man who dined with kings yet welcomed the pastoral visitors of England, was charitable to all and hailed in the street by the common Neapolitans. To see him supervising secrecy on his backstairs seemed out of sorts to Hazzard, yet somehow suited the reputation of the man.

'Quickly, sir, quickly,' urged Hamilton. 'It must be Mr Hazzard, is it not?'

'Sir, yes, my marines and Captain De la Vega of Barcelona.'

Hamilton took his hand. 'A surgeon has been called so let us be sharp about it, Mr Hazzard, lest our efforts for discretion come to naught – Sir Godfrey, if you please, let us convey them upstairs.'

Bronze and marble statuary glimmered in the candlelight, the housekeeper bustling ahead, insisting they should go to the servants' rooms in the attics but Hamilton not having any of it.

They turned a corner on the first floor and Sir Godfrey opened the first door. They put Cook in a wing chair near the fireplace as three footmen lay De la Vega on the bed. His breathing had grown erratic and Hazzard saw the dark spread of blood across his arm and shoulder. Sir Godfrey put a hand to his wrist. 'He grows cold, sir. The shock of the impact, I believe. Blankets, quickly.'

The footmen covered him as Sir Godfrey stipulated, and another footman appeared at the door with a grey-haired doctor at his side. '*Signore, il medico.*' He had evidently come in great haste, pulling coat and boots over his nightshirt and breeches.

Hamilton greeted him with a bow, apologies and thanks. Soon after him came two ladies in rustling evening gowns, the first bearing aloft a lamp.

'William? What has happened?' whispered the foremost. 'You are marked with blood...'

Hazzard stopped to take her in: a young beauty in silk and jewels, streaming the scent of blooms in her wake. He assumed she must be Lady Emma – Hamilton's society wife.

Hamilton looked at the smear on his sleeve with irritation. 'My dear,' said Hamilton, 'I bade you and Miss Lavinia remain with our other guests at that dreadful game of whist, lest they be overcome with some morbid curiosity – or, heaven forfend, go *home* at long last.'

The doctor knelt immediately at Cook's stripped and bloody leg and examined the wound, applying a damp pad of cloth and placing Cook's hand across it firmly. He gave Hesse and Kite a quick look-over, and saw their own bloodied arms and shoulders; he tore off wads of cotton, tipped them against a bottle of clear liquid and gave one to each and clamped it hard over their wounds to demonstrate, '*Sì? Forte. Bene.*' They nodded, taking the bandages and holding them tight, Kite reacting to the sting, '*Bloody 'ell, 'Erbert...*'

He then moved to De la Vega and Hazzard joined him. After a cursory check he beckoned Hazzard to hold a candle closer, and probed with a pair of instruments, then threw up his hands in defeat and shook his head, '*L'osso... la pallattola... troppo vicina all'arteria...*' The pistol ball was too close to the artery.

Hazzard said to him, 'No. You will *not* amputate,' his voice rose in staccato Roman insistence as he shouted, '*Non lo amputarai!* Do you understand? Do you! *Capisci? Sì o no?*'

The old doctor gawked at him over his spectacles. Hesse moved close, his reddened hands on the hilt of the bloody knife at his belt. Hamilton was astonished.

'Mr Hazzard, please!'

But the old doctor nodded in fear and reached for his bag with shaking hands. '*Sì, sì, capisco, capisco...*'

'Hazzard? *Captain* Hazzard?' asked Lady Emma. 'What on earth is happening here?'

'Madam,' replied her husband, 'I do wish you had not witnessed this—'

'I have witnessed more than you might wonder, William.'

Hazzard watched the doctor begin, talking rapidly to Hamilton and his wife in great umbrage, shaking his head, '*non posso, non posso,*' arguing to himself. A footman took the candle from Hazzard and offered a proper lamp in its stead.

As he watched the doctor, Hazzard felt the burn of his own wounds, and pressed the cook's cloth tighter into his jerkin, grateful for it. He pushed past them, the room suddenly too small, too crowded, and stumbled out. In the refuge of the corridor he stopped, took a breath, and leaned against the wall.

Christ...

All around him in the gloom of the lofty corridor he could see Corinthian black-figure vases and glazed Attic bowls from five centuries before Christ, figurines on plinths, niches filled with the treasures of Renaissance palaces – with De la Vega lying in there and Rivelli stone-cold in the back of a cart, for the first time these priceless objects seemed so much crumbling rubbish, without value, without meaning.

Lies.

He leaned against the wall and closed his eyes. *Just for a moment*, he thought, *just give me one bloody moment.*

After a time the door opened, then shut quietly with a click. He heard the rustle of silks, and pulled himself slowly upright. Lady Hamilton approached.

'Forgive me, ma'am...' he murmured. 'We are straight from a – a skirmish with the French.'

He stank of the sea, the sewers and streets, the odour of powder and violence still clinging to him in a cold haze. He wiped at his cheek and his shaking hand came away bloody – whose blood he had no idea.

'Captain Hazzard,' she said, examining him with concern. 'We had warning of you from the Admiralty.'

'Ma'am.' Hazzard was so tired he felt he might topple.

'But I did not expect...' She saw the slashed leather of his jerkin, a trailing bandage hanging from a cut sleeve. 'You are hurt.'

She put a hand to his arm and he flinched, his right jerking for his sword with a nervous twitch before he stopped it. He swore under his breath. *For God's sake.* 'I beg your pardon, ma'am.'

She left her hand resting on his arm, to calm him. For a moment he beheld the face that scandalised London had whispered about for so long. She was older than he had thought, not the simpering girl the press had so salaciously portrayed, but very much a woman, a caring beauty, a goddess.

'That man, in there,' he explained, 'saved me, saved us all, though it stood contrary to his duty. Because he believed in justice, and my honour. More than I did.' He righted himself and put a hand to the Lorenzoni in his belt. 'I will *not* lose him to a murder-gang in a Neapolitan gutter,' he said, 'I will not...' He tried to move past her, unconcerned with etiquette, her rank, but she stopped him with a hand. She was stronger than she looked.

'So, what, you would shoot a poor little doctor who came to help?' She watched him closely. 'I think you would not.'

Every word was suddenly a terrible effort and he felt as if he were falling to the cobbles again after Derrien. *Derrien, where do you go now, you bloody bastard...* 'I must speak with the Prime Minister − or Secretary of War...' he mumbled. '*Someone*, for God's sake.'

She considered it a moment and said, 'Done.'

He glanced at her. 'Easy as that?'

'No, but easier for me than you. You do not know Naples in the summer, Mr Hazzard. We are about to decamp to Posillipo for the season, and have dreary receptions planned for every other night this week. Sir John was not due till our last, but I shall invite him tomorrow, personally, so he cannot wriggle out of it.'

She looked at him with a sympathy and care he had not enjoyed for far too long, and part of him wanted to close his eyes and weep, for everyone, for himself.

'Do you recall,' he began, fearing to ask but knowing he must, 'an incident, of last March, of a coach attacked, its escort killed, a young Englishwoman captured?'

'A carriage?' She was shocked. 'There are highwaymen, but no,' she said, 'my husband would have rained fire and brimstone upon the court for it.'

He had known that would be her answer. *Known it.* The slaughtered Alberto, for all his deceit, had not been lying. 'When did Miss Sarah-Louise Chapel leave here? She stayed last year, a tourist, from Suffolk, joined a party for Athens. I received a letter...'

Lady Hamilton looked blank. 'I'm afraid I do not know the name, Mr Hazzard. Are you certain she went via Naples? Or was it Brindisi? Mr Hazzard? Can you hear me?'

She must have called out because Hamilton appeared with Sir Godfrey and they hurried because she was trying to hold him up as he slumped and stumbled, '*I am so very tired,*' and distantly he heard someone say, *must be wounded*, as they took hold of him.

But he was past caring, because now he knew: along with Blake and Lewis, Sarah had lied to him as well.

Palazzo

In the first glow of dawn, the *Volpone* slowed, gliding into the dark waters of the rocky Gulf of Malfi. Wayland let Handley clamber into the tops with the *Esperanza* crew to help douse sail, all chattering in their new bastardised Spanish and Catalan. Seabirds screeched, wheeling over the cliffs, white against bright blue skies, the scene watched over by a dilapidated medieval tower. A bell tolled, and small boats began pulling out towards them from the shingle beaches, eager to trade.

Acting Captain Alfonso remained as impassive as ever, Wayland frustrated with his unshakeable calm. 'It has been over a day. What if we are found by French ships, Captain? Or the Neapolitan navy?' He indicated the watchtower. 'And what if they decide we are not friendly and open fire?'

'Then we fight, as *El Capitán* would.' Alfonso was a quiet, almost dour man, but short and quick, and moved about on well-sprung legs, possessed of a limitless patience. He looked out again through his glass. 'Who is the more powerful, the old tower with the three guns, or us, with twenty-six, who move with the wind?'

Communication with Alfonso was an awkward business for Wayland. From Catalonia on the French border, as were nearly all the crew, Alfonso tried to speak to Wayland in a rough Languedoc French, pronouncing every E and S until it sounded like Spanish, yet Wayland somehow understood, thanks to his own French and Latin.

'Or we run, also as *El Capitán* would. *Volpone* is the ship with the most great speed on the sea, hm? We have copper, *cobre sí*?

Le cuivre, under the water, for to keep it smooth, no weed, *sí*? Just shiny *cobre brillante*. Very *rápido*.'

'But we can't leave him and the major behind, even to run—'

'We have the *rondezzavooz*, *Teniente* Ouayalande.' Wayland's name had also proved something of a challenge. 'We return the next night, or the next, or another. We have the habit, the system. We come here many times.'

He gave a command in Catalan and the *Volpone* dropped anchor. '*Señor el Teniente*,' said Alfonso to Wayland, watching as the local bumbling boats drew alongside, 'we shall not leave them. Elena, Christina, Maria-Luisa, they are my sisters, Rodrigo, Juan, Diego and Lluis my brothers. *El Capitán* Cesár Domingo, he is our father. We live and die together.'

Wayland watched him go, mounting the steps to the frigate's poopdeck. In the interim he did not see Warnock approach – but Sergeant Jeremiah Underhill did, and stepped smartly into the private's path, growling from the corner of his mouth.

'Now where might you be 'eaded, me beauty?'

Warnock grated at him in frustration, 'Just wanted... to *report*, Sarge. Wanted to *tell* 'im.'

Underhill looked out at the boats, at the coast, anywhere, to conceal this gross offence from Wayland. '*Tell* an officer, boy? You don't *tell* an officer *nothin'*. Chain o'command, Private Knock-bloody-Knock, chain o'command, and you knows it, too. You reports to me and I reports upp'ards and you never get so much as a sniff at the upshot, you got me clear as a *bloody bell*?'

Warnock kept his voice low, the tone of the conspirator. 'Sarge, we got Lambert up for'ard, Cocky to ring the signal, three hands ready to take the helm and the rest ready to take the capstan and tops—'

'*You mad bastard*,' hissed Underhill.

'It ain't *right*,' appealed Warnock, 'being ferried about by a lot o'*Dagos*. We can't *trust* 'em, Sarge.'

'Don't you bark at me, boy, or you'll get a nasty bite.' There was sudden laughter from above in the mizzenmast tops, and

Underhill jerked round to look: Porter and Napier were tying off a line with two of the Spaniards, getting the knot wrong.

'And what of the major? Eh?' demanded Underhill. 'Or you gon' to dump 'im over the side an' all?'

'Doin' it *for 'im*, Sarge, but the Dagos get off and stay 'ere with—'

Warnock stopped dead as Underhill moved nose to nose with him. Warnock looked down. In Underhill's hand was the sharp point of a thin-bladed stiletto, the tip pressing into Warnock's tunic. With only the slightest pressure it would be enough. 'Now,' said Underhill, 'I knows Mickey Kite ain't 'ere to old yer 'and, boy, and 'e'd've talked some sense into yer thick 'ead. But you get yourself back down yer 'ole with the rest of 'em and see to your kit, like a good soldier-boy, eh? And if I sees you on deck afore next watch I'll make sure our young professor there has no choice but to set you, and you alone, strugglin' from a topyard, got me? *No choice.*'

Warnock stared down at the stiletto and protested, 'He ain't got the *starch* for it, Sarge. Just a bloody kid—'

'Are you wet hindways your bloody ears? Doin' it *again*, talkin' o'yer officer, just like when Cookie laid into yer?' He put the knife away, keeping his voice low. 'The major will *shoot you dead*, boy. Like he did those murderin' scum from the *Stately* down the Cape. Put his pistol to a bloke's face he did, and pulled the trigger, no mistake, no trial, no questions. So you will *wait* for action till ordered. That's what we *do*, boy. We *wait*. We *stand*, till the enemy comes to bear and there's nowhere to run. That blood-red line of ours puts the fear of Hell into a Frenchie's shiverin' soul and ne'er you forget it. Y'understand me?'

Warnock nodded reluctantly, 'Aye, Sarge.'

'In your ma's *piss*, boy,' spat Underhill, his lips close to Warnock's ear. 'I *said*, you under*stand*?'

Warnock stiffened to attention. 'Aye-aye, Sergeant. Under*stood.*'

'Disperse then, and *begone.*'

Warnock stepped back smartly, turned and marched away. Some of the marines were on deck, on watch or performing routine duties, but all looking at the shore, as Underhill had said, waiting.

Wayland looked out at the horizon, at the watchtower, and Underhill came to stand beside him.

'I might suggest a boxin' match, sir,' he said. 'A friendly. Napier and Warnock, some of the Dagos an' all, that big bo'sun, Carlos. Get some heart back into 'em. P'r'aps that last side o'beef we got, do a big spit-roast at the galley fire, Spanish-style, by them *señoritas*.'

'Yes,' said Wayland, nodding, 'yes, jolly good, Sergeant, that's an excellent idea. You, er, set that up, yes. Jolly good.'

'Sah.'

Wayland gripped the handrail tightly, shaking with the fear of Warnock's threat. He had heard every word – and thanked God for Jeremiah Underhill.

–

Hazzard awoke the next day. His hand went for the Lorenzoni but he found nothing by his head but a feather pillow. Stiffly, he looked around. He was in a bed.

The dove-grey bedchamber was filled with soft light and gentle shadow, the walls finished in fine mouldings and decorative panels, a Mediterranean breeze wafting over him. He had rested. It felt like long shore leave. To his right, tall French windows led to a balcony, curtains blowing, the sun already high, the heat penetrating. Laundered and pressed, his clothes lay folded on a chaise, with his polished boots and sword. His skin smelled of lavender soap, and he felt clean – he had been bathed. After the sewers of Naples and weeks of hammocks, cots and mouldering damp, he felt refreshed, possibly for the first time in years.

He heard the bells outside strike noon. He was immediately seized by the memory of who he was, where he was, and what was going on, and threw off the bedclothes. He was pulled up sharp by fresh stitches straining at his ribs and arms and gasped, sitting on the edge of the bed. There were new dressings on his old wounds – and one by one, they came to life, each tugging with their own unique ache. He lay back and breathed slowly, coming more gradually to his senses.

A tray lay on his bedside table, a domed salver with cutlery, and he detected the long-forgotten scents of Gujerat *khitchri*. He lifted the lid and inhaled a memory of India. He set down the dome and took up a fork and ate, controlling the urge to wolf it down, the rice and smoked fish rich against his starved tongue. It was gone in minutes.

He heard a noise on the balcony. He rose from the bed, more gingerly this time, and pulled on his breeches, boots, and a fresh shirt. He found Cook at the balcony rail, looking out over Naples.

'First night's sleep in ages,' Cook said by way of greeting. 'Seemed a shame to wake you, sir.'

He stood in an old shirt and white ducks, a broad leather belt, his boots newly blacked and shining. He had been shaved. He looked a new man. 'How's the leg?' asked Hazzard.

'Hurts only when you mention it, thanks, sir.' He looked at him. 'The Captain's still resting. Sawbones did all right in the end. Saved his arm, sir.'

Hazzard nodded. They stood at the rail, looking out as if it were the quarterdeck of a giant ship of the line. The city looked different in the sunshine, dazzling white roofs, ornamental bell-towers, the fresh blue of the sea welcoming, hopeful. 'Could get used to this,' said Cook. 'Lady Ham's been taking close care of you, sir. Watched over you through the night, she did.'

Cook said it with some suggestion, and Hazzard saw her in his mind's eye. 'Sir William is the King's Envoy. I'd get thrown in the Tower.'

'Wish I'd been washed by sultry handmaidens.' He took a folded note from his pocket. 'She left this with the kedgeree, sir.

228

Reckon she's sweet on you.' He looked away discreetly. 'Should I give you a moment, sir?'

'Oh, belt up,' muttered Hazzard and tore it open: '*Your wish is my command. Hither comes Sir John to reception. Best bib and tucker this e'en.*'

'See? Very sweet.' Cook nodded at him knowingly. 'She's been in every hour, she has.'

'You going to stop harping soon?'

'Soon enough.' He looked out again. 'Remember that Maratha princess in Mamta? Ah, now there was a sweeter peach than ever—'

'Oh for God's sake.'

They dressed and found Hesse sitting on a chair outside De la Vega's room. He and Kite had shared the watch all night.

'I look disgraceful,' said the Spaniard, propped up luxuriously in bed. He wore a sling but was perfectly coiffed and shaved, and smoking yet another cigarillo. Though buoyant as ever, the pain from his shoulder was evident. 'And I have not yet had a maidservant. They send me a man to shave me. Do they think I am an *inglés*?' Hazzard smiled, and he continued, 'That was the Italian bullet, hm, hits like the *martillo*, the hammer. *El médico* is a true *caballero*, making only the little hole. I must pay him…' He put a hand to the bandage and sling but would never reveal the depth of his pain. 'So. Now I owe you my arm, *compañero*.'

'To repay a debt.' Hazzard held up Lady Hamilton's note. 'And tonight we have a soirée. But first you will rest.'

'Ha. I rest only if you get a maid to dress me for dinner,' replied De la Vega, drawing deeply on the slim cigar. 'You say this? Dress-for-dinner? It sounds very smart.' He looked about. '*Madre*, I am hungry. I could eat even English food.'

–

The evening heat mellowed to a glow of liquid copper, the sinking sun firing the stucco palaces of Naples into blazing

229

ochre. The Hamiltons' Palazzo Sessa occupied a choice position atop the Pizzofalcone Hill overlooking the city and the bay, and society clamoured for a seat at their table. The *piazza* in front of the villa filled with carriages, Vivaldi and Corelli wafting on the hot breeze, a private orchestra entertaining the city from on high. Fans fluttered at powdered breast and bare shoulder as guests exchanged the heat of their carriages and sedans for the relative cool of the house and refreshing *aperitivi*.

Sir William had rooted out appropriate evening attire for the five of them. In their new finery they reconnoitred the salons and marble halls of the house as if it were a field of battle – Blake might have been a liar, Hazzard decided, but his assessment of Naples seemed accurate. Émigrés rubbed elbows with diplomats and desperate, gossiping nobility – and faceless functionaries watched everyone with a calculating eye.

'Sodom and Gomorrah,' murmured Cook. 'Wigs as high as a horse's arse. And half o'the folk are bloody Frogs, if y'ask me…'

'It shall be an interesting evening, *amigos*,' said De la Vega and bowed. 'Keep the daggers close, and I shall see you shortly, as agreed. *Hasta luego.*'

De la Vega drifted off, humming a strain from the orchestra's efforts, plucking a glass from a passing tray, giving a sweeping bow to an elegant couple.

'Glad to see the captain on his feet, sir,' said Cook.

'He's in his element,' said Hazzard. 'And remarkably well dressed. Did he…?'

'Yes, sir. Teresa-Maria, house-parlour maid. She dressed him. Or *un*dressed him, I suppose.'

'Hm.'

They separated and moved through the crowd. The guests were ushered beneath the cavernous arches of the main hall to take their frosted glasses of chilled Fiano and Verdicchio. Alone, Hazzard found himself staring at still more of Sir William's antiquities, a Cycladic figurine in luminous marble, a funerary vase depicting a boy or young god receiving wine, perhaps from

Zeus. He thought of Cambridge, his academic peers and friends at the university, of Clarke, of teaching, and wondered at what might have been. He felt a fraud, and a fool, having squandered his life, wasting it on a fanciful duty that would never be repaid, indeed, had been rebuffed and scorned, rejected like so much waste. And here he stood, in the halls of the king, effectively a servant once more.

'Exits still clear,' said Cook, returning from a circuit. 'Back entrance taking deliveries. Hessy's watching the upstairs and Kite's making himself scarce with the cloaks or pinching the silver. The captain's somewhere in the crowd, telling everyone he's from the royal court in Spain.'

'Can't wait to see you dance.'

'Rather be boardin' a Frog man o'war under fire.' Cook shrugged into his undersized frock coat. 'An' this collar's ruddy tight…'

'Mr Hazzard?'

They turned to see Lady Hamilton, in a high-waisted Greco-Roman gown of shimmering silk. 'Ma'am,' said Hazzard with a bow. 'A familiar face.'

'Oh dear,' she said. 'Makes me sound like an old mare.'

'He has little truck with horses, ma'am,' said Cook, also bowing. 'Bein' a sailor.'

'What a pair you make. Will you take some wine, Sergeant?'

'No, thank you, ma'am – never one for the drink when I'm ashore.'

'It's against his Wesleyan principles,' said Hazzard. 'Carry on, Sar'nt.'

Cook happily withdrew. 'Ma'am.'

Lady Hamilton watched him go. 'Does he always look like that?'

'Always, ma'am. Frightens the enemy.'

She linked her arm in his and they ambled, skirting the crowd, in a world of their own. 'And do stop calling me "marm" in that flat military manner of yours. It makes me feel ancient.'

He nearly laughed. 'Madam, then,' he said.

'Worse by far. Why not "Emma"? But no, you wouldn't like that either, would you…'

He faced her, relaxed in an openness he had never known, not even with Sarah. 'My lady, then.'

'Very well, poetic indeed, I give in.' She smiled. 'I am so glad to see you recovered, William. There were moments last night when…' She stopped herself, flushing slightly. 'Well, you look better. I am pleased.'

'I cannot thank you enough,' he said. 'For everything.'

She looked at him and he wanted so very much for her to be someone other than the wife of Sir William Hamilton in Naples, in some other time or place. She shivered under his gaze. 'I suspect you will say something dreadful now.'

'No… but, if I must go suddenly, without a farewell—'

'I was right…'

'I wanted to tell you how very grateful I am, for bringing Sir John, for all of us. I doubt many will ever know how much you do here.'

She sighed. 'My dear William – or rather, "Captain Hazzard",' she spoke his name with a mock severity and a secretive smile, one hand adjusting his white cravat, part of the suit laid out for him, probably at her hand, he thought. 'How *ever* do you think treaties are forged and alliances made? Gossip, whispers after wine… it is what a lady in my place does best. I hear Josephine Bonaparte is an expert, but sleeps with them afterwards. And she has bad teeth and covers them with her fan.' She put a hand to her mouth. 'Oh dear. How catty I can be.'

They laughed and she dropped her hand, lingering a moment over his waistcoat, perhaps regretfully. 'But, thank you. And I am so very sorry we could not help with Miss Chapel. I think she is more than an acquaintance?'

His eye traced the delicate line of her jaw and pale cream of her throat, and he thought, *yes, she is very like in look, and spirit, yet so very unlike*. 'She was my world.'

232

She was pained for him. 'Oh, I am such a ninny at times. Forgive my idiotic prying, William, do.'

'There is nothing to forgive.'

For a moment he met her eye and she his, an intimate communion, born of unquestioning trust. Then, suddenly, he felt foolish and exposed, as if he had tried to make love to her, as he would have done had she been Sarah, and part of him felt he had. As did she, it seemed, for they both looked down and away, aware of something passing unspoken between them.

A servant interrupted with a tray of filled glasses and whispered in Lady Hamilton's ear. She nodded back and he vanished into the crowd. She clung to Hazzard a moment. 'Now it begins. Sir John Acton, the King of Naples' very own Prime Minister, has arrived and in his coach came the *comtesse* de Boussard. Quite scandalous, as she is without question a French spy as well as a complete trollop. They will enter separately, of course. Sir John will go to the east door and up to my husband's study, and she will come in here.'

There was a flurry of polite applause and excited whispers and she turned to him in sudden despair. 'I know this may be goodbye and I do hate it so, but promise me you *will* try to live, William, and one day be happy.'

With the same sudden unthinking honesty, Hazzard replied truthfully, 'If I can.'

'I do love my husband,' she confirmed in parting, perhaps more for her own sake, but added no more. She turned and smiled, feigning pleasure at the approach of a dark-haired woman acknowledging the compliments of the crowd. Behind came two men in close escort.

'*Chère madame la comtesse*,' trilled Lady Hamilton and they brushed cheeks carefully, 'may I present our Mr Hazzard,' she said, then added, 'a colleague of my husband's, from the Society of Antiquaries of London. And this, Mr Hazzard, is the *comtesse* de Boussard, *famed* throughout Naples,' she added with a laugh, not without barb it seemed, for Hazzard saw the reaction flash across the Frenchwoman's face.

'Not as famed as yourself, my lady,' the *comtesse* countered in English, her deep lustrous eyes feasting on Hazzard. She was captivating, the very antithesis of Lady Hamilton: dark-eyed and volcanic, a predatory beauty, a deadly Medusa.

'Countess,' he said and bowed to kiss her proffered hand. 'Delighted to meet you.'

'Ah, *mais bien sûr*, there are few gentlemen,' she drawled, 'like the *English* gentlemen.' Her fingernails traced a pattern in his palm as she withdrew her hand slowly from his.

'You are too kind, madam.'

'And you have made quite a study of gentlemen, my dear,' laughed Lady Hamilton, 'have you not?'

The countess joined her laughter and indicated the palace around them. 'But without your success, my lady,' and the forced laughter continued.

Hazzard watched the two men at her shoulder. One of them looked away too quickly. He had a fresh cut on his neck just above his tall collar. Hazzard recognised his own handiwork. He was one of the attackers from the night before.

'I shall leave you to become better acquainted,' said Lady Hamilton, then with a last look to Hazzard, '…though I insist on his safe return.' The two women curtsied malevolently to each other, displeasure seething with every glance, and Lady Hamilton gave Hazzard's arm a tight squeeze before moving off through her guests, the dazzling focus of all.

'Do you stay in Naples for long, *m'sieur*?' asked the countess, drawing his attention back to her hooded stare.

'Passing through, madam,' he replied, 'on studies of the triumvirate of Rome, you know, Brutus, Mark Antony, *I come to bury Caesar*, and all that. And the inevitable fall of the Republic.'

The irony was lost on her. '*Quelle dommage*,' she pouted, 'for it would be a shame not to see more of you.' She smiled archly. 'We go to Casserta soon, with the royal family, and you could have joined me for the long country nights. Do you say evenings? Or nights?'

Hazzard could hardly avoid her gaze. 'I'm sure you could say whichever takes your fancy, madam.'

De la Vega emerged from among the guests and stole up behind her. 'It is a closely guarded secret, *condesa*,' whispered De la Vega over her shoulder, putting a finger to his lips. 'Tell not a soul, but *this* man,' he said, taking her hand for a kiss, 'is actually a barbarian.'

She laughed and immediately turned her interest upon him instead. 'Oh *mon dieu*, two of you, how *delizioso...*'

Hazzard caught sight of one of Hamilton's servants under a distant archway, his eye searching the crowd until he saw Hazzard. He nodded once and turned away.

'*Comtesse*,' said Hazzard, 'may I present Don Cesár Domingo de Catalonia, personal adviser to His Majesty King Charles of Spain and importer of rare and fragrant cigarillos.'

'*Mucho gusto, Señora Condesa...* an honour,' he said smoothly, turning over her hand and kissing her palm. 'I was once a confidant of Queen Maria Luisa, and *Señor* Godoy, but that was some years ago.'

'Oh my dear,' she said, all but forgetting Hazzard, 'we *must* discuss the Spanish court *intimately...*'

'As *intimately* as possible,' he agreed. 'It would be my honoured pleasure, *señora*.'

De la Vega led her away as Hazzard turned, bumping deliberately into one of the French escorts and muttering, '*Mi dispiace*,' in apology but feeling the harsh ridge of both a holster pistol and dagger hilt in the small of the man's back.

He extricated himself from the gathering as the guests moved on to chilled Moët, the chattering noise almost too much, urging him to go. He marched quickly down the corridor beneath large hanging lanterns fluttering with moths in the evening heat. Kite emerged from a nearby doorway and fell into step with him.

'Ready, Kite?'

'Yessir. A stop 'n' drop. You keep the gaffer nattering an' I lift his tails. In a manner o'speakin'.'

235

'Just find something, documents, letters, I don't care. Anything. I want evidence, if there is any.'

'Right, sir.'

Kite peeled off smoothly to the cloaks cupboards as Hazzard headed up the main stairs. No one noticed Kite as he went through the back corridor, dressed as he was in footman's livery coat, stockings and buckled shoes, moving with complete confidence. Sir William's staff knew who he was, but he could be at risk from visiting servants, such as those of the *comtesse* or Sir John himself, and he had no idea how many were in their entourage, keeping watch.

He reached the rear quad where he found two waiting coaches. One was a small two-seater with the top down, making ready to depart after the horses were watered, the other the size of a four-seater English brougham; it was enclosed and curtained, and bore the heraldic sigil of the Kingdom of Naples on its shining black door. This he guessed would be Sir John's – the Prime Minister would not want to await the return of his carriage in case of an emergency of state, therefore it stood ready. The harnessed pair of black horses dined from nosebags and the coachman sat up top, swigging from a flagon of wine. Kite whistled at him from the back door. The man looked round, raising his hands.

'*Ehi, che cosa?*'

Kite shrugged, indicating the kitchen door, and shouted back in the very convincing Italian he had mastered at Hesse's tuition, '*Ehi, vieni – a mangiare, dice mamma!*'

Not wanting to miss his chance of a free dinner in a great house, the coachman climbed down quickly, overjoyed, and Kite moved out past the twin cab and back round the other side, and was in Sir John's carriage before the coachman had even reached the kitchen.

The interior was green brocade with gilt bullion-fringed curtains, smelling of heavy perfume and tobacco smoke. It was empty but for a silk-lined cloak lying over the rear banquette.

Working fast, he frisked the cloak, discarded it, then ran his hands along every surface looking for concealed cupboards, digging his hands into every opening, the folding pockets on the inside of each door, down the backs of the seat cushions. He tried lifting the bench seats, but they would not budge – until he found a clasp on just one, and flicked the lock open. Inside was a cased set of pistols, which he lifted out, several scraps of paper, and something which made him smile from ear to ear.

Within barely a minute he had locked the banquette, closed the door, pretended to wipe down the carriage coachwork and lamp with a cloth in case anyone was looking, and walked off past the corner of the house, the pistol case under his arm, the scrap papers inside. He turned the corner past the stables, Hesse approaching from the opposite direction, opening a sack. Without a word Kite dropped the case into the sack and they parted smoothly, heading back to different entrances.

–

Hazzard reached the top of the stone steps. One of Hamilton's Italian aides waited, an older, learned man in wig and spectacles. He led Hazzard down a broad, cool corridor of polished marble, their heels clicking as they headed to a set of tall double doors at the far end, guarded by a pair of footmen. The aide paused and apologetically indicated an ornate credenza set to one side. On it were laid several walking sticks and hats.

'*Mi dispiace*, forgive me, but, you are armed, *Capitano Hazzard*?'

Hazzard opened his coat to reveal the Lorenzoni in his old leather sling holster. He drew it, checked the action, and handed it over to the attendant, who examined it appreciatively. '*Complimenti, signore, magnifico. Italiano?*'

'*Sì*. Lorenzoni, of Florence.'

The man laid the heavy long-nosed pistol with care on the marble table. He bowed again, apologetic. 'The royal protocols, apologies, *mi dispiace*. Sir William say to remind you that Prime Minister Sir John, though he is, ehh, *inglese*, he serves Ferdinand, King of *Napoli e le due Sicilie*, the Two Sicilies, yes? And may have the agreements, *accordi, sì*? with the French to protect the kingdom.' He hesitated then added, 'In *Napoli, signore*, this is not shameful, not ehh, *disonorevole*. It is the politic, *prudente*.'

Hazzard did not share this view. 'Not to me it damn well isn't.'

The aide bowed, indicating the doors. '*Prego, signore*.' He nodded to the footmen and one knocked and showed Hazzard inside.

Sir William Hamilton stood at the window, talking to one of his guests, glass of white in hand. When Hazzard entered he turned with some relief and approached him at once. 'Mr Hazzard,' he said warmly. 'My apologies for today, sir, as I have been relentlessly engaged. What a pleasure to see you well. I do hope you are better rested, sir.'

Hazzard was humbled by his concern and bowed. 'Thanks to you, sir, I am, yes. And I apologise for being such a burden.'

'Anything I can do, sir, anything. It is my proud task and my honour.' He beckoned him in. Four other men waited by a breakfront bookcase, two dignitaries likewise holding glasses, and two with their hands behind their backs – personal guards, thought Hazzard. A balding, patrician figure smoking at the window turned and looked Hazzard over slowly, waiting.

'Prime Minister,' said Hamilton, 'May I present Captain Hazzard, a rare asset of the Admiralty in London. Captain, this is Sir John Acton, former Admiral of the Tuscan Navy, and Prime Minister to His Majesty the King of Naples.'

Acton gave him a sour look. He had a weight to him, the weight of accustomed power. He was in his early sixties and he seemed a complacent man, thought Hazzard, plump behind his sash and orders. Acton inclined his head briefly but regarded him blandly, uninterested, then sat, with a studied lack of haste, in the only available armchair.

'Mr Hazzard,' said Hamilton, 'perhaps you should explain.'

'Thank you, sir.' He turned to Acton. 'Sir John. I am here on Admiralty orders to seek out and destroy the French fleet which recently departed Toulon and currently threatens the Mediterranean.'

Acton said nothing. He took his time, his only reaction to sip slowly from his glass of Verdicchio. Hazzard continued.

'Admiral the Lord St Vincent at Cadiz stands ready to repel the fleet should it make an attempt to break through Gibraltar and head for England—'

Acton gave a brief snort at this and looked idly at Hamilton. 'Does he indeed? With only two dozen ships of the line at most?'

Hazzard could not have despised him more. 'Oh yes, sir,' Hazzard said, 'he needs no others. For these are British ships,' he said, 'not Tuscan.'

Acton flicked him a glance, his hostility rising. 'Then you hardly have need of me, Captain.' He softened slightly and looked at him with a tutor's frown. 'Captain of what? Post-Captain? Fleet Captain? Flag?'

'Former Captain-Lieutenant in the Bombay Marine of the East India Company and Captain in His Majesty's Marine Forces, sir.'

Acton was disappointed. 'Oh. A marine.' Hazzard recognised this reaction without surprise. Hazzard was not a naval officer. The worst naval officers regarded the average marine soldier as no more than a trained guard-dog. 'What could an officer of Marines possibly want of Naples?'

Believing he would at least respect it, Hazzard hit him with his broadside. 'Scout ships from the Neapolitan fleet, sir.'

The two associates drew in their breath and tutted, each taking a sip of their wine. Hamilton weighed in to support him: 'We have been through this before, Sir John, and here, as I reported, we have evidence of genuine need.'

Acton indulged his colleagues in some private joke, 'Surely *Nelson* is enough.' It was a pointless jibe and he sipped at his glass again, sniggering to himself. His two companions tittered obligingly.

'It would certainly aggravate Spain, Sir John,' suggested Hamilton, 'which is one of our aims at court, is it not, to turn Naples towards Britain and Austria, and away from France and Spain? And so we have, thanks to you and your efforts...'

Acton waved him away, 'Oh nonsense, Sir William, 'tis my duty.'

Hamilton was gracious, but still insistent. 'Indeed, and most nobly undertaken, sir. We signed the agreement on the 19th, and we are ready to face them, surely – here we may now put it into force and help Lord St Vincent and Nelson.'

'Agreement?' asked Hazzard.

Hamilton explained. 'Possibly while you were at sea, Mr Hazzard, it was agreed in Vienna that Naples will ally with Britain, Austria and Russia in a new coalition against France and Spain, but it has yet to be fully ratified.'

Hazzard saw the opportunity. 'Then Naples could open its gates to us once again. Lord St Vincent could bring the fleet in if Naples agrees.'

Acton grew restive, tired of the argument. 'How can I possibly sanction such a directive, Sir William? The Neapolitan fleet is as *nothing* compared to the French. Within a week of the treaty at Venice, Bonaparte annexed the Venetian navy without qualm. We have scarce 120 ships – with the French army sitting but days away in Rome, a sortie against their fleet would be a red rag, sir, a *red rag*.'

'It could serve to support Nelson's efforts, a few frigates or corvettes at least to scout the fleet's destination,' said Hazzard. 'After the storm his squadron was scattered—'

Irritably, Acton waved a hand at him. 'We know its destination, sir, all of us, surely – it goes to Malta.'

Hazzard glanced at Hamilton who shook his head from behind Acton. 'We cannot possibly know that for certain, Sir John...' Hamilton said, apparently just as mistrustful of Acton as Hazzard.

'It's what our fellows tell us, isn't it?' Acton replied, suggesting some personal source unknown to Hamilton or Hazzard.

Hazzard asked Acton, 'May I ask how you came by this intelligence, sir?'

'The *comtesse* de Biasi, if you must know. An *émigrée* from the Republic, dispossessed, husband killed on the guillotine. Dreadful.'

Blake's reports of Sarah burned bright in his memory: *...from Sir Wm Hamilton Kt, French informant the Countess De Biasi in company Englishwoman and agent 28'66'96: Boarded carriage Naples 11Hpm—*

Hazzard thought instead of the *comtesse* de Boussard, and her relationship to Acton. *Did Blake have the right comtesse?* 'Sir William,' Hazzard asked Hamilton, 'has the *comtesse* de Biasi been invited here tonight?'

'No, sir, for she left the city – a week, ten days ago was it not?' He looked to Acton.

'Possibly,' said Acton, uninterested.

'Where did she go, sir?' asked Hazzard.

'Really, I have no idea,' said Acton. 'The *comtesse* de Boussard could tell you. They are very close – or is she a spy now as well?'

'I could not say, sir,' said Hazzard, 'Is she?'

'Good lord *no*. The *comtesse* de Boussard has been entreating me to resist French forces in *any* way we can, and at the same time not to *anger* them. What would they do if they reached Naples? There would be a guillotine readied for the entire royal family – too *horrendous* to consider, sir. If their fleet goes on to Malta, all the better I say, and good riddance.'

Hamilton seemed very reluctant to accept Acton's view. 'This could be a clever feint, getting us to chase southwards while the French make a bid for Gibraltar and England. And if England falls,' insisted Hamilton, 'so falls Europe, Sir John.'

'Yes, yes,' said Acton, 'we have been over all this, *ad nauseam*, Sir William. But I happen to hold with the Malta idea. It is the perfect strategy to take Egypt.'

Hazzard felt a jolt run through his body.

Egypt.

'Why should they take Egypt, sir?' asked Hazzard, trying to maintain an even tone.

'Well, to attack India of course.'

Hazzard frowned. 'India…?'

An attack fleet, sailed through the desert to the Red Sea.

Good God.

Suez.

Hazzard could not believe it. 'They would have to cut open the ancient Suez Canal. It's been buried for centuries. They'd be mad,' said Hazzard, looking to Hamilton.

'No, sir, not mad, quite slim, in fact,' said Acton. 'It is a bold venture and will yield millions in revenue if they could cut a passage to the Indian Ocean and bypass the Cape of Good Hope. Jolly good luck to 'em if it keeps 'em out of Naples.' He drank again.

Hazzard's mind burst with a thousand probabilities: *Thirty thousand troops land at Alex, push south to Cairo, a mobile, modern army, fresh from endless victories in Europe.*

It would be outright slaughter.

Hazzard watched Acton. *He knew all about it*, he realised, *and agreed not to interfere.*

'That would suit Naples very well, sir, would it not,' said Hazzard. 'The wealth of India flowing into the Mediterranean. And Naples the portal to Europe.'

Acton lowered his glass. 'I beg your pardon?'

'Indeed,' continued Hazzard, 'what should it matter to Naples who controls such a canal? French or British, the millions would feather many Neapolitan nests, I am sure.'

Hamilton tried to intervene. 'That is unkind, Mr Hazzard, and would not be the case, I am sure—'

'Do you suggest we are *in league* with France, sir?' demanded Acton.

'Can you be surprised that I wonder, sir, when Britain stands alone, the world teetering on the precipice, while the royal court of Naples prefers to dance and sing?'

Acton set down his glass and got to his feet. 'Sir William. I do not need a *marine*, of all things, to teach me my duty or lecture me on republicanism, sir.'

But Hazzard would not let go. 'Perhaps you do need a lecture, sir. For it was the wretched *Lazzaroni* who saved us last night, commoners, not your plumed Royal Guard in their shining armour – none but they, the poor men and women of Naples, God help them, while French agents swagger through their streets at liberty.'

'That is monstrous untrue, sir,' blustered Acton.

'Is it? The Admiralty will certainly wonder whether the Neapolitan navy sits idle thanks to French coin. I hear the French Directory has little gold left for its mint – what then is the going price for a kingdom, Sir John? Thirty pieces of silver, is it?'

'I *beg* your pardon—'

'Or perhaps the First Sea-Lord should address these matters to the *comtesse* de Boussard, as she seems to hold most sway in this *rotten* borough.'

'You forget yourself, sir!' shouted Acton, red-faced.

'It is *you* who forget, sir!' retorted Hazzard. 'That we stand in the embassy of King George of England, not Ferdinand of Naples, and you, his subject by birth and title play him *false!* Had you offered haven to Lord St Vincent six months ago the French would have clung to the shores of Toulon like drowning men for fear of the English! An army of redcoats would now stand in line across the whole of Italy to protect you, and drive Bonaparte back to the Alps and out! Pray *God* those *four hundred* ships you let creep past your gates do not turn and level this pestilential *pit* as it so *richly deserves*.'

Hazzard stalked out, the door banging open, took back the Lorenzoni from the startled aide outside and strode down the corridor, regretting the outburst for Hamilton's sake, hearing him behind, '...*has suffered too much, Sir John... state of fever, shipwreck, wounds...*' the voice fading as he reached the stairs and paused to rest against the cool polished marble.

Four hundred ships. And they watched them sail by without a word.

He hurried down the broad stone steps, in his borrowed shoes and his borrowed coat, with his borrowed rank and his borrowed ship, feeling so very far from anywhere he could call home, or even a berth where he belonged. *Sir John Acton and his blighted king*, he thought. All he had ever known, all he had ever been expected to believe in, a king, *all* kings, their divine right, perforce greater than any mortal soul – now made so *mundane*, so much cheap profanity by their sloth, greed and duplicitous self-interest. *Damn them all. Sir John Acton, bloated baronet of His Majesty King George III by Grace of God.* As he crossed the main hall he could hear the strains of violins and laughter, the clink of cutlery, and the thought of it all made him ill.

Egypt.

Oh, Lewis, you utter swine, you knew all along.

'*You wrote a monograph on Egypt, hieroglyphs and so forth and, what was it?*'

'*Coptic, sir.*'

'*Yes.*'

Was this the great secret the missing agent was to convey? Passing it to Sarah and by association condemning her to, what was he to believe now, brutal destruction at the hands of Derrien?

Why had she lied in her letter?

He reached the south stairs, determining to retrieve his sword, find Cook and the others and *go*. As he got to the top and rounded the corner Hesse and Kite stepped out of the shadows.

'Sir.'

Hazzard nearly drew his pistol. 'God's *sake*. What is it?'

'The two French bodyguards, they are come to kill you, sir, I believe for revenge,' Hesse whispered. 'I heard the name

"Derrien" and talk of last night, but they do not know who you are. They spoke of an escape route and taking the countess with them. Sergeant Cook is waiting for you by the chambers, *Herr Hauptmann.*'

Hazzard took it in. 'Only two men? In the house?'

'Yessir,' said Kite, 'The ones what got away from you last night sir,' Kite reached behind his back. 'They won't do it with these leastways.' He held up the two daggers the French escorts had brought with them. 'Lifted 'em easy.'

'There may be others outside,' added Hesse, 'but we have friends – the *Camorra* watch the square for us, in repayment for Alberto's betrayal. The *Lazzaroni* send their compliments.'

Hazzard thought of the watermen from the previous night and was grateful. He looked at Kite. 'Find anything?'

'Found this, sir.' Kite held up a gold coin. 'From His Nibs' carriage.'

It was not a royal coin, but only five years old, from 'Year 2' of the Revolutionary calendar, 1793, emblazoned with the word *République.* 'It's not a Louis,' realised Hazzard, 'it's a Republican 24-*Livres*…' In Naples it could have been obtained only from a French republican, and they were not welcome. It was an agent: the *comtesse* de Boussard.

Kite pulled a few crumpled slips of paper, 'And these billy-doux is just old chits an' receipts for wine an' rubbish – nothin' else, but he did 'ave a fine cased pair of pistols, if'n y'don't mind, sir. French ones, o'course sir. Should fetch a bob or two. Essy's got 'em in the swag-bag, sir.'

'Right. Load and ram.'

Kite patted a gun under his livery coat. 'Cocked an' locked, sir.'

'Keep close.'

Hazzard hurried down the darkened passage, torches not yet lit, the clicking of his heels loud in his ear until he turned the corner to the gallery leading to their rooms and saw Cook further up ahead.

'That smoky Frog countess was the bait, sir.'

Hazzard could feel the rage welling up inside him once again. 'Where is she?'

'Captain's got her well occupied, judgin' by the noise. Reckon it was supposed to be you instead, so I wager she has something right nasty planned.'

With thoughts of Lewis and Blake, and Acton and his treacherous obstruction, of Derrieu, everyone playing him for a fool, he moved along the corridor to his bedchamber. Glowing busts of emperors looked down on him. He heard movement inside. Cook flattened himself against the wall and Hazzard likewise by the doorjamb. He held up a hand to Kite and Hesse, *stand by.* They separated and took up positions in the hall, Kite and Hesse ready, each with one of the French daggers.

Hazzard held up three fingers to Cook, then counted down, *three, two...* On one, he hit the latch and threw open the door, dodging back against the wall.

There was a muffled explosion. A cloud of feathers and down filled the air, a bullet smacking into the wall above a fluted column plinth on the opposite side of the corridor. They saw a man bending, coughing violently amid the gunsmoke and dust of the pillow he had used to silence his pistol.

Cook charged him with his shoulder and drove the heel of his hand up against the man's chin, snapping his head back sharply. He dropped to the floor, his neck broken. Kite and Hesse rushed in, keeping an eye on the corridor.

Hazzard retrieved his sword. 'Where's the other one?'

'Don't know...'

Hazzard looked at the dead man. 'Bring that bloody bastard.'

Hazzard hurried down the corridor, Cook behind, Hesse and Kite dragging the body. Hazzard reached the corner, the Toledo *ropera* blade ready as they approached De la Vega's room.

Judging by the sounds from within, there would be no waiting gunman this time. Hazzard kicked in the door. Among the rumpled sheets on the bed the countess was sitting naked astride De la Vega, her bare curves glowing in the candlelight – her moans of pleasure cut suddenly short. She whipped round, one arm rising to cover her breast, but too late, as Hazzard marched to the bed and smashed a bunched fist hard into the side of her head.

She flew from De la Vega, legs and arms splaying as she hit the wall and fell to the floor with a cry. Cook took the corpse from Hesse and Kite to the side of the bed and dropped the dead man next to her. She screamed, kicking, pushing the body away, not wanting to look, not wanting to touch. Hazzard stood over her and put the tip of the razor-sharp *ropera* to her throat.

'Cesár,' said Hazzard, staring down at her. 'You all right?'

'Why yes,' said De la Vega, wrapping his modesty in the bedsheet. 'Thank God you arrived,' he said, with some irony. 'Could you not have waited just two minutes longer…?'

Hazzard bent forward and thrust a hand into her thick, raven-black hair, shaking her like an animal, certain it was there – and finding it, an old favourite of the courtesan assassin: a heavy steel hairpin. He threw it to De la Vega on the bed. 'Your pleasure would have been short-lived.'

She writhed, trembling, trying to cover herself, her open groin, her breasts, the dead man preventing her, his open mouth on her shoulder, swollen tongue protruding, his sightless eyes staring. Hazzard put a boot on her hip. '*La comtesse* de Biasi,' he demanded. '*Où est-elle? Dites-moi ou mourrez!*' *Where is she? Tell me or die!*

'I – I do not know! Please, *m'sieur*,' then with sudden energy, '*Jean-Louis!*'

The door flew open and Jean-Louis, the second of the noble bodyguards, burst in, pistol drawn, but he hesitated when he saw Hazzard, Cook and De la Vega. He raised the pistol but Hesse stepped in behind him and slipped a dagger up and under his jawbone and into his brain. The Frenchman fell dead without a sound, Kite catching him and laying him on the carpet. Hesse withdrew his knife, wiped it, and spat on the body, giving it a kick. The countess screamed again, her voice trailing off to a croaking sob. Hazzard had not moved.

'I will kill Citizen Derrien, *madame*,' said Hazzard, 'and if need be I will kill *you*. Where did the *comtesse* de Biasi go when she left Naples last week? *Tell me!*'

The countess's teeth chattered and she stammered, 'N-n-north – to Rome! Please, *m'sieur, I know nothing!*'

'Who was with her?'

'She – she was alone—'

'Friends, servants, maids? *Come on.*' He ground his boot into her hip. '*Answer me, damn you!*'

'How can I know which servants!'

Hazzard looked over his shoulder at Cook. 'The other body.'

Kite and Hesse dropped the second dead man between the bed and the wall, half onto the countess. She screamed, in horror and helplessness, put a hand over the dead face, over her own and wailed, a hand to her mouth, the cords in her neck straining as she fought to look away, her words tumbling over themselves.

'*Je vous en prie, m'sieur!*' *I beg of you!*

'*Answer me!*' He pressed the tip of the sword further into her neck and it punctured the skin, a red spot appearing.

She shrank away, trying to fight for breath. '*Oui, oui, alors…* a – a maid, or companion, a friend…'

Une amie, she had said: feminine, not masculine. 'Friend?'

'I know nothing more – it is all!'

'Was there a *man*?'

The Admiralty agent.

'No, no! Only the companion!'

La compagne. Feminine again. *The agent*, thought Hazzard, *could be a woman.* 'Where did they go when they went north?'

She hesitated and he pushed on the sword. '*Where, damn you?*'

She clenched her eyes shut, forcing herself to resist, then failing, '*Civita Vecchia!*'

Lewis had said the armada was massing at different ports, Toulon, Marseille, Ajaccio, Genoa – and Civita Vecchia. '*Why Civita Vecchia? Details!*'

Her face contorted, her head thrashing from side to side, at last giving up her final secret. '*She went to the fleet! To Bonaparte!*' She put a hand over her face and sobbed. '*Jules was to take me! But you stopped him and he has gone! He left me! He left me!*'

'Jules? Who is Jules?'

'Jules-Yves! Citizen Derrien!'

'Take you *where? Tell me!*'

'*Valletta!*' she cried, 'To Valletta!'

Malta.

Derrien.

'We got the bastard dead t'rights now, sir...' muttered Cook. 'They're going for ruddy Malta.'

Acton was right. It did make perfect sense – to control Egypt, to control anywhere in the eastern Mediterranean, they would need an island base for resupply, for reinforcements. Sicily was too big to control without a vast garrison, but Malta was small, with a ready-made fortress harbour – occupied by nothing more than the rusting order of the Knights Hospitaller. How Bonaparte must have laughed and laughed.

The *comtesse* stiffened and started to gasp. De la Vega restrained Hazzard's sword hand. He had been pushing the tip into her neck. '*Amigo*, enough. The lady, she is done. *Volpone* will take us – I know where we can go, hm? I have a man in Valletta.'

Hazzard straightened and moved his sword away from the weeping Medusa. He looked down at her without pity. 'Gag her and throw her naked into Acton's carriage,' said Hazzard. 'With the dead men for company.'

Hospitaller

Baron Ferdinand von Hompesch zu Bolheim, Grand Master of the sacred Order of the Knights of Malta, of the Hospital of St John of Jerusalem, was dragged from a fitful sleep by his young Tunisian chamberlain servant, Ashaf – the only member of his staff innocent enough to agree to wake their lord on such a morning.

'Excellency…' he whispered, his voice shaking, 'Excellency? The ships…' He went so far as to touch the shoulder of the sleeping white-haired knight. The old man stirred and blinked awake.

'Ashaf?'

The boy could barely speak. 'Excellency, they say, *come.*'

Von Hompesch roused himself, the previous days of betrayal within the Order returning all too fresh to his memory. The French *Auberges* had claimed that the ships of Bonaparte would cover the waters from Malta to Sicily, and that when they did arrive, the French knights would refuse to take up arms against them – all nonsense, he assured himself, all nonsense.

And when the great fleet had arrived, it comprised a mere fifty merchantmen and a handful of warships loitering harmlessly at the mouth of the Grand Harbour. Having sent fifty thousand Turks to damnation two centuries earlier, Valletta could laugh at such a threat. But it had weakened him, this dissent, this… he dared not speak it, this… *disloyalty*.

Von Hompesch dressed in his silk robe and Ashaf pulled him by the hand, *This way, this way*, out to his private apartment and the palace balcony. The air was cool, and he felt refreshed. He then looked out over Valletta's vast stone bastions, its streets and quaysides, out to sea and the approaches to the Grand Harbour – and fell back into the doorway at the sight that greeted him.

'*Mein Gott…*'

Valletta had sprung to life with terror. Officers of the Maltese militia galloped along the roads and embankments, some knights among them, red battle tabards flying, leading the sparse militia battalions through the grid of streets in the Three Cities. Just beyond the harbour mouth out to sea, below a morning sun burning bright across the deep blue of the waters, there rode not fifty ships, but hundreds: the combined fleet of Napoleon Bonaparte, spreading larger than the capital itself.

Waiting on his balcony were three knights in breast-plate armour, black cloaks flowing overtop, the eight-pointed Maltese Cross emblazoned on their breast. The silver-bearded *Fra'* Rafaelo of the Italian *langue* rushed to support his aged commander and help him to a seat at the balustrade. The others, *Frère* de Fay, the Commissioner of Fortifications, and the glowering *Frère* Bosrédon de Ransijat, head of the *Auberge de France* and Treasurer of the Order, were not so sympathetic.

'*Now do you see? Now?*' shouted De Fay in accusation. He waved an arm at the sight before them. 'We are but *three hundred* knights, my lord. And they come with *tens* of *thousands*. We were warned of this!'

Rafaelo defended him. 'Warned! *You threatened*—'

'*Non*, Rafaelo, *par dieu!* You and I, we have met the Citizen Poussielgue together and undertook an agreement!'

'It is so,' confirmed De Ransijat. He was a careful, particular man, with watchful, politician's eyes. Older than most and a servant to the previous Grand Master, he was meticulous with records – good and bad. 'Have you forgotten his words, *Fra'* Rafaelo? The Republic marched through Italy in plain view, yet still, my lord, we did nothing.'

Rafaelo lashed back at them both, 'You will show more respect, brother, I demand it!' But when he looked at Von

251

Hompesch, the acceptance was clear in the old man's eyes. '*Eccellenza*,' said Rafaelo. 'The Devil, he has come. It is *Buonaparte*.'

The old man gasped. 'It cannot be true...'

De Ransijat had little mercy. 'We knew this day would come, my lord. We struck a bargain.'

'We struck no bargain!' cried Von Hompesch. 'Disloyal, inconstant!'

'You did, my lord, when you agreed to meet Citizen Poussielgue,' said De Ransijat. 'Europe will be aflame with this news. How can we fight such a force with scarce more than 330 knights – 50 of whom are old men, still a-bed with their mistresses as we speak?'

Rafaelo put a hand to his rapier. 'You *dare!*'

De Fay flapped out a despatch and held it up for him to see. 'The great general sent his aide, his Colonel Junot, with a demand to enter the Grand Harbour for water and supply, Rafaelo! You see? It begins!' He pointed over the balcony at the sea and the floating forest of masts. 'There are *four hundred* ships waiting – and by the statutes we may allow only *four* to enter at a time. Will he accept this? *Non!* We are *undone*, brother!'

'Never...'

De Ransijat was pragmatic but growing impatient with their inability to see. 'Shall we plead for help from the mad Russian Czar? Or surrender to save the city? To save the Order? And how can we spill the blood of Christians? It is forbidden, my lord, as I have made plain at Council. This is not Suleiman come to our gates but France – His Holiness would dissolve the Order or excommunicate us if we broke faith with God,' he concluded, 'but they have taken His Holiness as well, have they not.' He shook his head in pity. 'Why can you not understand?'

Rafaelo rounded on him, lapsing into his native Italian, '*Fra*' de Ransijat, do you quail before the enemy for fear of the *pension* they promised you, eh! *Infamia!*'

'Promised all of us, Rafaelo,' said De Ransijat, 'including His Lordship.'

Von Hompesch appealed to them, 'The guns,' said the old man bleakly, 'We must… man the guns, *Frère* de Fay, the Order begs of you—'

De Fay was outraged. 'The *guns*? *Quelle folie.* In the Fort Sant'Angelo, Fort Sant'Elmo, we have fifteen hundred men at arms to man only a thousand cannon! And the powder magazine, it is flooded, the powder *rotten*, as I reported before the council accepted their gold!'

'*Who*,' demanded Rafaelo, 'who could have taken their gold but *you*, Treasurer De Ransijat, *ehi! Well?*'

De Ransijat lost patience. 'It is my duty to inform you, my lord, that the French knights of the *Auberge de France*, Auvergne *and* Provence, will not take up arms against our fellow countrymen.'

'But… but…' gasped Von Hompesch, 'that is two hundred of the knights—'

De Ransijat had a deathly quiet about him. 'Our oath to God forbids the spilling of Christian blood. Our hands, they are tied, all. Castille, Aragon, Portugal, Bavaria, all. In permitting this, you have destroyed the Order, my lord. All we can do is save what remains.'

'*Traitor…*' grunted Von Hompesch, trying to rise. 'Traitor! Arrest him! Guards!'

But none came running. De Ransijat looked down on Von Hompesch, 'Your guards, my lord,' he said with disgust, 'are preparing to fight for no one but themselves.'

They turned to go, and Rafaelo called after them, 'You will not escape judgement for this treachery! Both of you! *De Fay!*'

'Ride then, *mon frère* Rafaelo…' called De Fay as they strode off, passing through the apartments, 'into the mouths of their cannon. *C'est fini.* Save yourself…'

The two French knights marched out, their black cloaks become vast shadows flowing across golden sculptures and chased urns, a passing darkness among the hanging silks and rays of the morning sun, their swords clanking, never to be unsheathed, never to contest an inevitable doom.

Von Hompesch tried to stand but sagged in Rafaelo's arms, struck by the revelation of his failure. He looked hopefully into Rafaelo's eyes. 'W-were the pensions they offered... w-were they generous...?'

Rafaelo lowered his head, spent, his gallantry wasted. But his oath to the Order was clearly more powerful than De Fay's or De Ransijat's, and the Italian knight held him fast. 'My lord,' he urged, a Percival at the side of his fading king, 'Rouse the men at arms, the militia, call them to battle. There must be time enough still – *in nomine Iesu Christi*, in the name of honour, and in the name of *God*.'

Von Hompesch seized on this frail, foolish hope, 'Yes... call out the remaining knights, this one last time... and we shall be De la Valette once again...' He sighed and collapsed into *Fra'* Rafaelo's arms. 'They were right,' he gasped, 'Bonaparte... he has darkened the seas.'

–

That night, *Sergent-chef-major* Achille Caron of the 75th Invincibles sat in the stern of a cutter from *Spartiate*, one of three boats rowing steadily across the mouth of the ancient capital. Beside him were St Michel, Rossy, a new boy called Antonnais, and the giant Pigalle, and half a dozen of the Alpha-Omega *chasseur* platoon. They were not in any recognisable uniform but each had brought a full pack. As they drew nearer to the harbour, the fug of Valletta's heat enveloped them in a thick, fetid miasma.

In their charge was a nameless creature Caron did not trust, a Maltese who had reported secretly to Command, and now guided them to their destination. He whistled at his contacts in the other boats to catch up; among them were a number of senior *savants* from the expedition, more diplomats and administrators than scholars, clutching their hats and turning their collars up, as if to avoid detection.

Caron looked up at the fortress walls of the Grand Harbour as the oarsmen pulled them past. In the harbour there were a number of broad inlets crammed with low-slung ships at anchor, antique oared galleys and old Porto caravels, many flying the black flag marked with the eight-pointed white cross of the Knights of Malta. Each promontory was studded with a small fortress, but none was larger than the slab-sided walls of the great Fort St Elmo in the centre. It looked down upon them all from the peninsula, jutting into the middle of the harbour, like a deadly tongue, thought Caron, gun emplacements and embrasures everywhere. The harbour was a death trap of over-lapping fields of fire. *How, by the balls of Pluto*, he thought, *shall we ever take this?*

Maltese civilians in rags came to the shoreline and the torchlit jetties, watching them with the dead expression of poverty untold – while in their midst stood shining crusader churches of gold and silver. Caron thought the place was ripe for revolution.

'*Mon dieu*,' he muttered, 'The truly wretched...'

'The Order,' said the Maltese spy in passable French, 'takes everything. But they have their price, no? Everyone has the price...' He laughed, a dry simpering hiss in the back of his throat. 'It pleases me to be home again... after all of the meet-ings with you Citizens, months ago.' He sniggered again and put a filthy finger to his lips, *shh*, as if it were his secret alone.

Caron saw nothing of any army, a few horse and foot perhaps but no guard – other than curious men in ancient breastplates holding medieval banners and halberds, gazing out at the fleet, unmoving.

'Who *are* they...?' whispered Rossy, as if seeing natives on an uncharted shore.

'They are the mad knights,' said the Maltese, touching a finger to his temple, 'still on crusade. They slaughter the enemy – *les Musulmans, oui?* – and enslave their captives. Soldiers of God. Ha.' He spat in the water, his allegiances revealed. 'Beyond here,' he pointed out at the sea, 'across the whole world, lies the infidel, *mon ami*, sons of their Prophet. Malta,' he concluded, 'is where Christ stops.'

A small group hailed them from the shore. The oarsmen pulled the boat in and the spy jumped out to greet them. The other two boats ground onto the shingle and scrub of the rock-strewn beach. A mule and cart waited nearby and some of the gathered young men became agitated when they saw Caron and the Alphas, and made aggressive gestures with their aged firelocks.

'*Sarti!*' ordered one of them angrily. '*Sarti!*' His skin was as dark as the twilight around them, a thin straggling moustache hanging over a scrap of beard on hollow, starved cheeks, angry black eyes shining. He threatened with his old musket, pointing it at them.

Pigalle climbed slowly out of the boat and stood full height. The Maltese gawped upwards in horror.

'I do not like this one,' grumbled Pigalle, looking down at him.

'Neither do I,' agreed Rossy, 'he is impolite.'

Pigalle reached down with a huge paw and took hold of the man's musket. Shaking with fright, the Maltese let him take it and stumbled backwards a pace or two. For a moment, Pigalle looked at it curiously, a Moorish flintlock with a Spanish mechanism. The other Maltese men rushed forward, their guns at the ready, but Pigalle took no notice.

He held the musket out in front of him, arms extended, and proceeded to break it in half. It trembled and shook in his grip until the forestock shattered with a bang, loud enough to make the Maltese jump back with a start, the wood cracking in long shards. The metal retaining bands pinged against the stones like so much grape-shot, and the barrel and ramrod collapsed in his hands like melted toffee until bent almost double. Pigalle then dropped it at his feet with a clatter, so much scrap.

The Maltese turned to run, crossing himself. '*Dio, dio…*'

'Stop,' said a low voice. There followed the unmistakable sound of a pistol being cocked.

Two men in black cloaks emerged from the shadows of the low scrub and trees behind the cart, one pointing a small screw-barrelled pistol. It was Jules-Yves Derrien, and Citizen Masson.

'Identify yourselves,' ordered Derrien.

Caron stepped forward. 'Who goes there? Advance one, and be recognised.'

Derrien noted Caron, his authority, the correct protocol, and addressed himself to him. 'You will first give the parole.'

Caron was disturbed by Derrien's confident indifference, and recognised the type at once. He was not a soldier. He was not an officer. He was something far worse: he was the unaccountable face of the State.

'*Alouette*,' said Caron. *Seagull*.

Derrien did not budge. 'Eagle. Who are these men? I requisitioned a platoon of the First Regiment of Guards.'

'They were busy,' said Rossy, 'doing their hair.' Some of the others laughed.

Masson growled like a restrained hound, but Derrien slowly switched his gaze. Unwavering, the pistol was aimed now at Rossy, dead centre.

'I am Citizen Derrien of the Ministry of the Interior. No man is busy unless I make him so.'

Rossy considered this seriously. 'Hm. You know, in Italy, we had these *delicious* little *mille-feuille* buns, with the peppers, garlic and olives baked *into* the pastry, ah, *mwah*.' He kissed his fingertips like a gourmet. 'You should try some, Citizen Interior. They say the garlic, it is very good,' he said in a stage whisper, waggling his little finger, '*for the impotence*, hm?'

'Impudent dog,' muttered Masson.

Caron intervened. 'Enough. I am *Sergent-chef-major* Achille Caron,' he said, '*Adjudant* of the 75th *demi-brigade de bataille*, the Invincibles. These are the *Alpha-Oméga*,' he explained. 'The first the enemy sees, and the last the enemy sees. So named by an Austrian colonel at the Adige in Italy, when these eight put an enemy company to flight at the bayonet, killing fifty.'

Derrien looked them over, absorbing the information. 'They look a disgrace.'

'Indeed. They are not soldiers, Citizen,' said Caron. 'They are killers.'

Derrien considered them once again, saw their mismatched equipment, Italian, Austrian, Swiss, their easy, insolent stance, their muskets held loosely at the hip like Prussian *Jägers*. They had moved imperceptibly into a rough semi-circle before him – he and Masson were now effectively surrounded. He put away his pistol. 'Very well. Transfer the cargo, *Chef-major*. Abuse the locals at your peril. They are now allies.'

'Yes, Citizen,' said Caron, and saluted.

The Maltese were now overjoyed that the giant was apparently on their side, and hurried to help Caron and the Alphas unload the crates of new muskets and ammunition. Derrien greeted the *savants* who handed over a roll of documents and a small case – *très bien, Citoyen Poussielgue, I fear there is nothing more to be done* – and Caron heard the clink of coins; another Maltese took the documents and case and headed to the main road. No one from the harbour approached or challenged them. The spy's colleagues seemed to have official status.

'Diplomacy?' asked Caron.

Derrien turned. 'Wheels must be oiled, *Chef-major*. For the sake of the people.'

Caron nodded. 'For someone's sake. But I doubt for the people.'

'Everything,' said Derrien, 'is for the people.'

Their Maltese contact ran to them, urging them to hurry. 'Come, come, we must go. Gejtano has bought us only little time here.'

'Why give them muskets?' mumbled Pigalle, already upset that he would not see a joust. He hefted three crates at once. 'He said they are knights. They need swords.'

'No, no...' Rossy put a tray of cartridge boxes on the top of Pigalle's load. 'We are not giving guns to the *knights*, Pig. But to their *enemies*, these brave republican fellows here with the bad breath.'

'Oh,' said Pigalle, lumbering slowly to the mule-cart. 'What about the knights? They only have swords. It is not fair.'

'No,' admitted Rossy with a philosophical shrug. 'You are right, Pig. It is not.'

Pigalle took the harness of the mule and clucked to him, pulling him along. 'What now, *Chef*?'

Caron watched as Derrien and Masson led the diplomat *savants* back to the boats. Within a few minutes they had shoved off, the oarsmen pulling back to the fleet, Derrien's black cloak swallowing his form in the darkness. But Caron watched him, and saw Derrien look back at him over his shoulder – Caron knew the man would never forget. The devil never did.

'We go, for oranges, *mes enfants*,' said Caron, a sour taste in his mouth. 'And wine. And Maltese beauties. *Eh bien*, and then we wait.' He looked out at Derrien, making for Bonaparte, with his secret messages and secret evils. 'Trouble, she will come for us soon enough.'

–

Général en chef Napoléon Bonaparte was not a good sailor. Later that night he rose gingerly from his sickbed aboard *Orient* as his young aide Captain Jullien put his head round the cabin door. 'We have a reply, *mon général*.'

Bonaparte nodded as he struggled to sit up but as soon as he did he felt the onset of nausea again and the chamber began to spin slowly round him. He steadied himself. '*Sacre*. They said it would be the most stable vessel on the water.'

He swung his legs over the edge and Jullien helped him on with his coat. The ship rocked gently and Bonaparte's bed rolled slightly on its oiled castors.

'Do they help, *général*…?' asked Jullien, looking at the brass wheels.

'No,' said Bonaparte bluntly. 'In bad seas when Bourrienne reads to me, I trundle about the room like a loose cannon, squeaking like an army of mice…' He got to his feet unhappily. 'It seems I must invade somewhere just to get off this infernal ship.'

He made it to the lamplit Great Cabin without showing too much of his *mal de mer* to the marine guards or officers who had gathered in the passages, and the fresh night air helped. Colonel Junot had opened the stern gallery windows – *just in case* – someone whispered, and the June breeze wafted in, warm and humid.

The General Staff had been called, some of the greatest generals of France – the uncompromising Chief of Staff, Berthier, in thunderous temper, awaiting the Knights' response; the snowy-haired Vaubois and Baraguey d'Hilliers, in command of the storming division; the tall, leonine Kléber of Alsace; the heavy-set, moustachioed elder 'Papa' Dugua, the gallant Reynier, and the grand *chevalier* Dumas, his braided Italian silk cavalry coat thrown over one shoulder; Vial, Bon, Lannes and others, including the calm, soft-spoken Desaix.

Admiral Brueys and Captain Casabianca attended, with the *savants* Poussielgue, Fourier, and his secretary, Bourrienne, taking notes. The wry, high-browed Swiss, General Caffarelli du Falga waited, standing resolutely on his peg-leg. As Bonaparte entered, they bowed. One man did not: unnoticed in the shadows of a dark corner lurked the grim figure of Jules-Yves Derrien.

'Maximilien,' said Bonaparte to Caffarelli, 'your leg, it causes you no pain in this sticky heat?' He asked solicitously, more to distract attention as he settled himself stiff-necked in his seat, a hand to his queasy stomach.

'Luckily not, *mon général*,' said Caffarelli with a rueful smile, commiserating. 'Though I'm green as a goose from these waves. *Mal de mer*,' he muttered. '*Merde du mal* more like.'

There were a few guffaws and Bonaparte smiled thinly. 'Most poetic. You can join me for barley sugar afterwards.' They laughed again. '*Alors.*'

They fell quiet. It was not good news. Colonel Junot stepped forward and delivered it. 'We have only now received a reply to our demand for water and resupply. To honour what they call their neutrality, the Knights will permit entry,' he reported with amused incredulity, 'for only four vessels at a time.'

Berthier shook his head and muttered, '*Idiots.*' Dumas laughed. Jullien and Junot watched but could not be certain if Bonaparte were pleased at Von Hompesch's refusal; it would give them the pretext they needed to invade. As it happened, it appeared he was not.

Bonaparte darkened with anger, his sea-sickness forgotten. 'Old *fool*. Sitting in his gilded little Jerusalem. He's been staring at the Civita Vecchia fleet for *three days* – and now *we* have arrived.' He waved a hand out of the window. He looked across at Derrien. 'This harbour is as deadly as the Dardanelles – I expected it to be *open. This nation has been bought and paid for.*'

Fourier indicated Poussielgue, who cleared his throat uncertainly. 'Citizen General, I am assured the knights are broken—'

'Broken?'

'Well, we promised them all pensions if they would accede to our demands, and the French knights now refuse to bear arms against us, the Knights' Treasurer, Bosrédon de Ransijat, now arrested for his loyalty to France.'

Admiral Brueys glanced at Casabianca. 'Are the squadrons ready to disperse to their landing points?'

Casabianca bowed. 'Marshalled and awaiting your signal, *mon amiral.*'

Derrien took a pace forward from the shadows. 'Citizen General, agents assure me there will be minimal organised resistance, if any at all.' The wound on his chin from Naples had barely healed, now a very obvious bruised red line – a burning memory of Hazzard. Perhaps to avenge his dignity, he urged, 'The Grand Master needs a sharp lesson, General.'

'Does he? A sharp lesson while the whole of Europe watches, ecstatic as France sacks the temples of holy warrior-monks! *Mon dieu…*'

He nodded to an aide, Duroc, who took up a pen and waited.

'*General Bonaparte,*' he dictated, '*will secure by force what should have been accorded him freely.*' Bonaparte looked at them, sullen, cold. 'Very well.' He nodded to Vaubois and D'Hilliers. 'Proceed. Trample his petty castle of sand.'

–

Once beyond the island of Capri, the *Volpone* caught fair winds to the western tip of Sicily. Ordinarily De la Vega would have gone south through the Straits of Messina, but he wanted to pass Sicily unnoticed. They struck a calm in the Aegadian Isles off Trapani to the west, and were soon swaddled in fog. The marines cared little: Cook drilled them in preparation for the fight they had been waiting for.

When the ship emerged from its blanketing clouds off the small island of Pantelleria, a northwesterly filled their canvas, and they soon found themselves in the midst of a local fishing fleet. One lugger drew alongside to sell them part of their catch, and De la Vega paid them with Neapolitan coin.

'And what of the *Francesi*?' he called down.

The fisherman shook his head. '*Non lo so, signore!* They pass Mazara yesterday.'

'Which direction?' asked Hazzard.

The fisherman pointed. '*Southeast!*'

Malta.

Volpone extended her yards, extra spars jutting far outboard, the nimble Elena and Maria-Luisa racing out along the polished struts to secure the sheets for stun sails, each taking a line and flying out over the sea, and swinging in again to land on deck, Carlos the bo'sun snatching each one up with a roaring laugh. Soon the spray blasted in clouds at the bows, the ship's copper flanks charging through the waves at a blistering twenty knots, dolphins leaping at the prow, the marines and crew cheering from the stays. At last, *Volpone* was on the chase – but they had lost precious time. Hours later, they reached their target.

They approached Malta at night, under cover of the north-eastern coast of the isle of Gozo. The sea was black and silent. They crept round Comino, the shoals treacherous, Handley hanging from a boat lowered over the side and calling his directions to Alfonso and Carlos the bo'sun, '*Steady... steady, two points a-starboard, estribor, estribor, starboard, rápido rápido...!*'

By midnight, a sense of unease had seeped into the crew, the marines tense, watching the darkness for hidden threat, the lookouts not exchanging a word. The northern ridges of Malta appeared in the eyeglass against the indigo darkness of a deep blue horizon, a low, dark mound dotted with firelight. Christina, all in black, floated across the decks to De la Vega at the portside rail, her pale face that of a disembodied spirit, and crossed herself as she looked out. De la Vega put an arm around her, then nodded to Alfonso, and they doused the running lamps. *Volpone* was rigged for a smuggling run, and everyone passed the word: *silencio.*

Hazzard joined De la Vega at the quarterdeck rail. There was no shipping traffic. Nothing moved, the only sound the wind in the sails above, and the whisper of the rigging.

'Something, *amigo*,' observed De la Vega to Hazzard softly, 'has frightened the seas.'

The *Volpone* hugged the black coastline, edging carefully southwards, every man straining to see and to listen. Someone muttered a word, and another hushed him. In the darkness someone dropped a tool and cursed. Then, once more, all was still. Wayland approached Hazzard and they both stared into the darkness, Wayland keeping his voice low.

'Captain Day reported approximately 350 knights, sir,' he said softly, 'Of whom at least 200 are French. He said they would most likely not take up arms to defend Malta if Bonaparte invaded.'

Hazzard nodded, 'So. He has been given the keys, it would seem.'

Wayland looked at him, hurt, misinterpreting his curt response. Since Hazzard's return from Naples and his report of Acton's declaration, Hazzard had been more withdrawn – but Wayland had been astonished by the revelations.

'I simply do not understand it, sir. I wrote a full report for Sir Rafe,' he insisted, his whispers growing with intensity. 'I – I examined old Turkish surveys of the canal levels leading to Suez and the Nile, extrapolations for silting, the drift of the banks, the difficulties involved, everything – and showed that it *could* possibly be done, and therefore that Egypt was the most obvious target according to Captain Day's intelligence reports. I passed all to him and he said he would take it to the First Sea-Lord. I assumed you had been informed,' protested Wayland miserably. 'I have failed you, sir, failed us all, not to have said a thing about it but I was told not to. Such a *fool…*'

'You are by no means the fool here, Mr Wayland,' said Hazzard, 'I should have known Sir Rafe Lewis was not to be trusted.'

Hazzard had worried at it for weeks. Did Lewis believe Hazzard would fail? The renegade 'tarpaulin' out of invalid retirement with his rag-tag band, bound to be killed or captured?

And what of Acton's assertion of Egypt? Lewis must have known it was possible, or was convinced of the likelihood, that it *could* be Egypt. He had sent Hazzard out to sea to find their agent, yes, and retrieve the agent's intelligence *in case the French were bound for England*, but also because Hazzard was the Egypt 'expert' – if Lewis were proved right, Hazzard would already be *in situ*.

Lewis, you conniving bastard.

Given the Admiralty's awareness of the very real threat of invasion, their awareness of the massing fleet, Hazzard concluded that their prevailing response to Acton's chance discovery would be simple: *Better Egypt than England.*

264

The inescapable conclusion was that Hazzard was not to *prevent* an invasion of a foreign land, but somehow *guarantee* it – to keep Bonaparte away from England.

And if Hazzard failed to find the agent, and indeed were captured, Lewis had fed Hazzard all the half-truths he wanted conveyed to the French. He would let Hazzard suffer under the knives, the burning slowmatch applied first to one eye and then the other, until the inevitable, *Yes, yes I'll tell you!* And in his despair he would spin them Lewis's yarn of a young woman on a tour, a fumbled relay of a vital despatch from a lost agent, convincing them of a confused, disorientated Admiralty – while Nelson, somewhere out to sea, was preparing to fall upon them with a dozen heavily armed ships of the line.

And young 2nd Lieutenant Wayland of His Majesty's Marine Forces and the men of 9 Company were an easy sacrifice: off the roll, non-existent, footsoldiers to be spattered against the bastions of enemy castles.

He looked out at the darkness, knowing they had bundled Sarah into this neat package of missing information and a lost agent, all to give Hazzard sufficient motivation to find them both.

Had anything been true? Had they known anything of Sarah?
Lies.

But now he knew. *Comtesse de Biasi. Bonaparte's fleet.*
Malta.

Oh, Lewis, you swine. You shall pay.

Once again he pictured the Admiralty buildings, the teeth of the Royal Navy. More than ever, Hazzard determined not to accommodate their lordships' wishes.

Volpone moved further down the coastline, the only light on deck from the small compass-lamp at the helm, big Carlos's grim features lit by its unearthly glow. They nosed round the Qawra promontory – to starboard the silhouettes of square-topped crusader towers rising black and sinister against the western sky. Hazzard leaned on the rail and steadied a telescope.

His plan was very simple. To find Sarah, to find the *comtesse* de Biasi, he still had to get at Derrien, whom he now knew had joined the fleet. Derrien would be at the centre of the command structure, somewhere within reach of Bonaparte – senior decision-makers needed constant access to intelligence officers. And he knew the principal objective of any assault on Malta would be to control the harbour and fortresses. To seize that control they would need the cooperation of the Grand Master of the Knights himself – one way or another.

If Hazzard could reach the Grand Master he might yet be able to save some small part of Malta from the wrath of the Republic – the attempt would at least provide him with suitable grounds for what he must now do. Though he had lost his false French identity papers he had written something more useful, and slipped it inside the lining of his Bombay coat. It was a form of insurance, but he would not tell Cook, Wayland or De la Vega – because they would try to stop him.

The black waters slapped against the hull and the spray hissed. The lines creaked overhead. The night stared back at them over an infinite sea, and devoured all things of Man. Abruptly, De la Vega moved to the portside rail of the quarterdeck and leaned outboard through the shroudlines, holding out his glass. Something had disturbed him.

'*Alfonso,*' said De la Vega, barely above a whisper, '*Cañones. Listos para la acción.*' *Guns ready for action.*

Alfonso snapped the commands. To the sound of running feet, the guns on the open deck before them were rolled back from the rails and loaded, then hauled forward into firing position, the crews working in whispers. Slowly, *Volpone*'s lower-deck gun ports opened in dead silence. Hazzard joined De la Vega at the rail and raised his own glass, sighting past the bows. It was clear the Spaniard had seen something.

'Cesár. What is it?'

De la Vega kept the glass steady, one finger held up for silence. Then shook his head. '*Nada.* Nothing. But – *listen...*'

Then they heard it. The faint, flat, bark of a cannon drifted towards them in diminishing echoes. A single shot. A startled seabird called, then three distant muted blasts.

'Fleet signal guns?'

'*Sí.*'

Handley gave a brief whistle from the tops. Hazzard looked up. Handley cupped his hands round his mouth and whispered down, '*Larboard bow...*' then pointed out to sea.

De la Vega followed the path of Handley's arm and raised his glass. After a few moments, he saw it.

'*Allí...*' he whispered. '*There, amigo.*'

Wayland, Cook and Alfonso clustered behind them and looked. The deckhands moved to the rails along the bows and fo'c'sle, some climbing onto the foremast rigging, all trying to see.

Lights flickered beyond the shoreline of Valletta. In his glass, Hazzard was certain he could see the torchlit glow of city walls, shadows, silhouettes. And something else.

'What is that...' mumbled De la Vega, '...another island?'

Hazzard focussed and saw it. It was not an island.

A dark mass lay spread across the water, its boundaries marked by lamps, hundreds of them: from masts, from rails, swinging over fo'c'sles, over quarterdecks. It stretched over the sea, a landmass of its own, casting a light as great as that of the capital city. Swaying from their anchor chains, the flanks patrolled by frigates and light corvettes, lay the invasion armada of Napoleon Bonaparte.

De la Vega lowered his telescope and crossed himself. '*Dios mío.*'

Hazzard handed the glass to Wayland. Seeing the fleet before them had brought Lewis and Blake's briefing to vivid reality. It had not all been lies, after all. Handley dropped to the deck and joined them, peering over his shoulder.

'Well, sir,' he said. 'You reckon them's for us?'

'Enough for you, Mr Handley?'

'Enough to put the wind up Nelly himself, sir.'

The marines joined the crew at the portside rail, leaning out, pointing.

Hazzard looked to Cook and said quietly, 'Jory. Ready?'

Cook nodded. 'Aye.'

De la Vega ordered the cutter swung out to starboard, over the landward side. A crew of Catalan oarsmen was assembled. Wayland watched, confused, aware he had been left out of a decision. 'Sir? What is to be done? Are we to make a landing?'

'No. Sar'nt Cook and I shall make a preliminary reconnaissance,' said Hazzard, 'with a guide provided by Captain De la Vega. We shall then return and report the situation.' He looked away, unable to say it to his face, even if it were for his own good. 'And then call in the remainder of the company if we can identify a clear objective.'

Elena moved behind Alfonso, watching Hazzard silently, as if catching him in the lie.

Wayland was aghast. 'Sir, I beg your pardon, but that, that is *short-sighted*. Yes, sir, *very* short-sighted.'

'It is better this way—'

'I – I beg your pardon, but that is nonsense, sir.' Wayland astonished even himself. 'If-if you would indulge me – we would be splitting our forces, without sufficient intelligence of enemy strength,' he protested. 'You could be overwhelmed and, and *lost* to us, sir, and us none the wiser—'

The marines gathered, looking at the empty boat, their muskets ready. Warnock said it first, Indian tomahawk in hand. 'It ain't *fair*, Sarge. Give us our shout – we've earned it.'

'*Mind yer tongue, boy,*' snapped Cook.

But Underhill looked uneasy with it as well. 'Jory, for Gawd's sake. These lads are sharp for it.'

'Let us guard your back, sir,' said Kite. 'Fast in, fast out. Like you said. Give you a fightin' chance, sir.'

'He is right, sir,' stammered Wayland, flushed, pointing at the men. 'Dash it, sir, they are *ready*. And, marine operations

268

require,' he stumbled, 'they, they *require* communication with the ship of origin, *constant* communication, it is said, and a-a *secure* landing point for evacuation, or reinforcement – and we can establish such a place, sir, and *hold* it until you return. And, yes, sir, dash it all, I would trust these chaps with my life, sir, and so should you.'

Hazzard looked at their faces. Unshaven and filthy, they looked back at him, grim, waiting, hungry for action. But he was spared an obstinate denial: at that moment, everything changed. Handley relayed a call from the lookout above. 'One, two, three enemy sail heading south – boats going ashore, sir. We've had it – they're goin' in.'

'They are *landing*, sir,' said Wayland. 'Or reinforcing. Any moment longer and they shall swarm across the island.'

Hazzard looked out to sea and saw the glow of white sails separating from the main body. There could be no covert operation now, only a heated infiltration under fire. Hazzard cursed that he had not gone alone when he had the chance. He made the decision. 'Very well. Mr Wayland, you have the landing party to secure a site. Sar'nt Cook and I will lead with the guide. If we are separated you will hold the landing site for a day unless discovered, then return to the ship and get the men to Nelson with the location of the enemy fleet. Is that clear?'

'Sir, *you* will do all that, sir, surely, when you return.'

Hazzard did not reply. 'Cesár, can you get us in close?'

De la Vega was busily removing his coat, a lit cigarillo clenched in his teeth. He drew on a pair of leather gloves as Carlos buckled his sword belt round his waist. The wound from Naples had left his right arm stiff and still obviously painful. 'Oh yes, we go very close,' said De la Vega, 'for I am the guide, *amigo*. I take you to the house of Luca, a Maltese, a good man, a good smuggler in Sliema. There is nothing he does not know.'

'Cesár, I cannot permit it—'

'You forget,' said the Spaniard, raising a finger, 'this ship, she does not belong to your mad King Jorge. He only borrows, for this short time.' He nodded to Alfonso and the ship nosed towards the shore.

Elena rushed to Hazzard, pressing a small rough-hewn crucifix into his hand. He looked into her deep, black eyes and saw more than simple concern; it was fear of the inevitable. She folded his fingers over the cross and kissed him.

'You see?' said De la Vega, 'Elena, she always knows.' He slung a cartridge bag over his shoulder and shoved a pistol in his belt. 'Now, *compadre*, *Volpone* shall taste French blood.'

–

Hazzard was out and into the surf first. They dragged the boat up the rocky beach to the lee of a leaning clump of thorn on the southern shore of a bay just north of Valletta.

The marines spread out and took up positions, crouching in the brush, only a few with their sawn Shorter Indias, most equipped with Spanish muskets from the *Volpone*. Wayland wore his newly cut-off Marine scarlet but, many having lost their uniform coats with the *Esperanza*, the men had donned smocks and jerkins, turbans and brimless caps – some looked Sicilian, some Greek – they would pass muster easily on Malta, where all lands met. Hazzard knew his own Bombay Marine jacket would stand out, but that was his intention.

'Mr Wayland, you will be supported by Sergeant Underhill. Do not engage the enemy unless forced, and then perform only retiring actions to fall back to this landing point, clear?'

Underhill glanced at the apprehensive Wayland and answered for him, 'Clear aye, sir.'

'Er, yes,' stammered Wayland. 'Clear aye.'

'Sar'nt Cook and I will follow Captain De la Vega into the town to find the contact. Do what you can for any locals in distress, but do nothing to jeopardise the *Volpone* or your escape. If I do not return here by nightfall tomorrow then you *must* get back to the ship and get word to Nelson. He will do the rest. Is that understood?'

Wayland nodded uncertainly. 'Yes, sir.'

Hazzard looked at them each in turn, Underhill, Pettifer, De Lisle, Kite and Porter, Hesse, Warnock, Cochrane and Napier. 'What do you do when you're caught in an ambush, Kite?'

Kite repeated by rote, 'Attack, sir, cut down the odds. Pick your man, head down and charge 'im like John bloody Bull, sir.'

Hazzard nodded. 'Good. Remember the Finger Five, scorpion style, fifth man on the stinger to come in blazing round the side like a snapdragon surprise.'

'*Aye.*'

'Keep to your formations, trust Mr Wayland, move fast, keep low. Remember: *we are the boat.*'

'*Aye sir.*'

De la Vega was ready. '*Vámonos, muchachos.*'

They followed the shoreline until they found a dirt track. As dawn began to break, they heard the first distant blasts of cannon, the musical howl of hurtling shells and muffled explosions. They hurried, the marines hugging the verges, ready to dodge into cover, Wayland in the rear, eyes bright and afraid.

After a mile they found the coast road and saw the few lights of Sliema – the town was little more than the northern outskirts of Valletta, its rock-strewn shores guarded by still more deserted towers and tangles of parched thorn and low stunted trees. The first rays of the sun streaked the coarse terrain with long, hostile shadows. They ran down a shallow rocky incline to a meagre thicket affording a view of the backs of mud-brick cottages and sloping streets. The cannon blasts grew louder.

'The guns. In the north,' said De la Vega, looking back the way they had come.

'And south,' said Cook. 'They're every bloody where...'

Hazzard could smell the ordure of the port. The streets before them shone with the dazzle of first light – but there were no fish stalls erected, no traders, no merchants. The eerie quiet was split by a sudden crackling barrage from the south, the thudding blasts palpable in the morning air. A door banged open and a man hurried out of a house, shepherding his wife and three children, urging them to hurry. They disappeared down a lane, the door to their home left swinging, and the street was once again empty. Then they heard the French guns again.

'The forts,' said De la Vega. 'They hit the castles on the harbour.'

Hazzard listened. 'Softening them up or cover fire for the first landing…'

The empty lanes began to flood with running people, pushing, screaming, some pulling carts up the road, mules braying, a single knight on horseback, red tabard flying, riding through them without care, *Out of my way!* all trying to get as far from Valletta as they could, the crash of cannon echoing through the network of streets, the people screaming louder with each blast.

'*Jaysus, shite an' all,*' murmured De Lisle.

'Mr Wayland,' called Hazzard, 'get back to the landing point. The worst has happened.'

Wayland nodded. 'Yes – yes, sir…'

'Hold the site but do not put the men or the ship in jeopardy, understood?'

'Yes, sir…'

Hazzard tried to reassure him. 'I *will* see you, Mr Wayland. I *will.*'

Wayland seemed distracted, confused. 'But, sir, *why*—'

'Mr Wayland,' insisted Hazzard, 'we could not have come this far without you. Remember that.'

Someone murmured *hear-hear.* Wayland nodded, a boy unhappily saying goodbye to a father. 'Thank you, sir…' He turned to Underhill. 'Marines, to me, Sergeant…'

'Aye-aye, sir.' He called to the others, 'On your landlegs and advance to the rear for Mr Wayland and be *flippin'* quick about it! Landing site to be held, aye, sir!'

The marines melted away, Wayland hanging back with Hazzard. 'Good luck, sir,' he said.

'Thank you, Mr Wayland.' It could be the last, he felt, he would see of his second in command. After a final look back, Wayland hurried after the men. In moments, they were beyond the dappled morning light of the trees. De la Vega checked his pistol. 'Come, *amigos*, it is not far…'

He led Cook and Hazzard at a run through the crowd and into the alleyways, the cries of the people echoing from nearby squares. The streets of Valletta and the Three Cities were in uproar, the populace running from the percussive blasts of French cannon. With every shot, the three ducked their heads out of reflex, Cook cursing '*You can't tell where the buggers're comin' from!*' They looked down into the centre, at the pinnacles of baroque churches, their bells clanging, and always a mass of people: desperate processions of the Virgin and saints jammed the hilly thoroughfares, clogging the church squares – they watched as another mob stampeded through the roads, priests among them, sacred effigies bouncing on the shoulders of running bearers. The fleeing Maltese militia ran after them in disorder, families racing before them in full flight south to the distant waterside, or east to the coast, and north to the fields, no direction better, no route safer than another.

De la Vega pulled them onwards. '*Come, this way!*'

They dodged into a back mews and saw a single man running, weeping, then gone, a group, the wailing of cornered animals, a girl in a headscarf, her bare feet slapping on the stones, seeing the three of them, their guns, and giving a scream of fright, then running off. De la Vega stopped at a terrace of houses and banged on a pair of ageing double doors. '*Luca!*'

There came no answer. Hazzard began to look for an alternative. 'Can we get to the back?'

'Luca!' De la Vega called and banged again then cursed, '*Hijo de puta…*'

Cook pointed at a pair of wooden gates at the side. 'Sir – listen…' They could hear voices.

'*Luca,*' called De la Vega at the gates. '*It is Cesár Domingo! Abra! Open the damned doors!*'

More cries came howling down the lanes, and De la Vega kicked the gate in, Cook and Hazzard following – to find two startled boys pointing muskets at them, and a girl clinging to an older man in a yard, all gathered round a barrow laden with belongings. The man's face broke into a smile of recognition. 'Cesár?'

'I have been banging and banging, *Malto estúpido*, where have you been?'

'We thought you were militia!' He laughed and they embraced. Luca Azzopardo shook his head. They spoke in Italian, their *lingua franca*. 'It is mad, the town. The Knights are *finiti*. Every Embassy, every *Auberge* and *Langue*, Castillian, Provençal, *le Tedeschi* Bavarians and *Inglese*, Portuguese – they hate the French knights, who do not take up the sword, and watch as De la Valette's castle will be broken down.' He spat. 'The people, they despise them more now.'

'Can you get me to the Grand Master?' asked Hazzard. 'Can we get him to safety?'

It took a moment before Azzopardo realised he was serious. He looked at De la Vega. '*È Romano?*' He is Roman?

Hazzard shook his head. '*Inglese.*' English.

Azzopardo laughed. 'Ha. Only an Englishman would ask such a fool thing. *No*, my friend, we go out *now* before the gate it closes on us all, *bouf*, and pray to the saints your *Nelsone* comes quick.'

More running feet passed the gate and another girl ran to Azzopardo and spoke quickly in Maltese, incomprehensible to Hazzard or De la Vega. 'They have landed the ships everywhere, some south, some north of here,' said Azzopardo, 'There is nowhere to go, *signore.*'

'But surely we can get to the water at least—'

'How? They attack, always attack, Marsaxlokk, down there, the water, *si*? San'Paulo, Birgu, Gozo too, everywhere already.

In Sliema, they come from San' Giuliano's Bay, yes? Just above us here? They march, shooting at the militia *baboom-baboom* then say, *come, come, we come to free you, libro libro.*' He put both hands to his head to pull at his hair to show his consternation, 'The militia taking our children to fight for the knights, it is all *confondendo*, madness, *sì*?'

'I'll keep a watch...' Cook ran to the gate and out to the street.

Hazzard needed Azzopardo to understand. 'Listen to me. Nelson will *not* come unless I report the strength of the enemy fleet, *capisci*? Can you get me to the harbour, or the fort?'

Azzopardo stared at him. 'Fort Sant'Elmo? You truly are mad. We must go *through the town*, the town where the French push the people, where the cannons fire—'

'Get me at least to the waterfront.' He needed somewhere under fire but also under control. 'Or Nelson could sail into a trap.'

Cook returned from his short reconnaissance, 'Bloody mad, sir – no Frogs yet, can ruddy hear 'em mind, but just folk runnin' every place.'

Azzopardo looked at Hazzard again, eyes wide, thinking fast. 'You bring *Nelsone*? The ships? You are with *Nelsone*?'

'I am. But I need to see the fleet and how many troops have landed – then I shall try to reach the palace to save the Grand Master.'

Azzopardo glanced at De la Vega, muttered something in Italian, and De la Vega shrugged with a nod, '*Sì, sì, la verità,*' *Yes, the truth.*

Azzopardo turned and gave orders to the children to leave the barrow and go to find their uncle in the next street, that he would join them. He looked at Hazzard, his humour gone. '*Signore*, I take you through Sliema, to water, harbour, *sì*? But not to *il gran maestro*, no. You see fleet, you go – and you bring *Nelsone*.'

'Very well,' said Hazzard.

275

They followed him out to the street and around a corner, then down, down through the panic of the town, ducking into empty lanes, until a flood of people fleeing the waterside hit them head-on, the street suddenly thronged with people, carts and animals. Between the buildings Hazzard glimpsed the bell towers of the distant churches on the spit of Valletta, jutting out into the Grand Harbour, the French ships manoeuvring into position, cannons blasting at a fortress on the far side and Azzopardo pointed. '*Birgu*,' he called. '*They shoot at Fort Sant'Angelo…!*'

A frigate and a sloop sliced across the harbour, racing to a distant inlet to threaten a fort, plumes of smoke billowing from the far side of the Grand Harbour. All the while the mighty guns of Fort St Elmo lay silent, its ramparts ridden by knights herding platoons of soldiers first this way, then that, no apparent order to be seen.

They burst through the crowd to find the harbour and shingle stretching down to quays and jetties, the Knights' galleys rocking on the swell caused by the French ships. Marsaxlokk harbour seemed filled with small boats, an armed merchantman disgorging troops from lines. A dozen cutters and jolly-boats rowed ashore and up the shingle, white-coated French grenadiers and light infantry pouring out and forming up.

'Storming troops,' said Hazzard.

Cook nodded back at Sliema. 'And behind us – line infantry, two hundred yards,' said Cook, 'or twenty in these bloody lanes. Bugger knows where.' A volley blasted nearby, followed by still more screams.

Azzopardo pulled them away, '*Dai, dai, veloci!*' Come on! Hurry! and they followed the flow of the crowd west towards Gzira, ever closer to the epicentre, to Valletta, the streets twisting, crammed with people and carts, no clear direction to safety to be found, the sound of horses' hooves clattering against the buildings, calls of French officers, *Deuxième bataillon! Formez!* and constant calls overhead, *Vous êtes libre! You are free!*

276

Up ahead, a platoon of French ran past the mouth of a lane; they waited, then hurried on, running with the crowd as cover, an old woman falling, crying out, Cook picking her up, *Come on, ma, King Georgie's got yer*, De la Vega nearly tripping over a child, scooping him up, handing him on to a gesticulating father already laden with two others. '*Amigo! This is too mad, even for Cesár Domingo!*'

'*Just get us somewhere we have room to move!*' called Hazzard.

Dilapidated terraces gave way to townhouses, baroque squares opened up before churches, each inundated by fleeing civilians and militiamen in disorder. Somewhere, troops were singing, the voices triumphant, infectious. A musket volley sounded several streets over and Azzopardo ducked. He turned wide-eyed to Hazzard, '*Signore.* Valletta *impossibile.* It is too far through these streets.'

They ran to the next junction where they found crowds, but Azzopardo drew back in sudden alarm. An aged knight in quartered red surcoat marked with a plain white cross appeared from a narrow lane, trying to hold back a platoon of running militia. He raged at them in Portuguese, blustering, waving a sword. In the adjoining square a column of French infantry were coming at the double – they stopped when they saw the knight and his men.

The knight pushed the Maltese militia in line to block the road, '*Preparai-vos!*' The Maltese raised their muskets uncertainly and he shouted the order to fire.

'*Atireh! Fogo! Fogo!*'

They did nothing, eyes tight shut, their raised musket barrels wavering. The knight had called in Portuguese. The French formed ranks in the square as the knight screamed again in Maltese, '*Nar! Nar! Miftuħa nar!*'

The quaking Maltese ranks fired, shots pinging off the church walls, hitting closed shutters, Maltese civilians running. The French faltered, some throwing themselves flat to the cobbles. The militiamen saw their chance, broke, and ran, knocking down the knight and throwing aside their empty muskets. A French volley followed them and a few of the Maltese cried out and fell, the others throwing up their hands in supplication, preferring to be French prisoners than followers of the Portuguese knight.

Azzopardo seized De la Vega's arm. '*Andiamo!* We go now! This way!'

Hazzard took his arm. 'No – Luca, can you get home from here?'

'*Sì, signore…*'

Hazzard nodded and shook his hand. 'Then go – while you can.'

The Maltese nodded in agreement. '*Sì, sì, signore.*' He embraced De la Vega. '*Vaya con Dios, amigo mío.*' Then he stopped and looked at Cook, at Hazzard, at his red coat, the braid, his sword. 'You promise? All this, it brings *Nelsone*?'

'Yes.' Hazzard was certain. 'Nelson shall not forget Malta.'

Azzopardo nodded. 'Then God save you, *signore inglese*. And I shall tell them. For hope.'

Luca Azzopardo checked the street, then dashed off, disappearing into the crowd. Hazzard made to go but Cook put a hand to his shoulder.

'Sir. Briefing.'

Hazzard hesitated. 'Check numbers, Sar'nt. Is it a raid or an occupation?' It was all he could think of. He could not give him the real reason.

Cook searched his face, Hazzard's eyes distracted, darting left and right – he was in the field and not prepared to speak any longer. 'Right you are, sir. Then out.'

'Then out. Clear?'

Cook nodded. 'Clear aye, sir.'

De la Vega grabbed at them. '*Amigos*, we have not the time for the sight-see of the pretty Maltese churches, *sí*?'

'Come on then,' said Hazzard, and they hurried to the next corner, echoing above their heads the sound of hundreds

278

marching in column, singing, all mingled with the wailing of canticles and crowds and the endless clanging of bells, calling for help.

–

Wayland took the marines back along the coast road. Barely halfway to the landing point, running militiamen burst onto the track, local residents running after, heading for the coast.

'Stand! *Stop*, I say!' called Wayland.

Underhill and Pettifer stepped out and fired a round in the air. '*Halto!*'

Some of the militia staggered to a stop as the marines grabbed at them but the people ran past. Behind came Kite at the double. '*Sir! Company o' Frogs hoppin' this way!*'

Wayland looked at the verges. There was not enough cover for an ambush, only thin stunted trees and low scrub, behind him nothing but the backs of fleeing civilians. The road could fit twenty men abreast at most, and did narrow, not much, but just enough – if a company were marching in formation at shoulder-dressing, he calculated, they would be entering a bottle-neck, not unlike Thermopylae – where numbers had counted for nothing. Wayland felt just as trapped, but the vulnerable Maltese civilians behind him made up his mind. Despite their discussions, despite their training in the theories of skirmish assault, he was going to order what he had once considered the unthinkable: an exposed defensive line, in the open.

'Sergeant Underhill! Get the militiamen and form two ranks, open order, arm's dressing, both ranks kneeling!' he called.

Underhill looked at Wayland, standing alone in the road in his scarlet, hand on his sword, then glanced at the cover and nodded with a grin. '*Aye-bloody-aye, sir! Marines! Open order, form line, arm's dressing, on yer rowlocks an' hop to it! Private Hesse, convey said order in the lingo, smartish!*'

'*Sì, sergente!*'

Hesse began to call out in Italian to the confused Maltese militiamen and Underhill shoved them into line across the road, pushing them down onto one knee, each between two marines. 'Come on now, lads, take yer guns, there ye go, cock yer locks an' lock yer cocks, that's it, get down there, good lad… King Georgie's gon' to give Froggie a nasty shock indeed, just you wait…'

French drums boomed in a slow, regular beat, drawing closer.

'Sergeant…' stammered Wayland, 'three volleys and retire, no more, clear?'

'Clear aye, sir! We'll give 'em a taste of it, aye!' He bawled out his firing orders, '*Double-shot yer Indies, lads, buck an' ball!*'

The drums grew louder. One of the Maltese beside Napier dropped his musket with a rattling crash. The huge broken-faced boxer reached forward and picked it up for him. 'Hold it *tight*,' he rumbled, 'an' *don't move, mush*. Right?' The Maltese nodded, not understanding a word, but heartened by Cochrane's mumbled blessing in Latin, his eyes closed, his head down, '…*benedicat, per Iesum Christum dominum nostrum, amen.*'

The drumbeat burst upon them, loud and sharp, thrashing at the surrounding trees, and a full company of the 19th *demi-brigade de bataille* lumbered heavily into view. They marched in line abreast, colours flying up front, a loose mob of Maltese civilians running ahead of them. The fleeing Maltese screamed louder still when they saw Wayland and the kneeling ranks formed across the road, blocking their path, and they rushed off to the scrub verges to get away, pouring round them as waters in a flood.

'Come on, Mickey,' said Warnock over the head of the Maltese between them. 'A shiny sixpence for whoever bags the first Frog.'

'Aw, bad bet, mate,' said Kite, 'cos you're such a rotten bloody shot…'

'*Nine Company His Majesty's Marine Forces!*' roared Underhill, '*Frenchies by the dozen, for the use of! Picks your man and makes your mark! Gawd bless King George and let's teach the dozy bastards a bloody lesson!'*

The answering shout came back, '*Aye-Ser-geant!'*

A Maltese beside Porter sagged in a faint, his musket drooping. Porter held onto his shoulder and pulled him upright. 'Come on, tha' lad, we can't be doing that now, can we. Looks bad in front of the French.' He produced a small flask and gave him a nip of whisky. The Maltese spluttered and coughed but nodded, taking up his musket once again.

The French came to an uncertain and confused halt, caught off-guard by this sign of resistance. The drum faltered and fell silent. A lieutenant in a white-faced blue tunic and tall cocked hat came jogging to the front of the line, perplexed at the hold-up. He saw Wayland and stared for a moment at the red coat.

Wayland took his moment. '*Front rank! Present!'*

Hesse called it out, '*Primo rango! Presente armi!'*

The muskets came up. The French lieutenant waved to the colour guard, who began to run off to the side, '*Vite! Vite!'* the heavy banners flapping, blocking the first line of infantry behind them as Wayland gave the order.

'*Fire!'*

'*Sparate! Nar!'*

The volley crashed out and the French officer lifted a protective arm and jumped back in alarm as his front rank fell, nearly all of them hit either by musket ball or spreading buckshot. He ran to the side, shouting, '*Anglais! Soldats anglais! Joue! En joue!'* English soldiers! Present! Present!

'*Front rank, reload!'* roared Underhill, '*Second rank, advance!'*

The second rank of marines shot to their feet and stepped through the kneeling front rank. '*Ready, aye!'*

The Maltese followed suit, more confident now. Warnock peered over his sights and laughed. '*Knock-knock…'*

Wayland gave the order, '*Second rank! Fire!'*

The volley burst, shredding the low-hanging leaves of the trees and more of the French flew off their feet. Underhill was ready immediately. '*Reload! Advance!'*

The French troops backed away, calling to each other, *Anglais, anglais!* Frantic, the officer shouting, *Retraitez*, as the reloaded front rank of marines and Maltese advanced through the second.

'*Front rank! Fire!*'

'*Sparate! Nar!*'

Still more fell, the French officer's commands ignored, the front rank fallen, many of the second calling out, beginning to turn.

'*Reload, advance!*'

Wayland gave the order again, '*Second rank! Fire!*'

'*Reload, advance!*'

The exposed ranks of French fell apart, some crashing into their comrades behind.

Wayland saw they were ready. '*Sar'nt! Will they break?*'

'*Like bloody matchwood, sir!*' Underhill stepped forward. '*Charge your bayonets and hold! Each marine will account for three Frogs or I'll scrag you like there's no tomorrah!*'

A dozen men of the French second and third rank stumbled forward, charging in ragged disarray, the officer calling to them to retreat, some stopping, falling back as their comrades turned and began to run – the remainder ran at the marines' bayonets, but they had miscalculated: Wayland's next rank had already reloaded. He let them loose.

'*Fire!*'

A final volley crashed into the French charge, Underhill bellowing out, '*Advance, and into 'em!*' The remainder tripped over their falling comrades, four speared immediately by the outraged Maltese as others came rushing at the British line.

Napier took one French musket by the barrel and jerked it forward, the muzzle flashing high over his shoulder as Warnock hammered down his tomahawk into the back of a skull, flailing right and left with it, taking a second and a third, '*How's that eh, how's bloody that!*'

Wayland stood, his pistol extended in his shaking right hand, '*Retire! We must retire…!*' Looking for a target, the sweat

282

streaming into his eyes, stinging, blurring his vision. A man in grey with full pack, bayonet waving, arose from nowhere and came straight for him, screaming. Wayland saw his contorted features in detail, his dark eyes, the unshaven jaw, the heavy moustache, detected the intimate stink of him, and he could not move, his outstretched arm locked.

The French bayonet sliced past his ear, the wind from the blow making him shiver, and he shut his eyes tight, feeling the jar of collision and a choking gasp. They fell, the Frenchman scrabbling for the pistol in Wayland's rigid hand – it had been driven against the man's chin and almost into his mouth. In fright, Wayland pulled the trigger.

The blast and recoil jerked the pistol from his fingers and the man's red face disappeared in a cloud of powder, a voice nearby shouting, '*You bloody got 'im, sir!*'

Shaking, Wayland fended off a blow with his sword that was suddenly in his hand again, he knew not how. *I am down, I am down, I am lying down*, his left hand thrusting upwards again and again as he screamed, '*Get it away, get it away!*' A body fell beside him.

He heard Kite, '*They're off!*'

Underhill was calling to them, '*Back with it! Back ye bloody lions, step smart into line, in line, in line! Look to it, ye bloody heroes! On p'rade!*'

Wayland pushed himself upright and put a hand to his face – it came away black and red, in his fingers a matted clump of the Frenchman's scalp smelling of burnt powder. With a cry of revulsion he flung it away. '*Disengage...*' he croaked from a dry throat. '*Disengage! Form line and retire!*' He spat and found his voice. '*Sergeant Underhill, retire and give withering fire!*'

Underhill formed the marines and militia into a rough line, firing another volley from the hip as they moved backwards, Wayland trotting alongside, turning, looking back at the retreating French, the bodies in the road, the French officer stunned, staring after them, his sword dragging on the ground.

Hazzard, Cook and De la Vega rounded a corner to find a jam of townspeople packed in a small church square. A priest led a procession of the Virgin in their midst, a choir chanting in Latin as they mounted the church steps, crowded with frightened worshippers, hands raised to its bell towers ringing in alarm. Behind them came the troops of General Baraguey d'Hilliers's storming division.

Two knights in the middle of the square waved their antique swords overhead, shoving their frightened militiamen into line, their muskets clumsy and unfamiliar in their shaking hands, '*Get in line, damn you all!*' – and all the while the people called out in hopeful revolt, '*Vive la France!*'

A French company blockaded the exits of the square, a mounted colonel at their head, calling out, *Vous êtes libre! You are free! Venez! Rejoignez la république du peuple! Come join us! Join the Republic of the people!* The trapped crowds turned as one, a flock of birds, darting first to one blocked street then another, the church doors forced open, the people rushing in for sanctuary. The French presented arms and Cook pushed Hazzard and De la Vega to the ground, *Hit the decks!* The people ran, trampling the wrong-footed – and the French fired.

But the shots went harmlessly overhead, and the colonel's call came again, *Vous êtes libre! Venez! You are free! Come, come!* Some ran to the French lines, arms outstretched, the soldiers passing them through to safety, some embracing them, others calling, *Vive la Malte libre! Long live free Malta! Your masters are our enemy! Not you the people!*

The two enraged and beleaguered knights tried to push the reluctant militia into position. '*Stand to! Get in line and fight!*'

The next French volley erupted, deafening in the confines of the square, the shots once again passing overhead, their cries to the disaffected Maltese echoing, '*Vous êtes libre! La république nouvelle est arrivée!*' *The new republic has come!*

Beating at the militiamen, the knights became more of a pressing threat than the French. The crowd turned on them.

'*Murderers!*'

The militia captain was seized by a group of black-garbed women and driven to the ground, and the knights turned to run. One became entangled in his tabard, tripped and fell. He was immediately kicked and struck by staves and stones, the other dragged off his feet. The women took up the militiamen's abandoned muskets and battered the knights to death as they twisted at their feet, crying out.

'That's it,' said Hazzard, 'we've seen enough!'

'*Sí amigo!* I think we have seen it,' agreed De la Vega, 'Malta has gone to France!'

Hazzard thrust the Lorenzoni into De la Vega's hands. '*Five shots left, Cesár, go! Jory, get the captain back to the* Volpone*!*'

'*Aye, sir…*'

He pushed the pair of them from behind into the crowd – when they turned, Hazzard had gone, clearing a path through the crowd in the opposite direction, towards the French line. '*Jaysus shite an' all the saints… I knew he was up to something! What's he doing?*'

De la Vega took him by the arm. 'Come*, amigo mío*, we must go—'

'He's never gon' to make that bloody palace through this lot!'

De la Vega took him by the shoulders. '*Amigo*, he goes to his lady! You know this – and we cannot stop him—'

'*I can't just leave him! Where's he gone?*'

Hazzard tried to fight his way to the edge of the square, anywhere to get him to a small unit of French and not face a full line in the heat of an engagement. A stray artillery round hurtled overhead and crashed into a townhouse and people screamed, slabs of shattered masonry falling into the square and narrow alleyways.

But it was not artillery. Hazzard saw a man in a tattered robe pull an object from a bag. It was a heavy grenade. Using

285

a smouldering linstock for a wick, he lit the short fuse and threw it at the edge of the crowd. It rolled to the foot of a doorway and exploded, blasting in the door in a cloud of stone. People fell in all directions, crying out, the square filling with smoke. Thinking they were under attack, the French commanders bellowed orders and fired another volley overhead, causing more screaming, more panic – they then advanced into the square.

Hazzard could see the lines of troops marching, crowds cheering, crowds running. The French company would be among them in minutes. The Maltese agitator took out another bomb and a French private in the front rank shouted *Le voilà! There he is!*

Hazzard charged for the Maltese, pulling people away, '*Everyone get down!*' he called first in English, then in Italian, '*Giù, giù! Rapidamente!*'

The Maltese saw Hazzard reaching for him and launched his grenade high over the crowd at the nearest townhouses, then turned to run but stumbled, falling over an old woman, shoving her away, and tried to push through the crowd. Hazzard caught him and he went down, an arm flung out and a cry as Hazzard fended off a swinging knife, someone crying in Maltese, *look out*, Hazzard's only thought: *grenade.*

A heavy man fell on the Maltese with a shout, '*Ho!*' and Hazzard dragged at the limbs of the people nearby to get them down, '*Giù!*' *Down!* and five toppled to the stones with him as he covered their heads. He then saw Cook and De la Vega appear in a doorway at the edge of the townhouse, and Cook saw him.

The grenade exploded. The blast blew in the door behind Cook and De la Vega and brought down a rotting wooden balcony from the corner of the house. They were hurled away, the masonry crashing and tumbling. When Hazzard looked up, there was no sign of either.

286

Hazzard tried to push himself up, lunging for the shattered façade, but his feet felt weighted, leaden, people in his path, '*Jory! Cesár!*'

A French soldier appeared out of nowhere, a look of surprise as he took in Hazzard's scarlet coat, and Hazzard drew the *espada ropera* as he charged into him, crashing the guard and jewelled knuckle-bow into the side of his feathered bonnet and he went down, his musket rattling to the flagstones underfoot. Another came from behind the first and Hazzard knocked his musket up and away, anger with himself setting in, *Jory, for God's sake, no!* and thrust his sword deep, jumping aside as he withdrew and another appeared, the *ropera* flying round in an arc, slashing at the man's face and he screamed and collapsed. '*Come along, damn you! How many shall you be! How many!*' Beating a bayonet aside, twisting, turning into the man's guard, ramming with the elbow, bringing him down, the sword tip flying and a cry.

A call went up in French, '*Un anglais! C'est le mien!*' *He is mine!* and a hand grabbed at Hazzard's shoulder. He whirled round, the sword-hilt smashing into an arm, the blade whipping round and slicing at a raised bayonet, his free hand knocking the forestock up and away, *too close, they are all too close,* and Rossy of the Alpha-Omega flew backwards, Hazzard in a rage because he *should have told him, should have warned him,* his foolhardy actions, the grenade exploding, the balcony collapsing, a reckless violence overtaking him, '*Only six of you! Is that all?*' Rossy threw a straight fist to Hazzard's sternum, missed, began to fall, the sword stinging across his sleeve, and he shouted out, *Putain!* A fusilier to their right seized an old man by the hair, a strangled cry, and Hazzard lunged, *Leave him be, damn you!* and the sword slipped through the fusilier's neck and he dropped, Rossy watching wide-eyed, calling, *Chef!* Another blow hard from the left, and he staggered, lights flashing in Hazzard's eyes, and he twisted away – until he came face to face with *Sergent-chef-major* Achille Caron. For that moment, they saw each other complete, Caron's grey coat, sash and pistol bandolier, Hazzard's

287

scarred Bombay scarlet, the black and gold facings, the sword, the posture – and their eyes met in immediate recognition: *old soldier.*

Caron shouted, '*Anglais!*' Englishman!

Hazzard shouted back, '*I am!*'

Caron drew a pistol but his wrist was immediately knocked away by the *ropera* and it fired; he brought it down at Hazzard's forehead, but Hazzard had already ducked low, slipping the spine of his sword-blade behind Caron's knee, and heaving. The heels of the stocky sergeant-major flew into the air. '*Putain!*'

Two other Alphas descended on him, one beating away the sword, the other pointing the gaping muzzle of a blunderbuss pistol, but Hazzard thrust it upwards and it discharged into the sky. He drove his elbow into the underarm of the shooter who grunted and collapsed, Caron crying above it all, '*Vivant! En vivant!*' Alive!

It was enough. Rossy put Hazzard down to one knee and knocked him sprawling with the butt of his musket. Another fusilier charged Hazzard at the bayonet but Pigalle stepped between them and crashed a heavy fist into the fusilier's head and he fell without a sound, '*Con stupide…*' Hazzard collapsed, the *espada ropera* tumbling from his fingers. Rossy and St Michel grabbed him up by the tunic, more infantry pouring into the square by the minute, some in the crowd cheering, some screaming, trying to flee. Caron and Rossy pulled Hazzard along, Rossy saying, '*Did you see, Chef? Did you see that? He stopped! He stopped for the old malt!*' Caron shoved a path through the mob, nodding, 'Yes, yes, *mon garçon*, I saw – quick – get him away – he is special, this one, *gardez-le… gardez-le bien.*'

Hazzard let his boots drag behind as Pigalle and the Alphas pulled him through the square past the French line. There had been only one sure way to reach Derrien, only one way to get inside, to find the agent, to find Sarah – and that was to be captured. The worst, he thought, was soon to come.

But in his mind's eye he saw only the crumbling house collapse above Cook and De la Vega, hurling them into oblivion, over and over again.

Captor

Several days later, Caron and his squad marched in escort with the gaoler to the cells in the depths of Fort St Elmo. It dominated the Grand Harbour, but in the battle for Malta its guns had remained silent and cold. However, its baking ochre walls had served its other purpose: a prison, its iron cells an infernal oven for despairing souls.

'They say to me, *open*,' mumbled the gaoler, a short, shambling, hunched Greco-Maltese who spoke an odd Mediterranean *Sabir* argot, 'I like it *no*.' He raised his hand several times in quick succession, as if hitting something, or someone. 'I say *no*.'

Caron shoved him along, 'Shut up.' The gaoler scurried ahead, seeking cover behind the warden – now under fear of sentence himself, his eyes darting nervously from left to right as they passed the vast cells. *Fear of the known*, thought Caron as they continued into the airless bowels of the fort.

Rossy stopped abruptly and retched. '*Putain de la merde. Chef*, that stench…'

'It is the smell of victory, Rossy,' rumbled Caron and led them on regardless. 'At least, it was for the *salaud* Christian Knights.' Pigalle and St Michel looked about as the corridor widened to a short row of mass cells beneath a low vaulted stone ceiling. Sunlight penetrated in dim orange beams from high grilled openings in the passages, but still the air hung heavily, lifeless and rank.

The prisoners inside began calling out and banging on their bars as soon as they saw the warden. The gaoler shouted and spat at them, lashing out with a short whip and many ran back into the deep shadows. Pigalle gave him a shove and the gaoler flew against one of the barred doors with a clang and scuttled away, bowing. The occupants laughed.

'There must be over fifty in each hole…' murmured St Michel, peering through his spectacles. 'Who are they?'

They had already been to the *bagnio* prison near the Lower Barraka Gardens – and despite the protests of the pompous *Prodomo* in charge, released some two thousand slave-workers there. But this, in the darkness of the fort, felt somehow worse to Caron.

'More slaves,' said Caron. 'Prisoners of war, captives of the holy Knights of Gold and God upstairs…'

The warden looked at him in wonder. 'But they are the infidel,' he said by way of explanation. 'And they pay the price for their sin in the galleys.'

Caron had once been posted as a guard to the old *Chateau d'If* in Marseille. It had been a calculated sentence of punishment for his own sins, which he had long forgotten, before France went up in flames. Since then he could not abide to see a man in chains. He had volunteered for this duty, pleased it had come straight from the *général en chef* himself.

'It is a Bastille,' said Pigalle. '*C'est la merde.*'

Caron nodded, moved by the big man's simplicity. 'It is, *mon garçon. Eh, tiens,*' he said to the gaoler. 'You, *salaud*. Start here.'

When the gaoler and the warden stopped at Caron's command the shouting of the prisoners died away and they watched. The gaoler kept a fearful eye on Caron, as if expecting to be struck at any moment, but Caron just called to the occupants, '*Vieni,* or *vai avanti,* or *yollah,* or whatever you say. *Come.*'

The keys rattled in the locks and the first door squealed open on its hinges. For a moment the prisoners inside stood and stared at them, then backed away into the shadows.

'Come,' said Caron, gesturing with his hand back up the steps they had just descended. 'Come.' He turned to Rossy, 'Your water bottle…'

He took it and poured a capful of water, held it out for them to see, and drank. He refilled it, then held it out again. 'Come. *Aqua. Venez, venez.*'

They looked to each other, then approached the open door. The first man to emerge, a tall, hollow-eyed North African, possibly Berber, thought Caron, looked at Caron and his men uncomprehendingly. Caron held out the cup and the man took it.

'If I drink,' he asked in rough Italian, 'am I yours?'

Caron shook his head. 'No. If you drink, you are free. *Libro.*'

The Berber closed his eyes and drank. He handed back the cup.

'Then I am free.'

He looked back at his cellmates, then made his way stiffly up the steps. Caron gestured to them. 'Go up. Men are waiting for you. Food, eat, water, *mangiare, aqua, sì? Tiens, allons-y, allons-y.*' *Let's go, let's go.*

The gaoler sullenly translated into Arabic, and the warden stood unhappily watching as they came out, at first in a silent and suspicious trickle, then a steady flow – there was no panicked flood, but Caron and the Alphas kept their muskets ready. The gaoler wisely feared for his life, and stood as close to the French as he dared. One cell after the other, they began to release the last slaves of Valletta.

When they had finished one wing of cells, they descended further to a lower level of the fort, and stopped at a broad landing, a high barred open window on one wall the only light, and saw a locked wooden door. It had a shutter over a barred viewing grille. Caron grabbed the gaoler. 'Eh, open. *Abierto, salaud…*'

The gaoler nodded, quaking, and slid back the shutter. Caron looked through the bars.

It was a large, long room with a high ceiling. There were steps down, and high on the far wall was a slim barred window opening at ground level. Along either wall ran long stone slabs, forming bench seating either side of a central aisle of sorts, large circular drains the size of vats set in one side, like an old bathhouse, or worse, thought Caron, a place for torture. The cell contained only one man.

In the middle of the room facing away from the door, his manacled arms pulled out like wings by chains fixed high to the walls either side, was William John Hazzard. The chains were too short to allow him to lie or sit, forcing him either to stand or crouch on one knee.

His head was hanging low. He had been stripped to the waist and beaten. Caron saw the crazed tracery of ancient scars across his back, old dead tissue white against the sunburnt skin, and fresh weals of clotted blood from new thrashings.

'*Sacre...*'

'*Chef,*' whispered Pigalle in recognition. 'Is it him? Our *anglais*? Look at his back...'

'Yes, he is one of yours,' said the warden with disapproval. 'To do this to a Christian... a terrible sin.'

Eager to please, the gaoler sought out the key from the collection on the large ring in his hand. 'He too?'

'Do the *anglais* beat their officers now...?' asked Rossy, looking in.

'I doubt that, *garçon,*' said Caron. 'But someone did, long ago. And someone else,' he said, glancing at the smiling eager gaoler, 'more recently.'

Hearing footsteps behind, one of the Alphas turned and cocked his Charleville musket. Caron looked round. With two escorting dragoon troopers behind, a figure in black approached. Caron knew him at once. He had since learnt his full name.

'*Le diable,*' he murmured, 'Citizen *Croquemort.*'

Derrien stopped. He tucked his hands neatly behind his back. '*Sergent-major.* We meet again.'

'*Sergent-chef-major,* Citizen. It is honorary. For service.'

Derrien stared back. 'You release prisoners today.'

293

'We release slaves, Citizen, as the general has commanded by proclamation.'

Derrien looked at them. 'This prisoner,' he said carefully, 'is mine.'

Caron said nothing. He looked in at Hazzard again. While Caron was proud that at least they had been able to take a genuine *anglais* alive, an officer no less, he regretted the result. He wished instead that he had despatched Hazzard with a clean shot. It would have been *un coup d'honneur*, and spared him Citizen *Croquemort*.

'Is it true, Citizen,' asked Rossy with apparent hearty interest, 'that the 9th *demi* in Gozo sang the "Marseillaise" as they scaled the walls of the fort?'

Derrien swivelled his gaze slowly, assessing the man's insolence. 'I am sure it is.'

'Very patriotic.' Rossy nodded. His sincerity fell away, dead. 'We didn't do that.'

Derrien met his challenging stare. 'Your work was equally patriotic.'

'Giving guns and bombs to mad Malts? To kill the women and children?' Rossy looked doubtful. 'We do not like the work of spies, and *cons*...' He nodded at the cell door. 'This one, even while fighting me, he broke off, you see? To save an old man from another soldier. *While* fighting me, Citizen. *Comprenez?*'

Derrien watched him, eyes a-glitter. 'Yes.'

'I do not think you do. It is not usual, for the common soldier, *hm*? We are fighting, most of us, to survive – but not this one. So, I am thinking, this *anglais*, he has much honour.' He looked Derrien up and down. 'More certainly than *some*.' He coughed and leaned forward, just over Derrien's shoe, and spat very carefully. The glob of spittle descended slowly to the ground with a wet smack. Rossy backed away and smiled briefly. '*Pardon*. The dust, Citizen. In this place of evil.'

A dragoon put a hand to a pistol but St Michel lifted his rifle-musket and cocked it, then pretended to examine its striking-plate curiously. The dragoon lowered his hand. Derrien said nothing but turned back to Caron.

'I have learnt something of you,' said Derrien. 'You have thirty-one years' service. From the King's own regiment.'

'I have,' said Caron. 'I am the old soldier, Citizen, who has seen the banners change, but never the result.'

Derrien did not so much as nod. 'How very philosophical.'

'An old soldier knows an old soldier,' said Caron. 'Such as this *anglais*. We captured him, took his sword in combat. By right of arms in this, this rotten *antique* place, he is ours.'

'No longer. He shall now be in my personal care.'

Caron met Derrien's blank look. There was nothing he could do to Derrien, but vowed that one day perhaps there might be. He indicated the cowering gaoler. 'Did this dog beat him?'

'Perhaps.'

'Really. A dog who beats a man.' Caron looked in again at the sickening sight of Hazzard's wounds. '*M'sieur* Le Pig,' he said to Pigalle with a nod at the gaoler, 'if you please.'

Pigalle drove his giant fist into the gaoler's face and the little man's nose burst with blood as his head cracked back against the wall. He fell in a heap, his head crooked, his eyes staring. He twitched several times, then lay still, dead. The warden and escorting cavalrymen stepped back, eyes wide. Caron looked at Derrien.

'What a dreadful accident.' He indicated the quaking warden. 'Now you and this holy *putain* may do your own heroic work, Citizen *Croquemort*, while we release the damned.'

The Alphas ported arms, Rossy brushing past Derrien and his dragoons, humming the "Marseillaise" as they filed away.

Derrien let them go, then moved to the cell door and looked through the grille. Hazzard was still as stone, his arms pulled outwards by his manacled wrists, one leg behind, one bent beneath his chest for support.

The warden looked down at the dead gaoler, trembling with Christian affront, 'This... this is *outrageous*...'

'Keys,' said Derrien. The warden recoiled from the order, then knelt with revulsion at the dead gaoler's foul bare feet to pick up the heavy iron key ring. The keys rattled like dry bones as he opened the lock with quaking hands. '*M'sieur...*'

The door swung inwards with a creak.

'You will wait here,' said Derrien.

The warden nodded. '*Oui, oui, d'accord...*' Muttering a protective prayer and crossing himself, the warden closed the door behind Derrien, the dragoons taking up station either side. One of them swore and kicked the dead gaoler's corpse to one side to make room.

Inside the cell, Derrien stood for a moment at the top of the steps. He looked down at Hazzard. This was to prove a first for him: he had never interrogated an Englishman like this, a captured officer. Dutch, yes, Germans, yes, and of course his own countrymen, but not an Englishman. Language would be only a minor barrier – Derrien had learned his English at the hands of a Swiss from Geneva, but had not ever conversed with a native. To question a genuine English officer, particularly this one, had brought a quiver of expectation.

He had not seen Hazzard's face clearly, that night in Naples, not entirely. But when he had heard what he had done in combat in Valletta, *with no more than a sword* – he had to admit, he had grown... *excited*. When he had seen him for the first time in the cell, he had no doubts. He *knew*.

He examined Hazzard from the door, the mass of scar tissue on his back and shoulders, great highways and canals in dead white and pale red carved by a merciless lash. There were more recent wounds, on his arms and ribs, well stitched, only partially healed amid the livid red of Maltese floggings. Overall, he was striped worse than a West Indian plantation slave.

Hazzard's head hung, his curling hair trailing low over his face. He did not move. He breathed tidally, the air whistling through swollen, cracked lips over a dry tongue and the crusted blood at his mouth. The cell was like a furnace.

Derrien descended the steps, watching him thoughtfully, and dusted off a spot on the stone slab against the wall, a small distance from the iron anchor ring holding Hazzard's right wrist in a manacle. On several old hooks on the wall hung various lengths of leather and rawhide, one of them braided into multiple flayed ends. He wondered which had been used most. He sat carefully, aligning his creases, his hat on his lap.

'Mister Hazzard.'

Hazzard jerked slightly then relaxed again. He had not expected English.

'You are William John Hazzard, an exploring officer of the British Marines.'

The bruised muscles in Hazzard's shoulders slowly bunched and flexed; his breathing quickened, then eased again. He tautened his grip, raising himself just sufficiently to relax his bent knee, then swapped legs, bringing the rear leg forward slowly, putting the other backwards. He settled again.

'We know this from sources in Naples, from within the household of Sir William Hamilton. You come from a single English squadron,' said Derrien, 'the squadron of Nelson. You sought our fleet. Well done. You found it.'

Still Hazzard said nothing.

Derrien withdrew from his pocket a folded page, dried from its evident soaking in seawater, its smudged ink staining the page. 'We discovered a document secreted in the lining of your red coat. Or is that *red*coat. I can never remember the idiom. You thought perhaps we would not find it – a very poor attempt at concealment. Or perhaps it is just the opposite, deliberately to be found, to appear important, but is indeed a lie. I wonder.' He glanced at the sloping hand, the neat letters in places illegible.

Society of Antiquaries of London
Somerset House
29ᵗʰ April, 1798

To Whomsoever It May Concern,

297

> *This is to acknowledge the commission of Dr. William*
> *John Hazzard, former Capt. HMMF (ret.), Ph.D*
> *(Cantab) MSAL, as agreed between the Society of Anti-*
> *quaries of London, the Royal Geographical Society and*
> *the Grand Master of the Order of Knights Hospitaller*
> *of St John of Jerusalem, to inspect and survey any sites*
> *he may find to be of antiquarian value or interest, in the*
> *city of Valletta, for the furtherance of scientific exploration*
> *and endeavour.*
>
> *Yours faithfully,*
> *John Herbert Eames, MRCS, FRS*
> *Society of Antiquaries of London*

Derrien watched him. Hazzard had not moved.

'I have shown this, this *letter* of retinue to Citizen De Ransijat, the administrator of the Order in Malta, and he has heard nothing of you.'

Hazzard's breathing remained a steady, dry wheeze.

'It is, but of course, a lie. You are not from the Society of Antiquarians and know of no such Member of the Royal College of Surgeons or Fellow of the Royal Society.' He paused, enjoying his knowledge. 'Yes, some of us have a grasp of such *English* things.'

No response.

'You know nothing of antiquities or museums. A brief conversation with any one of our *savants* would prove this. Shall I fetch one?'

No response.

'No, you are too rough a creature. Look at you, scarred, beaten, an adventurer, a swordsman – a night-ruffian, duellist, and rake, who frequents waterfront brothels with Neapolitan rebels.'

No response.

Derrien pursed his lips more tightly. His voice rose a fraction. 'You are an assassin, here to kill General Bonaparte.'

No response.

Louder still: 'You are an Admiralty assassin and spy, and you will be *shot.*'

No response.

Derrien changed tack. He mopped at his sweating forehead, reset his hat upon his head.

'A coincidence, I wonder, Mr Hazzard... I recall my time with a traitor to the Republic. It was a lengthy interrogation but thoroughly, how would you say, *satisfying.* A Citizen Hugues Bartelmi.'

The chains tensed, and Derrien noticed Hazzard was no longer hanging from his bonds. Instead he was restraining himself. He watched the scarred muscle move across his back and noted: *reaction.*

'Among his seditious correspondence were several letters, from a certain *"Madame d'Hazzard-Rémy"*, a woman of Lyons. Bartelmi had kept them for so long, they were evidently cherished. She refers to him as her beloved, and writes of his promise to educate her son, William.'

Derrien watched him.

'I wonder if this is you.'

No response.

'You had a benefactor who paid for your education in France.'

Hazzard's breathing had grown more erratic, but still he said nothing.

'There is further reference to her wounded husband, a Major Richard Hazzard, and Bartelmi's kindness for receiving them that year – for the summer months.' Derrien said reasonably, 'I must deduce that Hugues Bartelmi was more than a family benefactor.'

Derrien rose and moved in front of Hazzard and bent down to peer into his bruised face. 'It appears, Mr Hazzard, that you are not English at all. But French.'

Hazzard did not move.

'The officer, whom you suppose to be your father, was too badly wounded or… *impotent* to father children and died *before you were born*. He left you in the charge of your *true* father, Hugues Bartelmi, *counter-revolutionary and spy*.'

Hazzard shook his head.

A wet hiss sighed from Hazzard's mouth. Derrien listened again. 'I beg your pardon…?'

'*N'nch…*'

Still Derrien could not understand. 'I am sorry…?'

'*One… inch…*' enunciated Hazzard slowly, '*Fr'm… y'r… thr't…*'

Derrien's face betrayed nothing if Hazzard could but see it. 'One inch?'

''*Ap'les…*'

Naples.

The chains rattled and Hazzard surged towards him, arms reaching. Derrien leapt back, dropping his hat – then remembered he was safe, beyond Hazzard's grasp.

Confirmation.

'*You.*'

Hazzard grunted, his head hanging. Derrien lashed at him, 'You are condemned from your own lips, *fool*, assassin, *traitor*.'

Hazzard still do not reply.

'*Answer!*'

Derrien's voice was a thunderbolt in the stillness of the room and gave him strength. Soon he realised he was kicking Hazzard with frustration, *once*, *twice*, then a *third* time, his boot into Hazzard's midriff, his ribs, his chest, until he fell back, gasping, having to lean for support on the stone bench seat. Hazzard had collapsed, sunk lower on the one knee, retching.

After a moment Derrien straightened his coat, bent down, picked up his hat and dusted it down. 'The *comtesse* de Boussard was found dead,' he said, without interest. 'Naked, in a stable…'

Hazzard hung still, no movement.

'She had been beaten, raped, possibly by a local gang or even the idiot groom of the stable, whom we shot out of hand. Though knowing her as I did it could have been all of them at once with her willing consent. But we shall blame you, naturally, the British agent in the employ of Sir William Hamilton, consorting with thieves and pirates at the quays. A note of protest has gone to King Ferdinand that you assaulted her in the home of Sir William and that he was complicit. The civilised world knows British brutality and the royal court of Naples will believe it – or be made to believe it.' He leaned closer, 'You were *seen* with her, Mr Hazzard.'

Sir John Acton? His aides? Anyone could have informed France for another gold coin.

Hazzard let out a deep breath, tension released, but his head hung lower. Derrien remained philosophical about his progress but sounded optimistic.

'I believe the fear of pain will be of little motivation to you,' he said after some reflection. He examined his hat. 'I am the sole course to your survival,' he said, 'only I can save you.'

Hazzard shook his head, his lank hair swinging, sweat dripping off his chin. '*N'ne c'n save me…*'

Hazzard's torso began to convulse in quiet bursts.

Derrien watched him, surprised. He had not expected such a response. Hazzard was weeping.

Derrien had seen beaten men weep before, it was nothing new, but this was unusual. 'I do not understand this display, what is this, this nonsense, some new deceit?'

Still Hazzard shook with wracking gasps. '*L'ne. All… 'lone…*'

Derrien watched him closely. It was the cry of the agent, of the abandoned, the deceiver who sees his true rootless lack of place in a hostile world. Derrien knew it well himself. He pounced on it.

'Yes – *yes*, Mr Hazzard, you are *alone*. Forgotten, flotsam, you say, in the sea. Why then submit to your king? A king who allows the men, the women, and the children, I am told, to be

301

hanged for stealing bread, or a, what is it, a *farthing*? He orders the cavalry to attack the poor, to—'

Hazzard choked, '*Th… k-k'ng…*'

Derrien continued, the patient schoolmaster. 'Kings are borne aloft by the greed of those who serve them, the parasites feeding upon them. A king is without power of his own – strip him bare and what is he? A rampaging child, spoiled by endless privilege, who has never heard the word "no". But, those who support him wield all the power in the world, by pandering to the child's whims. Why then serve them, the, how would you say, the *lickspittles* who connive around him, press him to their own greedy ends?'

Saliva bubbled at Hazzard's dry, cracked lips. Then, bitterly, '*I h've… no king. D'mn all kings…*'

Derrien was not so conceited as to believe he had spawned sudden rebellion in Hazzard. 'You dissemble, Mr Hazzard. More nonsense. You think you are clever, Englishman with no king, who would yet die for him—'

Hazzard's body sagged, defeated. '*Damn the king… damn them all…*'

The dust and grit crunched under Derrien's boots as he took one pace, then another, then stopped, thinking. He knew the English had little care for the true religion, and therefore the divine right of kings, yet this was surely too much.

'You would turn your back on this king? Betray him and all his works?'

Hazzard's head hung low. He breathed and gasped, stricken. '*Damn… th' k'ng! M'rder'd m-my w'fe… m'rder'd m-me… damn them all!*' His breath was forced between his clenched teeth and along with the self-pity came the rage, spitting out, '*Trait'rs t'ke coin… I-need-no-coin! Damn th'r bloody empire! Damn th'm! Harry!*'

Hazzard had broken.

'*Harry!*' Then quiet sobbing, '*Harry…*'

Derrien looked at him. He opened his mouth to speak but stopped short. For a moment, he was lost.

302

Without Hazzard's resistance, Derrien's power dissipated, a mist evaporating before his eyes. He stood, waiting, waiting for something to reassure him of his purpose as Protector of the Republic, but nothing came. Momentarily, the two existed in a vacuum, the only sound the sighing of Hazzard's breath and his own, heavy in the still heat of the cell.

He stooped by Hazzard's head, then squatted, crouching low, looking up at the hanging, bruised face. 'But of course you despise kings. Misanthropes, self-enamoured monsters. Murderers of the weak and helpless. To do so is natural. It is in your *French* blood.'

Hazzard nodded, his back heaving once more, his breath coming in sobs born of the awful recognition of Derrien's truth. '*C'est vrai…*'

In French.

Derrien would not believe it. 'What did you say?'

Hazzard breathed in again and sighed, '*C'est vrai…*'

Derrien closed his eyes in exultation.

Triumph.

Frenchman.

In scarlet.

He took a steadying breath. He had done it.

Broken him.

He knelt by Hazzard, almost enthused at the possibilities before him – before them both. 'You will remember the France of before,' he urged, 'the oppression, the destitution of the people. *Now* see them. Citizens all, with the rights of law. We have freed the slaves of Malta, and we melt down the gold and silver of these, these *fatted* knights – to feed and clothe and educate the poor of this land. France is the only true leader of the oppressed in this world of tyrants – *and you can see this*. You are greater than this, this *red coat* you wear, and the *ancien* rule of brutality. You and I are not ordinary men, we are *thinkers*, with *hope*. Throw off your German king and come with us, your true family, where you will find a fraternity of brave, intelligent men like yourself. We shall pay the debts on your estates, give you and your family a civilised home in the new Repub—'

Hazzard had started to convulse again, his breath coming in short gasps. However, Derrien heard not a weeping self-pity any longer, but a dry, husking wheeze. Hazzard was laughing.

Derrien stopped talking.

Slowly, he straightened, on his cheeks the bitter blush of self-condemnation. *Merde aux yeux! Stupide! Tu crétin! Of course he lies!* With the passing of the moment, his vision of free thinkers in a harmonious world floated away, vaporous wisps of smoke, mere fool's mist, lost forever.

'Very well. We play fools no longer.'

He looked down upon him, his *hauteur* returning once again, stiffening him, supporting him. 'You are, then, no more than I thought, the assassin, the spy. The lowest form of political expediency. Nothing, a sword for hire.'

Derrien set down his hat. With sharp, angry movements he tugged off the sleeves of his black coat and tugged back his shirt cuffs. 'Yet you are not, are you, *M'sieur* French Englishman with no king and no God. You will tell me, Mr Hazzard. You will tell me all. About your Admiralty, your code, your Room 63 and Sir Rafe Lewis. You will yearn for my company, for the pain I inflict, and dream only of pleasing *me*, as my disgusting *slave*, begging for further humiliation. But I will never be satisfied with your screams, *never.*'

He reached for the braided whip hanging on the wall. Its split and frayed ends spread into a fan of hardened raw leather. He brought it down with all his strength across Hazzard's back, thinking of Caron, of Rossy and his *impudence*, of Pigalle striking the gaoler dead with a single blow and thought, *Now you shall see, now you shall feel,* and struck him again and again and again, until the grunts of pain blotted out the wheezing laughter still calling in his ear, *fool, fool, fool!*

–

The next morning Bonaparte's chief aide, *Chef de brigade* Junot, marched at the head of a small delegation heading to the palace of the Grand Master. Among their number were the best half-dozen marines of the *Orient* and *Sergent-chef-major* Caron, with his troop of Alpha *chasseurs*. Troops lined the quaysides, waiting, quartermasters and battalion commanders posting guards at billets, up and down the stunned, empty streets.

Along with Junot came the *savant*-diplomat Citizen Poussielgue, and, incongruous in their number, the white-haired geologist *savant*, Déodat Dolomieu. Caron moved up beside him, curious.

'What do you know of this, Citizen?' asked Caron.

Dolomieu seemed to have little interest in the sights around him. He explained, 'I was once one of them, *sergent-chef.*' He sighed. 'It is still a burden I carry.'

'And you come to parley with them?' continued Caron.

The old man shrugged. 'I must somehow smooth the path to their surrender.' He shook his head. 'I left for very good reason…'

'You are a real knight…?' asked Pigalle, very much impressed. 'Do you have a sword…?'

The old man smiled up at him. 'Even they do not, my boy, not anymore.'

Their Maltese guide smiled and bobbed his head, pointing, wanting to serve. Though they had taken the fort and there were troops lining the docksides, Caron kept one hand on the pistol in his belt. The Alphas were unnerved by the stillness, and stayed spread out in combat order, but nothing stirred in the empty city. Rossy and St Michel moved slowly around corners, gazing about like *sans-culottes* seeing Versailles for the first time. Junot was not so circumspect, his marines marching steadfastly. 'The streets will be clear to us,' he said to Caron. 'No resistance. It is a lucky thing,' he said with a rare smirk, 'that at least there was somebody to open the gates for us.'

'Is this how Malta is to fall, Colonel…?' murmured Caron. 'To the scurry of rats?'

'More to the scrape of a pen on a promissory note, *Chef*. And rats,' he noted, 'come in many shapes and sizes. As we shall see.'

Soon their heels were ringing along polished stone hallways and through ornamental gardens, to the echo of tinkling fountains. They approached an inner entrance of the palace, Halberdiers dotted at various doorways, their fearful eyes following them. The sights that greeted the delegation as they passed inside nearly stopped them dead in their tracks.

'*Mon dieu…*' said Junot. 'How *could* they,' he rasped with disgust. '*How could they*.'

Overhead, underfoot, everywhere, from gleaming marble up to soaring polished stone ceilings, shone the glory of the Order's holy crusade, the halls dripping with opulence. The passage was lined with suits of armour inlaid with gold and chased with silver, the walls mounted with bucklers, shields and gleaming crossed swords, vast tapestries, grand portraits, no surface without ornament, without excess.

'Who were they, these men…?' murmured Caron.

Junot stared, unashamedly hateful. 'The general should strip it. Strip it clean.'

Rossy and the Alphas gawped at the walls and ceilings, Pigalle pointing high above their heads. A single moulding bore enough gold to match the booty they had amassed between them over years of war. They moved through to another chamber, more polished stone, more treasures, and Junot called a halt. Clustered in the far corner was a group of elderly knights in uniform, some of it modern, but overtop some wore the grim black robes with the white Maltese Cross, others, more warlike, red tabards displaying the plain Latin Cross, watching their French conquerors in silence, like so many plotting senators. One of them bowed low. Junot did not return the gesture. Rossy and St Michel looked back at Caron, their eyes flickering about, as if wondering what would be best to loot first.

Their silent guide led them through the group and out to a cloistered courtyard studded with fruit trees and stone-lined ponds. At the far end of the cloister waited a small group of delegates from the Order, led by two figures, the Commissioner of Fortifications *Frère* de Fay, and the closed-faced Treasurer and Head of the French Secretariat, *Frère* Bosrédon de Ransijat. They watched Junot approach, his marines keeping time, their precision menacing. *Fra'* Rafaelo, the Grand Master's most loyal servant, edged forward with hostility.

'You said *nothing*, Bosrédon,' he accused, from the corner of his mouth. '*Nothing* to help the Grand Master. I would have left you in gaol…'

De Ransijat was unmoved. After his temporary imprisonment, the Council decided it was more prudent he be released, to treat with the foe. With the end of Von Hompesch tenure now in sight, De Ransijat had become one of the most powerful men in the Order. He held the keys to the greatest cache in the Mediterranean: the Treasury of the Knights of St John, and thus Malta itself – and the Council would never forgot it. Neither would Bonaparte. 'No, *Fra'* Rafaelo. Perhaps now all will be revealed.'

'You led the *two hundred* French knights to betray their oaths,' whispered Rafaelo to his colleagues, 'As I said, it is an *infámia*.'

De Ransijat bowed his head at the approach of Junot and the delegation. 'It is the will of God, *Fra'* Rafaelo.'

'Is it?' said the Italian bitterly. 'Or is it the purse of Bonaparte?'

Junot slowed and came to a halt and surveyed the group. Prepared for the ascetic republicans, De Ransijat wore a simple habit, while Rafaelo, De Fay and many of the Councillors were in full regalia, their black cloaks flowing over polished decorative breastplates, the white Maltese Cross bright in the gloom.

'Citizens,' said De Ransijat in French, bowing his head to Junot. 'The Commissioner of Fortifications, *Frère* de Fay, and a delegation of the Council of the Holy Order.'

Junot returned the bow curtly and nodded in recognition of De Ransijat's name. 'We received the petition of your Citizen

Mélan for the armistice. We bring a draft treaty for the liberation of Malta, *Frère* de Ransijat. You met Citizen Poussielgue here some months ago, I understand.'

With flushed cheeks, the thin-faced Poussielgue bowed. 'A pleasure, of course…' De Fay looked away, embarrassed, the implication of treachery clear.

'And we bring one of your own,' said Junot, indicating Dolomieu. 'At the request of the Grand Master, to ease the way in negotiations.'

De Ransijat bowed to Dolomieu. 'Brother. You are welcome once again.'

Dolomieu bowed to the knights, stiff and apprehensive, 'Commissioner, Brother Bailiffs…' He glanced at De Ransijat, an unwelcome memory. 'Treasurer.'

'Today will conclude the matter of pensions and payments if that is in order,' said Junot acidly.

De Ransijat nodded. 'All in order, Colonel, and I look forward to adjusting the Treasury to the demands of the Republic, personally, as promised.'

Junot nodded. 'Indeed.' It was their ultimate threat: De Ransijat would remain in power on Malta, or there would be no Treasury.

'Come,' said De Fay, 'the Grand Master is waiting.' He led them into a chamber off the passage. The marines turned about and stood guard outside the doors. The delegation of Knights Councillors gave them fearful glances and went inside to meet Von Hompesch.

As they went in, Caron and the others peered through the doorway at still more treasures, in black marble, Moorish ceramics and silks, jewelled cups, vases, urns, everywhere treasure. In their midst was an old man in cloak and armour, rising slowly from a grand chair – Dolomieu approached, removed his hat with ceremony, bowing. Caron watched as Von Hompesch became the benevolent father on the return of a prodigal son, and welcomed Dolomieu warmly, an act of dwindling hope.

'What now, *Chef*?' whispered Rossy.

Caron grunted. 'Now, *enfants*, we watch, and wait.' He looked out at the courtyard, the arches, the gardens, the balconies, all offering serene comfort, but Caron knew better. 'Trouble, she has not done with us.'

From inside, Junot gave Caron a look as the marines closed the doors, shutting him out. But it was over, Caron knew. Malta belonged to Bonaparte.

–

Two days later, Hazzard was released from his shackles hours earlier than usual. He collapsed to the floor into a crouch, hugging his knees to afford the greatest relief, his shoulders numb, his hands and wrists dead to the touch. He roared with shock as he was hit by three buckets of cold seawater, but instead of being kicked and beaten in punishment, he was brusquely towelled and his stiffened arms forced into his soiled red coat once again. They bound his hands behind his back and dragged him out of his cell. Citizen Masson in escort, two dragoons took him by the elbows and marched him behind Derrien through the twisting stone corridors.

Hazzard was in no state to resist. His head lolled, his senses fading from time to time – he stumbled along as if hobbled by chains, falling repeatedly. Over the two days, Derrien's rawhide scourge had nearly broken him, and every breath brought sharp pain, but the floggers were careful not to go too far – and Hazzard had learned how to feign unconsciousness.

But now it was a joy simply to be moving, through the dank corridors and into the sudden gasping heat of sunlight, then darkness again, the troopers pulling him along with curses. Marble floors flashed hypnotically beneath his blurred gaze, coats of arms of the Knights' *Auberges* and Secretariats of the different national embassies passing beneath. He could scarcely think beyond the dictates he had used to keep his mind whole: *feint, confuse, confound.*

Shadows flitted, a door opened and a fresh breeze blew off the sea. He sucked it in greedily, bright light dazzling, then into another hall. He was eventually thrust to the cool limestone floor on his knees. His captors would never know the blessed relief this afforded him, and he pressed the fire of his face eagerly against its smooth worn surface, until he was hauled upright.

His swollen eyes struggled to adjust to the light, and he saw distant figures moving in a haze within a gigantic chamber. He heard the low murmur of discreet conversation drifting upwards to soaring ceilings – the clink of a delicate cup on a saucer, the susurration of paper. A pen tinkled as it was rapped on the rim of an ink bottle somewhere in a great empty vastness all about him. He blinked. Great beams of sunlight slanted in from high windows, dust caught in their rays. Not far off was a black lacquered desk with bright gilt legs. Several men gathered round it, holding pages, waiting, sorting, deferring to the figure seated between them.

'Citizen General,' called Derrien, suddenly loud, from somewhere nearby.

The figure at the desk stopped writing. Hazzard tried to see through his crusted eyes as the man looked up from the page before him, interrupted.

'The prisoner you requested, Citizen General,' explained Derrien.

Hazzard tried to take in his surroundings, the stillness and silence of the chamber, of the man at the desk: *Citizen General*.

Hazzard wondered how long he had been here, or been at sea. Weeks, months – and brought here, to this cool stone floor.

Citizen General.

There was only one man it could be, only one man who could inspire such tension in Derrien.

Bonaparte.

The silence in the great hall hung over them all as they waited. Hazzard could hear his own coarse breathing, the creak of the dragoons' boots and belts. The figure at the desk moved.

Napoleon Bonaparte looked across the room at them, and laid down his pen. The secretaries waited. His chair scraped across the floor, and he stood. The men about him stepped back, bowing, and Bonaparte walked slowly round the desk, his heels echoing as he approached.

Masson's rough hand pulled at Hazzard's shoulder to hold him upright, his hands still tied, restrained by a dragoon, his arms gripped tight, one of the men murmuring, '*Attention.*' *Careful.*

Bonaparte stopped some distance off, hands behind his back. They waited.

'He is bound,' he said. 'Why?'

Above him, Hazzard could feel Derrien offer a discreet bow. 'He is a dangerous officer, Citizen General,' said Derrien. 'He tried to attack me though he was in chains.'

The rebuke in Bonaparte's tone was subtle but very clear, 'You put an officer in chains.'

'It seemed a wise precaution, Citizen General.' Derrien cleared his throat. 'He is an Admiralty assassin.'

'Not according to the letter shown me only this morning.'

The voice had the edge of a whiplash about it.

Derrien nodded, chastened. 'Citizen General.'

Hazzard squinted through watering vision. Soon the neat figure before him drew closer and appeared in clearer focus: the long hair, the thin, pale, handsome face, the dark cravat and high collar, a braided dark coat, a sash, and a dress smallsword. Bonaparte nodded in greeting. Hazzard tried to rise out of etiquette, but was forced back down. He nodded back, and spoke in English.

'*General. An… honour…*' His voice was a dry rasp, the sound of sand pouring through an hourglass.

'Speak French,' ordered Derrien. 'We know that you can.'

Hazzard sagged again.

Bonaparte flicked a glance at Derrien. 'He does not seem to agree, Citizen.'

311

'We have special intelligence to that effect, Citizen General. We also believe him to be half French.'

Bonaparte looked down at Hazzard. 'Who are you?'

Hazzard looked up, uncertain who was being addressed. Derrien jerked his shoulder. '*Répondez.*'

Answer.

Hazzard replied in English, every word an effort. 'W'lliam John... H'zzard, Captain, His Maj'sty's M'rines... retired, sir... but...' he paused for breath, 'I am Doctor... of Ph'los'phy and History, at... th'... the univers'ty of Ca–Ca'bridge...'

Bonaparte listened to the translation. He snapped at Derrien and the dragoons. 'He has identified himself as an officer and a civilian scholar, and should be accorded the appropriate treatment. Release him at once.'

The dragoons complied before Masson or Derrien could object. 'But, Citizen General, I...' protested Derrien. 'This is all but a deception...'

Hazzard's hands were untied and he fell forward gratefully. Bonaparte watched him, still for a moment, then frowned, searching his memory.

'Hazzard. I know this name.'

The room fell still, the secretaries in the distance now watching with interest.

Derrien was surprised. 'May I ask from where, Citizen General?'

'A paper – from...' Bonaparte then put a finger on it, 'from the Sorbonne. An historical work. About the Old Testament, and chronology. Yes, a paper. Free thinking, radical. Revolutionary.' He nodded, more certain, the details coming back to him. 'Yes. I do remember...' He nodded at Derrien. 'Translate.'

Derrien irritably translated Bonaparte's comments, but it was difficult for Hazzard to keep his head up to listen, his neck stiff and sore from his manacled posture and the floggings.

'Sir... *mon français est... très limité...* very lim-lim'ted,' Hazzard admitted with a sigh, keeping his accent thick as he

312

stumbled on, dispensing with grammar and idiom. 'I write…
inside the u-university, in England…'

'No, no,' said Bonaparte, sure of his ground. 'It was from the
Sorbonne.' He glanced at Derrien and saw him staring fixedly at
Hazzard. Bonaparte then moderated his tone, apparently giving
up. 'Indeed. But how could that have been.'

Hazzard said nothing. He looked back at him, and met an
intense stare. For a moment he felt as if they had participated
in some unspoken ruse, recognising something kindred in each
other, the only two men in the room who were truly alone.

Bonaparte waved a hand. Someone at the table poured a glass
of water. 'I am always interested in the sciences, of whichever
persuasion… as a Member of the Institute.' A secretary brought
him the water on a small tray. Bonaparte handed it personally
to Hazzard.

Hazzard took the glass with numb, shaking hands and drank.
It was gone in seconds and his throat swelled in relief. 'I hear
of that… of your election,' he faltered in bad French, 'in the
Institute, sir. *Mes compliments.*'

Bonaparte inclined his head in acknowledgement. Hazzard
could feel Derrien beside him seething with frustration. Bonaparte took back the glass and handed it on. 'So. Two scholars on
an ancient island. Have you explained your presence in Malta
to my officers?'

Derrien cut in. 'Only partially, Citizen General.'

Bonaparte ignored Derrien, keeping his eyes on Hazzard. 'I
am asking the captain, not you.'

Derrien repeated the question in English. Hazzard answered.
'It is… confidential, sir, though academic. A survey is all… for
the society.'

'And will you tell all?'

'Given the situation, it is… my duty… not to, sir, though
there is no harm in it…'

Bonaparte nodded. 'I understand. It is of little consequence,
Captain, as evidently not even the great Nelson could hamper
our progress.'

Bonaparte glanced back at the desk, at the work awaiting him, 'I am currently pressed, Captain. I must put this poor cousin of a nation on a proper footing, after the plundering of these knights. They believed they were still on crusade. But no more. Nevertheless, I should like the occasion to speak with a learned doctor again, if I may.'

Hazzard fought to keep upright, so that he might bow courteously, even while on his knees. 'I am… at your disposal, sir.'

'I would advise against such a measure, Citizen General,' interrupted Derrien quickly.

'I am sure you would, Citizen,' replied Bonaparte. 'But nevertheless I wish it.'

A door in the far corner opened, voices loud in the passage outside, a group arriving. An aide hurried in and spoke to the secretaries and they were forced to interrupt. 'By all means, yes,' said Bonaparte with some disappointment, 'we are finished here.'

But before he went he turned back to Derrien, not deigning to look upon him. 'You will see that he is billeted, bathed, paroled and afforded proper medical treatment and facilities, do I make myself clear?'

'Yes, Citizen General—'

'The entire world is watching us. If I must rely on reports from my own soldiers to learn of your activities—' Derrien's gaze flickered as he thought of Caron and the Alphas, '—or hear of night floggings and dead gaolers again, you will enjoy the view from a cell yourself and remain on this holy rock forevermore.'

Bonaparte walked off, one of the secretaries whispering, *The savants and ladies have come, General, I fear they could not be put off*, and Bonaparte retorted, *Ma foi – this is an expedition, not a pleasure outing…*

A flurry of visitors entered the far end of the hall and Derrien snatched at Hazzard's collar savagely, wanting to drag him outside, but it was too late to avoid the new arrivals. Masson and the dragoons moved in front of him, screening him from view and Hazzard heard senior officers and staff greet a number of ladies, '*Madame Dutoit, how charming, you have come for your tour.*' Hazzard noted Bonaparte's reluctant acceptance, and part of him sympathised and identified with the man all the more.

But, among the echoing, sibilant gabble of conversation, Hazzard registered a name, a name from Naples, and he reacted before he could catch himself, *Ah, Madame citoyenne la comtesse de Biasi…*

Derrien noticed this sudden flicker of recognition as the chatter continued in the background. He looked at Hazzard. 'What is it?' he hissed in English, 'you know someone – *who*?'

'*And my companion from the Comédie Française, of course,*' said the older lady, '*Jeanne-Marie Arnaud and Mademoiselle Isabelle Moreau-Lazare, of course you know, a dear friend to Madame Joséphine…*'

Derrien whipped round to look, his gaze searching the faces of the officers, *savants*, visitors, seeking out the conspirator, willing them to reveal themselves – then back to Hazzard, '*Which? Who is it – tell me! Dites-moi!*'

But there were too many people, too many faces, and Derrien would never know at which moment precisely Hazzard felt his worst fears realised, that he was now crushed by his most dreaded anticipation: Bonaparte bowing to kiss her hand, '*Of course, my dear, delighted that Talma could spare you from Toulon…*'

Fusing the last loose strands, checking and rechecking, Hazzard's mind hurtled down a twisting chasm to a sudden, blinding light as Derrien seized him in frustration, '*Quel! Dites-moi!*' *Which? Tell me!*

But Hazzard fell forward onto his hands, staring at the floor, his only hope the determination that he had to start working harder to stay alive, because he had found the Admiralty agent – when the old *comtesse* and her young companion saw him, and he looked up, straight into the bright blue eyes of Isabelle Moreau-Lazare: it was Sarah, and she was standing right in front of him.

Derrien snapped to the dragoons, '*Get him out of here – back to the cell!*'

The soldiers hesitated. Masson glanced at him, 'But the Citizen General said—'

'*Get him out of here!*'

Hazzard sagged like a drunkard, the dragoons fighting to stand him upright and Derrien tugged at Masson's topcoat. 'Your coat – *quickly, you fool...*'

They draped the black topcoat over Hazzard's shoulders to cover his English scarlet and moved along the edge of the gathering, Masson and the dragoons frogmarching Hazzard to the main door, the voice of the old *comtesse* clear to Derrien, *Isabelle, whatever is the matter, my dear? My dear? Are you unwell?* Hazzard wrenched round to look one last time as he was pulled out.

Derrien let them go, but stopped dead in the crowd. He turned slowly to look for the *comtesse*. The aged dowager *émigrée* stood in a circle of equally aged generals and senior *savants*, all consoling the younger woman, one of the officers holding out a glass of water for her. He stared.

She is here.

Derrien felt his limbs tremble, something powerful over-whelming his senses, until he found himself outside in the broad esplanade, the distant gates to Valletta just beyond. He waited as the visitors wandered about, looking up, pointing at the sights, and soon he came face to face with the old *comtesse*. 'Citizen de Biasi,' he said with a curt bow. 'An unexpected pleasure.'

The *comtesse* stopped, Isabelle pale with a hand to her mouth. 'Citizen Derrien,' announced the *comtesse*, so that all might hear her speak with the one that all knew as Citizen *Croquemort*. 'I was just introducing my *protégées* to the General,' she said, with a note of warning.

'Of course,' said Derrien smoothly. 'The Citizen General has told me often of the support you afforded us.'

'Indeed,' she said with restrained distaste. 'May I present my wards, *Mademoiselles* Jeanne-Marie Arnaud and Isabelle Moreau-Lazare, companions to *Madame* Joséphine in Paris.'

'But of course,' said Derrien, taking the shaking hand of Isabelle Moreau-Lazare and placing a discreet kiss on her tense, whitening knuckles. '*Mademoiselle*.'

The *comtesse* cut in, 'If you will excuse us, poor Isabelle is not well—'

'So I see...' But Derrien caught her eye and in it he read fear. 'I trust you will enjoy your afternoon in the city. Best not stray from the group,' he said, 'our glorious troops can be, how can one say, *impolite*.'

The *comtesse* held the two girls tight, and gave a brief curtsey. 'Thank you, Citizen, we shall. A good day to you.'

The three headed off down the road to the gate, two of the youngest *savants*, Jollois and De Villiers hanging back to enquire, *are you all right, mademoiselle, you look quite pale*, as Derrien watched, she shaking her head, the *comtesse* trying to comfort her.

The troops marched, the steady tramp of their boots in the June heat raising dust from the stones, ancient cobbles that had known the iron-shod thunder of the joust from days of chivalry, now gone, cast away for coin, by time, by pen and ink. The seabirds wheeled and shrieked to the bright skies, declaring to the world that Malta was now and forever the first outpost of the new French Empire.

Citizen Jules-Yves Derrien shook with pleasure, with satisfaction, feeling that electric *frisson* of triumph and relief – detecting in that final conclusive kiss of Isabelle's hand the same lingering scent from an abandoned boudoir in the home of Hugues Bartelmi: the fine work of the late *parfumier* Ablondi of Toulon.

At last, my dear, he thought, *you are mine*.

He looked out at the fleet in the harbour, the sailors, the troops disembarking, wondering how many knew, or at least

317

had guessed that Malta, this paltry conquest, was nothing by comparison to what glory was to come. He imagined the sight that would greet the inhabitants of Alexandria, and the alarm that would rise in Cairo, when Bonaparte's fleet covered the horizon from east to west – and they learned the futility of resistance.

He watched field guns swinging out on booms, gun carriages already waiting in rows, troops in line. This was the true power of the Revolution: *this*. Should Cairo dare raise a hand, he determined, it would be crushed beneath the wheels of the juggernaut.

And Egypt, land of gods and deserts, shall burn.

Derrien turned and headed back to the cells of the fortress, some part of him laughing deep inside, at the fate of Egypt, at the fate of Isabelle Moreau-Lazare – and at the despair of William John Hazzard, echoing from somewhere under the stones, so very far below.

Historical Note

Although this is a work of fiction, many of the events actually happened much as described, and many of the characters are drawn from real figures in history: from Nelson, St Vincent, Troubridge and Bonaparte, to Moiret of the 75th Invincibles, and Tomlinson of HMS *Valiant* – from Von Hompesch and De Ransijat of the Knights Hospitaller, to Luca Azzopardo, hero of Malta, who became a key figure in the resistance against the French Republic.

With a few exceptions, Bonaparte's officers and generals are depictions of real people, from the harsh chief aide Jean-Androche Junot, the great Kléber, and the one-legged Swiss, Maximilien Caffarelli du Falga, to young Capt. Jullien, beloved of the army's rank and file. Louis Antoine Fauvelet de Bourrienne was a diplomat, lawyer and civil servant, and Bonaparte's oldest friend, employed by Bonaparte on the expedition as his personal secretary. Just as Bonaparte complains to his aide Jullien at Malta, he did have brass castors fitted to his bed in the hope of off-setting the roll of the ship (and curing his chronic seasickness – it didn't) – and Bourrienne did indeed read to him at night aboard the *Orient*, doubtless trying to keep up as Bonaparte's bed rolled about the cabin.

Sergent-chef-major Achille Caron is a portrait of the best in the French Revolutionary army, combining the experience of the *ancien* French army before the Revolution with the sad recognition that change was necessary – yet hating the means employed by the *bourgeois* politicians who did it. The *Alpha-Oméga* suffer the typical shortages of uniforms and equipment of the growing Revolutionary army, which took in vast numbers of recruits without the means to sustain them – some were the poorest of the poor, in homespun or even sackcloth for months before they had uniforms, some entering battle without shoes or boots. What they all did have, however, was Bonaparte.

The Bonaparte of 1798 was not the round-faced, slightly overweight statesman common to popular imagination – instead he was a long-haired 28-year-old romantic hero, the idealised portrait of the Revolution, beloved of his men because he led from the front, and virtually unstoppable in the field. As Caron explained to Derrien, Bonaparte had to be pulled back from enemy fire as he charged the bridge at Arcole in Italy – then charged it again. At this time he is generally not yet referred to as 'Napoleon' – that was to come later, once he assumed the role of Emperor of France; here he is simply General Bonaparte, and on the rise. After victory in Italy in 1797, Bonaparte was too powerful for the Directory Government to control. They relied on his armies to provide loot for the treasury yet feared his growing success. With a snap of his fingers he could summon 20,000 men of the Paris garrison to the gates of the Tuileries Palace and change the government – which he had already done once, on their behalf. They feared he might do it again.

Having heard of the plan for Egypt from Foreign Minister Talleyrand, Bonaparte *wanted* to go – far more than he wanted to invade England, which he believed would have jeopardised his winning streak. After significant lobbying by Bonaparte and Talleyrand, the Directors acquiesced – and with good reason: to send Bonaparte a thousand miles away to a desert seemed a very sound solution to their problems. But they had no inkling of the consequences. Just like Caesar, he would return to cross the Rubicon.

Jules-Yves Derrien is the power behind the Revolution: faceless, dedicated, and implacable. As with many Revolutionary government structures, the Committee for Public

320

Safety and Committee for General Security were wound up before the Directory Government came to power, but the Ministry of the Interior maintained its own counter-intelligence unit. I have called this the *Bureau d'information*. Seventy years later it was divided into two, the *Prémier Bureau* and the more well-known *Deuxième Bureau*.

Derrien's reign of terror in Toulon is characteristic of the feeling of Revolutionary Paris for the *Toulonnais* who had sided previously with the royalists in 1793. Recorded barely a week before Bonaparte's armada set sail, an unnamed ministry official overreached his authority and summarily executed a citizen of Toulon for a breach of statutory regulations – just as Derrien did with Ablondi. When Bonaparte heard of it he was furious and as we shall see, publicly rebuked the official in question.

As to Derrien's quarry, there is no record of an Isabelle Moreau-Lazare on the roll of the *Comédie Française*, where the great actor François-Joseph Talma performed the heroic roles of Voltaire and Racine to the adulation of Paris and his key patrons: Joséphine and Napoléon Bonaparte, his very dear friends. Neither will there be record of Isabelle, (or Sarah Chapel), in Naples. Lady Emma Hamilton, the society beauty who married the much older Sir William Hamilton, British ambassador to the Neapolitan court, took great care of their English visitors, and had told Hazzard the truth. The famous diplomat couple lived in the Palazzo Sessa, on the Pizzofalcone Hill overlooking the great bay, and were renowned for their hospitality to society figures from all over Europe. Their world changes forever in the months to come, as we shall see, with the arrival of a certain house-guest: one Admiral Horatio Nelson.

What we do know of Admiralty agents is limited, but we certainly know that some were women, and some well-placed in society, part of networks that stretched from Naples to Hamburg. Agents were often given a numerical codename, just as Blake gave Hazzard. These most often consisted of three sets of two-digit numerals, some separated by an apostrophe, and looked very much like nautical Cartesian coordinates of latitude and longitude in degrees, minutes and seconds. Some did not follow this system and used three-digit numerals, which served to confound as efficiently as the impenetrable Admiralty ciphers themselves. Admiralty archives still contain recorded lists of agents' numbers from this period, much as Sir Rafe's personal reference book, *Mnemonics VI*, which he consults to confirm the identity of 28'66'96: *Op Cit. ref. Hazzard, Wm Jn (Chatham) HMMF (ret'd)*. Today's Admiralty Scale (or NATO code) uses a different alpha-numeric system of A–F and 1–6, appended respectively to sources and their information to denote reliability, A and 1 being the highest; as Wayland had learned in his first days in Room 63, Captain Day had been granted the 9-suffix in Sir Rafe's numerical system, 9 being '*most reliable*'.

Once decided on his course of action, Sir Rafe Lewis employs the Admiralty 'shutter-line' to send a signal. This was a large tower on the roof of the Admiralty building known as the Murray Shutter: coded visual signals, displayed on large revolving wooden panels, were passed via relay stations across the countryside to the ports and vice versa, enabling rapid contact between the Sea-Lords in London and the fleets at Deal, Yarmouth, Plymouth and Portsmouth, in some cases in just over sixty seconds.

–

The story of the armada begins with the British occupation of the Cape of Good Hope in today's South Africa, in August 1795. Six months earlier, a popular revolution had swept Holland, supported by French Revolutionary forces: the new Batavian Republic became a 'sister-state' to France, and William, Prince of Orange, turned to England for support. Fearing the same republicanism would spread to the Cape colony, a vital stopover on the route to India, England sailed a fleet to Cape Town with

William's sanction, to ensure the colony did not fall into the wrong hands. Negotiations lasted some two months.

On 7 August the British fleet moved along False Bay, just south of Cape Town, to attack the coastal batteries at Muizenberg, and some two hundred VOC (the Dutch East India Company) defenders retreated along the coast road back to the city. Only one Dutch officer, a Lt Marnitz, and a colleague called Kemper, stayed behind to man a single 24-pounder cannon. The barrage from the British fleet exploding all about them, Marnitz and Kemper succeeded in hitting both HMS *America* and *Stately*, causing two fatalities and four wounded before falling back: a unit of the 78th Highlanders, with a thousand sailors and marines, landed and marched from Simon's Town. After sporadic resistance, and with the intervention of the Scots VOC army commander, Colonel Gordon, the VOC surrendered the colony to British administration on behalf of the Prince of Orange. As a result, France was denied safe passage round the Cape, and was cut off from her colonies in India. Their only option was extreme: to invade Egypt, dig out a canal at Suez, and sail a fleet through to the Red Sea. Bonaparte seized upon the idea.

Three years later, in April and May of 1798, reports of a large French fleet massing in Toulon reached the Admiralty from Danish and American merchantmen in the Mediterranean, and by covert agents such as Captain Day, Britain's consul in Turin, who reported regularly to the Admiralty. Over these extraordinary weeks Captain Day's network intercepted letters from within France. They left him in no doubt that France intended to invade Egypt: the aged *savant* geologist Déodat Dolomieu (after whom the Dolomites are named) wrote to a friend in Austria, blurting out that he had 'agreed to go to Egypt' because he'd been promised he would find 'some interesting rocks' there. Further evidence came after the capture of Rome in February, when the Vatican Propaganda office was ransacked by French agents hunting for Arabic printing fonts – for Bonaparte's planned Egyptian proclamations. Even the appalling poet

323

Parseval-Grandmaison, badly wanting to go on the 'trip to Egypt', was heard to exclaim loudly to *savant* organisers, 'Of course you go to Egypt! The whole of France knows you go to Egypt!'

Actually, they didn't. No one did, least of all the 38,000 combat troops or 15,000 sailors, nor the other 167 *savants* who bravely signed on for an adventure that would cost some of them their lives. And neither did London – despite the rumours, they could not be certain England was not the target of a fleet twice the size of the Spanish Armada faced by Drake centuries earlier. It had been only a year since the defeat of the Franco-Spanish fleet at Cape St Vincent by Admiral Sir John Jervis – the massing at Toulon could be a second attempt to do the same. So alarmed was Captain Day that he carried despatches personally on the route through Hamburg to London, much as Isabelle had wanted to do. It would have been Day who sent her call for help to London and Lord St Vincent's fleet, to retrieve her from the safe-house of the ill-fated Bartelmi.

Admiral Jervis, now ennobled to Lord St Vincent after his famous victory, could not sail from his base at Gibraltar into the Mediterranean without great risk: Spain's treaty with France had closed all friendly ports to the British, including Naples. For a time, the Mediterranean was known as the 'French Lake'. It was the perfect moment for Bonaparte to launch his invasion.

St Vincent sent word to the Admiralty. Rear-Admiral Nelson was called off sick-leave, granted after his arm was amputated from wounds at the disastrous attack on Santa Cruz de Tenerife; he duly sailed to the Tagus and Cadiz with HMS *Vanguard*. St Vincent immediately outfitted a reconnaissance squadron, consisting of *Orion* and *Alexander* (two other 74-gun ships), two frigates, the *Emerald* and *Terpsichore*, and the war-sloop *Bonne Citoyenne*. There was dissent surrounding the decision to send Nelson instead of more senior officers, such as Admiral Orde, who went so far as to challenge St Vincent to a duel – and was sent packing back home to England. On

2nd May, St Vincent sent Nelson into the Mediterranean. As if by an odd telepathy the First Sea-Lord, the Earl Spencer, sent this message to St Vincent on that same day, delivered by Lt Tomlinson of the *Valiant*:

> *The circumstances in which we now find ourselves oblige us to take a measure of a more decided and hazardous completion than we should otherwise have thought ourselves justified in taking, but when you are apprized that the appearance of a British squadron in the Mediterranean is a condition on which the fate of Europe may at this moment be stated to depend, you will not be surprised that we are disposed to strain every nerve, and incur considerable hazard in effecting it.*

It is a matter of record that a Spanish privateer was spotted just off the Balearic Islands in the Mediterranean at the same time as our brig the *Esperanza* was headed for Toulon, suggesting a ship like the *Volpone* was lurking nearby. The French privateer *La Pierre*, mentioned by the Sardinian fisher-captain, was well-known on the sea-lanes around Corsica and Sardinia; it captured several Spanish vessels and commandeered them for use in Bonaparte's fleet – to De la Vega's fury. The pact between Spain and France was tenuous, and relations were fraught, as expressed by the noble Don Cesár and his attitude to Hazzard. De la Vega was later avenged: *La Pierre* was indeed captured, just as the Sardinian captain had said.

The great storm that caught the *Esperanza* was recorded on the night of 19–20 May 1798. It scattered Nelson's recce squadron, sending HMS *Orion* off course and blowing the two frigates *Emerald* and *Terpsichore* back to Barcelona. The gale threw Nelson's *Vanguard* and the *Alexander* 75 miles south-west, from Toulon to the rocks of Corsica. The *Vanguard* was dismasted, losing her tops with two men killed by falling debris, and the *Alexander* tried to tow her to safety, despite Nelson's angry signals to leave them. But Nelson was famous

325

for disobeying orders as well, and was grateful to *Alexander's* quick-thinking Captain Ball.

When the storm cleared Nelson had lost his two frigates, *Emerald* and *Terpsichore*, under Captain Hope, who had decided to return to Gibraltar instead of heading to Toulon to look for Nelson. Nelson's stricken vessels meanwhile lay under repair at San Pietro (as the French despatch-runner informs Capt. Casabianca in the presence of Derrien on the *Orient*).

After the report by Hope of the storm and the damage to Nelson's ships, St Vincent sent in reinforcements: eleven heavy ships of the line under the command of Sir Thomas Troubridge. No longer did they creep quietly into the 'French Lake', but rather thundered into the Mediterranean in line-of-battle. Lt Hardy, captain of the brig HMS *Mutine* (the same Hardy who went on to command Nelson's flagship *Victory* at Trafalgar), hunted for Nelson day and night; when he did find him, the new squadron reached Toulon on 27 May, but were too late – Bonaparte had sailed, just as De la Vega had said, for his ears were indeed better than those of *El Nelsón*.

Hazzard was understandably outraged at Naples – only a short time later, just as Hazzard predicted, the English would go to their rescue despite Acton's apparent reluctance to help. Hardy took the *Mutine* into Naples to ask for frigates, just as Hazzard had done, and Sir John refused again. Acton comes out poorly in this tale; in his defence he was in a difficult position, yet succeeded in aligning the court with Britain in a new coalition against France, a dangerous move in itself. However, had Sir John Acton done as Hazzard had suggested, and called for help to Lord St Vincent, the plight of Naples, Malta and possibly Egypt might well have been different.

Many are familiar with the name of the underworld society the *Camorra*, famed historically for their use of the Neapolitan sewers that gave access to nearly every part of the city, allowing them to appear from nowhere and vanish into thin air. *Lazzarono/a* is a term used in Italy even today, meaning 'troublemaker' – but in Naples in 1798 it was the royal court's term for 'rebel'. The *Lazzaroni* were the great resistors of the royal hegemony of the day, fighting for many things, for the poor of Naples, for freedom, for money, who can say, but they would certainly have come running to the aid of a swordsman fighting French agents in a dark alley. As we shall see, the *Lazzaroni* waterman was a true *uomo d'onore*, a man of honour, and never forgot.

The French fleet hit heavy fog at the tiny island of Pantelleria, just as De la Vega did in the *Volpone* – and there came the only clue, from the fishermen who had spotted the armada. Nelson meanwhile passed through the straits of Messina between Italy and Sicily, for resupply in Syracuse and Ragusa. The French meanwhile had only a few days' sail to their first target: Malta.

Grand Master Ferdinand von Hompesch zu Bolheim knew Bonaparte was coming to Malta, but ignored the threat. When first only fifty ships appeared he ignored them as well; he also ignored the reports of his seneschals that the powder magazines of Fort St Elmo had been flooded and were useless, and that the militia were unhappy falling in line with the knights.

However, when he awoke on the morning of 9 June 1798 and saw the fleet, he called out the army at last – but it was too late. The *savant* Poussielgue had already visited Malta months before, making contacts and promises, and had sounded out the French knights, learning they would not resist, especially if they received pensions. It was rumoured at the time that arms had been circulated to revolutionary elements within the city, just as Pigalle and Rossy had been ordered. Ignoring their populace to enrich themselves and their churches, the Knights of Malta had embarked upon a holy crusade the Pope had never sanctioned.

At dawn the next day, Malta was surrounded and invaded at four landing-points, the northern Maltese island of Gozo as well – and Rossy had been right: the 9th *demi* had sung the 'Marseillaise' as they scaled the fortress walls on ropes. Valletta was taken after minimal resistance but the city and the area around the harbour had been in uproar: French ships dominated the harbour, Fort Sant'Angelo on the southern side of Valletta undergoing a barrage for some days. The streets were in chaos, the people crowding into the churches as French troops marched in, often calling for the Maltese to join them – and many did. As Luca Azzopardo said, the knights had become the oppressors. The largely untrained militia surrendered where they could, and two of the knights were reported killed – some say by the people, others by the knights themselves, for desertion.

Though promised 500,000 francs and estates in Germany, Von Hompesch was ignominiously booted down the quayside steps to a waiting boat, never to return. Some 2,000 prisoners and galley-slaves were found in the cells of Fort St Elmo and the *bagnio* or '*bagno*' prison, (so named from an Ottoman bathhouse prison in Constantinople), a giant dormitory where the Knights billeted their galley-slaves and locked them up for the night. French troops found some 1,400 North Africans and 600 Turks. They were all set free at Bonaparte's order, as part of the French Republic's universal emancipation policy. Many joined his army in gratitude – though some were press-ganged into becoming crewmen in the fleet, to be released upon arrival in Egypt. All thanks to Bonaparte's new constitution, written in less than ten days, Malta became the first European nation formally to abolish slavery.

This was the end of the Knights of Malta, the Knights of St John, after nearly 700 years. We could claim Von Hompesch was betrayed by the French knights of the Order who refused to take the blood of Christians and fellow-countrymen, but in truth he was no Jean de la Valette, and had made no preparations. Those knights who did not wish to join Bonaparte's expedition were exiled from Malta; Bosrédon de Ransijat, Treasurer of the Order and leader of the French knights, accepted a post in the new Revolutionary government of Malta. The Knights Hospitaller went out with a scarcely discernible whimper, their anachronistic quest finally at an end, their flag passed incongruously to Tsar Paul of Russia, who became the next Grand Master. Within months the Royal Navy surrounded Malta, lay siege, and overwhelmed it, taking thousands of French prisoners, just as Hazzard had promised Luca Azzopardo – and Britain never forgot Malta again.

–

Perhaps it's hard to imagine, but the 74-gun warship was the 18th-century tactical equivalent of the nuclear submarine of today – a 'weapons platform' able to deliver the brute force of an entire artillery regiment anywhere the wind could take it. When war was declared in 1793, after the execution of Louis XVI, England had some 3000 warships. By 1800 this had risen to 9000. Ten years before the Revolution, the French navy was one of the finest in Europe, its ships easily matching the English at sea, under great captains such as Pierre de Suffren and others. But by 1798 the Revolution had so stripped its officer ranks, as it had with the army, that the navy was left in a dire state, poorly disciplined and untrained. They were often no match for the remarkably aggressive British, who routinely outgunned and outmanoeuvred their enemies.

All of this terrible power was controlled by the Lords Commissioners of the Admiralty, but doubtless piloted by the Intelligence service of a Sir Rafe Lewis – whoever he was. We shall never know Lewis's real name, nor Derrien's, and although we know Hazzard, Wayland, Sarah Chapel and others, they too are mere unknown soldiers, controlled by the unaccountable and the anonymous, from unremarkable places such as Room 63 – which really did exist: it was down the south corridor and up the back-stairs with the skylight, at the top on the left, the door marked by a small brass number-plate.

The Marines of 1798

In 1798, the British Marines were designated 'His Majesty's Marine Forces'. They were not given the title 'Royal Marines' until 1802, at the insistence of the indomitable Admiral John Jervis, the Earl St Vincent, who became First Sea-Lord. Viewed as a military branch of the navy, they first wore the army uniform of the day: this was usually a red tailcoat with white facings, a white waistcoat, breeches, and tall gaiters known as 'spatterdashes', and the tricorn or bicorn slouch hat – this later gave way to the distinctive black 'round hat', or 'topper', surmounted by a red and white hackle, worn by officers and men alike.

There could be anything from 30 to 100 marines aboard differently rated ships, often according to the number of guns: a First Rate warship could mount over a hundred cannon, and had a similar sized company of marines. Their ranks were arranged into army platoons, with privates and corporals under 1st and 2nd Lieutenants, and usually a single senior NCO, a Marine Sergeant. In command was a Captain of Marines – addressed as 'Major' while aboard to avoid confusion with the ship's naval captain. In 1798 they had just three depots, Chatham, Portsmouth and Plymouth.

Marines used the Sea-Service musket, a version of the Short India Pattern 'Brown Bess', a .75 calibre muzzle-loading smoothbore flintlock, more commonly known at the time as a 'firelock'. The Sea-Service musket was slightly shorter than the army's Brown Bess, though still some 53 inches (135cm) long, its steel parts replaced with rust-proof brass. The most recognisable aspect of this version was its square-ended stock and brass butt-plate. Sailors often blacked up their muskets with pitch (asphalt) to ensure seawater could not affect them – it's believed however that marines kept their musket brightwork polished for drill and ceremonial use, though for covert shore operations they would most likely have taken blacked weapons.

Their task, just as it is today, was shipboard security and amphibious operations – whether to reconnoitre, infiltrate, or cut-out (literally, to cut the moorings of an enemy ship and capture it), escort, seek-and-destroy or effect full-scale invasions.

Marines often helped load and fire naval guns, setting and dousing sail, and were often indistinguishable in 'Undress' or casual uniform from their brother sailors – who were called 'Jacks', and the marines 'Jollies'. Well liked and respected by the crews, their loyalties were split during the fleet mutinies at Spithead and the Nore in 1797; some marines sympathised and took part in the uprising, while other marines were deployed to storm the mutineers' ships. Thereafter, marines were billeted aboard ship in cabins separating the officers and crew as a protective measure, and paraded before the mainmast every day as a cautionary reminder to both groups of the captain's authority.

The 'Bombay Marine' mentioned here was the name given to the naval forces of the East India Company, (also known as the 'Honourable East India Company', the 'Honourable Company' and 'John Company'). It still exists today, having transformed over the centuries into the Indian Navy. Little is known of their origins or practices in the 17th and 18th centuries but, according to some sources, the Marine was headquartered in Bombay Castle, also known as the 'Black Castle'. They fought at sea and on inland rivers in sloops or more heavily armed frigates, escorting slow-moving 'East Indiamen', the cargo vessels that transported goods from India and China to England and her trading posts. Such ships were the targets of enemy colonies and non-aligned states within India, as well as privateers and pirates from Sumatra to Madagascar and the Arabian Gulf. Equally motivated by the lure of treasure and prize-money to be gained from their enemies' ships, the Bombay Marine became as feared as the pirates they engaged, and became known among the regular navy as the 'Bombay Buccaneers'.

Transferring from one branch of the armed forces to another was not an easy matter. His Majesty's Marine Forces were known to take soldiers from certain regiments at certain times, such as the 69th Lincolnshire Regiment of Foot (as with Kite and Warnock). Hazzard lost his rank of Captain-lieutenant in the Bombay Marine when he transferred, becoming a 1st Lieutenant in the HMMF.

With perhaps a few exceptions it was difficult for transferred troops to match the professionalism of the marines, who were considered the finest drilled troops in the world – no land regiment could drill on a rolling deck like a marine, and drill was vital to their ability to deliver concentrated musket-fire in battle. Their ceremonial duties had significant political value: when the king of Naples was uncertain whether to ally with England after the intermittent periods of peace in the Napoleonic Wars, a single British man of war docked in the Bay of Naples and landed its company of marines on the quayside. Before a welcome party by the royal court and a gathering group of Neapolitans, they performed their standard parade drill, butt-plates and boots crashing on the wooden planks. No one else commanded seaborne troops like these – not Prussia, not Spain, not Austria – only King George. So awe-inspiring was this spectacle that the King of Naples signed his treaty with England at once.

This discipline stood them in good stead, and was applied in the field regularly. During the Texel campaign in Holland in 1799, British troops evacuated Dutch royalist supporters fleeing in the face of advancing French Revolutionary forces. Seventy-five marines under the command of a young 2nd Lieutenant, barely twenty years old, were left defending the outskirts of the town of Helder, its docks crowded with terrified families boarding boats to reach the waiting British fleet. A large column of some 600 French infantry and light artillery was spotted marching towards the outskirts of the town. Using a low garden wall for cover, this young officer of only a year's experience rotated his men through firing ranks, loosing off volley after volley into the French front line; when the French column faltered, he led the marines in a bayonet charge, putting the French to flight, abandoning their arms and artillery in the process. It is on this incident that Lt Wayland's defence of the coast road on Malta is based. Wayland's diary entries, discovered by Hazzard late one night at his desk, are genuine extracts written by this same young officer.

Jervis called the marines the country's 'sheet anchor', to be relied upon in time of need. Much like today, they were a mobile army that could be dropped into the very heart of enemy country, ready to go anywhere and do anything – as their motto declares, 'By Land, By Sea'.

Cut off from their ship during shore operations, possibly for days or weeks at a time, and forced to fend for themselves in hostile territory, marines had to have an independent strength of mind, as well as an undying connection to their comrades in the field. All would agree there was only one rule, in the end, that really mattered:

Never give up the boat.

Jonathan Spencer, 2020

Acknowledgements

I would like to thank a number of soldiers, sailors, tinkers and tailors for their considerable help and guidance in the creation of the Hazzard series, including Michael du Plessis, Alistair France, Anthony Gray, John Rawlinson and Willem Steenkamp; linguists Diana Barlow and Monica Schmalzl; interpreters and transliterators Muhammad Wafa, Essam Edgard Samné, and former Naval Intelligence officer Hassan Eltaher; my editor at Canelo, Craig Lye, and agents Mike Bryan and Heather Adams.

And my father, who told me stories of the desert I will never forget.

Jonathan Spencer, 2020